"Say you want me as much as I want you."

Through the swimming of her senses, Leonie grasped at enough composure to answer, "I'll tell you that when . . . I'm in Wolfenberg."

A light came into Klaus's eyes. He thought he'd won. "And when will that be?"

"When I'm ready," she whispered.

"Little witch. I'll make you follow me."

"No man can make me."

"I can. I will. It will be a fine duel between us, Leonie. And I promise my victory will be as pleasing to you as it is to me."

She gave a slow smile of pleasure at the thought of that duel, and the arms that were holding her trembled. "Who is to say which one of us will win?" she provoked him softly.

"I always win," Klaus declared arrogantly.

"So do I," she assured him with a slow, beguiling smile. "So do I. . . ."

Dear Reader,

Welcome to another great month of the best in historical romance. With summer just around the corner, Harlequin Historicals has picked four titles sure to heat up your spring nights.

The *Royal Harlot* is Lady Leonie Conniston, a British spy whose assignment is to keep the enigmatic Prince Klaus from danger. However, when Klaus discovers her true identity, who will save her from his growing passions? A big book from author Lucy Gordon.

Newcomer Merline Lovelace gives us a sweeping tale set in ancient Britain. Lady Alena has no love for men after a brutal first marriage, but then why does she find passion and comfort in the arms of a *Roman? Alena* is the first installment of the Destiny's Women trilogy by the author.

In *The Fourth of Forever* by Mary McBride, Race Logan is looking for a harmless roll in the hay with "Kate the Gate," but is shocked to discover the woman in question is not at all what she seems.

And rounding out May, Kathryn Belmont's *Fugitive Heart* tells the story of Jeremiah Sloan and Sarah Randall, who pose as man and wife in order to pull off one of the biggest slave rescues of all time. Yet will their feigned marriage make them yearn for the real thing?

We hope you enjoy these titles. Next month, look for a big book by medieval author Claire Delacroix, and the next installment of the Warrior series by Margaret Moore.

Sincerely,

Tracy Farrell
Senior Editor

Please address questions and book requests to:
Reader Service
U.S.: P.O. Box 1325, Buffalo, NY 14269
Canadian: P.O. Box 1050, Niagara Falls, Ont. L2E 7G7

Lucy Gordon

Royal Harlot

Harlequin Books

TORONTO • NEW YORK • LONDON
AMSTERDAM • PARIS • SYDNEY • HAMBURG
STOCKHOLM • ATHENS • TOKYO • MILAN
MADRID • WARSAW • BUDAPEST • AUCKLAND

ISBN 0-373-28819-0

ROYAL HARLOT

LUCY GORDON

met her husband-to-be in Venice, fell in love the first evening and got engaged two days later. After twenty-three years, they're still happily married and now live in England with their three dogs. For twelve years Lucy was a writer for an English women's magazine. She interviewed many of the world's most interesting men, including Warren Beatty, Richard Chamberlain, Roger Moore, Sir Alec Guiness and Sir John Gielgud.

In 1985 she won the *Romantic Times* Reviewer's Choice Award for Outstanding Series Romance Author. She has also won a Golden Leaf Award from the New Jersey Chapter of RWA, was a finalist in the RWA golden medallion contest in 1988 and won the 1990 Rita Award in the Best Traditional Romance category for *Song of the Lorelei*.

To Shirley Russell, with love and gratitude

Prologue

In the chilly light of an English dawn, a proud, handsome man prepared himself for death.

He was unafraid, as befitted royalty, but he was angry with himself. He'd learned to use the blades under the finest masters in Europe and knew he was a skilled swordsman. But this duel had been forced on him, which meant that his opponent was a professional assassin, with orders to kill him at all costs. So Prince Klaus Friederich, hereditary ruler of Wolfenberg, had made his peace with his Maker before coming to this heath on the edge of London.

Two men stood a little apart from Klaus, never taking their eyes off him. The younger of them was his equerry and friend, Bernhard von Leibnitz. He was in his late twenties, with a pleasant, good-humored face, although just now it bore a worried look. He, too, had seen how the duel had been forced on his royal master, but his pleas to the prince not to go through with it had fallen on deaf ears. The other man was a doctor.

"We should have informed the British authorities," Bernhard muttered. "They'd have stopped this."

"But think of the scandal!" the timid little doctor exclaimed. "The Prince of Wolfenberg warned off breaking the law! It's unthinkable. Besides, he'd have been furious with us.'' He gave an eloquent shudder.

"I don't enjoy his royal highness's temper any more than you do," Bernhard admitted, "but it would be better than having him dead.''

"But surely it won't come to that. The prince is a fine duelist—''

"This isn't going to be a duel, it's going to be assassination," Bernhard said bitterly. "Gorstein has plunged his sword through the hearts of at least ten men—'' He looked up to see Prince Klaus approaching him. "Your highness,'' he pleaded, "it isn't too late even now.''

He inwardly braced himself for an explosion of the legendary family wrath that had helped to make the prince's ancestry so colorful. But instead, Klaus laid a light hand on his friend's shoulder and gave a brief smile. "Your care for me never fails," he said gently. "But it was too late from the first moment.''

"But if—''

"*If*—'' Klaus interrupted him, still in the same gentle tone. "Why then, my cousin Reinald will inherit my throne, and you will give him your loyalty...as you've always given it to me.''

The sound of hoofbeats made them all look up quickly. Three men were galloping toward them through the dawn light. The leading horseman swung down from his saddle. He was small and lithe, made of bone and sinew, and there was a cold glitter in his eyes as he confronted the prince. "Are we ready to begin?''

"Gentleman,'' Bernhard interrupted, "it's the duty of a second to attempt a reconciliation. Let me beg you—''

"No reconciliation,'' Gorstein interrupted. "No apology can compensate for the insult I endured.''

"And no apology will be offered, since there was no insult," Klaus declared quietly.

Gorstein gave a chill smile of satisfaction. "Then let us proceed."

The swords were produced. Gorstein swung his, making whipping sounds through the air.

"En garde."

The two men confronted each other, balancing lightly on the balls of their feet, their left arms held high. At that moment, the first rays of the sun appeared and touched the blades with a deadly gleam. There was a faint scratching sound as the lethal edges teased each other, and then an ugly clash as Gorstein thrust forward and was skillfully parried by the prince. He thrust again without pause, and when he was parried a second time, returned instantly. He was a machine for sword fighting, seeming not to need to breathe, his small, agile body presenting no target as he darted and turned. Klaus had power and a sound technique that carried him creditably through the first few minutes, but his aim was to disarm, rather than to kill, and against an unscrupulous opponent with murder in his heart, this put him at a disadvantage.

Thrust and parry, slash and drive. The two men moved back and forth, blades flashing in the fast-growing light. Bernhard held his breath, praying for some decisive movement that would help his sovereign and friend to seize the initiative and bring matters to a safe conclusion. But neither man could gain an advantage and the duel was turning into a slogging match.

Sweat began to run down Klaus's forehead into his eyes, forcing him to rub them with the back of his hand. Gorstein instantly danced forward with a vicious driving movement that would have ended his opponent's life if Klaus hadn't turned aside at the last split second, throwing up his arm to deflect the sword. Bernhard drew in his breath at this foul blow. Klaus gave a gasp as the blade pierced his flesh, then gritted his teeth to fight on, but Bernhard cried, "Halt!" and stepped in.

"Blood has been spilt," he declared sternly to Gorstein. "Be satisfied."

"Never!" Gorstein shrieked. "To the death."

"To the death," Klaus repeated, his face pale and livid. "Stand back, Bernhard. It's too late."

He launched onto the attack but his foe glided away like a snake, slashing viciously. Gorstein's eyes were glittering with mad pleasure as the final moment approached, a moment for which he was being well paid. A cunning flick of the wrist and Klaus's blade went spinning from his hand, leaving him defenseless against Gorstein's murderous attack. His enemy's sword was raised . . .

Then a shot rang out from the direction of some nearby bushes. The next second, Gorstein had fallen to the ground, an ugly crimson stain spreading over his white shirtfront. He had been shot clean through the heart.

Chapter One

That summer of 1865, society was dominated by the brilliant young Prince and Princess of Wales, who seemed set on turning everything into pleasure, and among the many shining lights of their crowd, none dazzled more brilliantly than Leonie, Dowager Duchess of Coniston. She was absurdly young for a dowager, being only twenty-seven, and in the four years of her widowhood she'd set international society alight with her beauty, charm and tireless energy.

Despite not having gone to bed until the small hours, she'd been up early this morning, advancing to meet the dawn in a tight-fitting riding habit that showed off every curve of her slim body, and enjoying a vigorous ride in Hyde Park. She returned to Coniston House, the palatial London mansion of the Duke of Coniston, to find the rest of the family at breakfast. Gwendolyn, the present duchess, turned acid eyes on her. It was the bane of Gwendolyn's life that her father-in-law had taken as his second wife a beautiful young woman less than a third his age, and that in consequence she had a mother-in-law twenty years younger than herself. It was worse still that Leonie periodically inflicted herself on her husband's long-suffering family, reducing the house to turmoil with her dashing ways.

"You have a visitor," she announced coldly. "Lord Bracewell has been awaiting you in the library this half hour."

"Oh heavens!" Leonie sighed. "Bracewell's such a dull man, always wanting me to join his wife's charitable committees."

"He's a worthy man and held in high esteem by your late husband," Gwendolyn reminded her.

"That's no excuse for interrupting my breakfast," Leonie observed with an injured air. "Oh, well, I suppose I'll have to see him."

She sauntered from the room in a leisurely manner that Gwendolyn considered highly improper. It might not be her fault that the tailored lines of her habit emphasized her tiny waist and the dancing movement of her flared hips, but it was hard to feel that anything the alluring Leonie did was entirely innocent. Not that Gwendolyn considered her alluring. She considered her scandalous.

As soon as she opened the library door, Leonie's manner underwent an abrupt change, and she advanced quickly to meet Lord Bracewell, her lovely dark eyes alight with greeting.

Lord Bracewell rose and gave a small, stiff bow. He was a man in middle years and of middle height, with bovine features that masked an icy genius. He was the head of the country's intelligence service, a fact known only to a few people, of whom Leonie was one.

"Welcome, my friend," she said. "I do hope this visit means you have work for me. I'm beginning to find London devilishly dull."

Lord Bracewell gave a small smile. "I'd heard that your admirers were turning the place into chaos."

She shrugged a pair of slim shoulders with the indifference of a woman who took admirers as a matter of course.

"One grows bored with the same words spoken in the same tone of voice, the same foolish vows that mean nothing."

"Aren't you being a little hard on poor Gregory Allsop?" Bracewell inquired. "I've heard he's constantly on the point of blowing out his brains for your sake."

Leonie gave a rich chuckle that one lovesick swain had described as being like the bubbling of old brandy. "My dear Bracewell, Gregory's brains would do me as little good as they appear to do him. He enjoys being suicidal over me. It gives him something to live for. Never fear. His brains— such as they are—will remain intact." She smiled mischievously at Lord Bracewell. "Can't you find me some more spirited prey?"

"I believe I might. Tell me, in your extensive traveling, did you ever visit Wolfenberg?"

Leonie frowned. "I'm not sure. There are so many of those little German states that it's easy to lose track. I know Coniston went to Wolfenberg a few years before we were married. That was just after the old prince died and the new one, Klaus Friederich, was proclaimed. Coniston said he was dreadfully pale and looked stunned by the whole business."

"Considering he was only twenty, it's hardly surprising," Bracewell observed. "He was surrounded by factions and intrigue, which he lacked the experience to deal with. Luckily he got his bearings, asserted himself forcefully and has kept a tight hand on things ever since. Wolfenberg is now a stable country with friendly ties with Britain." Bracewell's voice became judicious. "At all costs this situation must be preserved."

"But now Bismarck has his finger in the pie?" Leonie guessed.

"Bismarck has his finger in every pie in Europe," Bracewell said gloomily. "As the Prime Minister of Prussia, he's in a strong position to achieve his aim, which, as you know, is the unification of all the German states in what he likes to call 'a federation of equals.'"

"But which would actually mean getting them all under Prussia's thumb," Leonie said. This was familiar territory to her. Otto von Bismarck's plan to unify Germany had dominated the continent for the last few years.

Bracewell nodded. "The rulers would remain on their thrones, but real power would be drained from them. Prince Klaus wants nothing to do with it. He knows how little independence his country would have left, and he's made a solemn pledge not to yield. Bismarck was furious. He's tried to change the prince's mind by persuasion, and failed." Bracewell took a deep breath. "So now he's trying to have him assassinated."

Leonie stared. "Are you sure of that?"

"There have been at least three attempts on his life, the last one only this morning. Luckily it was foiled. If it had succeeded, Bismarck would have seized the excuse to invade Wolfenberg and 'restore order.'

Leonie frowned. "Is there no heir?"

"The heir is the prince's second cousin, Archduke Reinald, who also serves as his chief minister. He's even more opposed to unification than Prince Klaus."

"Is Bismarck trying to kill him too?"

"I believe so, but Reinald makes few public appearances, and he's much harder to reach. It's Klaus who causes us the real worry. If we could marry him to a member of the British court, it would act as a warning to Bismarck. But the Wolfenberg ministers won't consider anyone not actually of royal blood. The only possibility is Princess Louise, and her majesty won't hear of it."

"Louise is only seventeen," Leonie said. But she knew this wasn't the real reason for Queen Victoria's opposition.

Her eldest daughter had married into the Prussian royal family, putting the queen firmly in the pro-Prussian camp, to the dismay of her ministers.

"Prince Klaus is, of course, an object of interest to every royal house in Europe with a marriageable daughter," Bracewell continued, "not to mention some ladies of his own court with ambitious husbands."

"Does he take advantage of their...'ambitions'?" Leonie inquired with a twinkle in her eye.

"I believe he occasionally avails himself of a lady's charms. It would be incredible if he didn't. But he doesn't appoint his ministers on that basis. He's completely free from corruption and in some ways puritanical. I know of several beauties who offered themselves too eagerly for the royal bed and were snubbed."

Leonie's curved lips twitched with amusement. "Do I gather you wish me to throw my cap into the ring?"

Bracewell inclined his head toward her. "I certainly wish you to catch the prince's interest in your own inimitable fashion. We need someone close to him to help protect him until we can arrange the marriage. I don't think you'll find the task unpleasant." He opened his pocketbook and took out a photograph, which he passed to her. Leonie glanced over the face of a man in his middle thirties. It must have been a handsome face, she thought, before the mask of coldness and stern pride had settled over it.

"It's extremely fortunate that the Prince and Princess of Wales should have been blessed with another son just now," Bracewell continued. "At the prime minister's suggestion, they invited Klaus to be a godfather to the child. Officially, he's in England for the christening, but his real purpose is to negotiate a loan to strengthen his army. You'll see him at the baptism ceremony tomorrow, and again at the ball in the evening."

"And what exactly am I to do?"

Bracewell gave one of his rare smiles. "Just be yourself, Duchess. The rest will follow naturally."

"Hmm. Suppose I fail to arouse his interest?"

Bracewell rose and bowed low over her hand. "I have no fear of that," he assured her. "No fear at all."

When Lord Bracewell had departed, Leonie studied the portrait, noting the sensual mouth offset by wary eyes. She smiled to herself. This man would be a challenge, and she was looking forward to their meeting.

A little later that day, Prince Klaus Friederich received the British Prime Minister, Lord Palmerston, accompanied by Lord Bracewell.

"I rejoice to see your royal highness looking well," Palmerston declared as he made his bow. "It might so easily have been otherwise."

"The affair was supposed to be a secret, gentlemen," Klaus said coldly.

"It will remain so, to everyone except those in this room," Palmerston assured him.

"On the contrary. Whoever shot Gorstein, or sent someone to shoot him, knows all about it."

"There need be no concern," Bracewell said smoothly. "Gorstein was eliminated by one of my agents, with instructions to protect you from harm."

Klaus turned blazing eyes on him. "This is intolerable," he snapped. "Am I under surveillance by your spies?"

"Your royal highness must understand the importance placed upon your life by the British government," Palmerston said firmly. "Gorstein had orders to kill you. British agents had orders to prevent such a catastrophe."

Klaus's stern features relaxed a little. "My apologies, gentlemen. The blame is mine for having allowed such a situation to develop. I shall be more cautious another time. Now, I hope you've come to tell me that the loan has been agreed."

"There's no difficulty about the amount," Palmerston said. He paused delicately before continuing. "But I must insist that you take better care of your own safety. We foiled this attack because it took place in England. Once you return to Wolfenberg, it becomes more difficult."

"I've given you my word to be more cautious," Klaus reminded him.

"And naturally we have complete faith in your royal highness's word," Palmerston said. "But unforeseeable situations may arise. The fact is, the loan can only be finalized if you allow a British secret service agent to keep close to you when you return home."

"Out of the question," Klaus declared angrily. "I have a personal guard who can take care of my safety."

Palmerston shook his head. "With respect, that won't do. Your guards are answerable to you. You pay them and can dismiss them."

"And you prefer a man who's answerable to *you?*" Klaus snapped. "It's unthinkable. You can take my refusal as final."

"In that case, I'm afraid there can be no question of a British loan," Palmerston said.

Many men had quailed at the look Klaus turned on the prime minister and at the rage that broke over his head, but Palmerston was a wily old dog of eighty and he'd been dealing with royalty all his life. He waited until the storm was over and Prince Klaus said angrily, "It's clear that I have no choice. Nothing but necessity would make me accept such an intolerable arrangement."

"We're all the victims of necessity, your highness. But necessity in this case is called Bismarck. If we quarrel among ourselves, he will prevail."

"You're right," Klaus said more calmly. "In the face of that danger, nothing else matters. Very well. Who is the man to be?"

From an inner pocket Sir William Bracewell produced one half of a playing card which he handed to Klaus. "My agent will be carrying the other half of this card," he said. "The torn edges will fit perfectly together."

"Must we be melodramatic?" Klaus growled. "Why don't you just give me the man's name now?"

"Because I have yet to decide who will best suit your royal highness's particular requirements," Sir William replied untruthfully.

"George Frederick Ernest Albert, I baptize thee in the name of the Father, and of the Son, and of the Holy Ghost. Amen."

It was oppressively hot in the little chapel. Klaus had already played his part in the ceremony, standing as one of the sponsors to the baby prince. Now he was acting mechanically while his thoughts ran ahead. After the baptism there was only one more function to endure, the grand ball that he must attend that evening. Tomorrow he could leave for home.

He thought of his country with fierce protectiveness. At his coronation he'd sworn to protect Wolfenberg and its people with all his strength, with his life if need be. But yesterday he'd almost thrown that life away and plunged his country into chaos. He was still angry with himself.

At least he'd secured the loan he needed to fortify Wolfenberg's defenses, even if it meant a British agent dogging his footsteps, reporting back to London. He nearly groaned aloud. He was used to having his wishes obeyed, and to have such a situation forced on him against his will was galling. To divert himself, he glanced around the chapel. From his place near the altar he could see almost the whole congregation.

There were a few of the nine brothers and sisters of the young Prince of Wales. He didn't know them all by sight, but he recognized Alice, Alfred, Helena—and Louise, a sallow, seventeen-year-old girl with a prim face. His ministers were demanding a state marriage between them, and perhaps in the end, his duty would force him to oblige. But he didn't want a wife fifteen years his junior even if she did bring an English alliance as her dowry. He'd spoken twice to Louise and hadn't taken to her. Nor had she taken to him, if her manner was any guide.

Suddenly his glance fell on a young woman in the front row. He couldn't see her face properly, but there was something exquisite in the turn of her neck, the half-seen curve of her cheek. She had a tall, supple figure, tiny waist and high breasts, adorned with dove-gray velvet, set off by a tiny matching hat. A pearl clasp at her throat topped snowy lace ruffles. Her clothes were impeccably modest, as befitted the surroundings, yet somehow dashing and stylish, as though those qualities were so inherent in the woman that they must pervade everything about her.

He began to wonder about her features. Surely they must be beautiful, to fit the rest of her? If only she would turn her head.

At last she did so, but only slightly, giving him a clear view of her profile, with its high forehead, straight nose and neat, firm chin. It was an unusually determined chin for a woman, he realized, hinting at a nature likely to rebel against the sweet docility expected of females. His admiration dimmed slightly. He had little taste for argumentative women.

But then she leaned down to a little girl who was standing beside her, and who'd murmured something to her. She was making some reply, and she smiled as she spoke. Klaus drew in his breath at that smile. Even half-seen, it was like a miracle, radiating a warmth and charm that seemed to fill the chapel. Then she lifted her head, letting him see her face properly, and it was an incredible face, full of contrasts. The eyes, so dark and brilliant, could have come from a Gypsy, and her full mouth had a ripeness that made him think of succulent fruit. It was a wicked mouth, promising much, curling slightly at the corners, so that even now, when her smile had faded, there was still a hint of uncontrollable zest for life. And all this richness lay against a fair skin and hair of honey blond. She was wildly out of place in this sedate English chapel, as out of place as a diamond necklace worn over serge.

She was married, of course. The little girl beside her must be her daughter. Besides, no woman ever looked like that until she'd experienced a man. He felt a strange ache at the thought that some other man had garnered that lush harvest all for himself.

He was so preoccupied with the vision that for once he forgot to be cautious, and when she suddenly looked at him, he hadn't time to turn away. Caught! he thought furiously. Caught like a peeping schoolboy! But still he couldn't move. It was as though he was held against his will in a trap, unable to do anything but gaze at those marvelous glowing eyes.

He waited for her to give him a tempting smile, as women always did. He was free from vanity on that score, attributing their interest to his rank and not himself, but he'd grown unconsciously to expect it.

This woman was different. She didn't try to draw him on. Instead, she wore a startled look. Her lips parted and he could have sworn she drew in her breath in an echo of his own reaction a moment ago. Her clear, candid gaze met his without artifice or deception and he had the unnerving feeling of seeing to the bottom of her soul, and finding it beautiful. Suddenly she turned away. It might have been a casual movement. There was only his own inner certainty to tell him that she'd avoided his gaze deliberately.

He remained watching. He'd forgotten the service, the people around him. All his attention was concentrated on willing her to look at him, to give him the generous, enchanting smile she'd bestowed on the child. The force of his longing was so great that he could feel it reaching across the chapel to her, touching her....

At last she obeyed his silent command and raised her eyes to meet his. Now everything was different. There was steel in that beautiful gaze, and a challenge like a duelist's that took him aback. For a moment he felt he was back on the heath in the dawn, looking destiny in the eyes, his opponent's blade aimed for his heart....

He came out of his reverie to realize that the service was over. The young parents were leaving, followed by the sponsors. He fell into step, resisting the temptation to glance back. As they all moved through the wide doorway, he felt something brush past him. It was the little girl who'd been standing with the woman, but she was alone. She ran straight to the Prince of Wales, who pulled her ribbons affectionately. "Here's another member of my family," he said to Klaus. "Meet my baby sister, Beatrice."

"I'm not a baby," the little girl said indignantly. "I'm eight."

Klaus greeted her and said, "I saw you in the chapel. I thought the lady with you was your mother."

"Oh, no, that's Leonie," Beatrice declared.

She didn't elaborate and Klaus suppressed the instinct to ask further questions. He knew too well that if he showed any sign of interest in a woman, it would be common gossip in a matter of hours. If Leonie was a family friend, she would doubtless be at the ball tonight. Until then he must curb his impatience.

Coniston House was in turmoil, with maids, valets and footmen scurrying hither and thither. The ball to mark Prince George's christening was the social event of the season, and those who'd been invited were the elect. The Conistons, of course, had had no fears on that score. They knew themselves to be the elect of the elect, with only the royal family itself ranking higher.

One room of the house was notably free from hurry. The dowager duchess, having taken her bath and allowed Miss Hatchard, her personal dresser to attire her, was sitting quietly while her magnificent golden locks were piled into gleaming masses on her head, ready to receive the sapphire and diamond aigrette. Her expression was distracted, a little smile playing over her lovely lips, and Miss Hatchard, a grim-faced woman whose only joy in life was to produce this perfect work of art, was emboldened to say, "May I take the liberty of inquiring your grace's thoughts?"

"I was thinking of violins," Leonie said with a little laugh. "And how beautiful they are to dance to."

"Their royal highnesses will of course have the very best musicians," Miss Hatchard opined with satisfaction.

Leonie let it go at that. She hadn't been thinking of the liveried orchestra creating smooth sounds at the Prince of Wales's mansion, but of very different violins, played by Gypsy hands, making wild, thrilling music, long ago, in another world that sometimes felt like a beautiful dream.

How fast those musicians had played, fingers moving at incredible speed over the strings while the dancers spun madly and laughed in the light of the campfire.

There, in her memory, were her parents; her father, with his fair English looks making him stand out among the swarthy Gypsies, and his noble bearing marking him as an aristocrat, and her mother, with the turbulent dark beauty that had won him away from his background to follow the traveling people.

Even as a tiny tot, she'd known by heart the story of their romance, for she'd loved nothing better than to hear how her father, the younger son of an English marquis, had been traveling Europe to complete his education. In Italy, young Lord Gavin Markby had celebrated his twenty-first birthday in the house of a count, who'd thrown a party and hired a troupe of Gypsies to entertain the guests. And from the moment Nesta had leapt onto the floor, whirling to the beat of the tambourine, he'd been lost.

When the Gypsies left, he went with them, dodging and hiding to escape the pursuers who were intent on "rescuing" him and taking him back to live the dull life of an English country gentleman. By the time they were caught, it was too late. Gavin had married his Gypsy love. His father had cursed his favorite son and the woman who'd bewitched him, and blotted them out of his life.

Six months later, their daughter was born and there followed ten years of unclouded happiness. Leonie favored her father in her blond looks, and her mother in her fiery nature. The vagabond life had suited her. Papa had taught her to read and write and to speak his own language perfectly. Mama taught her about the herbs and spices that seasoned the pots hanging over the great fires. Old Meg, the troupe's wisewoman, instructed her in the spells and incantations with which trouble could be eased, but only for those who believed.

The little band rolled back and forth across Europe, always heading for the place where a better living could be earned. This town always had a fair on such and such a day. That circus often needed extra acts. Often they would find guidance along the paths where other Gypsy caravans had passed, plants hung on trees in a certain order, stones placed in a particular shape that seemed accidental, except to those in the know who would read in it a promise or a warning. By the time she was five, Leonie could read every Gypsy sign.

She had a dozen friends of roughly her own age, for the children all ran together. The boys showed her how to fight and she was soon able to aim kicks and thumps with the best of them. She learned to juggle, to tumble with the acrobats, to ride the swiftest horses, to speak French, German, Italian and Spanish in a higgledy-piggledy kind of way. She adored the whole troupe, but after Mama and Papa, she loved best Uncle Silas, Nesta's scapegrace brother. It was he who taught her how to pick a lock or a pocket, to throw a stone straight so that the highest fruit on the tree came tumbling down.

It was a strange beginning for the woman who now bore one of the most illustrious names in England. But the road from the Gypsy camp to a ducal coronet had been winding and tortuous, and sometimes tragic....

Her memories were abruptly cut off by an urgent knock on the door. Before she could reply, it was flung open and a girl bounced into the room. Leonie smiled at the sight of Lady Harriet, daughter of the present Duke of Coniston, and granddaughter of Leonie's late husband. Harriet stopped dead at the sight of Leonie and gasped, "You look *magnificent*."

And Leonie did indeed look magnificent in her dress of blue satin finished with silver. Silver roses adorned the skirt, draped over a huge, swaying crinoline, and a flounce of silver lace swept around the hem. There was more silver lace about the bosom, from which arose a pair of white, gleaming shoulders and a long, swanlike neck. For jewelry, Leonie had chosen to wear her husband's wedding gift of sapphires and diamonds. A heavy necklace hung about her throat, and pendant earrings shone from her ears. The set was completed by a flashing aigrette, adorned with two small white silk feathers.

They made a striking contrast. Harriet was delightful in white tulle with a modest neckline, as befitted a girl of her age. At seventeen, she'd just made her debut in society and the innocence of childhood was still on her face.

Leonie looked like what she was, a woman of the world, poised, beautiful and supremely self-confident in her dealings with both men and women. She indicated for Miss Hatchard to leave, and when they were alone, kissed Harriet on the cheek. "You look enchanting," she said. "Even your mama should be pleased with you."

Harriet sighed. "I wish she were. She criticizes everything, and I do my best to please her. I don't know what more she wants."

Leonie was silent. The Conistons were distantly related to the royal family, and the connection was dear to Gwendolyn's heart. Leonie had a shrewd suspicion that the duchess wouldn't rest until she'd married her daughter to royalty, however obscure, however decrepit. But she judged it wiser not to worry Harriet's guileless heart with hints of her mother's ambitions.

The door opened again and Gwendolyn entered without knocking. Her face was hard with displeasure. "I guessed I should find you here, Harriet."

"Why shouldn't my granddaughter come to visit me?" Leonie inquired languidly.

Gwendolyn's lips tightened. "I've asked you before not to refer to Harriet as your granddaughter."

"But she's Coniston's granddaughter," Leonie observed guilelessly, "and I'm so hopelessly fond of my husband's family that I want only to adopt them as my own."

"I think it's wonderful that Leonie loves us so much," Harriet said innocently, and was rewarded by one of her mother's most fearsome scowls.

"You, miss, can hold your tongue. Let me tell you that it does our family no credit to be connected with a woman who, whatever her title, is descended from—" Gwendolyn stopped, a sudden dryness constricting her throat at the gaze Leonie turned on her. The beautiful face had hardly changed. The lips still smiled, but the smile had faded from the dark blue eyes, to be replaced by a look of cold, deadly menace.

Gwendolyn gulped before continuing. "To be addressed in such terms by a woman in her twenties makes the family ridiculous. *I do not like looking ridiculous.*"

Leonie smiled as sweetly as a baby. "Well, there's nothing I can do about that, Gwendolyn dear," she murmured.

Harriet's little choke showed that she'd appreciated this sally. Gwendolyn controlled herself with an effort and spoke to Harriet. "Your maid says you rushed from your room so fast that you forgot to put on your diamond necklace. Hurry back now."

"Oh but, Mama, Leonie has told me that diamonds aren't appropriate for me just yet," Harriet protested.

A thunderous silence ensued. When Gwendolyn had mastered her temper, she said coldly, "I hadn't realized Leonie was such an authority on matters of taste and style."

"Not I," Leonie disclaimed with a hint of mischief. "The Princess of Wales told me herself that she never wore diamonds before her marriage."

Gwendolyn breathed hard. "I take it we're all ready to depart," she said.

"Perfectly ready," Leonie declared.

"Wait for us downstairs," Gwendolyn commanded her daughter. When Harriet had departed, she demanded, "May I ask if you intend to make an appearance like that?" Her eyes were fixed on Leonie's bosom.

"Naturally. Whatever's the matter with you, Gwendolyn? You're gobbling like a turkey."

"You shouldn't need me to tell you that your neckline is scandalous."

Leonie glanced down at the dress that plunged daringly, revealing the swell of her white, perfect breasts. "I consider it suitable," she said. "We're not, after all, going to church. And what's more, my dear Gwendolyn, it's highly improper for you to criticize your mother-in-law."

Gwendolyn's knuckles were white on her fan. "You may think you're very clever," she said, "but I refuse to tolerate your behavior. I insist that you leave my house."

Leonie's blue eyes glinted. "Your house? I thought it was the duke's, bequeathed to him by my late husband on the understanding that I should always have a home here."

"Some other arrangement can be made—a suitable dower house—"

"Oh, but I don't think it would suit me to live in an obscure dower house," Leonie observed. "And it would be obscure, wouldn't it—if you had your way?"

"If I had my way, you would be whipped out into the street!" Gwendolyn declared furiously. "Don't imagine you can defeat me so easily. I've seen my daughter coming under your pernicious influence, and it must stop. I shall not allow you to corrupt her.''

Again there was the cold look in Leonie's eyes, but Gwendolyn escaped by turning on her heel and flouncing out.

Chapter Two

When everyone was in place in the grand ballroom of Marlborough House, the majordomo thumped his staff on the floor, two huge mirrored doors swung open and the Prince and Princess of Wales appeared. Prince Edward was in his early twenties and hadn't yet grown the beard by which he was later known to the world. His plump, round face already showed signs of sensuality and over indulgence. Beside him walked Princess Alexandra, twenty-one, and exquisitely beautiful.

Behind them came Prince Klaus Friederich in the dress uniform of the Wolfenberg army, his face set in lines of cold hauteur that only his intimates knew was a mask to conceal intolerable boredom.

At a signal from the Prince of Wales, the majordomo announced the commencement of the ball. As the guest of honor, Prince Klaus danced first with his hostess, Princess Alexandra. "How serious you are," she teased as they glided and whirled in time to the music. After four years in England, she spoke the language well, but still with a Danish accent. "This should be a happy day."

"I assure you I rejoice in your happiness," Klaus said politely. It was hard to pull his mind away from the cares that absorbed it, but he made the effort, knowing that if he seemed worried or abstracted, there were eyes everywhere, and brains behind those eyes, making notes. Sometimes, being on permanent display was the most wearying part of his life.

Out of the corner of his eye he saw Prince Edward go whirling by. A frisson went through him as he thought he recognized Eddie's partner. He resisted the temptation to turn his head, but he gradually steered Alexandra to where he had a better view. It was she, the young woman he'd seen in the church that morning, clasped in Eddie's plump embrace. She was gone in an instant, spinning out of his view like a gorgeous blue-and-silver top, but there was no doubt. His heart beat faster at the thought that soon he would meet her, but he quickly brought himself under control. Self-discipline had been his watchword since he was ten and had fought back the tears over his mother's grave, knowing that his fearsome grandfather was watching everything he did. So nothing showed on his face now, but he was aware of every movement that brought him close to her, and away again.

"You're not listening to me," Alex chided him mischievously.

"Forgive me," he said. "My mind wandered for a moment."

"I was telling you about my good friend, the Dowager Duchess of Coniston. I would like to present her to you."

"I should be delighted," he said courteously. Inwardly he sighed. He knew all about dowagers, elderly ladies who charged through society like battleships, seeking positions for their sons, conducting complex marriage negotiations with a merciless eye for detail that would do credit to a government minister. Klaus knew of some dowagers that he'd be glad to have on his side in a fight, but none that he would enjoy being cornered by at a ball.

The music was coming to an end. "You must meet her now," Alexandra said, turning to look into the throng. "Ah, there she is." Klaus fixed a courteous smile on his face and assumed an air of pleased expectancy. "Your highness, I have pleasure in presenting my dear friend, the Dowager Duchess of Coniston."

He had a momentary glimpse of the woman in blue and silver as he inclined his head in greeting. Before he could understand what was happening, she was curtsying low before him. Her head was bent, revealing shiny blond locks piled high on her head, and a white, swanlike neck. As she raised her face to him, her eyelids glided slowly upward, so that the magnificence of her large dark blue eyes was only gradually revealed. Below them, the low cut of her dress showed off the tops of two of the most beautiful, milky white breasts he'd ever seen. He stared, thunderstruck.

"Your royal highness," she murmured.

He mastered his astonishment. "I'm enchanted, Duchess, to make your acquaintance," he said formally. "Perhaps you'll be so good as to honor me with the next dance."

"As your royal highness pleases."

She slipped easily into his arms. He put his hand around her waist, discovering it to be as slender as that of a young girl. But there was nothing else girlish about her. As he'd noted that morning, her face was that of an experienced woman, and her body moved freely and unself-consciously close to his. It was like dancing with gossamer, but gossamer infused with sensuality and erotic instinct.

A subtle perfume rose from between her breasts. It was one he'd never encountered before, and it was different from the usual creations women wore to allure. Beneath the slight trace of musk, it had a tang that hinted at wood fires and starlight, ripe fruit and hot summer earth. His head swam and unconsciously he tightened his clasp.

She was looking at him questioningly, and he remembered that it was for him to start the conversation. "You must forgive my surprise, Duchess, but I was informed that you were a dowager. Perhaps there's some mistake?"

She laughed and the sound sent shivers down his spine. "There's no mistake, your royal highness. My late husband was some years older than myself, which means I have a stepson and daughter-in-law twenty years my senior." She added impishly, "I believe I'm a great trial to them."

His severe face relaxed into a faint smile. "I can imagine that life with you could be unpredictable—Leonie."

"You know my name?"

"Does that surprise you? You saw me looking at you in the chapel this morning."

"I'd imagined your royal highness's mind was occupied with the solemnity of the occasion."

His grasp on her tightened again. "You imagined no such thing. You knew I was watching you. Admit it."

The last words were a command. To his surprise she merely shrugged her slim shoulders and said, "Perhaps. My eyes may have wandered, but I'm sure my mind was occupied with higher things. The service was quite beautiful, didn't your royal highness think so?"

His thoughts were clearing. She was a widow, experienced, a woman of the world, and free to travel. In short, the ideal mistress. "You needn't call me your royal highness every time," he told her. "My name is Klaus."

Instead of simpering at the compliment, she said directly, "I can't use your given name. Think of the scandal."

"You can say it when we speak privately, like this. And when we're alone."

Her eyebrows went up into two enchanting arches. "Alone? Are we going to be alone?"

"Yes," he said, holding her more tightly. "Yes, we will be alone—often."

"But how can that be? I understand you're returning to Wolfenberg tomorrow."

"But you're a free woman. You can follow me."

"Yes, sir, I'm a free woman. And because I'm a free woman, I'm not sure whether I'll be coming to Wolfenberg."

"Come, this is nonsense," he said peremptorily. "Why shouldn't you?"

"Perhaps because I don't follow tamely after any man—even a prince."

"I have much to offer, Leonie. Think of that."

"On the contrary, I'll do my best to forget you said it. If I followed you because of what you have to offer, what would you think of me?"

It hadn't crossed his mind. He was so used to women who were eager for the chance of a liaison with him that he'd never considered the world's opinion. It was no shame to be a royal mistress. But she forced him to confront the question, and to realize that if she were to do his bidding, he would think her just like all the others. And this woman was like no other.

But he answered, "I should think you an amiable woman, whose company I should enjoy, and who might, perhaps, enjoy mine."

"Charming. But a discreet woman had better not be too amiable, don't you think, sir? The world can be censorious."

"Not in this case. The prince's favorite is a position of honor." He looked down deeply into her eyes and his breath came raggedly. "I will make Wolfenberg bow before you," he said huskily.

"Until the day you become bored," she replied. "And then Wolfenberg will get up again, and laugh at me."

"No," he said seriously. "I'm a good friend, afterward."

"Afterward." She seemed to consider the word. "It has a melancholy sound. I don't like it. Perhaps it's better to have no 'now' than to endure an 'afterward.'"

"Are you teasing me?" he demanded.

A mischievous smile played over her lovely lips. "Perhaps. Do *you* think I am?"

He was taken aback at her impertinence. He wasn't used to being challenged, but there was a piquancy about it that teased his senses, blunting annoyance. While he was considering an answer, he realized that the music was slowing and the dance was over. "You will have the next dance with me," he commanded.

"Indeed I shan't. I've promised it to someone else, and your royal highness must have many duty dances still to do. My daughter-in-law, for instance, would be highly offended to be overlooked. Ah, I see her now."

He sighed and yielded to the inevitable. A sharp-faced woman with a military bearing was descending on them, with a middle-aged man and a younger girl caught in her wake.

"Your royal highness," Leonie said, "allow me to present the Duke and Duchess of Coniston, and their daughter, Lady Harriet."

Klaus inclined his head and repeated the words that had carried him through many such occasions. To his relief, he saw that Bernhard had appeared at his elbow and Klaus immediately presented him. The music was starting again. Since there was no avoiding it, he offered Gwendolyn his arm and led her onto the floor. The Prince of Wales, who had joined the group just in time to see Leonie direct Klaus to Gwendolyn, now claimed Leonie for himself, and Lady Harriet shyly accepted Bernhard's invitation. The duke escaped in search of a card table.

"That wasn't very kind of you," the Prince of Wales observed, laughing as he waltzed with Leonie.

"I had to give Gwendolyn her chance," Leonie said. "Think of the tirade that would have fallen over my head if she hadn't met the prince and danced with him."

"It's liable to fall still. She'll be furious that it was you who presented her."

"That's true. I think the time may be coming near for me to be off on my travels again."

"And London will lose your brilliant light. What shall we do without you?"

She chuckled. "You'll scarcely notice that I'm gone."

He made the reply of a skilled flirt and she listened with half her attention. The rest was given to considering the man she was pursuing like a hunter, hiding her intentions behind whatever foliage was available, but snaring his interest so that he couldn't escape. She'd made her first reconnoiter and the results had been interesting. Her prey was tempted by the bait, but she guessed he would toss it back at the first clumsy move.

Through her extensive traveling, Leonie had met all kinds of men. The woman who'd been born in a Gypsy caravan had danced in the arms of Otto von Bismarck, the gray eminence behind the Prussian throne. She had danced with Ludwig, the beautiful boy with mad eyes who'd recently become King of Bavaria, and with the handsome Emperor Franz Joseph of Austria. She'd learned to estimate their qualities quickly, and she found Prince Klaus intriguing. She knew that he wanted her, less because of his words than because he held her like a man in the grip of desire. As they whirled past each other, he didn't openly look in her direction but she sensed he was aware of her, that he knew at any given moment exactly where she was in the ballroom. She sensed all these things because it was the same with her.

Klaus's manner was reserved, but behind it she'd felt banked fires of passion, which perhaps had never been allowed to flare up in total freedom. The thought of being the woman to release those fires sent a tremor through her, and in the same moment, she recognized that she must suppress such feelings. They threatened her detachment and would get in the way of her job. And in her highly specialized sphere, Leonie was a professional who let nothing interfere with her mission.

The dance ended. The Prince of Wales released her with a reminder that she'd promised him the supper dance, but when the moment came, he approached her with Klaus a little behind him and declared, "I've been persuaded that as a good host it's my duty to yield up your hand to my guest. What do you say, m'dear?"

"I say that as a loyal subject I have no choice but to obey the royal command," Leonie responded, dropping into another curtsy that gave Klaus the full benefit of the vision she presented. Raising her eyes to him, she could see that he was in a fever for her.

The Prince of Wales took her hand, gave it to Klaus and tactfully vanished. The strains of a waltz drifted over the ballroom and she was in Klaus's arms again, swaying to the sweet rhythms, feeling the heat of his body.

"Your reception of me was ungracious, madam," he declared.

"It wasn't very gracious of your highness to make me a spectacle by claiming me so publicly," she retorted with spirit.

"Come, don't play the blushing violet with me. You're a woman of the world. Many men must have tried to claim you."

"Many have tried," she agreed. "But only one succeeded."

His arm tightened. "And that was?"

"Why, my husband, of course. Who else could I possibly have meant?"

He relaxed. "You little witch. Let there be an end to this. Tell me when you'll come to Wolfenberg."

"When I'm ready."

"And that will be?"

"Who knows? Some day perhaps, when I'm bored with England. I've never been to Wolfenberg and I'd like to see a new place." She sighed provocatively. "But then, there are so many new places to choose from."

His face darkened. "Don't play games with me, Leonie. I've offered you my favor. What more do you want?"

"Perhaps I don't want more, your highness. Perhaps I want less. I wonder if you would understand that."

His face showed that he didn't. It revealed also that he was a man at the end of his tether, strung on the rack of desire for a woman, aware that he had only a short time to secure her, yet unable to pin her down. The frustration was sending him to the danger point, and a wise woman would refrain from provoking him further. Knowing this, Leonie shrewdly provoked him a little more. "Isn't it a delightful ball?" she asked in her most innocent voice. "I declare there's no finer entertainment to be found than—"

It was enough. Goaded beyond endurance, Klaus began to whirl her faster, his eyes on the tall French doors that led out onto the terrace. In a few seconds, Leonie felt the cool night air on her bare shoulders and she was spinning along the terrace in his arms. When they stopped, they were way beyond the lights and she was alone with him. Until that moment, she'd been mistress of the situation, but now everything was rioting out of control. The arms that held her close brooked no refusal, and the mouth that crushed hers was hard and determined.

She felt her heart begin a sudden mad beating, greater than she'd ever known before. This wasn't how she'd planned it. She needed Klaus to desire her, the better to protect him, as she'd been instructed, but it was not part of the plan that she should desire him. Yet, without warning, she found her blood racing in response to the purposeful caresses of his lips.

"I warned you not to play games with me," he growled as he kissed her. "Now you'll learn that it's I, not you, who set the terms."

A flash of anger scorched across Leonie's brain. This man took too much for granted. He wouldn't be the first sovereign she'd had to remind that she wasn't one of his subjects. But she was strangely weak from the unaccustomed sensations that were chasing through her. She felt as if only his arms were holding her up, and her mouth had been made to respond to his. She fought for self-mastery. What was happening threatened the success of her mission.

But she couldn't stop him trailing kisses down her throat and across her bosom. Nor could she stop herself wanting this, craving for him to go on, burning her with his breath, bringing her flesh to life. Unconsciously, even against her own will, she clasped her hands behind his head, winding her fingers into the dark springy hair, and pressing him closer to her eager flesh. At the same time, a moan of pleasure escaped her, and her breasts rose and fell quickly in wild delight. She'd never before known such sensations, and she wanted them never to stop.

He raised his head and looked down at her flushed face. His own face was suffused with desire and he was breathing hard. "So many women offer me pretended passion to lure me on," he said. "Are you pretending, Leonie?"

"No," she murmured.

"No. No woman can force her heart to race as yours does. You like to tease me, but the truth is here in your lips."

"And *your* heart?" she whispered. "Does it, too, race?"

For answer he took her hand and laid it against his breast, where she could feel the pounding within. "Whatever is true, is true for us both," he said as he lowered his head again.

This time she was ready for his kiss, but nothing could protect her from its devastating force. Against her will, her very soul thrilled to him. This man's touch could make the air sing with danger and danger was her element.

He crushed her mouth beneath his own. He was in a fever of violent desire and it shocked him to the core. He was a sovereign. The watchword of his life was to remain always in control, but this woman had destroyed his self-restraint. He'd barely met her, but he felt as if everything in his life had been leading to the moment when he would take her into his bed and make her beautiful body entirely his own. She *must* belong to him. Anything else was unthinkable. If she fancied she could tease him like a callow boy, he would overcome her as he overcame all opposition.

He drew back, leaving her aching and deprived where he'd touched her. His face hovered in her consciousness.

"Say you'll come to me," he commanded.

She murmured, "Perhaps." It wasn't what she wanted to say. She longed to answer, "Anywhere," but she didn't give in so easily.

"Say it," he ordered. "Say you want me as much as I want you."

Through the swimming of her senses, she grasped at enough composure to answer, "I'll tell you that when...I'm in Wolfenberg."

A light came into his eyes. He thought he'd won. "And when will that be?"

"When I'm ready," she whispered.

"Little witch. I'll make you follow me."

"No man...can make me."

"I can. I will. It'll be a fine duel between us, Leonie. And I promise my victory will be as pleasing to you as it is to me."

She gave a slow smile of pleasure at the thought of that duel, and the arms that were holding her trembled. "Who's to say which one of us will win?" she provoked him softly.

"I always win," he declared.

"So do I," she assured him with a slow, beguiling smile that nearly sent him mad. "So do I."

"And what do you seek to win? What do you want, Leonie?"

"I'll tell you that when I'm in Wolfenberg," she repeated.

"Then you'll come. You *will* come."

"Yes...perhaps...when I'm ready."

Alarm swept over her at how far this had gone. She wasn't herself anymore. Without waiting for his answer, she wrenched herself out of his arms and fled.

As soon as Leonie was in her nightgown that evening, she dismissed Miss Hatchard. She was disturbed to the very core of her being. She needed to sort her disordered thoughts, and even more disordered feelings.

She could hear the music again in her mind, and she began to sway to its rhythm, the satin and lace nightgown swirling about her tall, slender figure. She was back in the ballroom, held by a man whose hands trembled and whose voice was husky with desire. She'd evoked desire in so many men before, and it had meant nothing to her, but tonight her own desire had come rushing up to meet his.

Suddenly the vision of the ballroom vanished to be replaced by another vision from long ago. It was the Gypsy camp where she'd first learned to associate dancing with love. Her mother had taught her how to whirl to the rhythm of the tambourine, but if Papa appeared, Mama would hold out her arms to him, and he would embrace her as they danced together, lost in a world where even their child was forgotten. Whenever Leonie thought of dancing, she saw her parents holding each other close as the firelight flickered over them, melting with the mutual passion that had survived time, marriage and hardship.

But Nesta had fallen ill. For three days, she lay burning up with a fever that nothing could ease. Sometimes she would reach out to caress the little daughter who nestled, terrified, by her side, but at the last moments, only her husband had existed for her. Her eyes had held his, her hand had reached up to touch his face, and her lips whispered, "My heart...oh, my heart..."

After her death, Gavin had been like a man in a trance. For six months, Leonie had seen him fading before her eyes, and had known, with a despair too old for her years, that soon she would be an orphan. One night he'd kissed her tenderly, left her in Silas's care and walked away from the camp. They'd found him the next morning, sitting beneath a tree, his flesh cold, his eyes open and staring, as if fixed on a vision that approached him with open arms and a welcoming smile.

There was no injury, nothing to show how death had come to him, and the Gypsies, with the instinctive wisdom of those who live close to the earth, didn't question it. He'd followed his beloved Nesta. That was all anyone needed to know.

Leonie had wept for the loss of her father, but in her heart there was an even greater grief. It was as though Gavin had abandoned her, choosing to go his own way, despite his child's needs. It was useless for Uncle Silas to explain that some things had to be. She felt betrayed.

Gavin's death had caused another convulsion to engulf her small world. Three months after they'd buried her father beneath the very tree where he'd died, Uncle Silas told her sadly and kindly that she must leave them. "Your father wrote a letter before he died," he explained. "He wanted you to go and live in England, in his old home, and learn to be a great English lady."

It was useless to protest that all she wanted was to stay with the Gypsy family she loved. Silas had cried with her, but he insisted she must obey her father's wishes. Next day, a man and a woman had arrived. The man was a lawyer, with many questions to ask. Silas's replies, and the papers he handed over, seemed to satisfy the man, and when he had his first look at Leonie he'd immediately said, "Oh, yes, definitely a Markby." Then the woman had taken charge of her. Her name was Miss Knole, and she was her governess. Miss Knole had explained that it would be some time before she was "fit" for decent society. She would live in a remote part of her grandfather's estate until she had learned civilized manners.

Even now, years later, she avoided thinking of the months of unrelieved misery that followed. She was heartbroken at the parting from those she loved, and desperately homesick for the free and easy life she'd known. She hated England, a chilly place where it seemed to rain most of the time.

Between herself and Miss Knole there could never be an understanding, which was unfortunate for them both, because they were imprisoned together in a small cottage, with only two maids and a manservant to save them from each other. Miss Knole was rigid, conventional and puritanical. Everything about Leonie shocked her, and she set about changing her completely. She had some success, for the Gypsy life had taught the little girl to be adaptable. She learned to dance in the polite English fashion, although it seemed abominably tame after the wild tambourine rhythms she knew, and her retentive memory enabled her to master her lessons with ease.

But although she could learn English style, she could never be at ease with English attitudes. After six months of daily battles, during which neither of them totally prevailed, Miss Knole had the folly to inform Leonie that she must never, *never* tell anyone that she was half Gypsy. "Gypsies are dirty, dishonest and immoral," she'd said in her tight voice.

She'd barely got the last words out before Leonie hurled her little blackboard at the wall, following it with every book she could find. She was screaming. She could not remember the words, but they must have been very wicked because Miss Knole nearly fainted. The maids rushed in and bore her, still screaming, to her room, where she'd burst into a fit of sobs for Mama and Papa.

When she'd calmed a little, she got up and pushed her bed against the door. For two days, she resisted all Miss Knole's commands to open up. On the third day, a magnificent carriage with a coat of arms drew up below, and out stepped a tall, elderly man. An hour later, the sound of a commotion took Leonie back to the window in time to see Miss Knole being conveyed away in a vastly inferior vehicle, which also contained her box. She was bonneted and shawled, and as she left, she looked up at the window and shook her fist. Leonie watched until she'd vanished among the trees.

After a short silence, she heard footsteps outside her door, and a gruff male voice said, "Miss Knole has left. She will not be returning. I shall expect you downstairs in ten minutes."

That was her first meeting with her grandfather. When she descended, she found him standing there, a tall, spare man with an imposing air and a severe face. Many people found him intimidating, but he reminded Leonie of a gentleman in France who'd caught her raiding his apple orchard. He, too, had looked forbidding, but instead of handing her over to the law, he'd lectured her on the dangers of eating green fruit, and shown her where the ripest apples were to be found. But what affected her most was the expression of intolerable sadness in her grandfather's eyes. She knew the reason. She was the image of the son he'd lost. In that moment, she forgot her own unhappiness and when he leaned down to her, she kissed him.

She became his darling, living with him in the great house because he couldn't bear to let her out of his sight. Leonie never spoke of her mother's family. She wasn't ashamed of them but she came to understand that any mention of Gypsies broke dear Grandpapa's heart. Gradually it became almost a forgotten subject.

Almost. But not quite. As she grew up and made her debut, society maintained the polite fiction that her mother had been "a continental gentlewoman," but behind their fans the women whispered, "My dear, there are the strangest rumors..."

Her beauty was her only advantage in the marriage market. With five children and eighteen grandchildren, the marquis could give her only a modest dowry, and her ancestry weighed against her. Except with Geoffrey.

The thought of her husband made her stop dancing. She opened a drawer and took out a shawl, which she unwrapped to reveal a large photograph. She set this on her dresser and sat regarding the face that looked back at her.

It was that of a man of about sixty-five, not handsome but with eyes that radiated good nature, and a kind smile. He was the late Geoffrey Alastair James Coniston, and this was just how he'd looked on that day nearly ten years ago, when he'd asked for her hand in marriage.

His proposal had thrown her into transports of mirth. But her grandfather had encouraged the match, urging that she'd never get a better offer. But at eighteen, Leonie was passionate, impulsive and wildly in love with Dudley Wemmingham, second son of an earl. Dudley had been boyishly handsome, and to her inexperienced eyes, he'd looked like an angel. She hadn't noticed that his charming mouth had an ominous touch of weakness.

She'd lived one summer in a delirious dream of love. Then, on his twenty-first birthday, Dudley had summoned the courage to confront his parents with the news of his intended marriage. And the heavens had fallen. Dudley's allowance was cut off, a severe blow, since he was extravagant and heavily in debt.

Fortified by Leonie's passionate love, he'd held out for a month before crumbling. Leonie received a letter breaking off all relations, written in Dudley's hand but couched in terms that made it clear he was writing to his formidable mother's dictation. He asked for the immediate return of all his letters, but Leonie was unable to do so, having burned them in disgust the night before.

The greatest pain came from the discovery that her love could turn to scorn. She'd offered him all her young ardor, and he'd scurried spinelessly behind his mother's skirts.

In addition, he'd confirmed, as no words could have done, that her choice of husband was severely limited. Whether it was chance that had made Coniston call that day, or whether, as she suspected, her grandfather had sent him a message, it didn't matter. He was a widower with two sons presented to him forty years ago by a lady of impeccable lineage, and two grandsons, so he could afford to overlook Leonie's ancestry. In a mood of bitter defiance, she consented to become Duchess of Coniston.

She never regretted her hasty decision. Coniston was a kind man, deeply in love with his young bride, and nothing pleased him more than to spoil her. The sapphires and diamonds that had been his marriage gift were worth a king's ransom, and the flawless pearls that adorned her wedding dress had caused gasps as she walked down the aisle.

He'd taken her abroad immediately and they'd begun a wandering existence that exactly suited Leonie. She soon perfected the languages that she'd spoken brokenly in her childhood, and in no time she was at home in international society. Her beauty flowered and ripened. She had admirers by the score. She flirted with and teased them, and allowed them to run her errands, but there was a line beyond which she never stepped. She'd developed a deep, warm affection for her husband, and she would have died rather than hurt him.

When they'd been married a year and she was the toast of Europe, she discovered that Geoffrey was in contact with British Intelligence. Under the guise of being nothing more than a beef-witted Englishman, he was secretly picking up information about the dangerous European situation and passing it back to London in the British diplomatic bag.

The discovery thrilled her. She had a natural gift for intrigue, and she plunged into intelligence work with delight. She'd already learned that infatuation could make a man stupid, and from there it was a short step to making him reveal things that he'd better have kept quiet about. She got possession of a steady stream of high-quality gossip, which she fed back to her husband.

After five years, Coniston suffered a heart attack on a visit to England, and in three days he was dead, leaving behind a beautiful young widow who mourned him sincerely. His love and kindness had never wavered, and Leonie's only consolation was the knowledge that she'd made him happy. She followed his funeral cortege swathed in black, the long veil hiding the tears that streamed down her face.

Gwendolyn, the new duchess, sneered acidly at that veil. "Of course she chose it to conceal the smile on her face. She married an old man for his money and now she's got everything she wants—an indecently lavish settlement, at *our* expense, and no obligations."

Her husband, Cedric, an inoffensive creature who would gladly have lived at peace with his young stepmother, had looked acutely unhappy and tried in vain to get his wife to lower her voice. Leonie had meant to remain at Coniston House for a while, but she and Gwendolyn were like two cats in a bag, and it was clear that the arrangement couldn't last long.

Then, Lord Bracewell, the man to whom Geoffrey had made his reports, had come to call. "It's an open secret that recently much of Coniston's information came from you," he told her. "The quality of the intelligence rose so sharply that I could almost put a date on your interest. You have unique talents, Duchess. It would be a pity if they were lost to the service of your country."

So Leonie's travels began again, apparently directionless, but actually guided from a government desk. On the surface she seemed to be exactly what men expected a woman to be, beautiful, frivolous, ready to be instructed by the "superior" male intellect, fascinated by clothes and scandal, not interested in serious subjects such as "boring" politics.

Those who acclaimed the young duchess sighed over her and wooed her, never noticed the shrewdness of her actions, so different from the giddy charm projected by her words. They knew nothing of the formidable memory that enabled her to recall whole conversations verbatim. Above all, they never suspected that she was sending back a stream of detailed information on the dangerous European situation to British Intelligence. She loved the work. It provided her with the excitement her Gypsy soul craved, and it helped to ease the ache of loneliness left by her husband.

Even now, four years after Geoffrey's death, the habit of taking all her problems to him was one she'd never entirely broken. The face looking at her from the picture bore the same kindly, good-humored expression she remembered and loved. It was easy to smile back at him and whisper, "Did I do well tonight? He took the bait. Do you remember how we used to laugh when they took the bait? I wish you were here now, and we could laugh together again."

Unbidden, Klaus's face came into her mind, the dark eyes glowing with passion, his voice husky as he commanded her. And she felt again the stirring deep within her that had so surprised her that night. It had alarmed her because it was out of place. She played love games for the sake of her country, but she remained unmoved by them. That was the only way she could work. But tonight she'd felt a fierce response go through her. She'd come to the edge of losing control and almost toppled over.

After a moment, she put the photograph away. For some reason, she couldn't laugh with Geoffrey about Klaus.

Chapter Three

It was no surprise to Leonie when Harriet sought her out in the garden next morning, and her first remark might have fallen from the lips of the most respectable dowager in England. "Four dances with the same young gentleman. Shocking." But Leonie spoiled the effect by a pair of twinkling eyes, and Harriet laughed joyously.

"Isn't he handsome, Leonie? Isn't he splendid?"

Leonie, who'd thought Bernhard pleasant but neither handsome nor splendid, concluded that Harriet was even more lovestruck than she seemed. "I thought him an amiable young man," she said cautiously.

"He was the best-looking man in the room."

"Better-looking than George Cannington, who's been trying to approach your mother?" Leonie asked mischievously.

"I detest George Cannington," Harriet declared firmly.

Leonie felt this was just as well, since Sir George, despite his legendary good looks and reputed wealth was a mere baronet, and nowhere near highborn enough for Gwendolyn. But neither, she suspected, was Bernhard. Luckily he would be returning to Wolfenberg with his royal master this morning. "I'm surprised your mother allowed you to behave so improperly," she observed, slipping her arm through Harriet's as they strolled under the trees.

Harriet giggled. "She didn't. She tried to prevent me from dancing with him the third time, but Prince Klaus kept asking her to dance and that distracted her."

"I observed that, too," Leonie mused. She'd watched Klaus requesting the second dance from Gwendolyn, and wondered if he was really performing an act of friendship. It seemed unlikely that this man with the proud, reserved face should condescend so far, yet there was no duty that obliged him to dance with any lady more than once.

"Oh, dear," Harriet murmured. "Here comes Mama now."

Gwendolyn was coming down the garden toward them, with a small package in her hand. She was moving in a manner that suggested she would have liked to run but was restrained by decorum. "Harriet," she said in a freezing voice, "you will go to my room and await me there. We have matters to discuss."

"Yes, Mama." Harriet moved as if to obey, but as soon as she was behind her mother, she slowed her step and looked inquisitively over her shoulder. Gwendolyn held out the package to Leonie. "This has just been delivered for you," she said coldly.

"And you brought it to me yourself instead of dispatching a footman?" Leonie queried, smiling. "How very kind of you, Gwendolyn, but quite beneath you, I'm sure."

"I brought it myself because I don't wish the servants to know the scandals that surround you," Gwendolyn snapped.

"Scandals in the plural, daughter-in-law dear? You credit me with too much energy. I assure you that one scandal at a time is as much as I can cope with."

"Don't bandy about words with me, madam. This was delivered by a man wearing the livery of Prince Klaus Friederich of Wolfenberg."

Leonie would have been disappointed to learn otherwise, but she let nothing show on her face as she opened the flat box, revealing a magnificent diamond necklace lying on black velvet. Harriet, who'd crept back to look over her mother's shoulder, drew in her breath in awe, but Leonie only shrugged. "Is it really from the prince?" Harriet breathed.

"Yes, it's from the prince," Gwendolyn informed her. "I told you to leave, but since you're still here, you may as well see what scandal and disgrace look like."

Leonie held up the symbol of scandal and disgrace, so that its million facets flashed in the morning sun. Harriet was pop-eyed. "It's beautiful," she whispered. "Can it really be scandalous, Mama, if he truly likes Leonie? I think it's so romantic."

"It isn't romantic, it's shocking," Gwendolyn snapped. "His royal highness—" she said each word with emphasis "—is not seeking marriage, but a liaison. Royalty marries only its own kind. We who have royal blood in our veins should never forget that."

Unwisely, Harriet tried to answer this. "But it's not very much royal blood, is it, Mama? I mean, if—"

"Royal blood is royal blood," Gwendolyn stated firmly. "One drop is enough to make the difference between royal and common. Never forget that. Prince Klaus would never make such a gesture to a woman of his own station."

Leonie's tone was bland and innocent. "It's your opinion that a respectable woman couldn't accept such a gift from a man she barely knew?"

"She would not even consider it."

Leonie gave her a sweet, mysterious smile. "Then it will delight you to know that I have no intention of accepting this." She dropped the necklace back into the box. "Is the messenger still here?"

"He's waiting for a reply," Gwendolyn said, taken aback, but still unyielding.

"Then I'll go and return this to him."

As she swayed gracefully along the path, she heard Harriet sigh, "You see, Mama? Leonie isn't at all like you say."

And Gwendolyn's angry reply, "Don't be deceived. She's holding out for better terms."

Leonie slipped into the writing room and sent for the prince's messenger. While she waited, a curious hesitancy came over her manner. Something told her she'd reached a crossroads, and on the other side lay peril such as she'd never known before. She enjoyed danger, but this was a new kind, one that threatened to break her heart and leave her devastated. Leonie was enough of a Gypsy to take premonitions seriously, and she didn't shrug this one aside, but sat considering it with dark, troubled eyes.

It would be simple to halt matters now, to go to Lord Bracewell and declare herself unsuitable for this assignment. But she seemed to hear Klaus's voice whispering, "It will be a fine duel between us, Leonie," to feel his hot breath burning her and the tremors of unaccustomed passion that he'd evoked. A shuddering sigh broke from her. Stopping now wouldn't be simple at all. It would be impossible. She'd set her foot on this path, and for good or ill there was no turning back.

Hurriedly she scribbled something at the bottom of Klaus's note and slipped it into the box. The messenger, arriving a moment later, was startled to find everything put back into his hands with instructions to, "Return this to your master."

"But—your grace," he stuttered, "there must have been some misunderstanding."

"There's no misunderstanding. His royal highness will find my answer in the box."

The messenger departed. Leonie remained where she was a moment, sunk in thought. She was trying to picture Klaus when he received his gift back and opened the box. Inside, there was a small card bearing his crest, and, in his own handwriting, the words, *"When will you come to Wolfenberg?"* Beneath them Leonie had written, *"When I am ready."*

For the rest of the day, the atmosphere in the house was sulfurous. Cedric, apprised of events by his wrathful lady, had hastily retired to the peace of his study to read a sporting newspaper. He groaned when his door was opened in the early afternoon, and looked out nervously from behind the paper. But it wasn't Gwendolyn.

"Poor Cedric," Leonie said, advancing into the room and closing the door behind her. "There's no need to be afraid of me."

"I assure you, my dear Leonie, that I'm complete master in my own house," Cedric declared with an attempt at dignity. But he added quickly, "She didn't see you come in here, did she?"

"No, I made sure the coast was clear first. I don't want to bring more trouble down on you. I suppose you've heard all about my shocking behavior."

"I've heard nothing shocking about you," Cedric insisted gallantly. "It's true that Prince Klaus behaved with a want of propriety that I find a little surprising—"

"Tut-tut, Cedric. And you related to the blood royal?"

"Oh, Lord, has she been lecturing the household about that again?" he groaned.

"Only Harriet and me."

"I wish she wouldn't put such ideas into the girl's head. Gwendolyn is only a distant cousin of the late Prince Albert, and I'll swear he'd never heard of her when she obtruded onto his notice a couple of years ago." He lowered his voice to mutter, "It was probably the shock that carried the poor fellow off to an early grave the following month. I just hope she hasn't set her heart on marrying Harriet to royalty."

"I'm afraid she may have. She's always been set on pulling off the trick with one of her daughters, and she failed with the other two."

"Yes, and look what happened. Poor Rose was kept away from every suitor until she became an old maid and had to seize her last chance and marry a man who was totally ineligible, and Antonia jumped at the first man who asked in order to escape her sister's fate."

"You should have put your foot down," Leonie admonished him.

"I know, I know. It's so easy to say that in here."

"It should be easy to do. After all, you're master in your own house."

Cedric gave her a speaking look, and filled two glasses from the sherry decanter.

"It's a pity you and she never had a son," Leonie mused.

"I assure you, I've never reproached her on that score," Cedric said quickly. "My brother's son will carry on the line."

"But that's exactly what Gwendolyn hates," Leonie explained. "It won't be *her* son who's the next duke, and that makes her feel diminished. I suppose she feels that some sort of royal title for Harriet would compensate her."

"Poor Gwendolyn." Cedric sighed. "She'll so hate being only a dowager duchess."

"In that case, you must live a long time, then she won't have to be," Leonie rallied him. "I wonder what that would make me, though. Can you have two dowager duchesses in the same family?"

"The question will never arise," Cedric assured her gallantly. "Long before then, you'll have remarried."

"I doubt it. Not unless I find another man like your father." Leonie gave a sudden chuckle. "One who'll let me have my own way all the time." Then she became serious again. "Don't let her bully Harriet."

Cedric sighed again. "I'll do my best but ... oh dear, oh dear."

"Well, I've come to ease your troubles. You'll be delighted to know, son-in-law, that I'm about to depart on my travels again." She watched his face with gleeful delight as his affection for her warred with his relief at the prospect of a quiet house.

"Really? What a pity," he said at last. "Can't I persuade you to stay a little—no, no, I'm sure you're keen to be gone."

"You're quite right," Leonie agreed. "I'll be off first thing tomorrow morning." She drank her sherry and headed for the door. With her hand on the knob, she turned and added mischievously, "I think I'll go to Wolfenberg."

Cedric covered his eyes.

The Duchess of Coniston traveled in style. Two maids and Miss Hatchard were necessary to attend her person, while an elderly steward called Kennett took care of all arrangements and ensured her comfort. He was assisted by an ox of a man called Masham, who rarely spoke but did the heavy work. It was Masham who manhandled the luggage, but it was Kennett who kept an eagle eye on the thirty-seven pieces and ensured her grace's privacy aboard the steamer across the English channel. When she alighted at Calais, a private carriage was awaiting her on the train.

Also traveling in the duchess's entourage was a thin, querulous-looking man of indeterminate age called Jackson, whom she swore was the only person who could make tea just as she liked it. In fact, he was one of the finest chefs in Europe, and on the payroll of British Intelligence.

Leonie remained with the train as far as Cologne, and from there she took a steamer along the Rhine, through Prussia toward Treuheim, the port that was also the capital of Wolfenberg. It was the only part of the country that touched the river. The rest stretched back in a strip, bordered on one side by Prussia and on the other by Bavaria. Wolfenberg was a small country, but its position made it strategically crucial.

At Treuheim, Leonie alighted in the early morning and went to the Palace Hotel. There she filled in a card, stating her name and place of residence. All foreign travelers made these declarations and they were collected by the police, who would report any interesting names higher up. By afternoon, Klaus would know she was here. It might even be sooner. It depended on how eagerly he was looking for her.

Within two hours, she had her answer. An imposing woman was ushered into the suite, introduced herself as the Countess Helga and claimed "the dear Duchess of Coniston" as an old friend. Leonie, whose memory for faces was as acute as her recall of conversations, was able to place her as a woman she'd met briefly in Paris four years ago.

"When I knew that my dear friend had arrived in Treuheim, I said to his royal highness that no court was complete without the Duchess of Coniston."

"You're too kind," Leonie murmured.

"Fortunately, an official court presentation is scheduled for this afternoon. I should be delighted to sponsor you."

Leonie thanked her sincerely. Without such sponsorship no lady could be admitted to court, but she'd been sure Klaus would manage it somehow. The result was that a few hours later she was collected by Helga's carriage and the two of them were borne the short distance to Treuheim Palace. It was approached via a long avenue that gave a perfect view. Like many other German princes, Klaus's ancestors had built for themselves a mini-Versailles, a place of elegance and grandeur. The building was made of light gray stone, with classical proportions, and was nearly a quarter of a mile long.

As the carriage rolled toward the grand entrance, Helga explained, "Presentations are conducted by the prince's aunt, the Archduchess Eugenia, and her daughter, the Princess Sylvana. His royal highness is naturally too occupied with affairs of state to be present."

"I've heard of the Princess Sylvana, of course," Leonie said, letting her voice sound languid and a little naive. "Wasn't she expected to marry the prince?"

"Hush, never refer to that," Helga protested with a sly, mischievous glance.

"But so many German royals marry their own relatives because they don't consider anyone else good enough," Leonie observed. "It's practically automatic."

Helga nodded and lowered her voice, her eyes on the coachman. "That's what Sylvana thought. Her mother raised her in the belief that Prince Klaus was bound to marry her, but he never encouraged them. He's gone out of his way to suggest suitable matches for her, all of which she's turned down in the hope that he would 'come to understand his obligations' as I've heard her put it. But he shows no signs of changing his mind."

The carriage drew up at the grand entrance. Footmen hurried forward to let down the steps. Leonie descended with care in the elaborate formal costume all ladies had to wear for a presentation. On her head she wore a white veil held in place by a diamond coronet. The white dress had a heavy train of four yards. It took a good deal of skill to loop it over her arm without dropping her fan or her bouquet, but by now she'd been presented at so many courts that she could carry it off in style.

About twenty ladies had gathered in the anteroom, all similarly attired. A signal alerted everyone to the fact that it was three o'clock. The doors were opened to reveal the throne room, occupied by the two princesses and members of their households. When silence had fallen, the first name was announced. Strict precedence was followed, which meant that Leonie came after the wives of diplomats and before the young debutantes. The debutantes from Wolfenberg would kiss the royal hands, but this wasn't required of foreign ladies.

It was her turn. Helga, her sponsor, was beside her as they made their way down the long crimson carpet toward the throne. A herald read out her name and a frisson seemed to go through the room. It was too subtle to be called a noise. Rather, it was a consciousness that passed through the little crowd, a swift turning of eyes. It was no more than that, but it told Leonie that rumor had gone before her, and all Wolfenberg knew that Klaus had shown an interest in her.

The faces of the two royal ladies were frozen as Leonie advanced the last few steps and gave Eugenia a curtsy that was acknowledged by the slightest of nods. Leonie stepped adroitly sideways and curtsied again to Sylvana.

Then a murmur of shock went around the room. Sylvana had put out her hand to be kissed.

Leonie drew a slow breath while she decided how to deal with the situation. She was exempt from this sign of deference and everyone there knew it. Looking up, she saw a woman in her late twenties who might have been handsome but for the hauteur that marked her face, and the hardness in her eyes. And now those eyes were filled with dislike.

For a long moment there was silence. Sylvana's hand remained extended, palm down, in an unmistakable demand. Leonie made her decision. With a smile that had steel behind it, she met Sylvana's eyes and shook her head almost imperceptibly. Then she kicked her train expertly out of the way and stepped back.

As she departed, she heard a buzz behind her, then the sound of a door slamming, and she knew that Sylvana had stormed out.

Lady Coniston had arrived in Wolfenberg.

Klaus, watching from a concealed gallery, permitted himself a faint smile. What a woman she was! What a mistress she would make!

He'd been in a fever for her ever since their meeting. On the journey home, he'd tried to concentrate on papers, but her face kept hovering before his eyes, and his flesh seemed to have received the imprint of her soft warmth. What had made her impact all the greater was the fact that for the first time in his life, a woman was keeping him in a state of uncertainty. It was a piquant, and even enjoyable sensation.

But she'd spoilt it. He wouldn't consciously admit it, even to himself, but she'd spoilt the new sensation by following him to Wolfenberg at once. So, despite her spirited, independent words, at heart she was no different from the others. His own reactions confused him. There was relief, because now their relationship could proceed along familiar lines. But there was also a strange sense of disappointment that he couldn't understand.

He quickly brushed the thought aside. He'd been foolish to expect too much from a woman. What mattered was that she'd followed him, and soon she would be here, in his arms, in his bed. He ached with need and anticipation. In a few minutes, he would have all he wanted from her.

A footman was waiting for Leonie when she left the throne room. Countess Helga smiled and vanished discreetly as the footman bowed and indicated for her to follow him. The route they took lay not through the official rooms, but through a rabbit warren of passages that were normally unseen, some of them actually within the thick walls. At last, the man opened a door, invited Leonie to step through and vanished. She found herself in a splendid but severely furnished room dominated by a massive oak desk. Some leather chairs were dotted around, and in one corner stood a narrow iron bed that would have been more in place in a soldier's tent than in a palace. Although everything except the bed was costly, there was an air of austerity. The man who occupied this room both slept and worked here, and seemed to have made it the center of his life. If so, it was a lonely life.

A slight click made Leonie turn her head to find Klaus standing there. There was a sudden tremor in her pulse at the sight of him. "Must you set my court by the ears as soon as you arrive?" he inquired, amused.

She curtsied, smiling up at him impishly. "If my arrival displeases your highness, perhaps I should go away."

His came forward to raise her. His hands were hard and possessive and a shiver of pleasure went through her at their touch and at the glowing light in his eyes. "Don't dare to try," he said. "You're here—and you belong to me."

On the last word, he moved too quickly for her to protest, pulling her into his arms and crushing her mouth with his own. Her head spun, and to her horror her senses instantly rioted. She made frantic attempts to cling to them, to retain some vestige of control, but it was impossible. This man wasn't like others she'd flirted with and kissed. He was no tool to be raised, lowered and manipulated in furtherance of her aims. He was in command, and something deep inside her responded with terrifying swiftness, both to his authority and the firm, athletic feel of his body. The hard movements of his lips over her own drew a soft moan from her.

But she forced some coolness back into her brain; not much, just enough to cause her to stiffen and withdraw somewhat. She knew her breath was coming in little ragged gasps that told the story of her arousal, but she managed to say, "I don't belong to you."

A cynical light came into his eyes. "Ah, yes, first we must discuss terms, mustn't we? Name your price."

For a blinding second, she was filled with such outrage that it was all she could do not to strike him. Then sanity returned, and with it the remembrance that this was the impression she'd striven to create. Suddenly she saw the trap she'd made for herself, a trap she must escape now, or never. "No," she cried. "*No*, I can't do this."

She tried to wrench herself free but his arms were like iron bands around her. "No false modesty, madam," he said. "I've agreed to your price in advance, so there's no more need for negotiation."

"Please let me go... you don't understand."

"It's you who don't understand. I'm not to be trifled with. You came here of your own free will, and now that you're here, you will stay. I never give up what's mine—until I'm ready."

She tried to protest but it was too late. He was kissing her lips, her face, her neck, murmuring hot words of desire and possession. Her heart hammered madly as she felt his mouth caress her. It was the mouth of a skilled lover, a man who knew how to seduce a woman, and was claiming her with determination and great skill. There was a hint of ruthlessness in the way his lips moved over hers, the way his tongue demanded entrance to her mouth. She opened for him helplessly and felt him thrust inside like a conqueror, brooking no refusal. She was on fire. Heat possessed her from the point where he was teasing the inside of her mouth with the tip of his tongue, down to her breasts, which seemed to have come alive with sensation, down farther to her loins, which clamored to have him there, to feel his invasion even as his tongue was invading her.

Her clothes constricted her unbearably. She wanted him to tear them away and touch the tender skin that ached for him, touch her with hands that knew what to do, where to go.

She became aware that he was undressing her, impatiently ripping aside the gorgeous satin of her gown. She managed to gasp, "Highness..."

"Don't call me that now," he said hoarsely. "You came here to give yourself to me, and I accept the gift. There'll be no titles when we're one, only man and woman giving and taking in passion. Come, we've delayed too long. I will wait no longer."

He lifted her in his arms, holding her hard against his chest, and carried her across to the bed. Her heart was hammering and the craving for him was almost unbearable. In a few minutes he'd done what no other man had been able to do, sweep away everything else but himself. She *must* have him, yet at the same time she *must* stop him. This was—she sought wildly for the word—unprofessional.

He set her down on the bed and loomed over her, still feverishly stripping away everything that covered her. A tug, and the pearls about her neck were scattered over the floor.

"Forget them," he commanded. "I'll cover you with jewels. But first, I will see you..."

He'd already ripped aside the satin that covered her bosom. Now his fingers were at the thin lawn of her chemise, wrenching the material away so that her breasts lay naked to his gaze. But something else was also exposed. A sudden silence told Leonie that he'd made the crucial discovery in the worst possible way.

Klaus lifted the half playing card that had fallen out from between her breasts. It was torn down one side, and he knew at once that those ragged edges would fit perfectly against another half card that he carried with him. He raised shocked eyes to her face. "What the devil are you doing with this?"

He seemed frozen. Leonie managed to get free and move away, trying to subdue the clamoring of her blood. "I believe your royal highness has one that matches it?"

"This—" he said blankly. "This is why you're here? You came to Wolfenberg—because of—*this?*"

"Because of this," she confirmed quietly.

And also, she thought, because you've haunted my dreams since the night we met; because you kiss me as I sleep and vanish when I awake, because I will know no peace until I have lain with you. But she kept silent.

He stared at her, then recovered himself with a great effort and went swiftly to the desk and pressed a button. At once, a concealed drawer sprang open, from which he drew the other piece of card. They matched perfectly. Klaus took a deep breath. "I understand," he said. "You've been sent on ahead by the British agent who is to work with me. This is to announce that he's here." The words were almost a plea for her to deny the monstrous suspicion forming in his head.

"No, your highness." She took a deep breath. "I *am* the British agent who's to work with you."

His astonishment was unflattering. "You? A woman?"

"Doesn't your own intelligence service ever employ women? You should think about it—"

"Madam, let me make it clear that I will not discuss intelligence secrets with you, now or ever."

"If you often make that much noise, I shouldn't think you've got many secrets left," she retorted crisply.

"This is a joke, isn't it? This is somebody's idea of a joke."

"I never joke about my job."

"Your job," he echoed scathingly.

"It's my job and I take it very seriously."

"I thought the British took my situation very seriously," Klaus said bitterly. "When Palmerston lectured me—actually dared to lecture *me*—on risking my life, I thought he was a sensible man who deserved my attention. Now I discover he was just playing games."

"It's far from a game. Your life *is* in danger."

"So you're going to protect me, are you? What with? Your hat pin?"

"With my freedom to stay close to you at all times, with my advance knowledge of your movements and my ability to liaise with a cell of agents nearby. They're picking up information about further possible threats, which they will relay to you through me."

"Let me make it clear to you that I'll agree to no part of this plan. You will leave this palace and you won't return to my presence ever again." Klaus's rage was growing as the memory of his own words and actions came back to him. He'd let his defenses fall, revealing his desires with a completeness that appalled him now. He'd thought he was with a hot-blooded woman who was responding to him as a man. But she was a spy, a professional who'd teased his passion alive as a means to an end. Shivers of shame went through him.

"And if I leave, what about the loan?" she demanded. "You need that loan."

"And I'll have it," he said through gritted teeth, "but I will not discuss it with you. Now, get out."

"I'm afraid your highness doesn't understand the situation. The first installment of the loan, fifty thousand pounds sterling, is waiting now, a few kilometers along the Rhine. When I send the signal, it will enter Wolfenberg. But if I don't send it . . ." She left the implication hanging in the air.

Klaus stared at her with loathing. The immediate use of that money was vital, and now here was this woman telling him that he could only have it if he did her bidding—*he*, who'd been able to enforce his own will since he was twenty.

"You devious, unscrupulous witch," he snapped in a fury. "Do you dare come here dictating to me?"

"Circumstances dictate to you, not I," Leonie declared.

"Be silent." Klaus's eyes had become deadly and his voice was full of menace. Courtiers had been known to scurry for cover at the sight of the storm about to break, but Leonie stood her ground, unafraid. "I think Palmerston did this to insult me," he raged. "Is this what the friendship of England means—to suggest that I let myself be protected by a woman?"

"I've already explained—"

"Oh, yes, you've explained. You'll really be a kind of governess, won't you? Spying on me to make sure I behave as London wants, because if I don't, there'll be no loan. Do you think I'll tolerate that?" He stopped pacing and faced her. "Do you know the risk you run by insulting me? This is a feudal country, not a nice, civilized democracy like England, but a place where the ruler's authority is absolute. For no more than you've already said and done, I could have you thrown into prison, and be accountable to no one, and right now I'm sorely tempted."

For a moment, she believed him capable of it. His eyes contained a reckless fury that suggested impulsive, headstrong action. But she refused to flinch. As his temper mounted, she kept her head up defiantly, and gradually it dawned on her that there would be no rash action, that his fury was all the greater because inwardly he'd recognized reality.

Klaus, watching her, waiting for her to bow before the storm that had cowed so many strong men, was baffled, maddened and filled with something like hate. But the little voice within him whispered, "What a woman!"

"Do you know where a female belongs in this country?" he snapped. "In a man's home, in the nursery caring for his children, and in his bed. *Nowhere else.* She doesn't dictate how he shall live his life, or attempt to meddle with politics."

"Is it meddling with politics to try to keep you alive?" Leonie asked mildly. She'd begun rearranging her clothes, fixing the torn edges together with a brooch, knowing that the sight of her disarray would infuriate him more by reminding him how he'd made the discovery.

"Such matters don't concern you," he said with biting emphasis. "Your very presence here is an insult to me and to this country."

"Nonsense," Leonie said calmly.

Klaus seemed almost too thunderstruck for words. At last he asked ominously, "What did you say to me?"

"I said nonsense, and it is. I'm here because I'm the best person for this job. My assignment is to remain with you at every possible moment, night and day, and only a woman can do that without arousing suspicion. If you kept a man

with you at all times, people would say you were afraid.
Would that be preferable?"

"Anything would be preferable to you," he asserted.

"You don't mean that. When the royal temper has cooled,
the royal common sense will assert itself and declare that this
is the most practical arrangement. No one will think it
strange if I stay by you. They'll simply assume that I'm your
mistress. After all, you've shown it's what you want."

"I did just as I was expected to, didn't I?" he demanded
bitterly. "You paraded your charms before me in the most
coldblooded, cynical..." He drew a deep breath and spoke
with difficulty. "Why the devil couldn't Palmerston have
been honest with me at the beginning?"

"You mean tell you about me? It had to look convincing," she argued. "The only way it could work was if you
didn't know and reacted naturally." She stopped, made
cautious by his thunderous face.

"Why, you scheming little— You and Palmerston between you have manipulated me like a puppet. Everything
about you is false. Everything."

His eyes held her, conjuring up between them the memory of her passionate response to his kisses, her heart thun-
dering beneath his burning lips, her mindless murmuring of
his name.

"Everything," he repeated bitterly.

"Not everything," she answered slowly. "There are some
pretenses that no woman can make...for any reason."

Klaus's eyes glinted. "Fine words, madam, but unnecessary, I assure you. As you predicted, the royal common
sense has asserted itself, and *for the sake of Wolfenberg* and
for no other reason, I'll accept your presence here."

"You understand the terms? I have to live close to you,
both physically and mentally. I must always know where

you're going and whom you'll meet. I need your word on that."

"Very well, you have it. It'll be a trial being yoked to you, but I'm used to bowing to disagreeable necessity for the sake of my country. Is that all?"

"One more question. Have you told anybody that a British agent is coming?"

"Are you mad? Do you think I wanted anyone to know the conditions London has imposed on me?"

"Good. You must stick to that. Absolutely nobody must know. Not your dearest friend, your most trusted minister. Not even Bernhard."

"Why do you mention him?" he asked sharply.

"Because he was with you at the duel. That means you trust him, and he probably knows what Bismarck's trying to do. But not even he must know about this."

"Very well," Klaus snapped. "And now I want to hear you say that you'll give the signal."

"It'll be sent tonight when I make contact with my colleagues. Tomorrow I should move into the palace, as close to you as possible."

"And how long is this farce to continue?" Klaus demanded.

"I don't know," Leonie admitted.

"You're not hoping Bismarck will simply give up, are you? He has only one aim—unlimited power for Prussia. He speaks of peace, unity and brotherhood for all the German states, but his true goal is total Prussian domination. He won't stop until he gets it, and that alarms me more than anything, because it means I could be burdened with you for a long time."

"Don't take so gloomy a view," Leonie advised him. "You'll probably negotiate a military alliance with England. You'll seal it by marrying Princess Louise, and produce an heir that's half-English. Bismarck would know that if he attacks you, he attacks England, and even he would think twice about that.''

The unconscious pride with which she said this stung Klaus. "To be sure, the whole world fears English strength, doesn't it?" he growled.

"Luckily for you, it does."

They faced each other, eyes sparkling with anger, and for once there was equal arrogance on both sides. "Let's hope I can marry Princess Louise soon," Klaus said, forgetting his earlier antipathy to the girl. "Then I can be rid of you."

"Lord Palmerston is trying to persuade Queen Victoria, but she's reluctant. Louise is only seventeen—"

"And besides, the queen is on the side of Prussia," Klaus said grimly.

Leonie sighed. "I'm afraid so. But perhaps Palmerston will prevail."

"I doubt it. Nor, to be frank, do I want to marry Louise. Only the pleasing prospect of being rid of you would make me consider it."

"But there's no other way. You need an English alliance."

Klaus regarded her coldly, eyes kindling with dislike. "I'll endure this as long as I have to," he stated, "but one day it will be over. When that day comes, beware. For then I shall remember every insult, every impertinence, every time you've cracked the whip over me and I've been forced to endure it. And then I shall enjoy demonstrating to you that *I* am the master."

"How ungrateful of you, when I'm here only to serve you and your country," she chided him.

He knew it and was furious at his own behavior. But he couldn't help himself. His naturally autocratic nature had been reared in a way that had encouraged imperiousness with men and women alike. He couldn't remember the last time a woman had so much as contradicted him, and to be held in check by one was a bitter gall to his pride. He said no more, but he silently promised himself that one day the account would be even.

"Very well," he said grimly. "If we must play out this charade, let's begin it now. Come with me."

He led the way into the next room, which Leonie saw at once was the official state bedroom. A huge gilt crown was supported over a double bed, which was hung with luxurious tapestries. At the end of the bed, a gilt rail marked the boundary beyond which only the privileged were allowed to step. "This is where I sleep, officially," Klaus declared. "In fact, I can't endure the place. I prefer the bed next door."

He pulled aside a tapestry to reveal a paneled wall, pressed a small knob in the carving, and part of the wall swung open, beyond which lay a staircase. He lit a candle and led the way down, Leonie following, until they'd descended about twenty feet. Here there was another door, which he opened to show her into a large, luxurious bedroom, similar to the one they'd left, but decorated in a lighter, more feminine manner. Several doors led off from it, and Leonie's exploration revealed that she was in a palatial suite of rooms.

"My great-great-grandfather visited Paris a hundred years ago, and was entertained by Madame de Pompadour in her suite at Versailles," Klaus explained. "He came straight back and transformed the east wing of the palace into something similar for his own mistress."

"But much more opulent," Leonie observed with a mischievous glance upward at the extravagantly painted ceiling and ornate gilding.

"Of course," Klaus agreed ironically. "We couldn't allow the French to outdo us. National honor was at stake.

Since then, these rooms have always been occupied by the favorite. I dare say that England, having a female monarch, wouldn't understand about such things.''

"The queen's ancestors understood it very well," Leonie said. "George I had two chief mistresses, one fat, one thin. They were known as The Elephant and The Maypole."

"I consider that being greedy. Besides, in Wolfenberg, the favorite is more than a mistress. She's more like an unofficial wife. It's an entirely honorable position, so honorable, in fact, that it isn't always filled. The last woman to inhabit these rooms was installed by my grandfather. She was a rapacious lady who got control of him in his final years and enriched herself at the expense of the country. I determined that it would never happen to me. You'll be the first woman I've ever allowed here."

"And yet, you haven't gone without female company."

A cynical smile touched Klaus's lips. "The court has its fair share of women who are ambitious either for themselves or their husbands. I've taken what was offered, made bargains and always kept my side of them. But such relationships have been very simple. I never promise more than I'm ready to give, and no woman has inspired me to give more than I promised. I've been content to leave these apartments vacant."

"Until now."

His expression darkened. "If I had my way, they'd stay vacant, but there are fifty thousand good reasons for deciding otherwise. You, no doubt, will find them convenient for your 'work.' "

"The closer my quarters are to your royal highness, the more convenient they'll be for my work," she agreed. "I'll move in tomorrow morning."

"Not until then?" he demanded sarcastically. "Suppose Bismarck has me assassinated tonight?"

Leonie's lips twitched. "Surely you can take care of yourself for one night?" she asked innocently.

Klaus drew in his breath sharply. "You will regret making fun of me," he said with slow emphasis. "It is something I do not allow."

"But it's one of the favorite's privileges," Leonie countered. "To be convincing, I must enjoy a joke or two at your expense." She smiled encouragingly. "But you can make fun of me, too."

"*Me?*"

"Don't you ever make jokes?"

Instead of silencing her, he was startled enough to reply, "With my friends, occasionally. But not with women."

"Why ever not?"

"Because I don't make friends with women."

"Not even with women you like? Or don't you like any?"

"I've never met a woman who wasn't trying to manipulate me for her own ends, so I was constantly on my guard. That doesn't make for a friendly atmosphere."

"You poor soul," Leonie said sincerely. "Geoffrey and I were always laughing together."

"Geoffrey?"

"My husband. We were the best of friends. It made for a delightful marriage."

"I suppose I should be thankful I don't have to marry you, as well," he said savagely. "That would be one sacrifice too many for my country."

Leonie gave him her sweetest smile. "Never fear, your highness. I shall personally ensure that you'll never be required to marry me. You wouldn't suit me at all."

"I've been away from my work too long," Klaus said with difficulty. "A carriage will return you to your hotel."

"And tomorrow night I hope you'll join me for supper. My cook is excellent." She added, "And his dishes are perfectly safe."

"Do you mean—?"

"That Bismarck might try poison? Why not? He showed his hand too plainly with the duel. He's got to finish you off soon. The more meals you can have with me the better. In the meantime, taste everything very carefully."

"Come," he said ironically, "how can I come to grief with you to protect me?"

"And I'll protect you, never fear. Your death would be a blot on my professional reputation."

Chapter Four

There was one trunk among Leonie's baggage to which only she had the key. It contained various costumes that were occasionally useful on her missions. Tonight she selected male garments, chosen for their conventional anonymity. Beneath them she wore a straight, stiff bodice to flatten her breasts, and over them a concealing cloak. Her hair was hidden beneath a wig. At close quarters, she knew nobody would be deceived about her sex, but that wasn't the purpose. The disguise allowed her to slip quietly through busy streets in dangerous places without attracting attention. Passing strangers might notice something odd about the "young gentleman" but wouldn't be allowed close enough to discover the truth.

That evening, she changed into these clothes and left the hotel by a side exit, accompanied by Masham. After a few minutes, she found a hansom cab and Masham gave the destination, a tavern known as The Black Dog. The driver hesitated at the name of a place in the most notorious part of Treuheim, but a gold coin pressed into his palm settled his doubts.

Leonie almost gagged on the smoky atmosphere in the tavern. The noise and heat were indescribable. Everywhere hot, flushed men sat with half-dressed women, alternately drinking and pawing their companions. Leonie's darting eyes soon picked out the man she wanted. At first glance, he looked as unshaven and villainous as the rest, but his eyes were alert and intelligent and he tensed when he saw her. She picked her way through the noisy crowd to sit at his table. "Good evening, Otto," she greeted him. "Or perhaps I should say good morning. Where's Jack?"

"He's gone to bed. We didn't think you were coming."

"You were told I'd be in touch immediately, and don't tell me you didn't know I'd arrived. Your contacts in the police department probably told you before it was passed to the palace."

"Yes . . . well, I can go and wake Jack up."

"We'll go together. I don't want to talk down here. Why did he pick this place?"

Otto gave an awkward grin. "He didn't think you'd dare come here."

"And then he'd have reported back to London that I wasn't up to my job?"

Otto shrugged awkwardly. "Well, he doesn't like working with a woman."

"He's not alone," Leonie observed with a wry smile.

"Can I get the gentlemen anything to drink?" the landlord inquired greasily at her side. He was staring at her garments. Plain though they were, they stood out as almost luxurious in these surroundings. Leonie slipped her right hand into her left sleeve and withdrew a long, wicked-looking stiletto. The landlord's eyes widened and he stepped back, but Leonie only used the knife to point to Otto's glass, full of strong yellow liquid. The landlord hastily produced another two just like it, which he gave to her and Masham. Sipping gingerly, she followed Otto upstairs, with Masham silently bringing up the rear.

Jack Blair, her contact in Treuheim, had taken a room. As they entered his room, they saw him stretched out, fully dressed, sleeping noisily on a dirty-looking couch. Three other men were sitting at a table, playing cards. Otto gave Blair a shove and he awoke suddenly. "She's here," Otto told him, indicating Leonie with a jerk of his head.

Blair's expression became one of weariness and impatience that only just stopped short of being a sneer. "So you're the fine lady who amuses herself playing at spies?" he growled.

Leonie made a quick decision. She'd encountered this attitude before and had a variety of ways of dealing with it, varying from charm and persuasion to no-nonsense authority. It didn't take long to realize that persuasion would achieve little with Jack Blair. Moreover, all the others were watching. "On the contrary," she said, deliberately brusque, "I find nothing amusing about this whole business, starting with your lack of readiness."

Blair's feet hit the floor with a thud as he leaped up to confront her. "I'm not taking that," he raged. "I told Bracewell I wouldn't work with a woman and I meant it." The sneer finally made it to the surface as he eyed Masham and said, "An agent who has to bring her private bodyguard! Get out of here and tell them to send me somebody sensible."

He turned away from her and headed for the door, but the knife got there first. With a movement so fast nobody in the room could follow it, Leonie sent the stiletto spinning past Blair to thunder into the door just ahead of his nose, stopping him in his tracks. The room was silent, electrified. Leonie considered her aim with satisfaction. Uncle Silas would have been proud of her.

"You'll have to be sharper than that," she observed coldly. "I could have taken your nose off, if I'd wanted to."

He looked back at her with coldly malevolent eyes, and she knew she'd made an enemy. It was a pity, but it couldn't be helped. "Let's understand each other from the outset," she said. "Masham isn't my bodyguard. He's my courier, and, when necessary, my voice. He'll contact you when I'm occupied elsewhere, but the commands he brings you will be mine."

"*Commands?*"

"I'm in control of this mission, Jack, and you'd better learn to accept it. You'll do as I say, or I'll certainly be contacting London, but it won't be me that's replaced. Now, we've wasted enough time on this. Listen, all of you. The prince has agreed to the plan, so you can send the signal for the first installment of gold to be delivered."

She fixed her eyes on Jack Blair until he gave a sullen nod of agreement, but he didn't speak. It was as though his bile choked him. Otto finally broke the silence. "Where are you staying?"

"I'm moving into the palace tomorrow. The world will regard me as the prince's favorite, so it won't arouse suspicion if I shadow him. I'll pass his schedule on to you, and I want any hint of danger that you pick up in good time to change his plans. Masham will drink here every evening, and you pass details on to him."

"I'm not putting anything in writing," Blair insisted with a truculent glance at Masham, whose size gave him a slow-witted appearance.

"No need," Masham said in an unexpectedly quiet voice. "I'll remember."

"He will," Leonie confirmed. "Don't judge by appearances—his or mine. Now, have you got anything for me?"

"Nothing specific, but that doesn't mean you can relax your guard."

"I've no intention of doing so," Leonie observed dryly.

"Bismarck isn't going to stop until he's killed him," Blair continued as if he hadn't heard her.

"Well, we won't let him," Leonie said lightly.

Her manner appeared confident but all the way back to the hotel in the hansom, she was brooding. Blair's words had given her a pang of alarm, which she tried to believe was merely professional. She roused herself to say to Masham, "You and the others must start gossiping to the other servants. See what you can learn."

Masham nodded. Although he was a man of few words, like all Leonie's servants, he could get by in several languages, and was devoted to her.

She fell back into her reverie, telling herself not to be foolish. She'd never allowed herself to be frightened by obstacles on any other job, and this was just another job.

But her heart was already warning her that Klaus was different. She'd seen behind his proud exterior, and glimpsed depths that made her long to explore further. There was an aching loneliness in him that seemed to call to her.

She was startled by the direction her thoughts were tending, and reproved herself. The first rule of the job was not to get personally involved. It had helped carry her successfully through a dozen adventures, and it would do so again. Marriage to a husband who'd indulged her every whim had left Leonie with the agreeable sensation of being in control of her own life. It seemed inevitable that she would remain in control.

The next day, she moved into the palace, entering by a stone staircase that led from the gardens to the private door to her second-floor apartments. As she climbed the steps, she was aware of faces at the windows above. Everyone wanted to see the first official favorite the prince had ever chosen. In her apartments she was greeted by Bernhard bearing a flat, black box, which he opened. Inside were the very diamonds Leonie had refused only a few days earlier.

"His royal highness also invites you to join him in the wolf hunt today," Bernhard said.

"Wolf hunt?" Leonie exclaimed, seeing horrifying visions of open fields and forests where an assassin could hide.

"This country took its name from the wolves," Bernhard explained. "Mostly we live in peace with them, but sometimes one of them turns vicious and has to be put down. Recently, a rogue wolf has been terrorizing the villages near Treuheim."

"By why does the prince have to go?"

"Because the people expect it. It's an honor to be invited to join the hunt. His highness told me to tell you that we leave in half an hour. I'm afraid that won't give you much time to—"

"Don't worry," Leonie said grimly. "I'll be ready." The message was like a gauntlet thrown at her feet. Klaus was still smarting, and he wasn't going to make her job easy.

Prodigious efforts by Miss Hatchard enabled her to be ready on time, attired in a tight black riding habit that showed off her curved figure to perfection. The snowy ruffles at her throat were held in place by one perfect pearl. Bernhard was waiting for her at the foot of the stone steps, and he led her to where the rest of the party was waiting. As they walked, he said with his gentle smile, "It's a pleasure to see you again, Duchess. I trust all your family are well."

"They're all splendidly well, thank you," Leonie said.

"I hope they enjoyed the ball the other night."

Leonie chuckled. "Coniston enjoyed it because he was able to escape and play whist. Gwendolyn enjoyed it because Prince Klaus danced with her twice." She added slyly, "I think perhaps he did that for you."

Bernhard smiled and nodded. "He's the kindest of friends," he declared.

"Indeed? But I hear other things of him, as well."

"Fearsome," Bernhard said simply. "It doesn't pay to cross him. I don't know which is more alarming, his boiling rages or his freezing ones. But he's the most generous man in the world—although he doesn't like that generally known," he added hastily.

"Then I won't tell him you told me," she promised.

Bernhard's manner suddenly became awkward. "You said—you said that *all* your family enjoyed the ball?" he asked, not looking at her.

Leonie took pity on him. "Lady Harriet had a delightful time—so she told me. But it was very naughty of her to dance with you so often."

He reddened like a boy. "I'm afraid I overstepped the mark in seeking her company so much. It's just that she— that I—" he pulled himself together "—if you write to her, I hope you'll convey my respects."

"I promise that I will," Leonie said. "I know she thinks very kindly of you."

About thirty lords and ladies from the court had been invited to join the royal wolf hunt. They all greeted Leonie pleasantly, and watched her covertly.

"This is Danza," Bernhard explained, indicating a mare that stood patiently. "Princess Sylvana selected her for your use." Leonie said what was proper, but she regarded Danza wryly. There was a mildness about the mare's eyes that verged on the insipid.

A clatter made everyone turn their heads to see Klaus riding toward them, Sylvana by his side. Leonie grew alert, watching the other woman, but Sylvana seemed to have forgotten their first meeting. She inclined her head toward Leonie and spoke with apparent affability. "I'm delighted that you're to join us. When my cousin said you were to be here, I went to the stable and personally selected your mount. Not knowing how good a rider you were, I chose Danza, a lady's mount who's very quiet and will give you no trouble."

The words were reasonable enough, but Danza wasn't a lady's mount. She was a mount for a nervous child, and everyone there knew it. Her rider would be left behind in the first five minutes, an object of ridicule and contempt. "You're very kind," Leonie responded with a smile, "but I believe I could cope with something a little more spirited."

"In that case, let me beg you to accept my own horse," Sylvana said. She held out her arms and Bernhard helped her dismount.

"Perhaps not," Klaus said quickly. "Sylvana, your generosity carries you away. Have you forgotten that Paprika doesn't care for strangers on his back?"

"Paprika," Leonie mused. "I like the sound of that."

"It's a name well chosen," Bernhard said. "He's hot and peppery."

Sylvana gave Leonie a smile that was like the clash of steel. "Forgive me," she said sweetly. "I was forgetting that only I can ride Paprika. Perhaps my original choice was the right one."

There was only one possible answer and Leonie gave it, vaulting lightly into Paprika's saddle without assistance. A tremor went through the large animal and he kicked out, but Leonie had ridden bareback in a circus when she was nine, and she kept her seat. "A beautiful animal," she said. "No words can express my gratitude for your generosity in lending him to me."

"This may be a rash decision," Klaus observed quietly. "Conditions get very rough when we're out in the country."

"Never fear," Leonie told him gaily. "My riding master was a Hungarian from the royal stables."

This was perfectly true. Leonie didn't think it necessary to mention that the man had been hiding from the law at the time.

Sylvana snapped out an order and another horse was produced for her. The party moved off toward the great gates of the palace. Leonie began to appreciate that Sylvana's scheme had been masterly. Paprika resented her and showed it by skittering here and there. Only her superb skill kept her in the saddle. She concentrated every fiber on keeping control while seeming to relax, knowing that all eyes were upon her, wondering if she would be made to look foolish.

The route took them through the town, where the people had come out-of-doors to witness the sight of their prince riding out in their defense. Now they had the additional delight of seeing the woman all Wolfenberg was talking about beside him, beautiful and splendid in her tight black habit, the white streamers of her hat flowing behind her. A rumble of satisfaction went around the crowd. She was a worthy favorite.

It didn't seem strange to them that Klaus showed no particular signs of pleasure in her company, indeed, hardly looked at her. That was royal decorum. A great prince wasn't a potboy slavering over a goose girl.

It would have surprised them to know that despite his air of indifference, Klaus was seethingly aware of the woman by his side. Since yesterday when he'd discovered the truth about her, he'd been possessed by bitter thoughts: humiliation that a woman had been sent to protect him; fury against her for tempting his desire for her own calculating purposes, for making him show weakness, for knowing she could provoke him to lose control; rage that he had no power to dismiss her. These were the feelings that tortured him as he rode out with a smiling face.

It would serve her right, he thought savagely, if she broke her neck on that dangerous brute. But in the same instant, he flicked his eyes in her direction to make sure she was safe. It was the briefest possible glance, but it served to burn into his consciousness the picture of her at ease on Paprika's back, her head up, her hands light on the reins. She was a superb rider, which aroused his reluctant admiration. And unbidden, the treacherous thought came again, "What a woman! What a mistress she would have made! If only..."

He shut the idea off before it could finish. He'd learned long ago to master his thoughts and instincts lest they master him, and so enable others to gain an advantage over him. She no longer attracted him and that was that.

But this time his thoughts broke free from the bonds he would have put on them. They reminded him of how she'd felt pressed against his body, of the softness of her lips, of the way her heart had raced as he touched her. They told him no woman could fake that soft, urgent pounding. He risked another glance at her and saw again the dazzling beauty of her face, the tiny waist and curved hips, the high breasts that moved slightly in the horse's rhythm. But the glance was a mistake. He knew it when he felt again the stirring in his loins that told him he desired her as much as ever. And that was the greatest bitterness of all.

They left Treuheim behind and began to gallop across country. Soon they were near the edge of the forest. Leonie looked around her at the wild, beautiful scenery. The foothills were covered in pines, and beyond them rose rocky crags, stark and forbidding. As she was regarding them, she heard a scream in the distance, and the next moment a woman had appeared from between the trees and was running toward them, waving her arms and wailing horribly.

Klaus slowed and approached her. Instinctively, Leonie kept close to him, which brought her a black scowl, but she refused to back off until she knew there was no danger. Her hand slid down to her boot where she kept a small gun.

As the woman got closer, Leonie realized that this was no assassin, but someone in terrible distress. Tears poured down her face as she flung herself forward to clutch Klaus's leg.

"My baby," she sobbed. "He's got my baby...the wolf...oh, your Highness, she's only four days old...." She began to scream dementedly.

Klaus leaned down from his horse and seized her hand tightly. "Calm yourself, Mother" he said, firmly but with kindness. "When did this happen?"

"Just now. He stole into my cottage while I was hanging out the washing...I heard my baby cry but it was too late...I saw him run away...dragging her by her clothes...he was huge...oh God, my poor little Gretl."

"Show us the way you saw him go," Klaus commanded. "And never fear. This is his last day, and your Gretl will be safe."

They followed the woman's directions to where the rocks arose, and as they looked, they could just discern the creature, far up, dragging a small object that looked like a rag doll. Leonie stared at the size of the animal. She'd seen wolves before, but never one like this.

"Come on," Klaus said quietly, and they moved off.

It seemed to take an age to reach the foot of the hills, and by then the wolf had vanished. They climbed until the grass began to fall away, leaving the ground stony and uneven. "The horses can go no farther," Klaus declared. "From now on, we track the beast on foot." When they'd dismounted, he said curtly, "The women will remain here."

"Oh, no, I won't," Leonie informed him under her breath.

She'd gotten close so that they could speak without being overheard. "Is the wolf one of Bismarck's agents in disguise?" he asked savagely.

"With Bismarck, nothing is impossible," she murmured. "Don't try to leave me behind. I've signaled for the first installment of the loan to be sent, but there will be others."

For a moment, anger flashed in his eyes, but it was replaced almost at once by cool amusement. "Very well, madam, if you think you can follow me up those rocks, you're welcome to try."

It was clear that he thought he'd defeated her, but as a child Leonie had climbed worse rocks than these in her bare feet. She answered his ironic grin with one of her own. "My devotion to your royal highness is such that I will follow wherever you go. Lead on."

There were some raised eyebrows among Klaus's companions when they realized Leonie was to join them, but their attitude changed when they saw that she could keep up and was ready for anything. She knew, from Lord Bracewell's briefing, that Klaus had been a climber from boyhood. To track an animal on foot over the hills and confront it directly was his preferred method of hunting. He was surefooted and fearless, and Leonie recognized that she would need her wits about her, and all her strength, if she was to match him.

The path grew steeper and more stony, until they were climbing as much as walking. Straight ahead of them a rock face reared up, almost sheer, except for an impossibly narrow path. "There he is," Klaus said suddenly.

Above their heads the wolf had appeared on a ledge. He was huge, and now that they could see him clearly, it was obvious that he was very old. One leg seemed to drag, suggesting a badly healed wound. This was a hurt creature, Leonie thought, old and crippled and abandoned by the others. He'd been forced to turn vicious to survive. As he leaned down to look at them, his lips curled back over cruel fangs. It was as if he knew his last moments had come and was defying them. At his feet lay a small bundle of rags. As they watched, it stirred and uttered a faint cry.

Behind them, someone raised a gun and pointed it at the wolf. "No," Klaus said sharply. "You can't risk the child. I'm going up behind him."

He was halfway up the rock before anyone could stop him. Bernhard made a move to follow but Leonie was there ahead of him. "The only other way up is the path," she said, "and my narrow feet are better than yours. If Klaus gets the wolf, I'll take the child."

The men fanned out in a circle behind them. Klaus picked his way purposefully up the rock while Leonie began to edge upward along the path, which was so narrow that she had to place her feet exactly in line, clinging on to tufts of grass in the wall. Faced with a choice the wolf turned his attention toward her, creeping forward, his lips drawn back over his fangs. Tension was in every line of the great bony body. Suddenly he seemed to gather himself together, ready to spring. Klaus acted swiftly, seizing a loose stone and hurling it forcefully to strike the wolf on the shoulder. It was an awkward shot but it achieved its effect. The wolf turned his attention away from Leonie and snarled down at Klaus. The next instant he had launched himself down onto him.

In a blinding moment of horror, Leonie saw Klaus release his hold and throw his hands out toward the animal, seizing the beast's thick fur and yanking his head away from his throat. Then man and wolf were hurtling down the rock face together. Swiftly she made her way up the rest of the

path to where the baby lay perilously close to the edge, and
snatched her up. The infant responded with a lusty cry that
eased Leonie's mind. With her heart in her mouth, she knelt
on the ledge and peered below to see the wolf lying dead on
the ground with Klaus's knife in his heart. Klaus glanced up
at her and there was a look in his eyes that was part triumph, part defiance and part respect.

He made his way up the path as she eased her way down,
and carefully took the child from her. The mother, who'd
followed on foot, had caught up with them in time to see the
final moments, and she snatched her baby from Klaus with
cries of gladness and gratitude.

Suddenly there was a crowd around them. Word of their
coming had spread to the little village that nestled at the foot
of the hill, and everyone had come out to see their prince
defeat the enemy that had terrorized them. They cheered
and danced over the dead wolf. Women wept, and children
regarded the body with awe.

Leonie was intrigued to see a change come over Klaus.
When one of his subjects had appealed to him in desperation, he'd been kind, strong and at ease. But surrounded by
their plaudits he seemed to become uncomfortable. When
the villagers begged him to come down to the tavern and
enjoy their hospitality, he agreed, but stiffly, and it seemed
to her that he would have gladly refused.

He watched her descend the final stage of the path, and
gave her a brief nod when he saw she was all right, but there
was no warmth in his manner and he quickly turned his attention elsewhere.

It would have been a merry party down the hill, but for
the rigidity of Klaus's manner. Leonie began to understand
many things. He was popular with his subjects, but at a
distance. They admired and respected him, but they didn't
love him because he wouldn't let them. In the tavern he did

his duty, accepting a glass of ale from the landlord and enduring a speech from the local mayor who'd been hastily summoned. But his manner, though gracious, was reserved.

She found herself thinking of the Prince of Wales back home, who'd once said to her, "There are chill winds blowing around the thrones of Europe. It's not enough to be respected. The day is coming when a monarch must be loved to survive."

How differently Prince Edward would have dealt with this situation. He'd have toasted them all, swapped stories with the men and flirted with the women, and everyone would have been delighted. When someone produced a fiddle, he'd have seized the prettiest woman in the room to dance with. He would not, as Klaus did, utter stiff words of thanks and depart.

As they rode home, Leonie edged her mount a little closer to his. "I must thank you," she said pleasantly. "It would have gone hard with me but for you."

"It often goes hard for a woman who interferes in matters that don't concern her," he said quietly. "Naturally I'm glad to see you unhurt—"

"And I am glad to see you unhurt," she said. "However would I have explained your death to London?"

"We must be glad that the blot on your reputation has been avoided," he said ironically.

"Your people are more than glad," she reminded him. "They want to thank you. Surely you can manage to smile at them a little?"

"You're impertinent," he said in a frosty voice. "What's more, your every word betrays how little you understand. I'm here to govern them, to think ceaselessly of their welfare, and if necessary, to sacrifice myself for them. I am not here to smile at them like a monkey performing tricks."

In his annoyance he'd forgotten to keep his voice down. Leonie realized that they were attracting interest from the others, puzzled by Klaus's air of hostility. If her being here was to appear natural, she had to change his attitude quickly. There was only one way to meet the situation. It was a gamble, but she'd never avoided gambles. Digging her heels into Paprika's side, she let the hot-blooded animal have his head. As he tore away, she allowed a cry of "Help," to float over her shoulder.

A quick glance back showed that her stratagem had worked. Klaus was in hot pursuit, his face set, the big stallion pounding the ground beneath him. Then she had to give all her attention to controlling Paprika, who was wild with joy at no longer being kept in check, and put out all his strength, eating up the ground, powerful, untiring. Klaus drew almost level, but Leonie managed to keep ahead just enough to stop him seizing her bridle. Together they flew over the land. Stone walls loomed ahead of them and vanished in a flash. Hedges and ditches slid away beneath, fields stretched ahead, then disappeared. Gradually she felt the animal grow tame and yield to her. She slowed, allowing Klaus to catch up, but wheeled away before he could take her bridle. His eyes were grim. "Very clever," he snapped. "The truth was you were never in any danger."

"Never," Leonie agreed, slightly breathless.

"And what, may I inquire, was the purpose of that little performance?"

"I needed to get you to myself. You're not playing your part properly. You've hardly spoken to me."

"I've been concentrating on the wolf. Does British Intelligence forbid that?"

"Only if it interferes with your infatuation for me."

"Oh, I'm infatuated with you, am I?"

"Wildly. Madly. To the exclusion of all else."

"Indeed? Then let me tell you that no female in the world evokes less ardor in my breast."

"I remember you saying differently."

"That was when I saw you as a woman," Klaus said acidly.

Leonie edged her horse closer to his, facing him. "And what do you see now?" she asked.

He regarded her bitterly. "London's paid hireling. A creature who uses her charms as tools for the job. Do I make myself clear?"

"Perfectly, but matters can't be left like this. If my being here is to look natural, you should seem enchanted by me."

"That will be hard when the only feeling you conjure up in me is cold rage," he snarled.

"Then I shall have to change that," Leonie declared. Leaning forward, she slipped one arm about his neck and pulled his mouth down to hers. He stiffened, and fearing he might resist her, she let her lips caress his softly, teasingly. It wasn't hard to make herself do the right things because every fiber of her being wanted to kiss him and feel him kiss her back.

She felt his arm go about her waist and the stiffness leave his body. Now his lips were moving against hers, harshly and with anger as if his own passion maddened him, but still he couldn't resist her. She parted her own lips softly, invitingly, and felt him tremble at the temptation she offered. The next moment, he was in her mouth, teasing her with his tongue, and she was challenging him in return. She caressed his face with her hand, wound her fingers in his hair, then let them trace patterns on the back of his neck, while heat coursed through her body and she tried to remember that she was only doing her job.

He raised his head to look down on her and spoke huskily, "Did your paymasters tell you to kiss me like that?" he demanded.

"They never interfere with decisions in the field," she whispered. "I do things my way."

"Don't you know that you're playing with fire?"

"I like fire. It's exciting."

He lowered his head. "Let's see if you're as brave as you think," he murmured as his lips covered hers again. This time it was his kiss, still angry but no longer fighting his desire. He began by taking his time, teasing out the sensations until she was wild. She clung on to him, fighting not to yield totally to her feelings as she was longing to do.

Suddenly his arms tightened and he pulled her sharply over toward him. The movement alarmed Paprika, who skittered. Too late Leonie remembered to tighten her legs on the sidesaddle. Paprika galloped away, leaving her helpless in Klaus's arms, clutching him to avoid falling to the ground. He drew her up firmly so that she was sitting on his horse before him, and cradled her in his arms.

"Is this what you wanted, baggage?" he asked harshly. "Or is it too much? Did you only want the appearance of my passion and not the reality? Do you ever stop to think that you might drive me too far? Suppose I dump you on the ground and ride off. What would you do?"

"You wouldn't do anything so ungentlemanly," she challenged.

"Don't tempt me to show you just how ungentlemanly I can be," he said bitterly.

She didn't answer directly, only lay in his arms and looked up at him with a little smile. His chest was rising and falling and there was a wild look in his eyes that matched something that was happening in her breast.

From a far place she heard the sound of a horse approaching. The next moment, Klaus exclaimed and looked up. His face was pale and his breathing ragged, but he regained control. Leonie realized that a third person was present. A tall man in his late thirties had appeared on horseback. In one hand he held Paprika's rein.

Klaus made a sound of annoyance and embarrassment at being disturbed. He released Leonie so that she slid slowly to the ground, and made a gesture for the man to come forward.

"My cousin Reinald," he explained briefly to Leonie, "and my chief minister of state. Also my most trusted friend. We're on his land."

The newcomer dismounted to face her, and Leonie regarded him with a languidness that concealed deep interest. Lord William Bracewell was anxious to know more about Archduke Reinald. Close up she could see that he was a coldly handsome man with a face that looked as if it never smiled, marked on the left by a savage scar that was evidently some years old.

"I'm flattered that you should visit me, cousin," Reinald declared smoothly, "but if you'll permit me to say so, the presence of the lady all Wolfenberg is talking about is more flattering still." He raised Leonie's gloved hand to his lips.

"And I," she said in her turn, "am flattered to meet the man the prince calls his most trusted friend. I know of no more honorable title."

Archduke Reinald acknowledged this courtesy with a slight bow of his head. "When I found Paprika riderless, I feared lest some harm had come to my sister," he said.

"She was kind enough to loan me her horse," Leonie said. "I thought it most generous of her."

"I think it most unwise," Reinald said. "You could have been killed on the brute."

"She nearly was," Klaus added. "It ran away with her, and she's lucky not to have a broken neck. Isn't that so, my dear?" he asked ironically.

"As your highness says," she replied demurely, but her eyes were wicked as they teased him, and after a moment he grinned reluctantly.

"My house is but a short distance," Reinald said. "Allow me to offer you some refreshment."

The three of them fell into step. Reinald inquired about the wolf, and the short journey was taken up with details of the hunt. Leonie was content to say nothing and study him. He had an intriguing face, she decided, the face of an inflexible man. He would be inflexible in everything, she felt, in friendship, in honor, in love. But it was hard to associate him with love. Certainly he was unmarried, so Sir William had said.

His home was a palace, set on the shore of a lake. As they turned into the long approach, Reinald called to one of the servants by the gate, instructing him to race ahead and make preparations.

"I'm surprised to see you out riding," Klaus said to Reinald. "When you refused to join the hunt, I pictured you pouring over papers."

"Rightly," Reinald said. "But I felt the need of a little air to clear my head. I'm glad you came this way. There are some matters I'd like to bring to your attention."

At the main door, grooms ran forward to take their horses. Reinald ushered Leonie in gallantly, where they were met by a stiff elderly man, wearing the archduke's colors. He bowed, but seemed uncomfortable. "Hugo, have you informed my mother of our arrival?" Reinald demanded.

The old man's discomfort seemed to grow. "Her highness begged to be excused. She has a headache and is prostrate with suffering."

Reinald's mouth tightened. It was clear that he suspected an excuse.

At that moment, Leonie caught a glimpse of herself in a huge gilt mirror. "Heavens, what a sight I am!" she declared.

A faint jerk of Reinald's head produced a plump, elderly woman in a white cap and apron, who greeted Leonie with a bob. "Alice will show you upstairs," he said. "She'll serve you refreshments and you can rest awhile. I deeply regret my mother's indisposition prevents her from attending you herself."

Alice showed her to a bedroom two floors up. As she climbed the stairs, Leonie became conscious of a presence on the landing just above her. Looking up, she saw a little man with an ugly face and eyes as sharp as a ferret's. He was watching her intently with an expression of curiosity and dislike, but as soon as she looked up, he scuttled clumsily away, revealing that his back was burdened with a hump, and one leg was shorter than the other. Alice hastily crossed herself, muttering. "Who is that?" Leonie asked.

The old woman crossed herself again. "The devil," she said. "I think he's the very devil himself. I wish master wouldn't insist on keeping him here. The archduchesses hate him, too, but his highness won't listen to any of us. He was always the same."

"He looks like a man who likes to have his own way," Leonie observed, encouraging the servant to talk.

Alice nodded. "Always. Right back to a baby. His father died young and he was the master here when he was only fifteen. He made us all feel it, too."

"A tyrant at fifteen?" Leonie echoed, as if amused.

"A little," Alice conceded, "but a more honorable boy you couldn't hope to meet. I remember when he was ten, he met a groom out riding his father's favorite horse. He insisted on changing mounts, but he couldn't hold the beast. The horse fell badly and had to be destroyed. Reinald went straight to his father and told him he was to blame. The old man flogged him till he was senseless, but he never once cried out."

"Inflexible," Leonie murmured.

"Oh, yes. But my lady, don't you go thinking he's cruel. He's kind and fair to them as serves him well. A year ago, my son Hans ran off to live in the city, and he got into bad company. He couldn't write, but he used to send me word by the carter who came every week. Then the messages stopped coming. Reinald put a man on to find out what had happened, and the man found Hans in jail. Reinald paid some money to have him released into his care and brought back here. He did that for his old Alice who looked after him when he was a baby."

"You must think the world of him," Leonie said, and the old woman beamed agreement.

A maid appeared with a steaming jug of water. Once she was alone, Leonie washed herself gratefully, and consumed the wine and cake that were brought for her. She felt exhilarated after her ride, but she knew the pounding in her blood wasn't all the excitement of the chase. Her mouth could still feel Klaus's kiss, the passion in his lips as they'd crushed her own. At that moment, she'd wanted nothing except to yield to him utterly. It was lucky that Reinald had appeared when he did. Yes, she told herself firmly, it was very lucky.

She didn't hurry down, knowing that Klaus and Reinald had matters to discuss. She moved onto the balcony and looked out over the lake, sipping her wine and drinking in the greens and yellows of summer.

"How dared you do such a thing!"

Startled, Leonie looked around for the source of the voice that had spoken these words, but could see no one. Then the voice came again, and this time she realized it was beneath her. *"You had no right to insult me."* It was a woman's voice, harsh and petulant.

Then Reinald, also speaking from below, said wearily, "I haven't insulted you, Mother. I had no choice but to invite her here. She's Klaus's guest."

"His harlot, you mean."

"I beg you not to shame us all by speaking like that in her presence."

"Don't concern yourself. I never intend to be in her presence."

"Do you mean to banish yourself from court, then?" Reinald demanded harshly. "The court will soon revolve around that lady, unless I'm much mistaken. Your best course is to put a good face on it."

"How can you say such a thing after she insulted your sister?"

"Sylvana brought it on herself. She had no right to demand that the duchess kiss her hand."

"You take this woman's side against your own family?"

"I take Klaus's side—and Wolfenberg's side. My only aim in life is to serve my cousin and my country, and I can't do that by falling out with his chosen favorite. Now, to please me, you will come down, announce that your headache is better and show our guest every courtesy."

Eugenia's voice rose to a shriek. "I will not do it!"

Reinald's tone grew ominous as he declared, "Then you will gravely disappoint me, Mother." There was the sound of a door closing, and Leonie guessed he had departed. Leonie stood, reflective.

After a while, she went downstairs without waiting to be fetched. Some French doors stood open, inviting her into the gardens, which the late-afternoon sun made warm and mellow. Almost at once she found herself confronting a maze made of tall hedges. She contemplated it in delight, for she enjoyed puzzles, and made her way inside.

The maze was deceptive, offering an appearance of simplicity until she was deep in, then revealing its true subtlety only when she was well and truly lost. After a moment, she heard voices, and realized that they belonged to Klaus and Reinald. She must be near the center.

Guided by the sound, she moved in until she could place the voices more clearly. She heard Reinald say, "You'll be glad to know that the agitator Crazne has finally been arrested and is under lock and key."

"At last." Klaus sounded relieved. "Let's hope the example will deter others who want to follow his path."

"Hallo," Leonie called. "Is anyone there?"

Both men answered her, and with their guidance she managed to get to the middle. They were sitting at a round stone table, covered with papers that Reinald was beginning to gather up. "I hope I don't intrude on affairs of state," she said, smiling.

"We'd just finished," Klaus informed her. "It's time for our departure."

As they left the maze, Sylvana galloped into view, accompanied by her groom. Klaus assisted her down. "I was concerned about you," she said to Leonie. "I blame myself for letting you ride a horse that was too much for you."

"I don't think you need to," Klaus observed. "She handled Paprika pretty well."

"But he ran away with me," Leonie said. "Don't forget that."

"Ah, yes," he said softly. "I was forgetting."

"You must allow me to provide a fresh horse for your homeward journey," Reinald said. "Perhaps you'll let me show you the stables. They are my pride."

She fell into step beside him. Klaus would have followed but Sylvana detained him, laughing archly and making teasing remarks that he answered with pleasant courtesy.

The stables were the finest Leonie had ever seen. Every animal was a Thoroughbred, groomed to gleaming perfection. They greeted Reinald with little whinnies of pleasure as he patted their noses and offered them tidbits. This surprised Leonie slightly. She hadn't estimated Reinald as a "tidbits" kind of man. But there was no mistaking the love in his eyes as he stroked the beautiful beasts and received their greetings.

"I'm relieved that you weren't hurt on that brute of my sister's," he said in a low voice as they moved along the stalls. "She should have known better than to let you mount him."

Leonie shrugged. "Sylvana was only being kind."

He gave her a telling glance. "It pains me to speak harshly of my own sister," he said reluctantly, "but I don't think she meant you well when she offered her mount. I hope you'll be careful."

Leonie laughed. "Do you think she'll poison my tea?"

"Not quite as bad as that. But her pride is formidable. I'm afraid it sometimes leads her to think of nothing else."

"And you?" Leonie asked curiously. "Isn't your pride equally formidable?"

He gave a faint smile that softened his face. "Yes," he admitted, "but it takes a different form. My only object is to serve Klaus, and for that, I sometimes have to take the long view.''

"And consort with scandalous women?" Leonie teased.

His smile increased, bringing a touch of real charm to his countenance. "No scandalous woman would be invited to set foot in this house. But *you* are always welcome, Duchess."

"Your highness is too kind."

"Reinald, if you please."

"And you must call me Leonie."

At the same moment, they both became aware that Klaus had entered the stable and was close enough to hear them. "I'm very sure that privilege is reserved for Klaus," Reinald observed.

"No, I call her 'you witch,'" Klaus observed wryly. "Don't be deceived by those melting blue eyes, cousin, or that soft voice. She's a devil sent to torment me."

Reinald's eyes seemed to scorch Leonie as he murmured, "I can believe it," in a voice just too low for Klaus to catch.

"No woman is what she seems," Leonie said lightly. "Men prefer us that way."

"Indeed, the world would soon be a dull place if women offered us no mystery to explore," Reinald agreed. "Leonie, will you oblige me by accepting the loan of Selma? As you can see, she's beautiful but—" he smiled slightly "—not dull, which I'm sure you'll appreciate."

Selma was indeed a beauty, but there was a spirited light in her eye that Leonie immediately took to. She thanked Reinald warmly, and waited while Selma was saddled. When it was done, he offered Leonie his arm and escorted her outside. Before bidding her farewell, he brushed his lips against her hand again, and waved aside the footman who would have assisted her to mount, offering his own hands for her foot. This time Leonie didn't reject the help.

As she settled into the saddle, she cast her eyes around and noticed the little hunchbacked man standing by the corner of the house, watching them. He backed hastily out of sight, but not before she'd seen on his face a look of the most vicious malevolence she'd ever encountered.

"Klaus must bring you here again soon," Reinald told her.

"I'll make sure that he does," she promised. The next moment, she was trotting away at Klaus's side.

"I'm glad that meeting went so well," Klaus observed when they'd gone half a mile. "Reinald's a stickler, more so than any man I know—including myself. I was afraid you'd throw him into a fit of puritanical gloom. Luckily he understands that it's wise policy to treat you with respect."

Leonie smiled wryly to herself. Reinald's hands had trembled slightly as he helped her onto the horse, and her instincts told her it wasn't with respect. But she judged it wiser not to mention this to Klaus. She wasn't sure yet whether Reinald's interest would help or hinder her mission.

"Who was that little man I saw?" she asked.

"That was Luther. He's Reinald's secretary. Don't be misled by his appearance. Inside that twisted body is a remarkable brain. Reinald discovered him being exhibited in a traveling fair by an 'owner' who forced him to perform memory tricks for the crowd. He had the man imprisoned and rescued Luther, who's been fanatically devoted to him ever since. As you observed, he hates to let Reinald out of his sight. He's like a dog, only happy when his master calls him. He'd give his life for him without a second thought."

"In that case, Reinald should be wary," Leonie observed thoughtfully. "Fanatical devotion can be a two-edged sword. For every person who loves you there's one who hates you, and sometimes they're the same person."

"You speak as if you know," Klaus said. He added slowly, "You're a woman who must have experienced a great deal of love and hate."

"Enough to know that it's hard to find one without the other," she agreed.

Between them lay the memory of the kiss they'd shared a few hours earlier, and which had blotted out all else for a few searing minutes. But his eyes, meeting hers, still bore traces of hostility, and she knew that his anger and his desire were still fighting a battle within him.

"I see the others coming this way," she said. "Now, do you remember your part?"

"I'm wildly infatuated with you," he recited ironically, "in between wanting to wring your neck."

"Your infatuation is for public use," she reminded him gaily. "Wringing my neck must be done in private."

He grinned. "I'll remember."

Chapter Five

That same night, Leonie accompanied Masham to The Black Dog, dressed, as before, in male garb. She found Jack Blair in an even worse mood. He'd cabled London for more funds, only to receive the reply that Leonie was the final arbiter in such matters, and that he should apply to her.

"You should have told me you needed more," she said quietly when they were settled upstairs. "Masham will bring you money tomorrow."

As she'd feared, her easy way of settling the problem merely inflamed his dislike. As soon as she could, she changed the subject and asked him what he knew about Crazne. "Why does Prince Klaus call him an agitator, and why was he arrested?"

"He's a radical," Blair growled. "He wants democracy and a free press. In this country, that sounds like a call to revolution. Prince Klaus is an autocrat, a despot who keeps power tightly in his own hands. Crazne's a threat to him so he had to be arrested. There'll be a show trial, he'll get a life sentence and the man we're all trying to protect will feel a little safer—until the next time someone dares to question his absolute authority."

Leonie was silent. She refused to let Blair see how disturbed she was by this. He painted an unpleasant picture of

Klaus, one she was reluctant to believe in. Arrogant, yes. Autocratic, possibly. But not cruel. Her heart rejected that idea.

"Now I'm going to tell you something," Blair growled. "And I hope it doesn't throw you into a fit of feminine flutters."

"Oh, my nerves are made of steel," she assured him, "as strong as the steel of my knife. You remember my knife, Jack?"

He flung her a black look, but didn't provoke her further. "Bismarck has troops massed on Prussia's border with Wolfenberg," he said flatly.

Leonie sighed. "That's common knowledge."

"But what isn't common knowledge is the fact that he's doubled them in the last twenty-four hours."

"*What?* Are you quite sure?"

"Certain as I'm standing here. He claims they're 'necessary defenses' against 'recent unfriendly acts' by Wolfenberg. Do you know what he means by that?"

Leonie had an uneasy suspicion that Bismarck had heard about the loan to reinforce Wolfenberg's army, but she wasn't going to reveal that to Blair. "Look," she said, "this is what I want you to do—"

Blair thumped the table. "Be damned to what you want, d'ye hear? I'll not take orders from a woman."

"You will if you don't want to be recalled to London with a black mark against you," Leonie said firmly. "I'm not wasting time having this argument again."

Blair looked murderous and for a moment she thought he would strike her. Masham had risen protectively but she kept him back with a wave of her hand. Blair saw this silent demonstration of authority and the venom in his eyes doubled. Leonie didn't appear to notice it. In a quiet voice she outlined her requirements, then rose to leave. "Masham will be here tomorrow night for a report on your progress," she said. "Good night Jack."

He merely scowled at her.

Instead of taking a hansom, she and Masham strolled back through the streets. As they walked, she brooded over what Lord William had told her about Blair. "A good agent in the field, capable of digging out first-class information. He's also as brave and cunning as any man I know. Unfortunately, he has a vicious streak and an unreliable temper, which is why he'll never go any further than being someone else's instrument."

After a while, she shrugged. Blair's attitude was a pity, but it was in his own interests to make a success of this job.

Treuheim wasn't a large place and half an hour's walk brought them to the neighborhood that adjoined the palace. It was a cheerful area, filled with the houses of doctors and lawyers and the workshops of skilled artisans. Here and there were taverns with tables on the pavement and light streaming from within. They sat down outside one and Masham ordered beer for both of them. In seconds the landlord had placed two foaming steins on the table and with one movement they raised them. Masham took three quarters of his in one gulp. "Better than the gut rot in the other place," he growled.

"The very finest," the landlord boomed. "I had it delivered today for the beer festival tomorrow."

"I thought October was the time for beer festivals," Masham observed.

"Oh, we have one in October, too," the landlord assured him cheerfully. "And in May. And September. But this one's the best."

The streets were bright with bunting and garlands hanging from the windows. Young couples strolled along the cobbled streets, the girls in skirts, tight black bodices and embroidered blouses. Although the festival wasn't until the next day, they were already anticipating it in their relaxed behavior, the ease with which they would stop and kiss beneath the lamp-hung trees. The sight gave her an unexpected pang of loneliness. Her life was rich and satisfying, full of excitement. But since her husband's death, it had been a life without love. She could recall many evenings when she'd poured out her thoughts and feelings under Geoffrey's tender eyes, relaxed in the certainty of his infinite loving kindness. Now she had no one to confide in.

And afterward, when he'd led her to bed, there'd been warmth and gentle delight, drowsy contentment and the sweet satisfaction of giving happiness in return for all he gave her. It had been enough at the time. There'd been no thrilling rapture, no ecstasy of the body, but she hadn't missed them. Not then.

It was only recently she'd looked back with the memory of Klaus's kisses burning her lips, and known that there was more, and that she wanted it; known also that her body had been brought alive by a man she couldn't have, except for a little while, and even then, not completely.

A young man began to sing. The refrain was taken up by the others, and soon everyone was singing. It was a song full of the delight of love, yet shot through with the knowledge of a parting very near. The sweet aching beauty of the tune possessed her, and Leonie, too, began to sing.

Sad is my heart beneath the silver moon,
Sad for soon I must leave you.
Soon there will be only the moonlight,
And my memories.

The song ended and the crowd immediately burst into a

different tune, jolly and rollicking, and out of keeping with her mood.

"Another?" Masham asked hopefully, displaying his empty stein.

"No," she said with an unconscious sigh, "we should be getting back."

Reaching the palace, she slipped quietly through the concealed entrance, up the stairs and opened the secret door into her bedroom. But she stopped on the threshold. There were no lights in the room, but every instinct told her that someone was here, waiting for her in the darkness. Her mind hurried over the possibilities. Was it possible that Bismarck had managed to get an assassin in place to dispose of her first? Quietly she slipped her hand into her sleeve and withdrew the stiletto.

"I wouldn't if I were you" came an amused voice. "You'd have a difficult time explaining my death to Lord Bracewell."

Her breath came in a rush. *"Klaus."*

He lit a small lamp. "Whom were you expecting?"

"No one."

"That's rather remiss of you, surely? My favorite should have been expecting *me.*"

"Why are you here? Has something happened?"

He regarded her satirically. "Can you have forgotten so soon that I'm wildly infatuated with you? Naturally we're expected to spend some part of each night together. I'll pass over my disappointment at finding the woman I worship to the point of madness not waiting to receive me."

She regarded him wryly. "The woman you worship to the point of madness has been out working hard on your behalf," she told him.

"Indeed? Hence your attire, presumably. Did you slay many assassins?"

"A few dozen. I lost count. Actually, I've been contacting my fellow agents, and I've learned something disturbing. In the last twenty-four hours, Bismarck has doubled his troops on your border." She saw by his face that he was as stunned as she'd been. "He claims to be acting in response to your 'unfriendly acts.'"

"That's an excuse," Klaus said harshly. "I've committed no unfriendly acts."

"You've committed one," she said. "You've negotiated a British loan to strengthen your army."

"But he doesn't know that."

"I think he must. Or at least he suspects. This place must be riddled with his spies. Whom have you told?"

"Only three men. Reinald, Count Halzen, my finance minister, and Baron Gruber, my foreign minister. Every one of them is beyond reproach."

"But what about their security? Suppose someone's been looking through their papers?"

Klaus shook his head. "They all have instructions to commit nothing to paper, and they'll have kept to those instructions. You don't know these men and I do."

"There's one other possibility," Leonie mused. "Perhaps Bismarck's heard rumors of your possible marriage to Princess Louise."

"Why should he call that an unfriendly act?"

"Because he must dread an alliance between Wolfenberg and Britain—the one country strong enough for him to fear."

"Of course," he said grimly. "British might, British force, British power to dictate how other countries behave! I can't forget that, can I?"

"Well, it's true," she said, stung. "Bismarck *is* afraid of my country. It's lucky for us all that he's afraid of someone."

"Yes, I suppose so," he said with a sigh. "Forgive me. I didn't mean to sound ungracious."

"But at this moment, I look like nothing but a damned Briton?" she guessed. "And you dislike the British with all the fervor of a man who's forced to take their help." An impish humor made her add, "You'd like my contact, Jack Blair. It's neck and neck which one of you hates me most."

"I don't hate you, Leonie," he said quietly. "I just hate the position you've put me in. It's a false position. Once, I hoped we could meet as man and woman, but how can we now?"

"Yes," she sighed, "how can we?"

Unconsciously, her voice retained an echo of the thoughts she'd been thinking as she sat at the table outside the tavern.

"Is something wrong?" Klaus asked, looking closely at her face.

"No, nothing's wrong. I walked back through the streets and everything was so cheerful for the beer festival—one of many, I gather."

"Wolfenberg produces excellent beer and people enjoy any excuse to drink it."

"Do you enjoy it?"

"I drink beer, yes."

"No, I mean the festival."

He shrugged. "I made an official visit to one in the first year of my reign. My presence ended the jollity very quickly, and I never went again."

"What a pity they can't be natural with you. It means you never see them as they really are, and so you don't really know them."

His face darkened. "You're impertinent. I've ruled my people for thirteen years."

"But do you know what they're thinking and feeling? I don't think so. Do you know what they think of *you?*"

"They know that my life belongs to them, that I think of nothing but what's best for them."

"But how do you *know* what's best for them? Do you think you find that out by sitting behind a desk? You make marks on pieces of paper until you come to believe that those marks are reality. You move this man here and that man there, and you imagine that's all you have to do. But if they don't *want* to go where you put them, you've left an important element out of your equations."

To her surprise she found him looking at her with quizzical amusement. "Have I just gotten myself thrown into prison again?" she inquired wryly.

"Without trial," he confirmed, smiling slightly. "You've questioned the prince's authority—"

"Not his authority," she interrupted quickly. "Only his judgment."

"Another serious offense. I warned you this was a feudal country. Wolfenberg isn't like Britain, encircled by a protective sea. We're surrounded by neighbors, most of whom have been hostile in the past. The prince has always needed to be a strong man who could make decisions quickly."

"But what does he know of the people whose lives his decisions affect?" Leonie persisted.

"What would you have me know—how they complain at paying taxes? Everyone complains about taxes. I don't have to hear them to know that."

"But which taxes, and why? Which are the unjust taxes—yes, yes, I know," she interrupted herself. "Go to jail for daring to suggest that the prince imposes unjust taxes." Klaus merely grinned. For the first time, she saw a hint of mischief in his face and it made her heart somersault. "I don't mean," she went on in a voice grown suddenly breathless, "that you tax your people unjustly—"

Klaus raised his eyebrows. "Come, Leonie. Have the courage of your impertinence. That was exactly what you meant."

"I didn't mean that you do it on purpose. But there are things that look reasonable on paper that are actually unfair in practice because of circumstances you can't imagine."

He frowned. "There are complaints procedures."

"Run by officials who know as little about these people as you do," Leonie countered.

"I suppose you'd like me to give you a free hand to go through the whole system shaking up my officials."

"No, I think that's something you should do yourself." Perceiving by his outraged look that she'd pushed him as far as was wise, she hastily added, "Besides, you don't just need to know your people's complaints. You should meet them in the good times, too. Hear them laugh and sing. That's when they're most truly themselves. If you don't know them at such moments, you don't know them at all."

"Laugh and sing," he echoed, savoring the words as if they were new to him. A touch of longing came into his voice. "Do people really laugh and sing? It's so long since I—" He broke off and sighed.

He became aware that Leonie was stripping off her outer garments. The cloak was tossed aside, then the coat, revealing her slender figure in a natty waistcoat and fawn trousers that revealed the length of her legs. The sight heightened his tension. He'd wondered whether her legs were as lovely as the rest of her. Now he saw enough to tempt and torment him further, but not enough to satisfy him.

"You take a great risk going out like that," he said with difficulty. "The moment you open your mouth—"

"Oh, Masham does the talking. I just look haughty," she said with a chuckle. She reached high above her head and stretched, unconsciously driving him to distraction.

"Will you go out again tomorrow night?" he asked.

"I think not. I've had enough of Jack Blair for a while. My real job is to stay close to you."

"But if I went out—say, if I visited the beer festival, you'd have to come with me."

"Yes," she said slowly, "but I'm not sure it's wise for you to go out."

"That's my decision," he declared firmly. "I shall attend the festival, incognito." Seeing her alarm, he added blandly, "I'm only taking your advice."

"But I didn't mean that," Leonie protested.

"You said I should see my people as they really are. How else am I to do it except by passing among them in disguise?"

"I was talking foolishly—"

"You were talking good sense. I'm not so set in my own pride that I can't take sound advice." He was enjoying shaking her composure for once.

"But anything could happen to you out there," Leonie said.

"Nonsense. If nobody recognizes, me I'm actually safer out there than in here," he observed. "Besides, I shall have you to protect me. Bracewell promised me the best agent London had. My safety is assured."

Leonie recognized that Klaus was beyond reason. His eyes had the glint of a man who'd been starved for normal human pleasure for too long, and now saw the chance to take it. She could do nothing but yield.

Klaus glanced at the clock. "I'll return to my own apartments now," he said. "My valet, who knows all my movements, will soon spread the word that I've been here long enough to affirm the—er—violence of my passion."

"By all means, leave," Leonie told him rather testily. The sarcastic way he spoke of passion was not at all to her taste.

Leonie had an early visitor the next morning. She'd barely finished dressing when Archduke Reinald was announced. She began to drop a curtsy but he took hold of her hands. "I beg you, don't curtsy to me," he said firmly, making her rise.

In the brilliant morning sun, the scar on his face was more visible, but it did nothing to mar his good looks. "State business obliges me to attend my cousin this morning," he remarked, "but I decided to give myself the pleasure of calling on you first. I'm delighted to see that your journey home was evidently a safe one."

"A very pleasant one on your lovely horse," Leonie confirmed.

"I'm glad you think well of Selma, because I wish you to keep her."

"You're too kind, but I couldn't accept such a gift."

A faint smile lit his haughty face. "There'll be many such gifts now, Leonie. You're the most influential woman in the country, and as such, you'll be courted by men and women alike. But my gift is not of that kind. I wish to be your friend."

"I never thought your gift was 'of that kind,'" she said at once.

"Klaus won't mind if I give you a horse. He and I have been close since boyhood."

"Then I accept," she said, smiling.

"The horse or my friendship?"

"Both."

"Good. I must leave you now, but I beg you to believe that I'm always at your service."

He stood upright and clicked his heels formally. But at the last moment, he raised her hand and brushed his lips against it. With a shock, Leonie felt the violent trembling in him, and the heat of his mouth, that contrasted so strangely with his chilly manner. Then he released her, bowed his head and walked away as straight as a ramrod.

Klaus appeared in her room that evening, dressed in an open shirt and leather trousers with embroidered braces. He might have been any one of his own subjects, save for an air of authority that sat on him naturally.

"It's nice to see you out of military uniform," Leonie observed.

He shrugged. "Usually I'm in uniform because I'm a soldier. My country has always needed soldiers, and never more so than now. You of all people should understand the danger."

"I understand it so well that I wish we weren't going."

A light came into his eyes as they rested on Leonie, who was in the traditional costume of Wolfenberg. The heavily embroidered skirt was very full, and short enough to show her trim ankles. Atop it was a black velvet waistcoat, laced down the front and cut away so that it fitted under her breasts, pushing them high. Her blouse was soft and white, pulled down to reveal her shoulders completely, and held by a black string in the front. Her glorious hair flowed free almost down to her waist, something Klaus had never seen before. He felt a constriction in his throat. "Perhaps we need not go," he said huskily.

He reached for her and drew her hard against him. "Let's see if my favorite can persuade me," he murmured. "After all, it's your job to offer me temptation."

Once again, there was the treacherous thrumming of blood in her veins and the racing of her pulse that threatened to overcome her reason. If she could have yielded to her sensations, Leonie would have returned his embrace with ardor, but she fought her impulse down and tried to pull away. "My job is to protect you," she insisted in a shaking voice.

"So, protect me by keeping me indoors," he said, leaning down to drop a kiss on her bare shoulder. She trembled, gasping with the desire that light kiss sent streaming through her body. Klaus had offered her an impossible choice: to let him risk himself in the crowd, or risk her own detachment by growing dangerously close to him. Which way did her duty lie? she wondered wildly.

But he solved the dilemma for her by releasing her suddenly and asking, in a mocking voice, "What's the matter, Leonie? Didn't your masters in London tell you how far to go? Very well. Let's go out and meet my people."

Reluctantly, Leonie touched the spring in the carving that made the secret door open, and walked out into the passage. Lighting their way with a lantern, she led him as far as the exit. "We come out beyond the castle," she said. "From the noise, I can hear the celebrations are in full swing."

"Then why are we standing here?"

With a sigh, she hung the lantern on a wall hook, blew it out and gingerly opened the door. They stepped out into a shabby, back street.

"Where are we?" Klaus asked, looking around.

"Near the edge of town," she told him.

A group of villainous-looking men stood loafing nearby. One of them glanced up as they appeared, his eyes glittering with ill will, and began to sway toward them. Klaus immediately put himself in front of Leonie to protect her. She regarded his back in exasperation. Apart from being well able to take care of herself, she'd recognized the man. "It's all right," she said. "He isn't a robber."

"How can you know?"

"Because he's one of us, and he's here on my orders."

Klaus swung around on her. "You mean that's one of my 'protectors'?" he demanded wrathfully.

"That's Jack Blair," she admitted.

"And the others?"

"And the others."

For a moment, she thought he would explode. But instead, he seized her hand and began to run, forcing her to run with him. "You mustn't—" she tried to say.

"Be silent, woman," he growled, increasing his speed.

She was lost. Shops and houses sped past in a blur, and she was running out of breath keeping up with him. By the time he stopped, she was gasping. "You shouldn't have done that," she panted.

"Sit down, shut up and stop telling me what to do," he ordered.

They were in a square, surrounded on four sides by brightly painted houses. Most of the square was taken up by the tables of a beer garden, lit by colored lamps in the trees overhead. Leonie made her way to a table, guided by Klaus's firm arm about her waist, and sat down with relief. Immediately two foaming steins were placed before them. Klaus downed his, wiped the foam from his mouth with the back of his hand and said firmly, "Just for this one night there are going to be no anxious observers, no protectors—just you and me. Tonight I'm a man enjoying the pleasures of the best beer in Europe."

"Don't say that," the landlord pleaded. "It could cost me money."

"Taxes?" Leonie asked impishly, with a glance at Klaus.

"It's always taxes," the man complained.

"Why shouldn't you want people to know you sell fine beer?" Klaus inquired.

"Because I'm not taxed on what I've sold, but on what the commissioners *estimate* I've sold," the landlord declared bitterly. "And their estimates are always weighted in their favor. My ale is divided into first-grade and second-grade, but will they recognize this? Of course not. I'm taxed as if it were all first-grade."

"And this isn't first-grade?" Klaus asked, tasting it.

"My first-grade has run out. It always does. But they're not interested. Of course they're not. They're paid by results. The more they can extort from me, the fatter their own pockets." He suddenly looked suspiciously into Klaus's face. "You're not a government inspector are you?"

Klaus drew back into the shadows. "No, only a man who likes good beer," he said hastily. "First-or second-grade." The landlord grunted and passed on. Klaus caught Leonie's eye and said, "Even the second-grade is a huge improvement on the stuff I get served in the pal—in my home. And it's a hundred times better than the weedy brew they serve in England."

"Have you been in England, friend?"

The question came from a man at the next table. He was dressed in the same style as Klaus, and was a little older. "Franz Schneider," he said, holding out his hand. "I'm a teacher."

"Friederich is a lawyer," Leonie informed him. "He was recently in England to meet other lawyers."

The two men shook hands. "I teach my pupils about England," the man said. "I say *there* is a country with good laws that everybody must obey. Not like here."

"You find fault with the laws of Wolfenberg, friend?" Klaus asked mildly.

"I say there are no laws here," Franz declared. "There are laws for some and not for others, and that is the same as no laws. If you're a lawyer, you must know about Crazne."

The name produced a murmur of interest and several other men and woman shifted closer so that they formed a little group.

"I know Crazne has been arrested, and will be tried," Klaus said, still in the same mild voice.

"Tried," Franz growled. "Now there's a fine joke. Oh, yes, he'll be tried, and if the magistrates are corrupt, they'll find him guilty, and if they're honest, they'll find him innocent. But the end will be the same. Whatever the verdict, the prince will keep him in jail."

"How can he be kept in jail if the magistrates find him innocent?" Leonie asked.

There was a rumble of laughter. "Your woman is a fool," Franz declared. "She doesn't know that the prince can take the law into his own hands whenever it suits him."

"Perhaps the law is safer in his hands than in anyone else's," Klaus observed.

"The law is never safe in the hands of any one man," said a man in the crowd. "Our prince means well, but times are changing, and he doesn't see it."

"Perhaps he'll be made to see it," Franz growled.

"Is that what you teach your students?" Klaus inquired. "Because if so, it's treason."

"I don't need to teach them," Franz said simply. "They can see the truth all around them. One day they'll rise up and speak it."

"And bring something worse down on us," said a woman close to Leonie. "I, too, think our prince is wrong about many things, but he's keeping us free from Bismarck."

There was a rumble of agreement. The next moment, an accordion had started to play, and with the lightning changes of mood that made the people of Wolfenberg so unpredictable, and often so charming, the little crowd around the table dropped the subject and turned to join in the singing. But Klaus didn't move. He sat staring into his beer, his forehead creased in a frown.

"What did they mean about Crazne?" Leonie asked him in a low voice. "Can y—can the prince really overrule a court's verdict?"

"Of course," Klaus said in apparent surprise, as though overruling a court's verdict were the most natural thing in the world.

She looked around. Their companions had risen to dance, nobody's attention was on them now. "And will you?" she asked urgently.

"Certainly I will. My people are like children. What do they know about political necessity?"

"Some of them seem very politically sophisticated."

"They think they are, but they see everything in simple terms. They know nothing of the crosscurrents and subtleties that I have to take into account with every decision. Crazne fills their heads with mad dreams. If I imprison him, it's to protect them."

"You're talking like someone out of the Middle Ages," she said, dismayed to find him fitting Jack Blair's derisive picture so closely. "No, don't have me arrested for treason, but listen to me."

He gave her a sly smile. "My dear, I wouldn't dream of having you arrested. You'd turn the guards' heads and be out in ten minutes. But I want *you* to listen to *me*.

"Seventeen years ago, there was a revolution that shook all Europe. It started in Paris, where they forced the king to abdicate. Then it spread across a whole continent—Berlin, Vienna, Rome, Prague, Budapest. Nobody was safe. There were even riots in Wolfenberg.

"The crowd stormed the palace where I lived with my grandfather. Some of them wanted to see us dead. We had no choice but to escape.

"It didn't last. No sooner had we gone than another group rioted, demanding our restoration to power. Luckily the army stayed loyal. It restored order, arrested the troublemakers, and within a few weeks, my grandfather was back on his throne. Things seemed to go on as before, but actually nothing was ever the same again.

"I was seventeen, reared in the belief that my life must be dedicated to the service of the people who would one day be mine. And then they turned on us. To the last moment of my life, I will remember the humiliation of being forced to flee like a criminal. Now, whenever I look into their faces—" he broke off.

"It makes no difference to my duty to them," he went on after a moment. "Or to my love for them. But I can't forget. How can I ever trust them again? You heard the way they talked tonight. Tell me, how can I trust them?"

"Yes, I heard the way they talked," she agreed, "and so did you. But you didn't *listen*. Perhaps they'd feel more kindly toward you if you acted less like an autocrat. You say they're children, but they're not. They're adults, and they resent you because you won't let them grow up."

"It's no blessing to grow up too soon, Leonie. I know that from my own experience. If only my father had lived, things might be different with me. But he died when I was a child, and I succeeded my grandfather when I was only twenty. I found myself confronting a council full of men twice my age and ten times as experienced. They tried to distract me with amusements so that they could get on with running the country their way. I had to fight to establish my authority. Perhaps it made me an autocrat, because autocracy was the only thing they could understand. If I held out my hands for friendship, they despised me as a weakling. So I slammed my fist down on them and taught them to respect me. It was the only way. Don't judge me for it, because you can't understand.''

"I don't judge you,'' she said softly. She felt strangely moved. As he spoke, she'd been able to see the shy, uncertain young man, little more than a boy, thrust before his time onto a throne, creating a friendless, loveless desert about himself, because it was the only way he could survive.

"I think it's sad that the actions of a few have been allowed to divide you from the bulk of your people,'' she mused aloud. "You said yourself, when you were gone, they wanted you back. *That's* what you should remember most.''

"It's so simple to you, isn't it?'' he said. "I can picture you as a little girl in the schoolroom, learning European history from your governess. I expect you had a book with a heading that said, 'The Revolution of 1848,' and explained everything in five lines. You read them with great concentration, and now you think you know what happened.''

Leonie's memory flew back to the year 1848, her last year with her mother's people. She knew more than Klaus could ever guess. The revolution had spread like wildfire from country to country, and the Gypsies had run before it, knowing that in troubled times they themselves could become easy targets for mobs wrought up to violence. They'd traveled by night, hidden by day, slipped across borders at the weakest points, laughed and sang for their suppers while their hearts beat with fear. Sometimes, men and women on the run had sheltered with them, appearing out of the night, then vanishing into the night when the danger eased. Terrifying times, but thrilling times—times when she'd felt alive. She sighed. "It was a little longer than five lines," she said with an abstracted smile.

Something in that smile intrigued Klaus. It hinted at subtle undercurrents, and made him feel he'd judged too hastily. "Why are you laughing?" he demanded.

"I'm not laughing."

"You're laughing inside, I know. Tell me why."

"Perhaps I'm thinking of the difference between what my life has been and what you think it has been," she said.

"Tell me about your life."

For a moment, she wondered if she could tell him about the Gypsies. The colored lamps softened his face and made him appear younger, so that she caught a glimpse of the boy who'd vanished long ago. But the accordion player was playing the sweet aching tune she'd heard last night, and she found herself swaying to it, watching the lovers dancing in each other's arms under the trees. Almost without realizing, she began to sing softly.

Sad is my heart beneath the summer moon,
Sad for soon I must leave you.
Soon there will be only the moonlight,
And my memories.

Klaus's eyes held hers and there was an uneasy stirring in his heart. Soon she would leave him and he might never know the secret of her mystery, the secret he'd once promised himself he would fathom. His hostility to her had largely faded. He'd distinguished himself before her in the hunt and eluded her spies tonight, both of which had improved his mood. Now, in the soft lamplight, he began to see her again as he'd seen her first, and to realize he didn't know how long he might have to discover her. As the song ended, he rose to his feet and took her hands, drawing her into the crowd of dancers. Without the huge crinoline as a barrier, there was nothing to stop him drawing her close to him, and he did so. The warm, sweet smell of her was in his nostrils, making his senses riot and his heart ache. "Look at me, Leonie," he commanded huskily. And when she did, his mouth naturally found its place on hers.

She kept her lips against his as she swayed in the dance, holding on to him. She knew she was dangerously close to becoming lost in the moment, forgetting everything else, even if it meant risking her mission. She fought the temptation, but her will was weak. She was aware only of this man, his closeness, his warmth, the scent of his body. And after all, he *was* her mission. How could it be wrong to think only of him?

Then strong hands seized her by the waist and swung her away. She gasped, realizing that one of the other dancers had claimed her, separating her from Klaus and whirling her off into the crowd. "Dance with me, *liebchen,*" he cried merrily. "Don't keep everything for that fellow there. Save some for Gunther." As he spoke, he pulled her close and made determined efforts to kiss her.

Gunther never knew how close he came to being knocked down. As a secret agent, Leonie was skilled in the art of self-defense, and she could have landed him on his rear on the cobblestones without difficulty. For a dizzy moment, she tensed to deal with him, but then the thought that a show of her skill would expose her identity made her relax and unclench her hand. "Let me go," she said, laughing. "My lover is very jealous—"

"Then we'll give him something to be jealous about, *liebchen*," he vowed and bent his head to try for a kiss.

But his lips never touched Leonie's. A strong hand on his shoulder swung him around, a fist connected with his chin and sent him flying against the wall. A bellow of laughter went up from the crowd as Klaus stood over his rival, his eyes glittering, his chest rising and falling. "Be off with you," he said grimly.

Gunther rose to his feet, rubbing his chin. "No offense, friend," he said amiably. "Don't blame a man for trying his luck."

"I said be off," Klaus repeated.

Gunther took a step backward, his gaze fixed on Klaus's face. His eyes were full of curiosity, as though he was amazed by something. Alarm stirred in Leonie's breast. One of the colored lamps was shining directly onto Klaus's face, a face his people knew well from their stamps and coins. Gunther was still retreating, still regarding Klaus. Suddenly he turned and vanished into the crowd.

"Let's go," Leonie urged, touching Klaus's arm.

He didn't seem to hear her. He'd recovered his temper and was grinning at the crowd's cheers. Many a love rivalry came to a head at festivals, and they all respected a man who could reclaim his woman with such a punch. They were laughing as they cheered, slapping him on the back, pressing beer onto him, offering bawdy congratulations. And he was loving it, Leonie realized. He was among his people, one of them, laughing and drinking with them, just as she'd urged him to do. And he was happy. It was a pity to drag him away, but she knew she had to do so. "We have to go," she said in his ear.

He seemed to become aware of her. "Go?" he cried. "We've only just arrived. I'm here to enjoy myself."

"Yes, but don't you realize..."

He wasn't listening. He had a huge stein in his hand and was starting to drink from it. He drank without pausing for breath, leaning his head back and bending his knees slightly in the effort to get it all down in one go, while the crowd shouted encouragement and the musicians played.

When Klaus was on the point of collapse, he lowered the stein so that they could see it was empty, gasping heavily as he acknowledged their roar. "Landlord—your best beer for all these good folk," he shouted.

"No," Leonie whispered frantically.

"What do you mean, no? These are my friends, and if I want to treat them, I shall."

"But—"

"Woman, be silent," he roared, picking her up suddenly and seating himself on a nearby bench with Leonie on his lap. She struggled, but he kept both arms tightly around her, making her helpless.

In despair, Leonie recognized that Klaus had been carried away by the novelty and excitement. This would be the ideal way for him to meet his people if she hadn't been so horribly aware of danger. "Stop wriggling," he commanded. "I came to your rescue. The least you can do is be grateful."

"I *am* grateful," she said, "But—"

"Perhaps she preferred Gunther," someone shouted, to the accompaniment of laughter.

Without hesitation, Klaus tightened his grip, turned her face up to his and covered her mouth with his own. Leonie's head swam. If things had been different, she'd have asked nothing better than to be in Klaus's arms.

He released her long enough to roar, "Do you prefer his kisses or mine?"

"Yours," she said breathlessly, "but—"

"Good." He returned to the attack, crushing her mouth with his and making her head spin. Overhead, the landlord was distributing the huge steins of beer around the crowd, who were beginning to bang them on the table, chanting, "One—two—three—four—five—" as the seconds ticked by and the kiss went on and on.

When Klaus allowed her to come up for air, his eyes were glittering. "How delightful," he said so that only she could hear, "to get you in a position where you can't answer back or give me orders. How I shall enjoy making the most of it."

"You've got to listen to me!"

"Ah, but I haven't got to do anything you say. Not now. Not tonight. I'm Friederich," he raised his voice, "a free man, who does what he pleases—as each man should."

There was a yell of agreement from every man in the crowd, followed by some ribald suggestions as to how he should assert himself. "I've got an empty room upstairs," the landlord hinted.

"We'll take it," Klaus said at once.

"We will not," Leonie protested.

"Woman, don't argue," Klaus commanded masterfully.

Before Leonie knew what he meant to do, he rose to his feet, seized her in powerful hands and tossed her over his shoulder like a sack of meal. She was helpless, trapped by an arm held across her legs like an iron bar. She hammered his back uselessly as he turned toward the inn, calling, "Show me the room," and strode purposefully into the building. The crowd cheered them on their way.

A little maid showed Klaus upstairs and threw open a door. When it had closed behind them, Klaus set her on her feet. His face was glowing like a boy's and her heart gave a lurch of tenderness. If only they could stay here together. "Now," he said significantly.

"Now it's time to stop acting like a madman. We have to get out of here," she urged.

"When I'm ready," he said firmly, trying to take her into his arms.

But Leonie had regained her wits. Seizing him by the shirt, she fended him off with a practiced movement that sent him flying backward across the bed. He lay there staring at her, a prey to amazement and indignation in equal parts. "Where the devil did you learn to do *that?*"

"In the service. You never know when the strangest skills are going to be useful."

It was borne in on Klaus, with horrible clarity, that she could have freed herself from Gunther with equal ease, and his "rescue" of her had been less glorious than he supposed. "Why you teasing little—why did you let me think—?"

"What else could I do? If I'd sent him flying, it would have exposed my identity. As it is, I think it's exposed, anyway. That man got a good look at your face and he was very interested. What's more, he vanished immediately. I think he's gone to tell someone, and that means we've got to get out of here quickly.

"Woman, are you mad? After the way I came storming up here, do you think I'm going to walk tamely down those stairs with them all standing around grinning?"

"Do you have any money?"

He looked surprised. "I never thought of it. I seldom carry money."

"Then how were you going to pay for those drinks for everyone you ordered, not to mention this room? Tell them to send the bill to the palace?" She enjoyed the sight of Klaus's jaw dropping as realization dawned. "You won't need to walk tamely downstairs," she assured him. "We'll have to escape through the window."

"Run away without paying my bill, like a common criminal?" he demanded, aghast.

"All right then," she said, exasperated. "Go downstairs and pay it."

"We'll go through the window," he decided hastily.

The window looked out onto a small enclosed yard. Klaus went first, climbing over the sill and hanging by his fingertips until he was steady enough to drop. When he'd landed, he put up his hands to take Leonie's waist as she swung down. In another moment, she was on the ground beside him.

"Hey."

They looked up to see the landlord staring at them indignantly through the downstairs window. "Run," Klaus said, grabbing her hand and heading for the gate.

They found themselves in an alley, blocked at one end. The only way out lay through the crowd. Heads down, clutching each other, they dived into the throng of dancers. "Stop them," the landlord yelled. "Stop, thief! Stop, I say."

Luckily the dancers and drinkers were too busy enjoying themselves to heed him, and they were able to weave through. In a moment, they were running down a side street leading to the square. A few stragglers watched them go by, taking little notice until the cry of "Stop, thief!" reached them. Then their eyes lit up at the thought of something fresh to to, and they gave chase. The fugitives picked up speed, running until they were breathless, clutching each other's hands for dear life.

At last, they found a small alley where they could stop for breath. "If we're caught," Leonie gasped, clutching her side, "can you prove who you are?"

"No. And I'd rather not have to try."

"Then let's not get caught."

"This way," he said, pointing to the end of the alley.

But Leonie's sharp eyes had pierced the gloom to notice something ominous. "It's a dead end. We'll have to go back."

"Hurry, then."

They whirled but almost immediately found themselves confronting a young man in the uniform of the Wolfenberg police. "Ah-hah!" he announced in satisfaction. "Thought you'd escape me, did you?"

They looked at each other, then at the policeman, whose youth and braiding revealed that his was the lowest rank, and whose country accent proclaimed him a newcomer to the city. He was almost dancing with joy. "Look what I've got!" he exclaimed. "Two hardened criminals. Let them laugh at me now!"

"Who laughs at you, friend?" Klaus inquired sympathetically.

"*They do.* The others. They say I'm not suited to police work. But they won't say that when I walk in with you two." He moved closer to stare at Klaus. "I know your face," he yelped.

"You do?" Klaus asked cautiously.

"Yes, I do. You're the *chicken thief.*"

"I beg your pardon!" Klaus said.

"You're the thief who made off with Frau Mantel's chickens last week. I saw your face as you escaped. And now I've caught you."

He was too preoccupied with his discovery to notice that Leonie had moved behind him, but Klaus saw it, and his eyes met hers over the young policeman's shoulder. A moment of perfect understanding passed between them. Then Leonie moved fast, swinging her leg across the back of the constable's knees so that they buckled. In an instant, Klaus hauled the hapless young man up and dumped him, flailing, into a nearby horse trough. His yells of indignation followed them down the alley.

This time they were in luck. There was no sign of their pursuers and they were able to run the last half mile to the palace without interruption. They got through the secret door, slammed it behind them and stood leaning against it.

"Let's get on," Klaus said at last. "I'll feel easier when I'm in my own surroundings."

They hurried the last few yards to emerge in Leonie's bedroom. Her heart was thumping with dread at the danger they'd so narrowly averted. Looking up, she saw dawning realization and dismay in Klaus's eyes. "Do you realize what I did?" he demanded, aghast. "I assaulted an officer of the law. At my coronation I pledged to support law and order, and tonight, *I threw a policeman into a horse trough.*"

Leonie ran a hand distractedly through her hair. "That's the least of it," she said. "When I think what might have happened... You could have been caught, imprisoned, and it would all have been my fault."

He gave her shoulders a little shake. "Stop being a secret agent for five minutes. It wasn't that bad."

"It could have been. We should never have taken such a risk."

But Klaus's face was lightening. "I wouldn't have missed it for the world," he said. "To be mistaken for the Treuheim Chicken Thief." Suddenly he began to laugh. "Poor fellow! Did you see his face?"

"It's not funny," Leonie said worriedly.

"But it is," Klaus insisted in the tone of man who'd made a discovery. He looked into her face. "And you have to admit that as thieves we make a wonderful team."

His eyes were gleaming with fun, something she'd rarely seen in him before. And suddenly she was swept by an aching tenderness for him. He lived in luxury, but he had so very little of the things that mattered. "Yes," she agreed. "We make a wonderful team. The Treuheim Chicken Thief and his doxy."

Klaus let out a bellow of laughter and pulled her against him, not kissing her, but sharing his mirth with her through the contact of their bodies. She laughed with him, until a thought came to her. "And his colleagues say he's not suited to police work," she said. "I wonder why."

That set them off again and they rocked back and forth in each other's arms. She looked up and saw again something of the boy he must once have been before too much responsibility crushed him too young. Tenderness for him was like a pain in her heart.

"Thank you," he said gently, cupping her face between his hands. "Thank you for showing my people to me."

Chapter Six

Next day, the *Treuheim Gazette* thundered against "anarchic elements in society who used innocent celebrations as an excuse for lawbreaking." This was illustrated with the story of the unfortunate landlord of The Golden Bear, the victim of two hardened criminals, a man and a woman, who ordered massive amounts of beer before retreating to a room in the inn, "ostensibly for purposes that it would be unbecoming to discuss in a respectable newspaper," but actually as a cover for their escape. The two had subsequently been apprehended by a brave officer of the law, but they had foully assaulted him and escaped, leaving him for dead.

Klaus read the story behind closed doors, noted the name of the inn and dispatched a servant to pay the bill. When that was done, the servant, following orders, sought out the unfortunate policeman and offered him a donation sufficient to enable him to leave the police force and return to the country, "where he might be happier." He had strict instructions not to reveal whom he served, but the landlord had seen him before, knew he came from the palace and lost no time in spreading the story of how Wolfenberg's gracious prince, acting like a true father to his people, had come to the rescue. In this way, Klaus's popularity was enhanced.

With the dawn, he'd reverted to his old self. Nonetheless, he unbent sufficiently to tell Leonie what he'd done, and even to laugh about it with her, which she felt showed a decided improvement in his character. "I have to thank you again," he said. "I learned a great deal about my people and the way they live and think. Never before have I realized the importance of money." He fell silent for a moment before saying, "I wonder what would have happened between us if we hadn't been forced to escape."

"Nothing," she told him. "Nothing would have happened."

His eyes met hers. "Don't be too sure, Leonie."

"It would be irresponsible of me to forget my job like that," she protested.

"And are you always responsible?"

"Always."

"Always an agent—never a woman?"

She gave a little sigh. "I can't afford to be a woman. When I'm working, the woman doesn't exist."

He touched her cheek lightly. "One day I'll put that to the test," he promised.

As he returned to his own apartments, he tried to put thoughts of her aside. His morning would be occupied by a discussion with his finance minister, and with the memory of last night still in his blood, he found the prospect more than usually tedious. But none of this showed in his manner as he welcomed Count Halzen to his study with his usual courtesy. The elderly count had overseen Wolfenberg's finances for twenty years and was one of the few who knew about the British loan. He was spare, efficient, rigid of mind and manner, discreet and honest. Klaus trusted him totally but had never felt entirely at ease with him.

"Even with the loan, the treasury is still depleted," Klaus observed, studying the figure again.

"That will improve soon," Count Halzen observed in his dry manner. "The tax collectors have just begun their semiannual rounds, so your royal highness should rapidly see an improvement in fiscal levels."

Klaus suppressed a sigh. Suddenly, the old man's way of talking like a textbook was irksome. He stayed silent, however. "I feel bound to say," the count continued, "that but for the system of appeals, money would reach the treasury sooner. Your people take advantage."

"Surely they're supposed to take advantage of their right to appeal?" Klaus objected. "How exactly does it work, for the landlord of an inn, for instance?"

Count Halzen sniffed. "Landlords are the worst. Taxes are levied on the amount of beer estimated to be sold. They always try to pretend it was less than it was."

"But not just on the amount, surely?" Klaus said. "The quality of beer also affects the figures."

The count looked slightly ruffled, as though this unexpected knowledge on the part of one he'd instructed since childhood was disconcerting. "Disputes about quality are also a way for these people to defraud the Revenue," he conceded.

"But if the figures are only an estimate, how do we know the landlords aren't telling the truth?" Klaus persisted.

"The estimates are compiled with great statistical precision by men who are experts in handling figures—"

"But are they expert in drinking beer?" Klaus couldn't resist asking.

Halzen stared at him in disbelief. Klaus found himself wishing Leonie were there to appreciate the sight of the old man's astounded face. No matter. He would tell her later. "They're not just figures, are they?" he persisted. "There's a reality behind them. If a man isn't familiar with the inside of an alehouse his estimate is almost certainly mistaken."

"Mistaken?" Count Halzen sounded as if he'd never heard the word before.

"I mean," Klaus amended carefully, "that in their concern for the well-being of the country, they may sometimes overestimate."

"I can assure your royal highness that these people are perfectly able to pay, despite the exaggerated protests with which they waste the appeal commission's time."

It was obviously useless to persist. Klaus tried another tack. "How often do the appeals succeed?" he asked.

"Virtually never. There was one unfortunate occasion about two years ago, but the circumstances were exceptional. I am happy to be able to assure your royal highness that your commissioners know their duty."

"Meaning that they see their duty as refusing to correct estimates that are clearly too large?" Klaus asked in a strange voice.

"But I have already assured your royal highness—"

"Yes, indeed," Klaus checked him. "Clearly, my commissioners are excellent men. I should like the opportunity to observe their diligence for myself. Please arrange for me to be present at a hearing, unobserved."

The finance minister's jaw dropped.

"It took me half an hour to persuade him that I was serious," Klaus told Leonie over supper that evening, "and a further half hour to help him recover from his shock. The poor fellow is now convinced that Wolfenberg's fall is imminent since the prince has lost his wits."

"So what are you going to do?" Leonie asked, pouring him some wine.

"There's an appeals hearing at the town hall tomorrow, and a place where I can sit in the shadows." He saw her frown, and added with a touch of mischief, "It's perfectly safe, unless you think Count Halzen is in touch with Bismarck. I promise you, a less likely traitor I never knew. He was my grandfather's minister, as well, and if he has a fault, it's that he can't forget he knew me when I was a boy."

"I'm surprised you didn't appoint your own man," Leonie observed.

"I'd have liked to, but his grasp of finance is phenomenal. Until today, I thought that was enough..." Klaus's voice trailed off uneasily.

"What is it?" she asked gently.

"We were like two men shouting to each other from across a chasm. His sole concern was to reassure me that all appeals are ignored, however just they might be. Not that he would recognize any justice in a complaint against the government."

"He's an old man," Leonie reminded him. "Some of them get hidebound."

"Yes, but I should have known. And I didn't." He sighed unhappily. "The blame is mine."

Leonie had argued to bring him to this point, but now that he was here, she wanted to shield him from pain. "Don't judge too soon," she said. "He may be right. Perhaps the people who complain are all crooks, after all."

"Perhaps. We'll find out tomorrow."

"We?"

He grinned. "You don't think I'd dare go without you to protect me, do you?"

She half expected him to forget the idea, but when Klaus set his mind to something, he carried it through. The next morning, Leonie joined him in his study where he was wait-

ing with Bernhard. He was not in uniform. Both he and
Bernhard wore sober civilian garb, such as any lawyer might
have worn. She, too, had dressed demurely, and the three of
them went through the streets in a plain carriage without
attracting attention.

On Klaus's orders, they were let into the town hall by a
side entrance, and slipped quietly into the appeals court. It
was a gloomy, oak-paneled room, with a high dais for the
commissioner, from which he could look down loftily on the
appellants. "Are all appeals held in these surroundings?"
Klaus queried the chief clerk.

"I can assure your royal highness that every care is taken
to ensure that those who come into this room are fully aware
of the dignity of your royal highness's commissioners," the
clerk asserted fussily.

Klaus looked at him with displeasure. "You mean it's
designed to intimidate them?" he asked coldly.

The clerk looked bewildered. "I can assure your royal
highness that—"

"Never mind." Klaus cut him short grimly. "I'll see for
myself."

The three of them sat well back in the shadows as the first
case started. The appellant was a butcher whose tax assess-
ment had doubled. He arrived armed with account books to
show that his sales were nowhere near what was claimed.
The commissioner glanced at them, but Leonie, watching
closely, was convinced he couldn't follow them. At any rate,
it made no difference. He dismissed the case. Bernhard was
earnestly taking notes. Klaus watched the proceedings with
a black scowl.

The scowl deepened as the morning wore on. Some of the
folk who appeared had the look of rogues trying their luck,
but most seemed to be honest people fighting oppressive
decisions. They fought valiantly but with a kind of hope-

lessness, as if they knew the battle was lost in advance. And if this was their thinking, they were right. The commissioner seemed to be a well-meaning man who tried to be kind. He had endless patience for explaining gently to appellants why they were wrong, and seemed convinced that such explanations made their burdens easier.

"Is there anyone else?" he asked at last in a weary voice.

"Hal Kenzl, innkeeper," intoned a voice from outside in the corridor.

The next moment, a large man had appeared in the doorway. Leonie's touched Klaus's arm urgently. "Do you see who that is?"

He nodded. "We'd better move back a little."

They slid their chairs back as the landlord of The Golden Bear strode into the room. He carried piles of account books, which he set down with a thump, and looked up belligerently.

The commissioner beamed. "An old friend, I perceive," he said genially. "Good morning Herr Kenzl. I hope your arguments are better than they were last time."

"My arguments are the same as always," Hal growled. "Your assessors know nothing about beer or innkeeping. They pick figures out of the air. My accounts show conclusively that second-grade beer has been estimated as first-grade."

"My dear Herr Kenzl, I'm very sure your accounts show whatever suits you..."

They settled in for a long dispute. Hal thrust his books under the commissioner's nose and the official waved them away. It was plain his mind was closed and his decision made. Klaus turned his head and spoke softly to Leonie. "It pains me to admit it, but you were right. It's worse than I could have imagined. This is nothing but tyranny exercised in my name. I should have known. I blame myself that I didn't."

"Don't feel badly about it," she urged. "At least you know now, and can do something about it."

She'd meant that he could change the law, but to her surprise, Klaus said grimly, "You're right. And I'm going to."

Before she realized what he meant to do, he was on his feet, striding forward. "If I may take up the commission's time," he said politely, "I should like to speak a word on behalf of Herr Kenzl."

The innkeeper glanced up to see who'd spoken. Then he blanched with shock, dropped a heavy account book on his foot, and exclaimed, *"You!"* His voice rose excitedly. "Arrest this man! He's a thief!"

"Be silent or I'll have you removed," the commissioner ordered.

"I tell you this is the man who ran off without paying. Arrest him. I demand that you arrest him."

The commissioner raised his voice. "This is His Royal Highness, Prince Klaus Friederich. For the last time, be silent, or *you* will be arrested for treason."

"Treat Herr Kenzl gently," Klaus said. "He's been most shamefully treated, isn't that so, friend?"

He moved closer, giving Hal a good look at his face. The inn keeper paled again. "But—but you—"

"Sometimes like to enjoy a glass of ale with my people," Klaus finished for him.

Hal thrust a hand into his pocket, brought out a coin, examined the head on it and gulped. "Your—your royal highness," he stammered. "I could have sworn—"

"I know Herr Kenzl," Klaus informed the commissioner. "His beer is excellent—" a faint smile touched his mouth "—even the second-grade. I believe that very excellence has caused the assessors to mistake second-grade for first. In these circumstances, it will be right to grant the appeal."

"But, your highness," the commissioner wailed.

"That is my wish," Klaus declared quietly.

A muscle twitching in his cheek, the commissioner wrote out a certificate, declaring the appeal granted. Hal was still staring at the coin. Klaus moved closer and spoke to him quietly. "Even if I were the man you thought, I understand that you've since been well recompensed."

"Yes, yes indeed...." Some hint of the truth dawned over Hal's broad face, and with it came total speechlessness. Klaus permitted himself a grin, and prudently retired before the innkeeper recovered his voice.

In the carriage, Bernhard flicked through his notes, frowning. "I could hardly believe such injustice," he murmured.

"Nor I," Klaus told him. "I want every one of those cases investigated by people who understand what they're doing...if you can find any," he added grimly. "Then make me a full report. But that's not enough. The whole system must be overhauled. These officials bully my people in my name and they expect me to be pleased. I want a commission of state set up to look into everything to do with taxes. Anyone with a grievance will be heard."

Bernhard grinned. "That'll set the cat among the pigeons."

"Good. It's about time some of the plumper pigeons had a scare."

Bernhard looked puzzled. "How did Hal Kenzl get you confused with a thief? I couldn't understand a word he was saying."

Klaus's eyes met Leonie's and his lips twitched slightly. "It's a long story, Bernhard," he said. "I only hope he doesn't go blabbing all over town, although I don't count on it."

He was right. Hal told the story—with embellishments—to his family and his customers, who spread it in their turn. Soon everyone knew that Klaus had personally intervened to make the taxes more fair. This increased their goodwill toward him. But the story that really delighted them was of how their prince had mingled with his people for the beer festival, and had had to flee the law. That tale spread far and wide until it had covered the whole country. Songs were sung about it. A theatrical troop turned it into a drama which played to packed houses until the scandalized magistrates closed it down. But the good was done. Klaus's popularity was established in his people's hearts as never before.

Only one person refused to believe a word of it. In a village on the extreme edge of Wolfenberg's most distant province, a man who'd exchanged a policeman's uniform for the coat of a Town Cryer enthralled them in the ale houses, telling tales of his past glory, and in particular, of the great night when he'd almost apprehended the Treuheim chicken thief.

As Reinald had predicted, the court had begun to revolve around Leonie. High-ranking ladies deferred to her for fear of the royal displeasure. Ministers sought her attention because they assumed she had the prince's ear. One notable exception was Baron Gruber, the foreign minister. He'd been spending a couple of weeks at his country house and didn't return to Treuheim until several days after Leonie's arrival. He visited her apartments, ostensibly to pay his respects, but actually to declare war.

Like Count Halzen, the baron was an old man, and had held his position under the last prince, Klaus's grandfather. In appearance, he resembled Santa Claus, with fluffy white hair and twinkling blue eyes. But Leonie soon realized that behind the worldly charm, he was implacable. "The court of Wolfenberg is graced by your presence, Duchess," he declared. "A beautiful woman is always an adornment."

Leonie's eyes gleamed. As a duelist, she appreciated this subtle method of putting her in her place. "You're too kind," she murmured. "I was in dread of not earning your approval."

"Come, Duchess, let us be plain. Since you've won the prince's confidence, I imagine you know already that I have tried to have you ejected from these rooms."

Leonie nodded, watching him with a little smile just touching her beautiful lips. That smile had been known to make strong men tremble. On Baron Gruber it was wasted. "I believe it was news of my presence here that brought you back to Treuheim yesterday, and you lost no time approaching the prince to demand my immediate dismissal," she said.

"Not dismissal, Duchess," the baron corrected her with a twinkle that was at odds with his words. "As befits the sovereign of Wolfenberg, his royal highness is a man of lusty appetites. He needs a woman to satisfy them, and were you accommodated elsewhere, I should have no objection. But to be installed in these apartments—*no*. That is unsuitable, and I said so to the prince."

"I understand the last occupant was a disastrous choice," Leonie observed, refusing to be provoked.

"She tried to meddle in politics," Gruber declared. "Something no woman should do."

"And you attribute that to these apartments?"

"They are the apartments of the *official* favorite. That's a title that encourages meddling. It gives the illusion of grandeur." He gave her a conspiratorial smile. "It gives the illusion of *intelligence*."

"And in your opinion, no woman can be intelligent?" Leonie asked sweetly.

Baron Gruber gave her a beaming smile that ill concealed the steel glint in his eyes. "Let us say that I believe in a kind of womanly cleverness that works splendidly when it's limited to a female's natural sphere." He patted Leonie's hand in a fatherly way. "What would we men do without women to oil the wheels of society and provide us with the background against which great matters are decided, eh? Oh, yes, you have your place. But you ladies, you want more. Isn't that so? You want to be involved in the great matters, assisting with the decisions, or even making decisions yourself. And it leads you to do things that are quite unsuitable for the delicate female constitution." He beamed at her triumphantly. "In short, Duchess, I have guessed your real reason for being here."

Leonie managed to keep all trace of reaction out of her face. "Indeed? May I offer you some more tea?"

"Thank you, yes. I maintain there is no drink in the world more delicious than English tea. If only the English would confine themselves to tea, and not meddle in the affairs of other countries."

A flicker of serious alarm flared up in Leonie's breast, but she merely contrived to look a little stupid as she poured the tea. "I fear you have quite confused me. I assure you, I'm not here to meddle."

He chuckled and patted her hand again. "But of course, you're only the instrument. Palmerston's the real meddler, trying to interfere with Wolfenberg's historic destiny as part of a greater Germany. Naturally, Britain doesn't want to see Germany strong and united. It threatens British power. So Palmerston interferes. He sends you to come between the prince and his proper wife, the Princess Sylvana."

"Sylvana?" Leonie echoed, astonished. "He's never intended to marry her."

"They were destined from the cradle," Gruber asserted loftily. "His grandfather and I made the match then, and he's honor bound to it. Unfortunately, the late prince died before the wedding could take place. Now comes Palmerston, with the offer of Princess Louise to cement an English alliance and wrench Wolfenberg away from the glory that awaits her."

"In a united Germany?"

"Precisely. You've stumbled into matters too deep for your comprehension, madam, and I advise you in future to confine yourself to the proper concerns of ladies. I thank you for the delicious tea. I've so enjoyed our little talk."

When he'd gone, Leonie sat considering. Her alarm had been needless. Gruber suspected she was sent by Palmerston, but he had guessed incorrectly as to her mission. Unless...

Unless he was behind the assassination attempts. She'd discerned the fanaticism that underpinned his avuncular charm. She told Klaus about the conversation that evening as they had supper together, but he dismissed her fears. "Gruber comes from the old school, which saw a nation solely in terms of its glory," he said. "He's got a fixation about the German union but he's in a minority. I suppose I ought to replace him as foreign minister, but to be honest, I lack the heart. His wife and children are dead, and his belief that he's serving Wolfenberg is all he has left in the world." He looked closely at her face. "You really took against him, didn't you?"

"Well, I don't like men who pat my hand and talk to me as if I were mentally deficient," she said crossly.

"But surely you're used to that? I mean," he amended hastily, "in your job. Isn't that how you make men talk—by appearing stupid?"

"It's a valuable technique," she agreed.

"Among others," he reminded her with a faint ironic edge to his voice.

"I was certainly never silly enough to try stupidity on you."

"No, with me there was another technique, even more certain to succeed, hmm?" His eyes glinted. Although Leonie and he were on good terms these days, the true facts behind their relationship were always there, never quite forgotten, and sometimes they pricked him into a flash of resentment.

"We're losing sight of the point," Leonie said. "It's true I dislike Gruber, but that's not why I think he's dangerous."

"How wise of you to change the subject, Leonie," Klaus told her affably. He'd taken her hand and now turned it palm upward and began to brush his lips against the silky skin. Tremors went along her arm. The touch of his lips was so light, yet it had the power to send violent sensations rippling through her body.

"I'm not changing the subject," she said. Her voice shook, despite all her efforts to keep it steady. "I'm keeping to it. The subject is Gruber."

"Is that the subject?" He let his tongue flick against her palm.

"Yes."

He glanced up, his eyes alight with a hint of amusement, and something else that wasn't funny at all. "I have to admire you, my dear," he murmured. "You're so involved in your mission that you let nothing get in its way. Here you sit, letting me do this—" he trailed his tongue over her palm again and she took a shuddering breath "—pretending that you don't mind, even pretending that you like it. And all the time you're merely a good agent who feels absolutely nothing. Isn't that correct?"

"Correct," she agreed raggedly.

"Nothing at all?"

"Nothing at all." It was hard to get the words out.

"Such dedication earns my respect." He was playing with her fingers. "Perhaps I should give you a decoration.... How about the Grand Order of Wolfenberg? Second-class, of course."

"Don't I merit first-class?" she asked, trying to talk lightly.

"You haven't yet proved your dedication quite enough for first-class."

"Then I think I'll manage without, thank you."

"I wonder," he mused out loud, "just how useful a weapon is that maddeningly desirable body? How far have you gone in the past to get a man to talk?"

She immediately picked up the faint change in tone. This wasn't just a prince struggling against the bonds that constrained him. This was a man in the grip of jealousy. "How far, Leonie?" he asked again. His hold on her hand was no longer soft and teasing. It was hard and tense.

"As you said, I'm a good agent," she reminded him, pulling her hand free. "I go as far as is necessary for the performance of my duty, and not an inch farther."

"And how do you decide how far that is?"

"Well, I have to weigh up the man." She spoke teasingly. "To be honest, most men are such dunderheads that a very little is enough."

"And me?"

She gave him a seductive smile. "No one could mistake you for a dunderhead."

"And a very little will not be enough," he said huskily.

"I knew that from the first."

"In that case . . ." He reached for her but she rose swiftly from her chair and went to stand by the window. He followed her. "Don't play with me, Leonie," he ordered. "You've as good as told me that one day—"

"One day," she interrupted him softly. "One day I shall go away from Wolfenberg and never see you again. One day we shall all be dead."

"But we're not dead now," he said, taking hold of her. "We're both very much alive, flesh and blood, and we want each other." He pulled her close. "You do want me," he said against her lips. "Why try to pretend that you don't?"

It would have been easy to melt in his arms, but some corner of her mind was irked by his arrogant certainty. "But how do you know when I'm pretending? Am I pretending when I kiss you, or when I refuse to kiss you . . . as now?" She freed herself.

"Don't play with me, Leonie," he repeated harshly.

"Why shouldn't I? For fear of finding myself in your deepest dungeon?" She gave a theatrical little shudder. "I swear I'm quite overcome with terror."

He seized her. "Stop that!" he barked. "I'm no boy to be trifled with. I'm a man who's used to having what he wants. Right now, I want you. Don't act surprised. You've done your damnedest to make me want you, for your own ends. Well, madam, you're going to discover that you've unleashed more than you expected. You're my official favorite. I've installed you in sumptuous apartments, showered you with jewels and made my court bow before you. And what do you give me in return?"

Her pulse was racing. "I protect your life," she managed to say.

Before the words were out, he'd covered her mouth with his own. "Be damned to that," he said against her lips. "The life you protect is hollow and bleak if I don't have you in my bed. And by God, I'm going to have you there tonight!"

He kissed her ruthlessly, a suffocating kiss that swamped her senses and made her head spin. Now his passion was hard and driving, refusing to accept rejection. "For too long you've been free to tease and torment me," he growled, "to dangle what I want before me, then snatch it away. Not this time."

His lips crushed hers again. Pleasure and excitement surged through her. The Gypsy in her loved a battle and this was the most thrilling battle of all, between man and woman, each one in the grip of desire, moving toward the moment when all barriers were down, yet still testing each other for supremacy. She wanted him, but she wouldn't submit to him as other women had done. He must be made aware that she wasn't his subject, and then, if he was very lucky, she would take him on her own terms.

His tongue was exploring her mouth with wicked seductiveness, inciting tremors of delight inside her. For all her resolve to stay in control, she couldn't help giving a little gasp of pleasure, and starting a return invasion. She could feel his hand on her neck, sliding down to caress her shoulder, then tugging at the dress, pulling it lower. Her breath began to come deeply as her passion rose. She was taking risks. The proximity of the bedroom shattered her resolution, making her want only to melt to him. The thought of what could happen at any moment fired her unbearably. Her body had been made for physical love, but until she met this man, she'd never known what it was to be swept away by desire. Now her adventurous spirit was driving her on to new discoveries. And if they were dangerous, so much the better.

She murmured his name, and at once he was looking deep into her eyes. "Yes," he said huskily. "You want me, don't you? Let me hear you say it."

"I—"

"Say it. I command you to say it."

She lay in his arms and smiled up at him provocatively. "I take no man's commands."

"You'll take mine. This has lasted long enough. Say the words, damn you. You know they're true." When she still hesitated, he laid his lips on hers, caressing her slowly, seductively, driving her to the edge of insanity. "Say the words," he murmured.

She could feel herself yielding, giving him the victory she wasn't yet ready to give. Her proud spirit rebelled, but the craving of her flesh was louder, more demanding.

"I—"

"Yes? Yes, Leonie—yes . . . ?"

Into the silence there dropped a small, terrible sound, the click of a door. It froze Klaus. When he could make himself move, he raised his head, aghast. "What the devil was that?" he snapped.

Reluctantly, Leonie rejoined time and looked around the room. "The door's closed," she said raggedly.

"I can see that."

"But it wasn't closed before. I think—I think a footman must have looked in and, seeing us occupied, retreated."

The thought of being observed by an outsider turned Klaus's body to ice, while having the opposite effect on his temper. "You should train your servants better, madam." He released her abruptly.

"Yes, I'm sorry." Her head was still spinning and she swayed slightly, clutching the mantelpiece. Courtesy obliged him to offer her his arm and lead her back to her chair at the table, but after doing so, he moved away from her at once. "Thank you," she said meekly. "Let me pour you some more wine."

"I want only to leave you immediately."

"Don't do that," she begged. "Think of the damage to my reputation." Her lips twitched. "Think of the damage to yours."

He stared at her through narrowed eyes. "Are you daring to find this amusing?"

"Well, you must admit it has its funny side," she said unsteadily. She was recovering her composure faster than he. She glanced at his unyielding face. "What a pity you don't have a sense of humor," she said on a sigh.

"There is nothing wrong with my sense of humor," he countered through gritted teeth.

"Yes, there is. It doesn't exist."

"I forbid you to say so. *I have a perfectly good sense of humor.*"

There was a thunderous silence during which their eyes met, his full of rage, hers full of merriment. Then, incredibly, his face lightened and the tension seemed to drain out of him. "You witch," he murmured. "You disgraceful, enchanting witch. What have you done to me?" Her chuckle told him the answer and he sat down, burying his head in his hands. "I ought to send you away and damn the consequences," he groaned. "But what would I do without you?"

"Who would make you laugh?" she teased.

"Yes, who would make me laugh?" He accepted the wine she poured but removed himself to safety a few feet away. "Let's talk about something else," he said. "Something that isn't . . . provocative. What were we discussing before—before we—"

"We were talking about Gruber."

"Then continue talking about Gruber," Klaus said a little desperately. "He's a nice safe subject. You were saying that he's dangerous, and I was disagreeing."

"I think his *ideas* are dangerous. He believes in Bismarck, and he wants to see this country part of the German union. Isn't it possible that he's behind the attempts to kill you?"

Klaus frowned. "I won't believe that of a man I've known all my life, a man I know to be rigidly honorable."

"But he defines honor as the honor of Wolfenberg," Leonie reminded him. "And he thinks the honor of Wolfenberg depends on union with Bismarck. He also says you're 'honor bound' to marry Sylvana. You were, apparently, promised in your cradle."

"That's impossible. Sylvana wasn't born until I was eight," Klaus said, exasperated.

"*Her* cradle then."

"I never had any intention of marrying her, whatever they may have hoped when we were children. She was thirteen when I came to the throne, far too young to be regarded as a jilted bride, and I've introduced her to a hundred suitable matches since."

"Ah, but did they have thrones to offer?"

"Unfortunately, thrones are in short supply," Klaus said dryly. "They all had royal titles and dignity, and there were a couple I hoped might attach her heart. But nothing came of it."

Leonie wasn't surprised. She seriously doubted that Sylvana had a heart capable of an honest, unselfish love. Raised in the expectation of a throne, she would settle for nothing less. And some of the blame for that lay at the door of Baron Gruber, who'd encouraged her to go on hoping beyond reason.

For the rest of the evening, they discussed neutral matters, careful not to get too close to each other. When the time came for Klaus to leave, he murmured, "I think you've developed a headache."

"Have I?"

"A very bad one. It will prevent me from visiting your room tonight."

"Yes, I'll feel safer that way too," she said in an amused tone.

"Witch," he said again. "Do you know the risks you take?"

"Perhaps not. But I have a delightful time discovering them."

"Good night," he said unsteadily, and departed.

When she was alone, Leonie summoned Masham. "Get a message to Jack Blair tonight," she told him. "I want him to find out all he can about Baron Gruber. Perhaps you should also become friendly with Gruber's servants, but be very discreet. He's already suspicious of me."

Masham bowed. Before leaving, he asked, "Will your grace require the carriage tomorrow morning?"

"Naturally." Her eyes twinkled. "We mustn't deprive the gossips of Treuheim of their chance to goggle at me."

Like every great lady of Wolfenberg, Leonie was frequently driven through Treuheim Park at the fashionable hour of eleven. Knowing what was expected of her, she made these trips in Klaus's most regal carriage, drawn by two perfectly matched blacks, with Masham on the box. Fascinated crowds lined the broad alley that cut through the park to see the beauty who'd captured the prince's heart. The women sighed enviously over her clothing, and several new fashions were started by her whims. The men nudged one another and growled that the prince was a lucky fellow to be able to buy a woman like that. Doubtless he was spending a fortune on her, and equally doubtless she was repaying him with a sizzling performance when required.

Because the park was open to everyone, she was watched by rich and poor alike, and no one thought it strange when she ordered the carriage to stop in order to bestow a coin on a shabby-looking man. "Bless you, ma'am," he muttered sarcastically.

"What are you doing here, Jack?" she asked. "Why aren't you investigating Gruber?"

"I *am* investigating him. I've already been watching him for weeks. I didn't need you to tell me that. By the way, I need money."

"Masham took you some last night."

"I need more. I've had . . . expenses."

"You mean, you've been gaming," she said furiously.

"A man has to get around if he's to learn things. I can't spend all my life in The Black Dog. It's a stinking hole."

"It's not the only thing," Leonie said, recoiling from the beer on his breath. "Stand back."

Blair laughed nastily. "You only like to play the game your way, don't you, my fine lady?" he sneered. "Everything laid on." He reached out a hand to touch her. Leonie instinctively drew back, but the next moment, a whip cracked. Blair let out a yelp of pain and grasped his wrist where Reinald's whip had circled it. In an instant, the archduke dismounted, freed his whip and lashed Blair repeatedly. Blair gave a howl of agony as the whip caught him full across the face.

"My lord," Leonie said urgently. She managed to seize Reinald's arm and he turned his eyes on her. They were cold and brilliant and he seemed in the grip of some powerful emotion. She tightened her grip on him. "Enough, I beg you," she said in a low urgent voice. "People are staring."

He was breathing fast. "He dared lay his filthy hands on you...."

"But I'm unharmed. See, he's running away now. Let him go."

Reinald's chest still rose and fell violently, but he obeyed her. Leonie saw Blair turn once more to gaze on her with a face full of hatred, before he vanished between the trees. Gradually, the color faded from Reinald's face, leaving it lividly pale, the scar standing out. "I shall do whatever pleases you," he said stiffly.

"Then it pleases me for you to ride beside my carriage for a while."

"Would that really please you?" he asked in a low voice, the intensity of which startled her.

"Of course," she declared lightly, offering him her most mischievous smile. "There are so many people who still think I'm slightly scandalous. Your company is bound to raise my standing."

He gave her no answering smile. Humor appeared to have no part in his nature. But he bowed to her, bending his head a little more than strictly necessary, and rode beside her all the way back to the palace. Once there, he helped her alight, declared himself forever her servant and hurried away, leaving her looking after him. Inwardly she was furious with Blair, whose behavior had been unprofessional and could have exposed her identity.

Leonie had spoken no more than the truth when she said Reinald's approbation was as valuable as Klaus's. He was known for his rigid virtue and the puritanism of his views, and his friendship was the seal on her acceptance.

He intrigued her. Although his manner was punctilious, he went out of his way to be pleasant, even taking time from his work to visit her. He called on her the next day to ask solicitously after her welfare. On being assured that her nerves were unaffected by her ordeal, he begged her to walk with him a while in the palace grounds. They were magnificent, a collection of gardens, each with its own theme and predominant color, and everywhere peacocks wandered, trailing glorious trains of feathers and uttering their melancholy screams.

"I brought you here because this place is private," he said to her when they reached the rose garden. "And there are things I must say to you."

Leonie braced herself for difficulties. She was too worldly-wise not to understand the light in Reinald's eyes, and a scene would be a complication she would rather avoid. But he went on, "You have Klaus's ear. I beg you to make him take better care of himself. I don't want to alarm you, but his life is under threat."

Leonie stared at him with wide eyes. "But who could possibly want to kill him?" she asked innocently.

"The life of a sovereign is never entirely safe," Reinald said. "Bismarck would like to see him dead because Klaus is holding out against Prussian domination. In England, one of Bismarck's agents lured Klaus into a duel."

She clasped her hands to her breast. "A duel! How terrible."

"Don't distress yourself. It didn't succeed."

"But to think of him risking his life..."

"Klaus has the reckless temper of our forebears," Reinald admitted. "Luckily it seems to have passed me by. I do nothing without calculating the consequences. It's why I'm valuable to him."

She nodded. "I can believe it."

"Has Klaus never told you about this?"

Leonie made a pretty assumption of bashfulness. "He doesn't believe in discussing affairs of state with women," she said with perfect honesty.

"But his life is at stake, and that's more than a state matter for those who care for him. For me...and for you. He's too proud to take precautions for his own safety. But you could protect him."

"I?" Leonie echoed breathlessly. "A mere woman?"

He smiled. "You are no mere woman, Leonie. You're a supreme woman, a woman who could so obsess a man that he would—" Reinald drew a shaky breath "—that he would do anything you asked."

"Not quite anything," she said. "Klaus is a very stubborn man."

"Anything. If a man loved you, you could make him please you. You could make Klaus promise to be more careful. Won't you do that, for all our sakes? Please, Leonie, say you will care for his safety, and ease my mind."

"His safety will be my first concern," Leonie promised.

"God bless you," he said fervently. "Now, if you'll take my arm, I'll escort you back to the palace before I leave." As they walked, Reinald said, "I've been meaning to speak of the ball tomorrow night. Whatever his feelings for you, protocol obliges Klaus to dance first with Sylvana. May I hope that you will honor me with the first dance?"

"I shall be delighted. How my enemies would have laughed to see me a wallflower."

"No one will dare laugh at you while I'm there," he declared firmly.

They'd reached the stables where Luther was waiting for his master. The ugly little man watched impassively as they came into view, arm in arm. Reinald disengaged himself and bowed low over her hand before mounting and riding away without so much as a glance at Luther. Only then did the dwarf's mask slip, and for a moment she saw the malevolence flash from his hard little eyes. Then he was galloping away in pursuit of Reinald.

* * *

They reached Herrenhaltz at the same time as a carriage bearing Eugenia and Sylvana drew up at the door. Reinald dismounted and gallantly gave them his hand to alight. "I'm exhausted," Eugenia declared. "I shall go straight to my bed and stay there until tomorrow afternoon. But I'm sure I shan't sleep a wink tonight for thinking of the ordeal we must undergo. The very thought of that woman lording it over her betters is enough to make me ill."

"I assure you, the Dowager Duchess of Coniston has no such intention," Reinald replied. "She's a woman of elegance and refinement."

"She's a vulgar adventuress," Sylvana snapped. "If I had my way, she would be horsewhipped. How can Klaus so lower himself as to favor her?"

"Klaus doesn't lower himself," Reinald said in a freezing voice. "He's chosen a woman who surpasses all others, and who would grace any position to which she was elevated. Let it be clearly understood that I forbid you to insult her."

The women stared. A fierce and terrible light burned in Reinald's eyes and his face was deadly pale. But he recovered himself quickly and said in a more normal tone, "Try to understand that I only wish to protect you from Klaus's displeasure. If you offend her, you will alienate him. Now, for pity's sake, let's have no more of this subject."

Without waiting for an answer, he strode off to the stable. It didn't surprise him to discover Luther hidden just within earshot. He knew Luther overheard most of his conversations, and it didn't trouble him. Or rather, he considered the little man so negligible that it was as though a dog had eavesdropped.

Luther fell into step beside his master. "Their highnesses are right," he said. "She's a witch, that one."

The next moment he was sent spinning by a blow from the back of Reinald's hand. His master followed him in two strides, seized him by his collar and struck him back and forth, finally letting him fall to the ground.

"Master—master," Luther sobbed, though he seemed hurt more by Reinald's displeasure than by the blows.

"Take yourself out of my sight," Reinald said in a low voice. "And don't dare approach me until I give you leave."

Luther set up a wail that drew laughter from the stable boys. They hated him because of his arrogance, and not one was sorry for him. "Be silent, all of you," Reinald snapped. "Get to your work."

He strode away. Luther immediately began to lope after him, careful to stay at a safe distance. He followed Reinald as far as his study, but when the door was shut in his face, for the first time ever, he dared not go farther but stayed outside, a wretched, shivering mass of misery.

The evening passed with no word for him. Darkness fell. Still, Luther didn't move. At last, Reinald emerged and made his way to his bedroom without a glance at his servant. Luther crept as far as the closed bedroom door, where he stretched out on the cold floor, and lay motionless until morning.

Chapter Seven

The summer ball at court was one of the social highlights of the year. For weeks beforehand, unattached young ladies pored over their attire in collaboration with their mothers.

But this year, there was an additional excitement. Everyone knew of the favorite, and of the fabulous jewels that had been showered upon her, and no great lady wanted to be outdone. The family vaults were plundered for the finest gems. A profusion of diamonds, rubies, sapphires and emeralds adorned necks, bosoms, ears, wrists and fingers until the effect was blinding.

Archduke Reinald had ventured to protest at the sheer number of costly baubles that smothered his sister, but to no avail. "For your sake, I'll be polite to her," Sylvana had said. "But I shan't yield to her in anything."

The ball was held in the Glass Room, so called because the walls were lined with mirrors. Even the huge double doors had mirror panels. Everywhere there was gilt and glass. The million crystal facets on the chandeliers had been polished until they reflected a blinding light back and forth from mirror to mirror. Halfway along one of the two-hundred-foot walls was a raised stand for the orchestra, dressed in the blue-and-silver uniforms of the royal house.

When the evening came, there were some who'd never seen the favorite and couldn't identify her in the crowd. While they were searching, the master of ceremonies rapped his staff on the floor and footmen pulled open two huge doors at one end of the room. To the accompaniment of a fanfare, the prince entered the room, his cousin Sylvana on his arm, followed by Archduke Reinald, escorting his mother. As they made their way down the room, women curtsied and men bowed, until they reached the dais at the other end on which stood a throne.

Klaus stood for a moment, to be seen. Leonie, curtsying with the others and watching him from beneath her lashes, thought how handsome he looked in the dress uniform of the Wolfenberg army. The white jacket with silver epaulets, and dark blue trousers with the silver stripe down the outside, might have been designed to set off his tall, athletic figure with its broad shoulders and hard muscles. His face was set in its usual lines of aloofness.

At last he nodded to the master of ceremonies, who conveyed a signal to the orchestra. The strains of a waltz filled the ballroom. Klaus turned to Sylvana, bowed and opened his arms. Then Reinald, whose eyes had been swiftly covering the assembled ranks, stepped forward and bowed low to a lady, who curtsied to him. And a buzz of astonishment went up.

"Can that be her?—Surely not?—Yes, I know her by sight—But she's wearing *no jewelry.*"

It was true. But for her wedding ring, wildflowers provided the favorite's only adornment. Small white flowers were wreathed into the heavy mass of her fair hair, and more flowers formed a corsage at her waist, trailing down the skirt of her gleaming white satin gown. And suddenly every woman there knew that her carefully chosen jewels were a vulgar excess.

Reinald's gaze was full of admiration. "Only you would have dared," he breathed. "Only you have the beauty to carry it off. You are beyond all women."

Leonie laughed. "I wonder how many enemies I've made tonight."

"You don't care for enemies," he said. "Why should you?"

Again Leonie felt the trembling in his arms and saw the burning light in his eyes. Reinald might be the most puritanical man at court, but she had shaken him to the soul, and he couldn't hide it from her. As the music came to an end, he said, "May I take you to my sister?"

"Will she like that? The Princess Sylvana hardly regards me in a kindly light."

"But that was a misunderstanding that I'm sure you're both eager to put right. More than anything, I should like the two of you to be friends."

Leonie gave an inward sigh, half amused, half exasperated. Only a man could have so blinded himself as to imagine friendship between herself and Sylvana. But she accompanied him to where Sylvana stood chatting with Klaus, detaining him with a hand on his arm, now that their dance was over. Sylvana was dressed lavishly in a low-cut gown of crimson velvet. Rubies set in gold adorned her hair, her neck, her wrists, her fingers.

"A delightful ball," Reinald announced pleasantly as they approached.

"Delightful," Sylvana echoed, addressing only her brother as though Leonie weren't there. "We were just saying—" she smiled archly at Klaus "—what a splendid evening it is. My cousin was kind enough to inquire after the slight chill I suffered recently. I was happy to be able to tell him that I'm completely recovered."

"We must all be glad to hear that," Leonie said, though try as she might, she couldn't keep the irony from her voice.

Sylvana turned glacial eyes on her. It was clear that she'd heard the irony, but was too shrewd to retaliate before Klaus. "How lovely to see you here, Duchess," she intoned.

Leonie murmured something proper. Sylvana continued to chatter, her hand possessively on Klaus's arm, her conversation strewn with references to shared experiences and acquaintances. Then something unfortunate happened. The crowd parted and gave the two women a clear view of their reflection in the nearest mirror. The contrast between Sylvana's gaudy excess and Leonie's elegant simplicity was startling. If Sylvana hadn't known before that she looked like a tinsel chandelier, she knew it now. Her bosom swelled with fury, and her skin turned an ugly mottled red that was exactly the wrong shade to go with rubies.

By now, even Reinald had realized that the encounter was a disaster. "The musicians are ready to start the next dance," he announced smoothly.

"Yes, indeed." Klaus held out his hand to Leonie.

"May I hope for another waltz later?" Reinald inquired.

"You know you may," she told him, smiling, but her attention was already on Klaus. His face was expressionless, the mask of a man trained from childhood to conceal his feelings in public, but Leonie knew better. In his eyes burned the same ardent light she'd just seen in Reinald's. Nothing could hide that.

"Your social success is now assured," he informed her as they whirled about the floor. "Reinald is such a stickler that his approbation gives you far more cachet than mine ever could."

"Is that a royal joke?" she teased.

Klaus looked startled. "I believe it is."

She laughed, and after a moment he laughed with her. "What have you done to me?" he asked, as he'd asked the other night.

"Improved you, I'm beginning to think," she dared to say.

For a moment, his frown made her wonder if she'd gone too far, but his features lightened. "Perhaps you have," he murmured.

The room seemed to be spinning around her as she danced in his arms to the strains of the latest Strauss waltz. Every eye was upon them but she found that the huge crowd seemed to have faded. There was only Klaus and the feel of his arms about her, his gaze burning through the white satin of her dress to the skin beneath. She knew he was mentally undressing her, and the knowledge made every inch of her body come alive. Unconsciously she allowed her hips to move with a new provocation, making the gorgeous crinoline swirl against his legs as they danced. She was teasing him, reminding him how much he desired her, how impossible it was for him to have her. To what end she did this, she didn't know. Or so she told herself. She only knew that some devil impelled her to heighten his desire, especially when circumstances made it impossible for him to call her bluff.

"You should smile at me adoringly," she whispered. "People are watching us."

His lips moved, saying soundlessly, "Don't push me too far."

But she wanted to push him too far, and then push him further beyond that, and wait for the explosion to engulf her. She'd always enjoyed playing with fire, and this particular fire was especially inviting. Her eyes met his and the world seemed to turn into a furnace about her.

"A delightful dance," Klaus said formally. "Perhaps you'll be so good as to honor me with another, later."

She hadn't even realized the music was slowing. What was happening to her wits? "Yes," she said distractedly. "Later."

She barely knew whom she danced with after that. Ministers competed for the honor of taking her around the floor. She waltzed and flirted with Gruber, exchanging compliments, the extravagance of which couldn't hide the keen edge of mutual suspicion beneath. It was the kind of conversation that normally found her in her element, but tonight it was hard to be alert. Every nerve, every sense, was sharpened, aware only of Klaus.

Halfway through the evening, the master of ceremonies banged on the floor with his staff. "Your royal highnesses, lords and ladies, I beg your attention for the dancers who are here to entertain you."

The glass doors were flung open again and a stream of colorful figures poured through, flying and whirling, spinning and leaping to the beat of a tambourine. They were dressed in vivid costumes with streaming ribbons and multicolored stockings. Fiddlers danced as they played, their fingers never missing a note as they flew over the strings. An accordionist brought up the rear, and beside him, a man with a long drum that he held under one arm while the fingers of his other hand beat out a complicated rhythm. And suddenly something stirred in Leonie's heart. She knew those wild rhythms. She'd danced to them often enough as a child. These were Gypsies.

She sat entranced as they filled the hall with zest and light. They were all young and their movements were full of the joy of life, youth and freedom. Leonie was swept by a bittersweet wave of conflicting emotions, aching happiness and blissful yearning, a delight in sweet memories and a longing for what could never be recaptured. Those days had been so free, so lighthearted and full of camaraderie, and it was all lost to her now. She'd exchanged her rags for satin, a caravan for a gilded apartment. On the surface, there was nothing to connect this brilliant woman with a court at her feet with the ragamuffin who'd raided orchards and scuffled with the boys. But for an anguished moment, she would have given it all in exchange for the freedom she'd lost. She put up a hand to her eyes, which had suddenly blurred with tears.

Recovering herself, she saw that Klaus was regarding her with a puzzled expression. She smiled hastily and returned her attention to the Gypsies, but she could sense that Klaus's gaze was still on her.

A boy and girl had separated themselves from the others and were dancing together, their bodies entwined in a theatrical simulation of passion. The young man was extravagantly handsome, with black hair and a wild face. Something about that face caught Leonie's attention. Something familiar...

With a surge of delight she recognized Toni, dear friend of her childhood. They'd been born only a week apart, and they'd grown up doing everything together, playing, fighting, raiding orchards. Both hot-tempered, they'd had frequent fights in the dust with no quarter given on either side. But a hint of censure from outside could unite them against the world. She'd last seen him when they were both ten, but though the years had changed him, she still knew his face.

She remembered Paquita too, four years younger, but desperate to be admitted to their friendship, crying when Toni scolded her away. And now, surely, that was Paquita dipping and swaying in his arms. The discovery sent her searching through the rest of the Gypsies, and her excitement grew as she picked out other familiar faces.

To a crash of tambourines, the young couple threw themselves into an abandoned pose in each other's arms.

The applause was loud and enthusiastic, and the whole troop of Gypsies bowed and smiled. Leonie beckoned a footman, and spoke a quiet word that sent him over to where Toni and Paquita were just leaving the floor. They looked up to see her disappearing through the French doors onto the long terrace. A moment later, they were with her, bowing low.

"Lady, you honor us," Toni said respectfully.

"Oh, Toni, don't talk to me like a stranger," Leonie begged. "I remember when you called me a thief and a witch because I ate all your blackberries." Startled, he looked at her with doubt in his eyes, but still he couldn't believe the truth. "Paquita knows me," Leonie added mischievously.

Paquita took a step forward. "He's mine now," she said firmly.

And suddenly the years were swept away, and they were three carefree urchins again. Leonie laughed with delight and kissed Paquita on both cheeks. "He was always yours," she said.

"Mother of heaven!" Toni breathed. "Can it be true? Can this great lady really be the little girl I knew in rags?"

"The very same," Leonie confirmed. "Oh, tell me about the others. Is everyone I knew still there?"

"Some of the old people have gone," Toni said. "But Meg is still with us."

"Meg?" Leonie cried in delight. "Praise be! But she must be a hundred."

"Uncle Silas says she's always been a hundred and she always will be," Paquita said wisely. "Uncle Silas?" Leonie echoed eagerly. "He's there?"

"He's our leader now, and grown very wise. He'll laugh when we tell him we saw you looking so fine."

Leonie sighed. "If only I could see him again. Where are you camped?"

"Not far from here, in the woods."

An ache of yearning was growing in her breast. "Will you be there for long?" she asked anxiously.

"Uncle Silas spoke of moving on in a few days, but I'm sure he'll wait when I tell him we've seen you."

"Oh, yes, tell him to wait. Tell him I'm coming," Leonie said in agony. "Don't let him go until I come."

They promised, and impulsively she opened her arms to them, first Paquita, then Toni. He hesitated, seemingly nervous of her finery. "Ignore it," Leonie pleaded. "It isn't real. Inside, I am still *myself*."

His face lightened and he threw his arms about her, holding her in an eager embrace. They were standing like that when Leonie heard Paquita give a little gasp. She turned to see Klaus and Sylvana standing at the open French doors. Sylvana looked like the cat that swallowed the cream. Klaus's face was rigid and expressionless, a sure sign of anger. Leonie extricated herself from Toni's arms and turned to Klaus, smiling in reassurance, but he didn't relax. The two young Gypsies bowed and he gave them the briefest of nods. Sylvana retreated a little but stayed where she could see and hear.

"I was concerned when you left the ballroom," Klaus informed Leonie coldly. "It is *not expected*."

Of course, she'd committed a breach of protocol by leaving while the prince was present, and he was clearly furious. "Your royal highness," she began, "if I might present Toni and Paquita, who—"

"I've already had the pleasure of seeing their performance, upon which I congratulate them," Klaus declared stiffly.

Toni and Paquita backed away until they reached the steps to the lawn, and scuttled down them to join the rest of the troupe. Leonie watched them go, feeling a sudden intense loneliness. The old life had briefly been revealed to her again, warm and free and joyful. But in a moment it was gone.

"And now, madam, perhaps you'd favor me with your complete attention?" Klaus demanded.

"Of course. If I could only explain to you—"

"We should return to the ballroom," he interrupted in an icy tone.

Sighing, she took the arm he offered and let him lead her back. Through the material of his dress uniform she could feel that he was stiff with anger. Sylvana gave her a look of malice and triumph and slid out of sight.

When the music struck up, Klaus bowed and indicated that they should dance. But when Leonie went into his arms, she found no softening. His face was still cold and unyielding. "Why do you dance with me if you're still angry?" she asked.

"Because it's expected. People wish to see you in my arms."

"But you haven't forgiven me."

"I won't tolerate being made a fool of."

"I know it was a breach of protocol—" she began to say.

He wanted to shout, "To hell with protocol. I was afraid for your life." When Sylvana had told him where Leonie had gone, his first thought had been that Bismarck had sent the Gypsies to lure her away and assassinate her. His nightmares had driven him to forget the detachment expected of a prince, and he pursued her. He'd feared he would find her dead or vanished. Instead, he'd discovered her eagerly embracing a handsome young man, and the revulsion had been like a blow to the heart. In self-defense, he'd assumed his most frozen and lofty aspect. It was the only way he could cope with the turbulent feelings in his breast. "But you're now going to tell me that they were more of your associates from British Intelligence," he said ironically. "Perhaps one of them was Jack Blair in disguise?"

"Certainly not," she said tartly. "Hell will freeze over before I put my arms around Jack Blair. They weren't my associates. They were my friends."

"Undoubtedly, from the way you abandoned yourself to that man's embrace," he said bitterly.

Leonie's face lightened a little. "A vain woman might wonder if the prince was jealous," she hazarded.

"The prince is never jealous," Klaus asserted firmly. "Such feelings are beneath him. He neither knows them nor understands them. Nor does he care sufficiently for any woman to risk his happiness over her fidelity."

"I see."

"But dignity is another matter, madam. While you occupy the position of my official favorite, you'll oblige me by controlling your behavior." He gritted his teeth. "My cousin Sylvana observed you leaving and remarked that you seemed ignorant of the customs of our court. She took great pleasure in telling me that you'd slipped away with a young man."

"Only a young man?" Leonie inquired. "She didn't mention that a woman was with us?"

"Obviously she failed to notice her."

"Come, you know better than that. She was trying to make trouble for me. And she succeeded, didn't she?"

"If anyone else had seen you in that man's arms, I would have been a laughingstock, and *that I will not tolerate*." He took a deep breath. "Now, why are you looking at me like that?"

"The truth would probably offend you."

"That's never stopped you before," he snapped.

"Very well. I was feeling sorry for you."

"You're right. That does offend me. I need no pity."

"But how can I help it when you show me how empty and loveless your life is? You live in this beautiful palace, but inside you there's a desert."

"It has to be so," he declared somberly, no longer trying to dispute her reasoning. "I'm a prince. I can't afford the feelings you regard as natural. There are too many people ready to exploit those feelings, and so I put them aside too long ago to remember. It's better that they stay aside. Now the dance is ending and we're both free to seek other partners."

She curtsied to him, and immediately found her hand claimed by Reinald. Her heart ached for Klaus, and she would have been glad to be alone. She managed to smile, as was expected of her, but found Reinald looking at her with sympathy. "I'm afraid my cousin can make himself very unpleasant when he's angry," he said gently.

"He was a little annoyed," she said, trying to pass it off.

"Don't be too distressed," he advised. "Klaus demands perfection, but he's a generous man." He hesitated, then spoke quickly, "Leonie, if Klaus's rages ever become too much for you, will you—" he seemed to check himself forcibly "—will you remember that I'm your friend?" he finished with an effort. "I might be able to assist you."

"I'm sure I'll always be glad of your assistance. But don't fear for me." She gave him an impish smile. "I'm very well able to take care of myself, much more so than I look."

"I know you're very brave and gallant," he said gravely. "Sometimes I don't think you fully comprehend how vulnerable a woman can be."

She made another effort to tease him. It would be a triumph, she felt, to make Reinald laugh. "That's true," she said with a chuckle. "I'm more used to discovering how vulnerable men can be."

"You mean that many men fall in love with you?" he asked, still in the same grave tone.

"I'm afraid I do," she confessed, her eyes dancing. "I'm sure it's very improper of me to enjoy it."

"Nothing you do is improper," he said at once. "You enjoy it because your heart is innocent. How could you know the world, Leonie? A sheltered girl, married young to a man who might have been your grandfather—what do you really know of men?"

She sighed. Reinald's determination to think the best of her was charming, but his utter lack of humor could sometimes make him hard to talk to.

At the far end of the ballroom, Sylvana was dancing with Klaus, and contriving to keep Leonie in view from the corner of her eye. "I feel for you so deeply," she murmured to Klaus. "How hard it must be to discover that you were mistaken in her."

"I don't believe that I was mistaken," he declared in a voice that warned her to say no more.

"Oh, my dear, you're so loyal, but can't you see the truth? She's done nothing but expose you to ridicule from the first moment tonight. Look at the vulgar way she's dressed."

"She seems to me to be dressed with great restraint," Klaus observed. "I find her lack of jewels far less vulgar that some of the excesses here tonight." He purposely avoided looking at Sylvana's riot of rubies.

She gave a soft laugh. Some men would have found the sound alluring, but not if they had ever heard Leonie laugh, Klaus thought. With Leonie, it was more of a chuckle, rich and inviting, floating from her throat in teasing amusement at the follies of her fellow humans. It made a man want to explore her fully, and maddened him that he couldn't. Klaus wondered what everyone here would say if they knew the truth, that he'd never yet enjoyed the glorious body that was swaying so irresistibly in Reinald's arms, that she kept him at arm's length, and it was driving him crazy....

"I beg your pardon," he said hastily to Sylvana when he realized that he'd been looking over her shoulder.

"I was observing how generous you are," she remarked, trying to keep the edge from her voice but not entirely succeeding. "Too generous to divine her real intent. Her attire is silently telling the world that you're mean, that you don't give her enough jewels."

"I'm very sure the whole court knows by now of the diamonds I gave her when she arrived. In fact, she originally refused them."

"Holding out for better terms," Sylvana said in an unconscious echo of Gwendolyn.

"No, I don't think so," Klaus mused out loud. "I don't think she cares for such things. She's unlike all other women."

"Dearest Klaus, you're so blind," she said soulfully on a sigh. "But one day you'll see her as she really is. And when that day comes, I promise you I—"

"Don't abuse her to me," Klaus said tensely, his eyes blazing. "I know what to think of Leonie far better than you do." Then, to soften the harshness of his words, he kept hold of her hand as the dance ended, and drew it to his lips. "I realize that your words spring only from your concern for me. I think no man ever had a kinder or more beloved sister."

"But I'm not your sister," Sylvana said sharply.

He kissed her hand again. "In my heart, you will never be any less than my dearest sister."

He released her and bowed slightly, leaving her no choice but to curtsy and say, "You're always too kind, *cousin*. If you'll forgive me, I feel a little unwell."

"I'm sorry to hear it. You have our permission to leave."

The dancers drew back as Sylvana departed the ballroom, her head high, her jaw set firmly. It was only close observers who saw the touch of furious color in her cheeks, or the hint of flounce in her step.

The ball was over, and a somber hush had fallen over the palace. Those who had danced beneath the glittering chandeliers had retired to brood, in pleasure or dismay, over the events of the evening.

He wouldn't come to her apartments tonight, Leonie thought. He was too angry with her. She could slip out and see her friends, and perhaps return without his ever knowing. The temptation was suddenly overwhelming. Moving quickly, she took out the national costume she'd worn for the beer festival, and put it on. But as she turned to leave by the secret door, she checked herself with a small gasp.

"May I ask where you're going?" Klaus asked coldly. He was standing in the doorway, barring her way. "I doubt you're on your way to see Jack Blair dressed like that."

"No," she said hesitantly. "I'm not going to see Jack Blair."

He stepped closer. "Then who is it, Leonie? Who do you hurry out to see with your hair streaming free like a river of gold? Who matters so much that you neglect your duty and leave without telling me?"

"I didn't think you'd be down here tonight," she said.

"You mean you hoped I wouldn't." His eyes were hard. "Tell me about the man I saw you embracing," he said with a touch of bitterness that not all his years of self-control could keep out of his voice.

She regarded him with raised eyebrows. "I thought the prince was never jealous."

"He can't afford to be. But if I were like other men, and could admit to jealousy, what would you say to me, Leonie?"

"I'd say that Toni was my childhood playmate, and I was hugging him with joy at meeting him again after so many years."

He looked at her wryly. "Your childhood playmate? A Gypsy? Very well, keep your secrets. I was foolish to ask."

"But it's the truth," she insisted. "Until I was ten, I played with Toni every day of my life."

"A well-bred English child played with a Gypsy?" he said with derision.

"But I—" She broke off and laid a hand on his arm. "Can you keep a secret?"

"Can the prince keep a secret? Have you any idea how many secrets I carry every moment of every day?"

"Then keep this one, for you're the only person I've ever told. For the first ten years of my life, I wasn't a well-bred English child. My father was the son of a marquis, but my mother was a Gypsy. I was born among Gypsies. It was only when they were both dead that I was sent to England to become a lady."

"You—a Gypsy? That's impossible."

But even as he denied it, his mind said, of course. That explained her brilliant dark eyes and the wildness he'd found in her from the first moment. That was why beneath her fine clothes he had always sensed a woman of the earth, unlike all other women, so that losing her would be an ache that would never leave him.

"Impossible," he said again, but his voice lacked conviction.

"It's not impossible. I've got more in common with them than with you. When I watched them tonight—so wild and free—I felt weighed down by my fine clothes. *They* don't need satin and lace. They know what's important." For a moment, her eyes glistened with tears and he stared at her, thunderstruck.

"I believe you'd give all this up to be with them," he said slowly. "Is that the truth, Leonie?"

"Perhaps," she said in a husky voice. "I only know that I have to see them again...all my old friends. Uncle Silas...how I loved him. I don't know how long they'll be there. *I have* to find them. It's not far. I can be there and back by day. You mustn't try to stop me."

He was swept by a terrible fear that she might vanish with them into the night. Gypsies were strange, different. The legends said they could do magic, appearing out of thin air, then disappearing into it again. And although, as a rational man, he naturally believed none of this, he had a sudden illogical dread. There'd always been something magical and mysterious about her, and now he had the key to it. "I won't try to stop you," he said. "But I won't let you leave without me. We'll go together."

"You—in a Gypsy camp?" she asked, startled.

"Why not? They're my subjects, aren't they?"

Leonie shook her head. "Gypsies are nobody's subjects," she said. "We are a free people, wandering everywhere, tied to no country, beholden to nobody. I'd lived in fifteen countries by the time I was ten."

It was marvelous, he thought, to watch the glow that came into her eyes whenever she spoke of her Gypsy childhood. Marvelous and disturbing. Unconsciously, perhaps, she'd said, "*We* are a free people," not, "*They* are…" "You speak as though you're still one of them," he said.

"I *am* still one of them," she said passionately. "My father's people tried to turn me into a fine lady, but I'll be a Gypsy until the day I die."

The fear was with him again. "I'm coming with you," he repeated. When she seemed about to protest, he silenced her with a raised hand. "You say they're not my subjects, but they're living here under my laws. So I want to meet them. Consider this another aspect of my education. Besides," he said as he touched her face with hesitant fingers, "I don't want to let you out of my sight."

She understood and her heart was suddenly light. "It's all right. I'll come back."

"Will you? How can I be sure?"

"Because I can't stay away from you," she whispered. Seeing his startled look, she added quickly, "I mean, I mustn't stay away from you too long. That's my job."

He seemed to come out of a dream. "Of course. Come with me." He took her hand and led her back up the secret stairs to his own room. There he slipped into an adjoining room and put on the clothes he'd worn the night of the beer festival. "We'll need horses," he said. "I know another way out that will bring us to the stables."

She followed his lead until they were outside in the dark courtyard of the palace. They found a hostler asleep on the straw and Klaus awoke him quietly, pressing a coin into the man's hand and putting his finger over his lips. The man brought two horses out, smiling to show he understood that the prince might want a midnight ride with his lady. A few minutes later, they were galloping away from the palace.

* * *

It was very quiet in the woods. Above them, the moon gleamed through the trees. "We should find them easily," Leonie said. "It's a large camp."

"Did the dancers tell you that?"

"Not in words, but they're telling me now."

"What do you mean?"

She stopped her horse near a clump of trees and pointed upward. "It's lucky there's a full moon," she said. "Look."

He looked up to where three plants hung suspended from the lower branches. "Gypsies leave these messages for one another as they pass," she said. "Each plant means something different to those who can read the signs. This is a big friendly crowd, ready to take in those who need a home and friends." She sighed reminiscently. "There was always great excitement when strangers arrived. Especially if—" She seemed to remember whom she was speaking to and stopped.

"Especially if . . . ?" Klaus prompted her.

"If they were rather disreputable. Those people were the most fun." She added, "I'm afraid I'm really rather a disreputable person myself."

"I wouldn't have you any different," he said quietly. In this unearthly atmosphere, he found he could say things he could never have said in the brilliant light of the palace. This was her world, where magic happened, and the magic was happening inside himself.

She smiled at him, and he waited eagerly for her answer, but instead, she sat up tense and straight in her saddle. "Listen," she said urgently. "*Listen.*"

He strained his ears, but heard nothing, although he was beginning to see a faint glow between the trees some distance off. Then, he heard the sound of a violin, floating softly on the night air, rising and falling with an aching sweetness that seemed to go through his heart. There were a thousand things in that music, freedom and laughter, wine and love—all the things that had deserted him on the day he bowed his neck to the yoke of duty. Now they all seemed to lure him on to where that glow lit the night.

"Let's hurry," he said, hardly aware that he spoke.

They urged their horses forward. The music was becoming louder and the glow brighter. Then, all at once, they were in the clearing, and the sounds burst over them. The light was coming from a campfire, its red and yellow fingers dancing up into the darkness, tossing restless shadows on the couples who whirled and turned in each other's arms. Sweet music came from the fiddler, who stood on the steps of a nearby caravan, his fingers racing over the strings, his eyes bright in the firelight. Leonie drew in her breath with joy, forgetting even Klaus, who watched her closely.

One or two of the Gypsies noticed the newcomers, then a few more, and as they noticed, they became still, drawing closer together defensively. The music stopped and for a long moment there was silence. Unable to bear it any longer, Leonie jumped to the ground, crying, "It's me, Leonie. Does nobody remember me?"

Toni gave a yell of delight. "I told you she'd come," he said. He seized her in his arms and swung her around and around. A roar went up from the rest of the crowd, and the next moment they were milling about her, reaching out to touch her. Those who'd known her as a child hugged and kissed her.

Klaus sat silently on his horse, taking in the whole scene. He was used to being apart, watching the lives of others as an outsider. That was a prince's fate. But it was somehow harder to watch this scene of warmth and joy and know that he was excluded. It was because of her. She belonged here among that laughing throng, whose ways were so carefree and natural. She'd said, "I have more in common with them than with you." It was true, and the knowledge hurt him. He sat there, feeling lonelier than at any time before in a lonely life.

A gigantic, booming laugh crashed over everybody, and they all fell silent to look at a man who'd just appeared. He was the biggest man Klaus had ever seen, with a bushy moustache and beard split by gleaming white teeth. There he stood, arms akimbo, his feet planted in the earth like tree trunks, bellowing a welcome. "Leonie!" he roared. "Leonie, my child."

"*Uncle Silas.*"

In an instant, Leonie was in his arms, almost vanishing in the exuberant bear hug he gave her. "My child, my child," he repeated. "My little Leonie, after all these years. And not changed a bit."

"Am I really not changed?" she asked eagerly.

"Not in the least," he reassured her. "Except perhaps that you've grown lovelier, more truly my sister's daughter. Ah, my poor Nesta. Poor Gavin. If they could see their child now, they would be so proud."

Without warning, the huge man began to cry. He made no effort to stem the tears that streamed down his face, but drew Leonie close again, sobbing like a child. "Dear Uncle Silas," she said, hugging him, "I've missed you so much all these years."

Suddenly they were all in tears, weeping as freely as they'd laughed. Klaus, to whom the free flowing of emotion came very hard, watched in envy. At last Leonie brushed her tears away and came to him. "Don't sit up there above us all," she begged. "Come down and join us."

He dismounted, but said quietly, "Join you? If only I could."

She seized his hands in both of hers. "You can if you want to. My people have never yet turned anyone away."

But at first it seemed as if he were right. Toni had spread word of Klaus's identity and they looked at him in awe, stepping back and bowing respectfully. But Leonie cried to them, "He is my friend. I promised him warmth and friendship, things our people have never denied to anyone. Will you deny them to him?"

But authority had never shown a kind face to them, and despite Leonie's words, they regarded him with apprehension. Klaus understood and sighed inwardly, wondering why he'd exposed himself to unnecessary pain. The sharpness of that pain took him by surprise. Then Uncle Silas stepped forward and held out a hand. "Friend!" he boomed. At once Klaus seized the great fist with both hands. That was the signal for constraint to disappear. The others crowded around, and some of them ventured to touch him. But he flinched instinctively for he was unused to being touched by strangers. They felt his recoil from them and backed off in fear. Leonie was watching him tensely. Suddenly Klaus knew he was at a decisive moment of his life. This was a chance that might never come again, and he'd nearly let it slip away. But there was still time to retrieve it.

"Friends," he cried. "Be my friends."

He opened his arms to them, and when they still hesitated, he came to them, seizing their hands. A low rumble broke from them and they gathered around him. Over their heads he could see Leonie's smile of joy and relief. Their hands felt strong as they clasped his. They were hard hands, toughened by toil, but they were warm and eager, outgoing, welcoming him to life in a way he'd forgotten. Or had he ever known?

A man thrust a mug of ale into his hand. It was rough and bitter, but nothing in his life had ever tasted so good, not even Hal Kenzl's best second-grade. As he lowered the mug, he found that Leonie was standing before him, her eyes shining. He looked at her questioningly and she nodded. Relief flooded him. It wasn't until long after, and with a sense of shock, that he realized he'd been seeking her approval—he, Prince Klaus Friederich, who'd sought no one's approval since he took the throne.

She put her hand on his shoulder. "They've accepted you," she whispered. "I'm so glad."

Before he could answer, he became aware of a murmur running around the crowd, then a silence. Looking up, he saw a woman approaching. Her lined face was shriveled, her eyes shrunken, and she seemed so old that there was no way of guessing her age. Young women supported her faltering steps on either side, and as she came into the firelight, Klaus saw that she was blind. "Who's here?" she asked. "Who comes among us from the past?"

"Meg," Leonie said in a voice full of gladness. "Meg, it's I, Leonie, returned to my home."

She put her arms around the old woman and after a moment Meg put her own arms about the strong young body. Tears streamed from her blind eyes. Watching them, Klaus felt an unaccustomed pricking behind his eyelids. He turned his head, lest anyone should see the disgraceful sight of the prince overcome by emotion. But the Gypsies were all around him. There was nowhere to hide. And he knew suddenly that there was no need to hide. These people weren't afraid of emotion.

Meg was running her fingers over Leonie's features, and gradually her face was wreathed in smiles. "Leonie," she whispered, "Leonie, home again, and unchanged."

"Yes," Leonie said through her tears. "Unchanged."

"Our Leonie has brought a friend," Uncle Silas said huskily, for he, too, was still weeping.

"Let him come forth," Meg commanded in a voice that suddenly resonated with authority.

There was a nervous ripple among the Gypsies at this ordering of the prince. Uncle Silas dropped his voice to mutter, "Mother, he is—"

"Hush!" Meg silenced him. "*I* will tell you who—and what—he is."

Before they could protest further, Klaus stepped forward and stood before her. He took her hand in his and raised it to his face. At once her look became concentrated as she ran her fingers over his features. "There is strength in this face," she said at last, "and harshness, but it is a harshness created by circumstances, not by nature. Nature's gifts are kindness and generosity. Warmth and tenderness live here, too, laughter and eagerness to love, but they hide. They fear to show themselves." She sighed. "They have hidden too long. Beware, lest they forget how to speak."

"I know the danger," Klaus told her.

"Yes, I can tell that you do. You know the danger, and in your heart you know how to fight it, but you're not yet ready. Hurry, hurry. Time is passing, the door closes, and once closed, it can never be opened again."

"Now tell me who I am," Klaus said.

"You're a friend. It's hard for you, but the friendship is there."

"You're a wise woman," Klaus said quietly. "Your blind eyes see everything."

"My ears hear everything, too," Meg said with a cackle. "Since I was a girl, I could judge a man by his voice, judge him as a *man*. You understand me?"

"Perfectly," Klaus said, embarrassed but grinning.

She dropped her hands away from his face to rest on his broad shoulders. "There's a certain vibrant note—I was never wrong—I hear it in you. Ah, but Leonie's a lucky woman."

"Meg," Leonie protested.

"Silence," Klaus said at once. "Let Meg speak."

Meg cackled again and addressed Leonie. "If I were a few years younger, I'd give you a contest for him. Ah, but my time is gone, taking my lovers with it. Wonderful lovers they were, strong-limbed and smooth-skinned. Now they are as old and stringy as me, those that are still alive. I tell you, too, that time passes. Such a man comes once in a life-time."

A fiddler stood nearby, instrument at the ready. Uncle Silas made frantic signs to him, and the next moment, music thrilled through the air.

Chapter Eight

It was fifteen years since Leonie had danced with Gypsies, yet it might have been yesterday. The rhythms were in her blood, sweet, singing and urgent, melting her body into movements that only Gypsies knew. Nesta had been the supreme dancer, whose fluid suppleness had made onlookers fall silent and won the heart of the man she loved. And she was Nesta's daughter, with the same instinctive knowledge that the body could speak so much more eloquently than the mouth.

Klaus's eyes were on her. In the glow of the campfire she could feel them burning her, stripping her naked. The physical craving for each other that they'd thwarted had turned into a fire ready to engulf them both, and Meg, who had the wisdom of the earth, had sensed it at once. Leonie wanted him with all the passion of her nature, and that same nature told her that his desire for her was fast becoming uncontrollable. How many nights had she lain alone in her cold bed, wanting him, aching for him, railing against the common sense that kept them apart. Now she'd had enough of being sensible. Her body's clamor for fulfillment was the only thing in her consciousness, blotting out caution, blotting out professional pride, leaving only the driving need to have him. Tonight she would take him, not blatantly, but by provoking him to take her.

Her movements became wilder, more daring. She whirled and spun in the firelight, sometimes raising the hem of her skirt to tantalize him with a glimpse of her long, beautiful legs. The tambourines crashed as Toni came in close, put one brown hand in the small of her back and pulled her hard against him, looking down into her face with a practiced simulation of passion. She answered in kind, sliding her fingers up his cheek and into his black hair, and drawing his face close to hers.

Like her, Toni was a master of illusion, and he knew exactly the game that was being played. "Tell me, dearest Leonie," he murmured, "just how jealous do you want him to be?"

"Very jealous."

He sighed. "My Paquita will kill me."

She laughed. Immediately he laughed with her. They looked like a couple sharing a love joke that excluded the rest of the world. Klaus's nails ground into his palm. Uncle Silas, who saw everything, grinned, and whispered in Klaus's ear, "If you want her, you must fight him for her."

"How can I break up a dance with a fight?" Klaus growled.

"Look." Silas pointed. "See how Brak fights Donner for Elaine." A young man, evidently Brak, had leaped into the throng and touched another man on the shoulder. It was clear that Donner didn't want to give up Elaine. He held up a hand and immediately Brak seized it and began arm wrestling. Elaine watched with delight, cheering them both on equally, until at last Brak forced his opponent's arm down. Their companions applauded this triumph, and Elaine flung herself into Brak's arms. Donner grinned and made a gesture of respect to his victorious challenger, then promptly claimed another woman by the same method. "That's how it's done," Silas said, adding significantly, "among Gypsies."

Klaus stood up. The blood was thrumming in his veins and he felt light-headed. Leonie had teased and tormented him long enough. The time had come to assert himself against her power, while at the same time letting that power carry him to the inevitable conclusion.

The other dancers drew back as he tapped Toni on the shoulder. At once Toni released Leonie and turned, his right arm held up in challenge, his eyes alight. Klaus gripped the young man's hand in his own, and cheers broke out all around them as they strained against each other. Toni had the strength of a man who had lived a hard life, but Klaus was a fencer whose arm muscles had grown steely after many bouts with the foils. They strained against each other, bodies taut, each surprised by the other man's strength.

Toni was in a fix. He knew Klaus was supposed to win, but Paquita was watching. He couldn't afford to be shamed. So he tensed his shoulders hard against Klaus's hand, and felt the surge of resistance come back against him. All around them the dancers had fallen silent, watching in delight as one of their own challenged the prince and gave as good as he got. Somebody yelled a word of encouragement, then another, then cheers broke out as the locked wrists went back and forth, each man in turn gaining a temporary advantage, but unable to press it home.

Klaus began to think he might lose. Toni was young and slim, but his muscles were pure steel. The thought of the Gypsies seeing him fail filled Klaus with dismay, but in the same moment he knew it wasn't the others who worried him. *She* was watching. The prize was to take her in his arms and claim the beautiful body that tormented him. She must be his tonight. *She must.*

Toni was prevailing. Klaus could feel his arm being bent slowly backward. His shoulders were aching, but it was now or never. He put out all his strength, thrusting back, forcing his hand upright again, then over to the other side. And down. The cheers rose to yells. Painfully the two men untangled their fingers and shook hands. Klaus looked about him. He was no longer aware of his surroundings or the Gypsies thumping him on the shoulders. He saw only her.

He'd thought Leonie would throw herself into his arms, but she didn't. She stood apart, watching him with a little smile curving her beautiful lips, part invitation, part triumph. He saw only the invitation. He was too blinded by desire and exaltation to realize that things were working out according to her plan. He took a step toward her and swept her up into his arms, holding her high against his chest. His eyes were burning.

"Now," he said. "No more games. No more teasing. *Now.*"

And she murmured, "Yes, now," in a voice that was dark with desire. The next moment, he was striding away toward the trees, still holding her. Some guardian angel must have guided his footsteps for he never looked where he was going. He walked on and on, his eyes fixed on her face as she lay contentedly in his arms, gazing up at him. At last he stopped and laid her gently down on the soft moss. He lay beside her and took her into his arms.

Their kiss was different from any other they'd shared. The others had been filled with frustration and sometimes anger as they yielded to feelings they both knew it would have been wiser to fight. Now there was no more fighting, only eager anticipation of what had to happen. But even through the passion that dazed her, Leonie feared for him. "We shouldn't have done this," she murmured. "To wander so far... It isn't safe for you."

But he laughed. It had a reckless sound that was new from him. "How can it be dangerous when I have you to protect me?" he whispered.

The prince had vanished. Only the man remained, and that man was half-crazy with desire. A lifetime's control fell away from him as he rained fierce kisses on her face, her neck, her shoulders. His lips burned her, sending trails of fire along her satiny skin, and she gave herself up to that heat in ecstasy. Nothing in her whole existence had felt like this moment when she was possessed by passion and about to unite with the man her body was made to love.

He pulled the soft blouse away, baring her breasts in the moonlight. The touch of his lips on her skin sent tremors of delight through her and she moved swiftly to pull at the strings of her tiny black waistcoat. A tug and it was gone, then the blouse itself. She sighed his name and ran her hands through his hair. Then she yielded to the rage that possessed her, too, tightening her hold and arching against him. Meg had divined that this was a man skilled in the art of physical love, and the hint had been the last ember tossed on the fire of Leonie's passion. Now she wanted Klaus with an all-absorbing need that drove out thought. She moaned as he kissed her breasts. They ached for him, and the feel of his tongue rasping across the nipples was unbearably good.

He was discovering the way through the petticoats beneath the brightly colored skirt. He'd seen her bare legs in the firelight as she danced, and knew she wasn't wearing the long lacy drawers of a fine lady. He came to the scanty undergarment that was all that stood between him and the satisfaction of his desire. It disintegrated under his rough grasp and she was there, ready for him. He thrust his way between her legs and drove into her blindly, mindlessly. The sensation that went through his whole body as she received him almost drove him mad.

He was a man of experience and skill, but he found himself slaking his desire like a green youth, abandoning caution, and with it, restraint. With lesser lovers, he'd been careful to offer an expert performance, for no woman must be disappointed by the prince. But this time, he was with a woman that he wanted too much to think about how he appeared. Now he could truly believe she was a Gypsy a wild creature, made of earth and fire, loving him fiercely, burning him up in a volcano of passion. She was a tigress, concealing her claws in silk but never entirely sheathing them; she was a bird fluttering in his arms, straining for freedom at the very moment she offered herself; she was the wind sweeping across the land, coming from places unknown, vanishing into eternity. She was all these things. She was Leonie.

He gasped when he drew back to look at her. The violence of his passion had drained him. She lay on her back on the moss, her breasts bare in the moonlight, and stretched her arms luxuriously above her head. Her face was blissful and satiated, echoing his own feelings.

But as he watched her, the drained feeling left him and her beauty began to work its magic again. He longed to caress her breasts and lay his face against that flawless skin, longed for it as heatedly as if they'd never made love. She turned her head lazily to meet his eyes, and he saw in her expression that it was the same with her. She, too, was only just beginning.

But there was more than passion in her face. There was humor. She regarded him satirically as she murmured, "Meg was right."

He began to laugh, clasping her to him. "Enchantress," he said. "I want to make love to you for the rest of the night."

"I want it, too," she whispered in his ear. "But not here."

"Let's hurry back."

As they got to their feet, he glanced in the direction of the Gypsies. Leonie smiled. "Don't worry," she said. "They're not expecting to see us again tonight."

They found their horses and slipped away into the woods. They rode quickly, eager to return to the palace and the pleasure that awaited them. As they rode, they exchanged the glances of joyful conspirators.

The trees began to get thinner, and through them Leonie could see the trail that led to Treuheim. There was just a little light, turning the sky from black to dark gray, throwing into silhouette a huge oak tree that stood on a small incline on the very edge of the woods.

Suddenly she was swept by a sensation of such bitter grief that she involuntarily jerked on the reins. A tremor went through Selma and she slowed to a walk, then halted as Leonie pulled the reins again. Leonie sat there, trembling, shattered by the waves of misery that went through her. "What is it?" Klaus asked anxiously.

"I don't know," she whispered. "Suddenly I—such misery—there's something terrible about this place."

Klaus looked about him at the gentle scenery that was just becoming visible. "I don't understand you," he said, touching her hand gently. "This is normally held to be a beauty spot."

"Yes, but...it fills me with such pain. I don't understand." Uncontrollable tears were pouring down her cheeks.

"Then let's leave quickly," he said. "Come, my dearest."

She urged Selma forward, glad to escape the ache of grief. Soon they'd left the place behind, and as it disappeared, she felt the strange mood lift. Sadness was banished, and again she was full of joy at being with him. In the stables they handed the horses back to the groom and hurried into the palace without being seen. As soon as the door of her bedroom had closed behind them, Klaus took her into his arms, and all else was forgotten.

Their loving had become different. Now they knew what it was to yield to their bodies' fever and unite in the fire of passion. They'd had a glimpse of what more their union could give them, and they reached out for it eagerly. Klaus's hands trembled as he undressed her. In the forest he'd known her body by touch, catching brief glimpses in the moonlight, discovering her elusiveness even while she was in his arms. Now he uncovered her beauty with joy, reveling in the richness of each new discovery. She was his, yet not his, and that sensation was the most mysterious of all. For the first time, he'd risen from a bed of desire feeling even more tantalized than before.

But this woman's gifts were like a two-edged sword. The more she gave, the more she revealed what she was withholding, and the more he had to follow her lead through mist and mysterious landscape. He had a mad instinct, dangerous in a prince, to put his hand in hers and beg her to show him the world, because he sensed that only she had the key.

When they lay naked together, he held her close, adoring her body's perfection. Leonie saw it in his face and offered herself up to him joyfully, wanting him in the deepest heart of her being. She murmured his name, and at once he began to stroke her hair back from her face with gentle fingers, watching her intently. "I've thought so often of having you in my arms like this," he said. "How it would be...how you would look and feel when you were naked... But no imagining was nearly as beautiful as the reality. You're the most peerless of women."

"And I'm yours," she said softly.

"Yes. Mine to hold. Mine to adore."

He was stroking her as he spoke, letting his fingertips caress her softly, outlining the curve of her breasts, her hips, the length of her thighs. Their lovemaking in the woods had been thrilling, but now, safe in the warmth and comfort of bed, she could relax and take her time to enjoy the sensuous delight he offered her. She took a long, deep breath as the warmth began to spread through her flesh, making her skin tingle with expectancy.

Klaus looked at her with brooding eyes. No other woman had made him wait so long, teasing his desire to madness with her impudent games. She was different from the rest in so many ways, but mostly because there was nothing she wanted from him. She wasn't seeking money or favors for herself or her family. She wasn't anxious for his approval. In fact, she often made him feel that he needed her approval, a novel sensation that sometimes enraged, sometimes amused him. She couldn't be bought. She could only be won.

But tonight he'd won her, wrestling among her own people, and claiming her by right of conquest. And the victory was sweeter than any a thousand compliant court ladies could have given him.

The round perfection of her breasts tempted him and he dropped his head to enclose one proud nipple between his lips. He felt the tremor go through her as he began to tease it with his tongue, and knew that her passion was ready to break out at any moment. The wildness of Gypsies was in her, and tonight it had been roused after a long sleep. Her fingers moved softly in his hair, holding him close, urging him on.

Leonie felt as though she were drowning in a sea of sensation. Forks of lightning flashed out from the place where he was kissing her to encompass her whole body, making it vibrate as never before. She was humming with desire, pulsating with it, giving herself up utterly to the man who could inflict such glorious ecstasy and torment intermingled. She arched her back, wanting more, yearning to be possessed and to possess him in return. He was an adventure of a new kind, and nothing attracted her so much as adventure.

As his lips loved her, his hands explored her. His fingers traced her voluptuous shape, leaving trails of excitement wherever they went. She was burning in the fire of her own eagerness, anxious to take him inside her. "Klaus," she breathed.

He didn't seem to hear her. His tongue flickered over her breast, causing sparks to shimmer through her. He seemed to be in no hurry, but she could feel his manhood against her leg, hard and powerful, driving her mad with impatience. "Klaus," she said raggedly, "I...want you...now—*now*."

The moment he entered her, she cried out. It was so good, so right. Her body had been made for him. It was moving now in the rhythms of love, responding with passionate intensity to the hard thrusts that carried him deep into her. She met his thrusts, deepening her own sensation, feeling herself become one with him in ecstatic union.

He was looking down into her face, smiling a little, but also searching for something. "Is this what you wanted?" he murmured.

"Oh yes...yes..." She wrapped her legs around his strong body, imprisoning him for her pleasure. *"Yes,"* she breathed wildly.

His loins and thighs were like steel, hardened by hours in the saddle. Her own hips had the same strength and she forced herself up against that hardness, trembling at the power deep within her, rejoicing in it and what it could do for her. All the things of her life that had seemed so important before—her work as an agent, the thrill of danger, the pleasures of success—they were all nothing beside what was happening to her now. She was soaring into the heavens, borne aloft by a magic carpet.

His movements became faster, stronger. The pleasure shook her whole body. She felt as if she might fall apart from the force of it. A cry broke from her as the universe exploded, sending her spinning back to earth. Gradually she became aware of her surroundings, the feeling of the sheet beneath her back, his weight between her legs, and the unutterable joy and peace that pervaded her.

She felt liberated by what had happened. Images of freedom flitted through her brain. She was the eagle, flying high over the world below, the gazelle dancing through the forest. She was fire, answerable to no man. All the life of the earth seemed to run through her, because in the end, all life came down to this moment, when a man and a woman lay, exhausted and triumphant, in each other's arms.

He looked down on her, his eyes glowing with a look she had never seen there before. As he moved away, he kept an arm around her, and soon they were both asleep, still curled in each other's arms.

Leonie awoke first and propped herself up on one elbow to look at him. In sleep, the tensions were drained from his face, leaving it relaxed and softened, almost like a boy's. A lock of hair had fallen over his face, and she brushed it back softly, so as not to awaken him. It was the first time she'd ever seen him so totally vulnerable and it made her heart ache with tenderness.

The strangeness of the sensation brought home to her how much her life had cut her off from a woman's normal feelings. Men had been foes trying to trap her, or prey to be trapped by her and compromised into indiscretion. She'd flirted, made half promises and evaded them, teased, pretended, and in private had mocked them for being so easily deluded by her. They'd been children to be led by the nose, danger to be courted and then escaped. It was all in the service of her country, but she was too honest not to admit that she'd thoroughly enjoyed herself.

Only two men had called forth her softer feelings. One had been her grandfather, the marquis, whose sadness had touched her heart. The other had been her husband, whose loving-kindness had made her life sweet, and whom she'd repaid with gentle, constant affection.

But he'd never caused in her the storm of passion that Klaus could provoke. The combination of tenderness and wild desire she felt for Klaus was new and almost shocking in its intensity, shocking because it showed her a path before her she'd never trodden before, a path that could bring only heartbreak, for it led to love for a man who could never be hers.

Klaus stirred in his sleep and flung an arm over her. Gradually his hold grew tighter, drawing her to him until his face was buried against her breasts. His breathing resumed its deep, steady rhythm, and he relaxed again, as though he'd found comfort. Leonie stroked his tousled hair. A tempest of feeling swept over her, buffeting her, taking her breath away.

And suddenly she saw what a fool she'd been. The path of love didn't lie before her. She was already far along it, too far to turn back. She, who'd always stood aside and watched others in the toils of love with a merry, half-cynical smile, had been caught in the trap that had sprung before she knew. It was too late now. It had been too late from the first moment. This was the man she loved, the man she'd been born to love and would love until she died.

A shudder seemed to go through him, but then he opened his eyes and relaxed when he saw her. "I was afraid you weren't here," he whispered.

"But of course I'm here," she said, smiling. "Where would I go?" She added with a teasing note, "I'm always at your royal highness's command."

"Don't joke," he said. The laughter died from her face as she saw how he was looking at her. There was amazement in his eyes, bewilderment, disbelief, and yet a recognition that exactly mirrored her own. "It's true, isn't it?" he said at last.

"Yes," she said slowly. "It's true."

When had she begun to love him? Perhaps from the very start, but passion had blinded her to the true nature of her feelings. But with passion slaked, there was nothing to hide the truth.

He sat up and took her face between his hands. "Tell me that you love me," he pleaded.

"I love you. I mustn't . . . but I do."

"Yes. We mustn't love each other, but we can't help it."

"Perhaps it isn't really love?" she said as if seeking escape. "Perhaps we're only deluding ourselves."

"It isn't a delusion," he said insistently. "I'm not a boy and you're not a girl. You know that what's between us is more than desire. Why shouldn't we give it its real name?"

"I think I'm afraid to."

He looked at her intently. "You're not afraid of anything. I don't believe you're afraid to love me.'

"No," she said, facing the inevitable. "What's happened has happened, however unwise we were to let it."

"Did we 'let it'?"

She shook her head. "It's like the wind that blows. There's no way to stop it."

But try as she might to be philosophical, Leonie was a Gypsy, and sometimes the curtain that hid the future slipped aside for her. She felt now as if a small tear had opened, giving her a vision of fleeting joy, terrible fear and unimaginable grief. "Oh, my love," she cried, "my dearest love. What are we to do?"

"Love each other," he said somberly. "There's nothing else to be done."

Chapter Nine

Leonie's apartments were a hive of activity. The hands of the elegant gilt clock were moving toward nine p.m. and within a few minutes her guests would begin to arrive.

The favorite's intimate supper parties had become legendary at court, and invitations were much sought after. The rules of protocol were relaxed to an extent that no one could remember before. At normal gatherings, royalty arrived last and left first, but here it was understood that the prince appeared before all other guests in order to have a moment alone with his favorite. At table, anyone was allowed to introduce a new topic of conversation without, as was usual, waiting for the prince to do so.

Leonie never invited more than twenty guests. There were usually a couple of government ministers and their wives, but the others were chosen for their wit. Serious subjects were forbidden, since the favorite had declared them beyond her understanding. Fun was the order of the evening, and she was always pleased when his royal highness laughed. Some wondered if she feared that her hold on his heart was merely a light one. Others decided that she was just incurably frivolous.

Twice, Leonie had made a point of inviting Baron Gruber. Both times, he'd accepted and been superficially the perfect guest, but beneath his smiles she could see the glint of steel, and his courtesy barely disguised his contempt. Tonight he would be there again, and they would duel silently across the table.

As she prepared to receive her guests, she was a vision. Her dress was cloth of gold, specially designed to set off the gold necklace and earrings Klaus had given her. Even her skin seemed to have a golden glow, although this owed less to her jewelery than to the perfect fulfillment, both emotional and physical, she'd found with the man she loved.

She made a final check of the dinner table, pronounced everything perfect and gave smiling thanks to her anxious servants. As they melted away, she heard a slight altercation from the entrance to the apartments. A man's voice demanded immediate entry.

"You can't come in now," her majordomo replied indignantly. "Her grace cannot be disturbed." This was followed by forceful protests.

"Come in, Masham," Leonie called. She nodded to the major domo. "You may go."

He left reluctantly. "What is it?" Leonie asked.

"I've brought news from Blair," he informed her, putting papers into her hand. "As you ordered, he's been investigating Gruber. This is the result." She read the papers in silence. Their contents were explosive.

"Now, let me tell you what I've discovered myself," Masham said when she looked up with a tense expression.

She listened to him gravely. As he finished, the tiny gilt clock on the mantelpiece struck nine, which meant that Klaus would be here at any moment. "Get yourself something to eat, but don't go far," she commanded Masham. "I may need you tonight." He left quietly, without another word.

A few minutes later, footmen opened the gilt and cream-colored double doors. The majordomo cried self-importantly, "His Royal Highness, Prince Klaus Friederich," and Klaus entered, his face impassive.

But as soon as they were alone, he relaxed, took her into his arms and kissed her deeply. Her head swam and she melted against him. It was hard to think of professional matters when she was intoxicated by his touch. "Send all the others away," he murmured. "Cancel the party. I want to be alone with you."

"My love, we must talk seriously—"

"Later."

"No." She pushed against his chest with an urgency that made him look down on her in surprise. "I have to talk to you about Gruber," she said.

Klaus sighed and released her. "That poor old man," he said with a grin. "He thinks you're just a giddy female. If he knew how dedicated you are to his overthrow, I think he'd have nightmares."

"Not nearly as dedicated as he is to *your* overthrow," Leonie said grimly.

"Come now—"

"Where was he while you were in England?"

"Visiting his estates and checking our defenses along the border."

"Exactly. His estates are near Wolfenberg's border with Prussia. While there, he made at least two trips into Prussia, *at night and in secret*."

The good humor vanished from Klaus's face. "He'd never have done such a thing without my knowledge and consent. Why should he?"

"To meet Bismarck."

"Gruber? A traitor? Meeting my enemy behind my back? My love, I know you care for me, but it's led you astray this time."

"Then read this," she said, holding out a paper to him. "It's a copy of a letter he sent Bismarck three weeks ago. It mentions meeting him while you were in England. But it says much more."

Slowly Klaus took the paper and scanned it. Leonie saw the color drain from his face. "He's dared to tell Bismarck about the British loan," he said with bitter fury. "He warns him that it's to be used to strengthen Wolfenberg's army."

"That's why there are now twice as many troops on the Prussian border," Leonie said angrily.

Klaus was still staring at the letter in disbelief. "Yet he advises Bismarck to take no action, and to ignore a communication from me, restating my opposition to the union. He says he's confident of being able to overcome 'such shortsighted stubbornness' and bring me to a knowledge of where Wolfenberg's true destiny lies." He raised his head, staring into space, stunned. "This is impossible. Even with the letter in my hand, I feel it's impossible."

"That letter is Gruber's own copy in his own handwriting," Leonie emphasized.

"How do we come to have it?" Klaus asked.

Leonie gave a whimsical smile. "I don't like Jack Blair," she said, "but I have to admit that within his limits, he does his job thoroughly. He says that all those papers come from Gruber's desk, and you can rely on that."

Klaus nodded. "I know his writing," he said slowly. "Still, I can hardly believe it of Gruber. A man that my grandfather called friend, a man I was raised to admire, who taught me when I was a boy."

"A man who's been trying to have you killed," Leonie reminded him.

He didn't answer. She laid a hand on his arm, hurt by the pain in his face at this betrayal by a man he'd trusted. He gave her a twisted smile, and for a moment she thought he would go into her arms, but as he turned to her, there was a noise from the hall, and the sound of Reinald's voice.

Reinald also sometimes appeared before the other guests, though never before Klaus. He would offer her a small corsage, or a gift of bonbons. He performed many such acts of gallantry, but always with such discretion that he couldn't be accused of competing with Klaus. He was simply there, ready to step in should Leonie need his services. Now and then she saw in his eyes the same disturbing light she'd been surprised to find there on the first day, a hint that his thoughts and desires were very different from what appeared on the polished surface. But he kept himself well in check.

She went to greet him, and at once he carried her hand to his lips. "Dare I ask you to accept these?" he begged, revealing a small posy of yellow rosebuds. "I think they'll go with your gown."

She gave a forced laugh. "They go with it so perfectly that I'll have to suspect you of spying on Miss Hatchard."

"Not at all. I knew Klaus had given you gold jewelery, which you were bound to wear. The rest was easy."

"They're exquisite. See, I'll pin them here at my waist."

Reinald seemed to become aware of the strained atmosphere. He looked up to where Klaus was standing with the papers in his hand, his face still pale. "Cousin," he said urgently, "in God's name, what's the matter?"

Klaus's eyes met Reinald's steadily. "We have a traitor," he said. "A man I would have trusted with my life... wrongly it seems."

Reinald became deadly still. His face, too, had lost its color, and when he spoke, his voice had a strange note. "A traitor? I don't understand you."

"Gruber," Klaus said heavily. "He's been conspiring with Bismarck, meeting him in secret."

"No," Reinald said at once. "There must be some mistake. I know Gruber's a fanatic who thinks he's always right, and he hasn't always respected your authority as he ought, but conspiring with Bismarck? I can't believe that."

"I'm afraid this leaves no doubt," Klaus said, handing him the paper. Reinald read it in silence, then made a sharp exclamation.

"He actually told Bismarck about the loan," Klaus said. "I needn't tell you how serious it is that this information should have reached our enemy."

"My God, it's horrible!" Reinald's shoulders seemed to sag as though an unbearable weight had just descended on them. "I'm disgraced," he said heavily. "My intelligence network should have discovered this, and it failed." He straightened, his face grim and determined. "I offer you my immediate resignation," he said in a voice that was harsh with effort.

"No, cousin," Klaus said at once. "I shall need you now more than ever."

"But I'm useless to you," Reinald declared bitterly. "It shames me even to be in your presence. Let me go, I beg you."

"Never," Klaus insisted. He rested his hand on his cousin's shoulder, a silent reminder of years of comradeship. Reinald raised his head and studied Klaus's face, and Leonie could have sworn she saw the glint of tears in the archduke's eyes. The next moment, the two men were locked in a fierce embrace.

When Reinald had recovered himself, he said in a voice that still sounded husky, "May I ask how this information came into your hands?"

"I, too, have an intelligence network, cousin," Klaus said with a faint smile. "Not the equal of yours, admittedly, but as you can see, it has its moments of brilliance."

"Is that all you'll tell me?" Reinald asked. "Well, perhaps you're right. Despite your kind words, we both know I've failed you, and must earn your trust again."

"I trust you completely," Klaus declared firmly. "But the secret isn't mine. Don't press me, but remain my dearest friend."

"Gruber must be arrested immediately."

"No," Leonie exclaimed. Both men turned to stare at her. "I have twenty guests arriving at any second," she went on hastily. "Among them, Gruber himself. If you arrest him now, the talk will be all over the palace within five minutes."

"I agree," Klaus said. "I want this dealt with quietly. We must get the evening over first."

"Are we to sit down at dinner with this man?" Reinald demanded, aghast. "A traitor to Wolfenberg—to you?"

"There's no choice," Klaus told him. "Leonie is right. We must behave as if everything were normal." A murmur announced the arrival of the first guests. Klaus thrust the paper into Leonie's hands. She quickly locked it away in a small gilt desk and handed him the key. The next moment, the double doors were flung open to admit two of the younger diplomats from the British embassy, with their wives. Leonie advanced in welcome, and while greetings were exchanged, more guests arrived.

Gruber was the last to arrive. He strode in, white-haired and proper, the picture of innocence as he bowed over

Leonie's hand. She gave him an impersonal smile and hoped her manner betrayed nothing.

The evening was an ordeal, but she was an accomplished dissimulator and managed to don her usual frivolous mask. The two men were less at ease, retreating behind formal courtesy that seemed out of place in this setting. Klaus spoke little to Gruber, but now and then his eyes were on him, bitter, brooding.

At last Klaus rose to depart, thus bringing the evening to an end. After his formal departure, everyone knew they were expected to leave quickly, so that he could return in private. Before he left, he exchanged a quick glance of understanding with Reinald.

Reinald had recovered his poise. When Gruber prepared to depart, he said, "Stay a moment," in a tone that betrayed nothing but impersonal cordiality. Gruber sat down again, his face its usual cherubic mask.

When the last guest had gone, Leonie said, "I'll leave you." She was longing to hear what transpired, but even now she must protect her cover. She slipped into her bedroom where, as she'd guessed, she found Klaus, who'd come down by the secret staircase. Normally he would have changed, but now he still wore the formal clothes of the evening. His face was stern and sad.

"He's there with Reinald," she said.

Klaus sighed. "I wish this interview could be avoided. But it must be faced." He smiled at her wearily. "To think I doubted your ability when you first came. Yet you've done your job and uncovered the traitor in our midst."

He kissed her briefly and left her. Leonie stared after him, feeling a dreadful chill invade her heart. She was sure Klaus hadn't realized the implications of his own words, but they'd hit her like a blow. *Her job here was finished.*

She'd discovered the traitor who was threatening Klaus's life, and now she would probably be recalled. Somewhere there was another mission waiting for her, but how could she undertake it when her heart was here? She'd fallen into the trap, abandoned her professional detachment, and now she would pay the price. Hurriedly she sat down and began to pen a report to Lord Bracewell describing the latest development and explaining that it was still vital for her to remain in Wolfenberg. But after two pages, she abandoned it. No matter how hard she tried to sound dispassionate, her love for Klaus breathed through every word. She lit a candle and burned every last scrap of the report. After thinking carefully, she began another one, but an hour later, that, too, was ashes.

The waiting was becoming unendurable. She drew a shawl around her shoulders and slipped out onto the terrace. Most of the palace lights were out, but all around her the grounds were bathed in moonlight. It lit up the terrace and the stone steps leading down to the lawn. It was only a few weeks ago that she'd climbed those steps to take over these apartments. Now perhaps she would soon descend again to leave Klaus forever. This was her night of triumph, but her heart was heavy. Slowly she wandered down the stairs to find a seat tucked away in a niche in the wall. She was dazed by the suddenness of what had happened.

From above she heard the sound of a French door being violently opened and shut, followed by quick footsteps. Looking up, she saw Reinald hurrying down the steps, scowling furiously. He saw her watching him and some of the tension went out of his body. "If I'd stayed, Klaus and I would have quarreled, and that I couldn't endure," he growled, coming to sit beside her.

"Why? What's happened?"

He stared out over the moonlit grounds. "Gruber's a clever man," he said at last. "Clever as a snake. And Klaus is too generous for his own good."

"You don't mean—you *can't* mean that Gruber is protesting his innocence?" she demanded.

"Essentially, yes. Oh, not the meeting with Bismarck, or the letter. Even a barefaced villain such as Gruber can't deny those. But the attempts on Klaus's life—he swears he knew nothing about them."

"Of course he did," Leonie said in disgust.

"Of course," Reinald agreed. "It's obvious to us, but Klaus doesn't see it like that. To him, Gruber is nothing worse than a stiff-necked, overbearing old man who went too far in trying to get his own way."

"You don't mean he's going free?" Leonie asked, aghast.

"No, he's been arrested and is on his way to The Fort, under guard, at this moment. He'll be charged with treason, but there'll be no mention of attempts on the prince's life, because Klaus simply refuses to believe it."

"He must be out of his mind," she breathed.

Reinald grimaced. "Not out of his mind, merely too noble and generous to comprehend genuine evil. He finds it hard to think the worst of people, especially those he cares for. He's furious at what Gruber admits to, but he won't face the worst of the truth. I'm afraid we exchanged heated words and I stormed out before I said something unforgivable." He rose and carried her hand to his lips. "I must go now. See if you can persuade Klaus to see reason."

As he vanished into the shadow of the trees, Leonie flew up the steps into her apartments. A moment later, she was in Klaus's arms, holding on to him tightly, full of dread. "I suppose Reinald has told you," he said wryly.

"Yes. Neither of us can understand how you can be so blind—"

"My darling, I understand Gruber. He's a fanatic, convinced that his way is the only way. I should have dismissed him long ago, and I blame myself that I didn't. But he's been Bismarck's dupe. In his own blinkered, unyielding fashion, he believed he was serving his country."

"Revealing state secrets to your enemy?" Leonie reminded him fiercely.

Klaus sighed. "He didn't see Bismarck as the enemy, but as Wolfenberg's best friend, leading it along the path of true glory. He saw his own role as guiding me along that path, helping me to see the greater truth. It led him to treason, but not to murder. When I told him of the attempts on my life, he was devastated."

"Or he pretended he was," Leonie cried angrily. "Reinald was right. You're generous to the point of madness."

"He'll spend the rest of his days locked up in The Fort. Is that being generous? Are you like Reinald, who wants me to set that deluded old man in front of a firing squad? I haven't the heart to do that. In his time, he's done this country great service. He went astray, and he'll pay for it—but not with his life." He gave her a faint smile. "So you see, my darling, I shall still need you."

Then she thought she understood. He wasn't fooled, but he was seizing on the excuse to keep her. He, too, couldn't face a parting just yet. Her spirits rose with relief, and she threw her arms about him.

The Fort, where Gruber had been taken, was a place Leonie had heard about, but glimpsed only briefly in the distance. It stood at the extreme edge of Treuheim, a huge, dark, sinister edifice that had been built hundreds of years ago by the first princes of Wolfenberg. From here they'd defended their country from enemies and controlled their subjects. To be sent to The Fort was a terrifying fate. Over the centuries, men and women had been swallowed up by its cold, stone walls and never seen again. Once, there had been stories of torture and terrible screaming, and it was said that the walls ran with blood. When continental Europe had opened up to English travelers, those who lived in The Fort's shadow had made a good living retelling legends of reproachful ghosts that appeared wailing on the battlements, always in places that could be conveniently seen from the street.

Now The Fort housed the crown jewels and most of the royal archives, and was only occasionally used as a prison when tight security was needed. Prisoners were rare, and the arrival of one very late at night had caused great excitement. Two hours later, the sensation had died down, but the guards were still tense and suspicious. The sight of two figures coming slowly out of the darkness on horseback made them stand alert, bayonets at the ready. Brasch, the senior guard, called, "Halt and declare yourself."

There was no answer, but the leading figure dismounted and stepped into the lamplight. "My lord!" The guards stood to attention as they recognized Reinald.

"Can you be trusted?" the archduke asked softly.

"Give me the chance to prove it, my lord."

"Good. Then conduct me to the governor, and do so without rousing the whole place. I'm here on the prince's most secret business." He lowered his voice still further. "Most secret," he repeated. "So you will send no message on ahead to inform the governor of my coming, but simply take me to him now."

Red with importance, Brasch saluted. He ventured to give an inquiring look at the other arrival, a small man with a hunched back, but Reinald didn't enlighten him. He merely spoke curtly to his companion. "Follow six paces behind, and make no sound."

Brasch escorted Reinald and the small man deep into the heart of the castle, to the rooms occupied by Captain Leven. At the door, Reinald spoke to the guard. "Now return to your post and speak to no one about this," he ordered. "You've served Wolfenberg well."

Disappointed but thrilled, Brasch turned away. But he walked slowly, and could hear Reinald command his misshapen companion to remain outside the door, before he entered without knocking.

Captain Leven, the governor of The Fort, roused from his bed to receive an unexpected prisoner, had just managed to get back to sleep when he was roused a second time and, in his dressing gown and slippers, was forced to confront Reinald. He began to sputter apologies, but the archduke silenced him graciously. "Not a word, Captain. It is I who should apologize for disturbing you without warning, but the prince's business must be conducted privately, between men of discretion." His nod seemed to invite Leven into a charmed circle. Leven sighed inwardly with relief. The archduke was a great man.

"You've received a prisoner tonight," Reinald continued. "A traitor to the state, who's conspired against the life of our prince. Be sure you keep him safe."

"I couldn't believe it. Count Gruber—a traitor?"

Reinald nodded. "A man the prince trusted. He must be made to talk. I'm here to interrogate him, but for reasons of state, it must be done in the strictest secrecy. I know I can rely on you."

The captain nodded, but a frown creased his forehead. "I had orders to allow no one to talk to the prisoner," he ventured timidly.

"So I should hope," Reinald said at once. "I urged the prince to sign such orders. I'm happy to know that he took my advice. You're a good fellow, Captain, and I shall commend you to his royal highness for your devotion to duty. No doubt you're overdue for promotion." His friendly smile encouraged the captain to mutter something about disappointed hopes. "An oversight," Reinald declared. "It must be remedied immediately. Come, we'll drink to your success."

He took out a silver flask and poured a measure into the little cup, handing it to Leven. "Success should be toasted in the finest brandy," he declared. "Your health, Captain."

Pop-eyed with wonder at this magnificent condescension the Captain downed the measure in one gulp. It tasted a little sweet for brandy, but that might have been the effect of his heady delight. Reinald grinned at him in a comradely fashion that made his heart swell. "Another?" he said, and filled the cup Captain Leven held out. "To your success."

"But you do not drink," Leven pointed out timidly.

Reinald smiled and upended the flask. "There's none left. But I drink to you in my heart, and to all good fellows like you. Now, if you've finished, you may conduct me to Gruber."

It would have taken a braver and cleverer man than Captain Leven to press the point that his orders made no exceptions. He hurriedly pulled on his clothes and conducted Reinald up a flight of stairs, followed by the little man who had waited outside the door. "The count is in our most secure cell, overlooking the courtyard where the executions have always taken place," Leven prattled as they went.

"A most suitable place for him," Reinald agreed.

"If he's conspired against the prince's life, perhaps his own execution will follow soon?" Leven suggested, smothering a yawn.

"There's no doubt of it," Reinald said grimly.

They came at last to a cavernous antechamber, furnished only by a chair and table, at which sat a rat-faced man, playing solitaire. Reinald stood back in the shadows. "Who is he?" he inquired softly.

"Turpitz. An excellent man, your lordship."

"Without arousing his suspicions, find a way to be rid of him."

Reinald remained in the shadows while the captain sauntered forward with contrived casualness. "Any trouble from the prisoner?" he asked.

"Not a thing, sir," Turpitz snickered. "He's started writing something. I shouted through the bars to him once but he didn't look up. He writes as if the devil were driving him."

"I'll take over for the rest of the night. Be off to your rooms. And not a word to your wife."

Turpitz vanished down another corridor, and Reinald emerged, followed by the little misshapen man. "Leave me the key, and disappear," he said. "When I depart, I'll return the key to you." Then, seeing doubt on the captain's face, he clapped him on the shoulder, declaring, "Rely on me to see to your promotion."

Another yawn overwhelmed Leven, this time too big to be smothered. He smiled vaguely and left. Reinald took up the key and turned to Luther. "Stay here and make sure no one approaches," he ordered, and turned without waiting for an answer.

When he entered the cell, it seemed as if Gruber didn't hear him. He was sitting at the small wooden table, scribbling madly. Reinald stood before him. When Gruber still paid him no heed, Reinald contemptuously sent the pen flying from the baron's hand and forced Gruber to his feet. "Let me look at the traitor," he said disdainfully. He waited for an answer, but Gruber didn't speak, although he turned wild eyes on his tormentor. "A man so eaten up with pride that he tries to force his will on the prince."

"Before God, I am no traitor," Gruber declared hoarsely. "I did what I believed right for Wolfenberg. In the past . . . the prince was guided by me. . . ."

"The prince was a boy when he came to the throne," Reinald snapped. "But he's been a man for a long time now—a man ordained by God to lead this country. What you have done is not merely treason, it's sacrilege."

"I meant . . . for the best," Gruber said heavily. "I dreamed of Wolfenberg's glory—"

"By conspiring with our enemy?" Reinald sneered.

A fanatical light came into the old baron's eyes. "Bismarck isn't our enemy," he insisted. "If there have been assassination attempts, I do not—*cannot* believe that he's behind them. He's Wolfenberg's truest friend. He dreams of a united Germany, a great, brilliant nation, showing the world the path to the future. I wanted Wolfenberg to be part of that dream."

"So it was idealism that caused you to betray state secrets?" Reinald demanded caustically. "It was highmindedness that made you tell Bismarck of a loan to strengthen the country's army?"

"Bismarck already knew that."

Reinald stared at him. "He *told* you so?"

"Not in so many words, but . . . there were little signs. He wasn't surprised."

Reinald strode to the window, his long cloak swirling with every step, and stood, arms akimbo, staring down into the courtyard. "What else did he tell you?" he asked over his shoulder. "Or rather, what other 'little signs' did you imagine you detected?"

"Only that."

"Come, there must be more. You trusted him with Wolfenberg's secrets. He must have trusted you with some of Prussia's."

"He told me of his vision for Germany. It seemed a great enterprise—"

"What else did you talk about?"

"Nothing else. I swear it."

Reinald swung around. His face was livid, making the scar stand out. "That won't do. You gave him information about us, now you must give us information about him."

"I have told all I know," Gruber said stubbornly.

"What else did he tell you?"

"Nothing. Nothing. It was a great and glorious dream."

"You vain, stupid old man," Reinald sneered. "Your 'glorious dream' was to be nothing but a monument to yourself."

"It *is* glorious," Gruber insisted fiercely. "Germany must unite, must become a great power to counterbalance England. All my life I've seen the continent dominated by English might, English wealth, English arrogance. Of course they want to keep Germany fragmented, so that we can't challenge them. They see Wolfenberg as the weak link, and they're using every unscrupulous means to keep it weak. They've even sent their agent to help lure Klaus Friederich into their clutches."

"Their *agent?* I assure you, Gruber, if there was an English agent in Wolfenberg, I should know about it."

"Would you? Aren't you also enchanted with her?"

"Who?"

"A light woman, who distracts the prince from his duty, because she's been sent to do so."

"Good God, what madness is this? Are you suggesting that the Duchess of Coniston works for British Intelligence?" Reinald demanded, almost amused.

"Of course not," Gruber said impatiently. "She's a mere woman—and a remarkably foolish one at that. The duchess is an adventuress, living on her wits and her erotic charms. She plainly has no idea of how she's being used. But when I saw her installed in those apartments, I understood the conspiracy. Until an English princess can be sent to marry him, they keep him in thrall to an English mistress."

His voice became higher in pitch, urgent. "This woman lives in a sink of depravity. I've had her watched. At night, she dresses in male garb and goes out to the most notorious part of the city, accompanied only by her groom."

"I think you must have taken leave of your senses," Reinald said impatiently.

"I tell you she's been seen going to The Black Dog, a haunt of disreputable characters—a place no decent woman would know about, much less visit wearing immodest attire."

There was a silence. Only the slight tightening of the mouth betrayed that Reinald recognized the name of The Black Dog, and in the half-light, Gruber didn't see it. Nor would it have availed him anything if he had noticed. His life was drawing to its close.

"So it's come to this," Reinald said at last. "In your desperate attempts to mitigate your crime, you seek to blacken an innocent woman. You're unfit to live."

Gruber's head went up. "But I *will* live," he declared, "because I must. One day soon, Prince Klaus will see how he's been deluded. Then he'll summon me, and together we shall guide Wolfenberg to her destiny. I'm writing him a letter—"

"So I see. You think he cares for your excuses?"

"I make no excuses," Gruber declared proudly. "This letter is my *justification*. When he reads it, he'll understand where his duty lies."

The archduke gave him an ironic look. "I'll leave you to your delusions, old man," he said. "You may find they make cold bedfellows."

It was about ten minutes later that Reinald let himself quietly out of the cell. The antechamber was dark and, apart from Luther, empty. Luther watched as his master locked the door, and crept silently after him as he returned to Leven's room and entered without knocking. The captain was slumped over the table, snoring loudly. "I've come to return the key, as I promised, Captain," Reinald said.

A sleepy groan was his only answer. Reinald surveyed him for a moment. "You're an excellent fellow," he said gravely.

"And it was excellent brandy," Luther snickered. "It'll be hours before he wakes."

"What's more important, it'll be hours before he sends the guard back to Gruber's cell. It wouldn't suit my purpose at all for anyone to look into that cell before morning." Reinald laid the heavy iron key down carefully, without a sound, and stood listening. All about them The Fort seemed to be sleeping. He thought of what he'd left behind him in the cell, and for a moment his eyes were hard. Then he strode away, followed by Luther.

As he rode home, Reinald was sunk in thought, and Luther stayed silent. But he kept close to his master, and his gaze never left him. After a while, Reinald raised his head and spoke without looking at his servant. "You heard everything?"

"Everything," Luther confirmed.

There was another long silence before Reinald said. "You know The Black Dog?"

"I know it well, master."

Reinald spurred his horse forward and put a distance between them. Nothing more was said. No words were necessary.

Chapter Ten

Leonie was with Klaus next morning, at the very moment the news came. The messenger arrived while they were visiting the stables together to inspect a new horse that Klaus had acquired, when a guard appeared in the stable yard. Leonie discreetly drew aside while the man spoke. She couldn't hear the words, but she discerned the guard's pallor and the fact that his message terrified him. As he listened, Klaus's face became suddenly haggard. "How could this have happened?" he demanded harshly. "I gave orders that he was to be watched." The wretched messenger looked helpless. "The governor of The Fort is to attend me at once," Klaus snapped. "Why isn't he here now?"

"Captain—Leven—is on his way," the messenger stammered. "He sent me on ahead to—to—"

"To tell me what he lacked the courage to say himself," Klaus finished bitterly. "You may leave."

The man mopped his forehead and departed. Leonie came quickly to Klaus's side. "What's happened?"

"Count Gruber was found dead in his cell this morning," he told her in a strained voice.

"Dead? But how?"

"He used his belt to hang himself from the bars. I gave orders that anything that might be used as a weapon should

be taken away from him, but I supposed no one thought—
Oh, my God!" A shudder went through him. Then he
seemed to become aware of the stable hands nearby. He
lifted his head and his jaw set. "Not here," he said. "Come
inside with me."

Together they went to his official apartments. As soon as
the door had closed behind them, Leonie threw protocol to
the winds and put her arms around Klaus, unable to bear the
look of agony on his face. "I never sought his death," he
whispered, holding her close. "He had to be punished, but
not—not like this."

"You're not to blame," she urged.

"I'm the prince," he said fiercely. "I'm responsible.
Don't you understand? There's no burden that I can refuse
to shoulder."

"But you don't have to seek them," she said, firm in her
turn. She drew back to look into his face. "He nearly caused
your death. Whether you believe he conspired in your assassination or whether you think he was only Bismarck's
dupe, it makes no difference. He revealed a chink in your
armor through which you could be killed. I can't forgive
him for that and I won't pretend I'm sorry he's dead. It's no
more than justice."

He looked down into her face and his own softened into
tenderness. "My dear defender," he murmured. "I've never
known you to speak so harshly. I think you'd take on the
whole country for my sake."

"The whole world," she said passionately. "Oh, my love,
don't blame yourself. It wasn't your fault."

"All roads lead to the prince. I can't escape that." He
pulled her hard against him. "Thank God I have you!" he
said. "You make it bearable. Without you—" He broke off
and buried his face against her hair as she tried to give him
all the comfort in her power.

A small click drew her attention to the door. Reinald had just appeared and was about to retreat. "Forgive me," he said. "I heard the news and hastened here. I should have knocked but—" he gave Leonie an apologetic smile "—I'm so used to being free to enter unannounced—"

"And you always will be," Klaus said at once. "I would have sent for you directly. I just needed a moment to come to terms with the horror of what's happened."

Reinald grasped the hand Klaus held out to him, then he held out his other hand to Leonie. She took it, enjoying the sense of three-way comradeship that Reinald's presence could give. He smiled, but he was looking at her with an expression she hadn't seen before. She was used to his suppressed longing, but now his brilliant dark eyes held a new look, appraising, almost puzzled. The thought passed quickly. Her mind was full of other worries. "Klaus blames himself," she told Reinald. "Tell him he mustn't. Gruber deserved the worst that could happen to him."

"I agree," Reinald said at once. "There should be no mercy for such as he. Why should you blame yourself?" he demanded of Klaus.

"I feel I didn't deal with him last night as well as I might have done," Klaus said heavily. "I was shocked and disillusioned. It made me cruel. But I never meant to drive him to suicide."

Reinald shook his head. "If he was driven to this act by anyone's intemperate words, they weren't yours, but mine. I have a confession to make. Last night I went to The Fort."

"And saw Gruber?" Klaus asked sharply.

"Yes. I know your orders were that no one should speak to him, but I assumed that didn't apply to me. Perhaps I was wrong, but you've often made me an exception in the past, and my rage and scorn were such that I couldn't rest until I'd confronted him."

"And what passed between you?"

Reinald grimaced. "Nothing satisfactory. I wanted to know how he could have brought himself to do such a thing, but he only poured out fanatical nonsense. He was maddened by his own pride."

"Did he admit to conspiring to have Klaus killed?" Leonie demanded.

Reinald's eyes rested on her, and for a moment the appraising look was there again. If she hadn't been so preoccupied, she might have thought he seemed like a man embarking on a desperate but calculated gamble. "No," Reinald said at last. "He didn't admit that. He swore he was Bismarck's dupe. But perhaps his letter will be more revealing. He was writing a long 'justification' when I left. No doubt it will have been found by now."

There was a noise outside, and the sound of Captain Leven's high-pitched voice. A footman opened the double doors and announced the captain who strode in with an appearance of confidence that vanished almost at once. In a stammering voice, he reported going to Gruber's cell that morning and finding him hanging. "What time was that?" Klaus demanded.

"About . . . nine o'clock," Leven confessed.

Klaus stared. "Nobody looked in on him until nine o'clock?" he demanded.

"I—I overslept this morning, your highness—the disturbances of the night, I—somehow—found it—hard to awake."

"So, your prisoner was left unattended until nine o'clock?" Klaus repeated grimly. "And when you visited him, he was dead."

"Yes, highness. He was quite cold and stiff," Leven added placatingly, as though fearing that someone might have expected him to bring Gruber back to life.

Klaus regarded Leven with disdain. "My orders were to have him closely watched *at all times*," he snapped. "Was there no man on duty?"

"Indeed there was, your highness," Captain Leven said eagerly. "A most excellent man, named Turpitz, loyal and conscientious."

"Then why didn't he discover this before? If Gruber had been dead long enough to become cold and stiff, what had Turpitz been doing?"

"But—when his lordship—that is—" Leven looked miserably at Reinald.

"I had Turpitz sent away so that I could talk to Gruber without an eavesdropper," Reinald intervened. Leven nodded and mopped his forehead, but his relief was short-lived, for Reinald's next words were, "But the guard should have been returned to his post when I left. You may recall, Captain, that I reminded you of that fact when I brought you back the key?"

Leven, who'd certainly found the key on his table that morning, regarded him in miserable confusion. "You may also recall the conversation we had before I saw Gruber," Reinald added quietly.

"Yes, your lordship." Any further protests the captain might have made were drowned in the elusive hope of promotion.

"And the letter he was writing when I left?" Reinald asked. "No doubt you've brought that to give to his highness?"

The captain put his hand into his pocket and brought something out. He seemed about to expire from misery as he opened his fingers to reveal a mass of tiny pieces of torn paper. "I found this on the floor," he whispered.

The paper had been destroyed with great diligence. Scarcely a single piece was larger than a grain of rice. To fit it together would be an impossible task.

Klaus's face was dark with fury. He barked out an order, and the two guards on duty outside the room immediately appeared. "Arrest Captain Leven," he commanded. "He is charged with dereliction of duty." He tore the epaulets from Leven's shoulder and turned his back. The hapless captain cast a beseeching look at Reinald before he was escorted away, stammering protests.

When they were alone, Reinald said heavily, "Perhaps you should arrest me also. I brought much of this about. My condemnation must have driven him to this. If I'd acted with more restraint—"

Klaus managed a faint, wintry smile. "I'll swear that's the first time you've ever acted without restraint," he said. "My grandfather used to hold you up as an example to me when my temper got the better of me."

"Even the most reserved of men can allow his feelings to get the better of him," Reinald said in a strange voice.

"Evidently." Klaus sighed. "It would have been useful to know what more he had to tell, but there's no point in fretting about what can't be changed. I'm more concerned with the danger Gruber has caused. At least the British loan gives us a stronger army. It could even be useful that Bismarck knows we're less vulnerable."

Reinald nodded. "There are three battalions of mercenaries heading for the border this minute. I've hired the best, and believe me, Bismarck knows the best when he sees it. But it will take money to keep them loyal. When does the next installment of the loan arrive?"

"Any day." Klaus's tone became guarded. "I'm reliably informed that the signal for its release has already been sent.

Money alone isn't enough, however. I plan to go to the border myself to inspect the troops.''

"An excellent idea. In the meantime, may I ask what you intend to do with that fool, Leven?"

"Court-martial him," Klaus said harshly.

"He undoubtedly deserves it," Reinald conceded. "But I feel some responsibility here. I was also to blame, and it troubles me that he alone should bear the brunt of your anger. If he were quietly dismissed from the army, surely that should meet the case?"

Klaus considered. "I suppose there's some justice in that," he said at last. "Very well. Just get him out of the army and don't let me see him again."

While this exchange was taking place, Leonie had remained discreetly in the background, although in earshot. Now she dropped a brief curtsy and asked permission to leave. Klaus pressed her hand and murmured that he would see her later.

In her own rooms she made another attempt on the report that she'd abandoned the previous night. It was easier now to show that matters were still unresolved, and her continued presence here was essential.

Later that afternoon, Masham collected the letter from her. He would take it to the embassy, from where it would travel in the diplomatic bag, courtesy of an agent who'd been placed on the embassy staff. No one had felt it necessary to inform the ambassador about this, Lord William having a tolerably accurate idea of the man's mental abilities. When he had delivered the letter to the embassy, Masham would proceed to The Black Dog with instructions to Blair to move some men nearer the border, in preparation for the prince's inspection of his troops.

* * *

There was a mysterious postscript to these events. The wretched Captain Leven, dismissed from the army, was relieved to receive a visit from Luther, with news of a lucrative appointment on one of Reinald's more distant estates. Luther gave him money for the journey, and told him to start immediately. Eagerly Leven did so, but he never reached his destination. Since nobody there had been told to expect him, no questions were asked, and Leven was never heard of again.

It was Lady Coniston's habit to receive visitors early in the day while the prince conferred with his ministers. One morning, the last person to be announced was Lord Hadden, British Ambassador to Wolfenberg. He was a tall white-haired man with an imposing air, who looked the part completely, but the diplomatic grapevine called him a buffoon. This morning, however, he was all charm and affability as he extended an invitation to a formal reception at the embassy. "My secretary had instructions to include you at all costs," he said, beaming. "I thought I'd make quite sure."

Leonie, who'd not only received her invitation but formally accepted several days ago, was instantly alert. Plainly, Lord Hadden had another motive in calling on her, and by letting him bumble on while she served him tea, she would soon discover what it was.

Her patience was rewarded when he cleared his throat and said, "Lord Palmerston writes that he's delighted by the lucky chance that led you to gain such influence over the prince." He spoke without irony. Nobody would have been so foolish as to confide the true situation to this vacuous timeserver. "I won't trouble such a gracious lady with dull politics—"

Straight-faced, Leonie replied, "How kind."

"Suffice it to say that anything that advances the British interest in Wolfenberg is to be encouraged." Apparently fearing that this last sentence might be too sensible for her to comprehend, he chuckled and added, "Although you didn't suspect it, dear Duchess, while following your own—ah—amiable inclinations, you have been incidentally serving your country."

Leonie commented that there was no knowing how life would unfold.

"Quite...ah...quite! The fact is I had another reason for coming to see you. Under cover of an invitation, I wished to ask you to join me in a little conspiracy. There. What do you think of that?"

Leonie professed herself overwhelmed at the thought of assisting a man who moved among great affairs of state, and Lord Hadden preened. Privately she was wondering how quickly she could get him to the point.

"But I beg you not to be alarmed by the mention of a conspiracy," he bumbled on. "It's a very charming little conspiracy, one that I know will appeal to a lady. In fact, it's about marriage. Yes. That's right. Marriage. In fact, the prince's marriage. To Princess Louise, you know."

An observant man might have noticed the small clatter as Leonie laid her teacup too quickly in the saucer. Luckily, Lord Hadden was off on a flight of his own. "It must be an English wife, you see, if only to stop him marrying a pesky foreigner. And then there's the heir. Half-English. Oh yes, the ideal marriage."

"Except that Princess Louise is fifteen years his junior," Leonie said, a mite sharply.

"Best thing in the world. Her mind will be wide-open like a flower, ready to be molded by her husband." Lord Hadden mixed his metaphors with abandon.

"I heard rumors of a possible marriage while I was in London," Leonie said cautiously, "but my impression was that the queen was not in favor of the match."

"Nothing to worry about," Hadden declared with airy condescension. "Just a whim of the kind you ladies are prone to. I'm sure you won't misunderstand my saying that."

"Not at all."

"Palmerston is determined about this marriage, and in the end, the queen will bow to wiser counsels. In the meantime, we rely on you to keep the idea to the forefront of the prince's mind, and promote it whenever possible." It plainly didn't occur to him that Leonie's own relationship with Klaus might provide any complications.

She murmured something about being glad to serve her country, but the words were mechanical. Inwardly she was stunned. If only he would go so she could be alone with her tormented thoughts.

It took another half hour to be rid of him, a half hour during which she put on a sweet guileless face, uttered inanities and endured the agony of the dying. At last Hadden bowed himself out and she was free to confront her own feelings. She was angry with herself. She had no right to be so taken aback. She'd always known that Klaus must make a state marriage soon, but she'd blinded herself to the thought while her feelings for him escalated out of control. Such a loss of detachment was shockingly unprofessional.

She told herself this with great firmness for a while, but at last the front collapsed and she was forced to see herself as she was; not a secret agent lamenting a professional mistake, but a woman who loved a man who could never be hers. She was too much of a realist to think Klaus could marry her, however much he might love her. Now she must try to make him marry another woman.

They were to dine alone together that night. Leonie supervised the dinner, tasted each dish, and dismissed the servants. She'd lavished every care on her appearance. Her gown of black satin had been delivered only that morning, and the prince's diamonds adorned her hair, wrists and bosom. She looked every inch the favorite.

But Klaus, accustomed to seeing the woman rather than the favorite, had a strange sense of something wrong as soon as he arrived. He could feel the tension in her slim, beautiful body as soon as he took her in his arms. She came to him quickly, but she didn't melt with joy in the way he was used to. Her kiss was passionate but without tenderness. Rather, it had something fierce and purposeful about it, and her eyes, when he drew back to look into them, were wild.

"Tonight we're completely alone," she told him as she led him to the table. "No servants. I shall serve you myself."

"That will be delightful," he said, turning to watch her graceful movements as she worked. This wasn't the first time she'd served him, but still he couldn't rid himself of an odd feeling. There was a cold brilliance about her that made the very air seem jagged.

"I haven't seen much of you today," he said. "I'd hoped we might go riding together this afternoon, but my messenger couldn't find you." He tried a familiar joke. "How can I be safe if no one knows where my bodyguard is?"

She flung him a dazzling smile. "But I have so many things to do. To be the official favorite is a great responsibility. Don't you realize that fashionable society can take not one single step without my leadership? Why, with a wave of my hand I could decree that each woman must pad out her shoulders to a width of six feet. The strain of making such decisions gives me constant headaches."

"Let them pad out as much as they like. I shall see only you," he responded gallantly.

"For as long as I'm here," she agreed, nodding in recognition of his compliment. "But when I'm gone...think of the hideous legacy I might leave behind me."

"Are you planning to depart?" Klaus inquired. "I didn't know."

She gave an elegant shrug that caused the rivière of diamonds to flash and sparkle in the candlelight. "Some day I must leave. Someday you will marry."

"Someday." He growled a reluctant agreement. "Let's leave it there. Someday in the distant future." Something in her silence made him look at her sharply. "What's happened? Has Queen Victoria consented?"

"No."

"Thank heavens for that!"

"But I gather it's only a question of time. After all, how can a mere woman hold out against the will of men?" She gave a tinkling laugh.

"I wish you'd stop this," Klaus said quietly. "You're not like yourself tonight."

She made an elegant gesture of submission. "As my prince commands."

"I'm suspicious of this meekness," he said, trying to tease her. "It's so unlike you that it leaves me feeling lost in a strange country without a map."

"But I'm your favorite," she reminded him. "And the favorite exists only to please."

"It doesn't please me to hear you speak of leaving me."

Leonie shrugged, but her eyes were watching him guardedly. "I'm a professional, doing my job. Eventually this assignment will be finished and I shall pass on to the next."

In the silence, he looked at her strangely. "And how do you feel about that?"

She shrugged again. "All assignments are alike to me."

"That isn't true," he said quietly.

"It has to be true. I'm a servant of my country. I never forget that and neither should you."

"And what has England told you to do now?" he demanded with an edge to his voice.

"To encourage an alliance between your country and mine, an alliance that can only be forged by marriage. Personal considerations don't come into it. How can they?"

"How can they?" Klaus echoed, staring at her.

"So you see, my time here is nearly up. It only remains for me to bring matters to a satisfactory conclusion." She moved away to the mantelpiece so that she wouldn't have to look at him.

"Do *you* consider it satisfactory?" he asked.

"A successful mission is always a feather in my cap," she told him lightly.

"And that's all this is—a successful mission?"

"You're alive, aren't you? It was my job to keep you so, by any means in my power. And you must admit, I've done my work brilliantly."

"Oh, yes," he murmured, not taking his eyes from her. "Brilliantly. There's nothing you won't do in the furtherance of your professional aims. Is that what you want me to think?"

She was racked by indecision. It was a torment to think he might really believe what she was telling him. He rose and moved closer and looked down at her. "Answer me, Leonie," he insisted. *"What are you telling me?"*

She couldn't endure that intent gaze. It threatened her resolve. She turned away from him and spoke over her shoulder. "That my job here will be done when I've persuaded you to press England for a quick marriage." She gave a brittle laugh. "Perhaps then, you'll award me the Wolfenberg Order of Merit, *First*-class—for services above and beyond the call of duty."

Goaded beyond endurance, he pulled her around to face him. "*That's enough.* Do you know what you're saying?"

"I always know," she said breathlessly. "I'm a good agent, always in control—"

The words were cut off by his mouth on hers. "Are you in control now?" he demanded angrily.

"Yes...yes—" she tried to say.

"And now?" His arms crushed her, while his slow, suffocating kiss nearly made her faint. "Are you in control now?" he whispered.

"Yes—"

"And now?" He lifted her in his arms and strode toward the bedroom.

"Klaus," she protested faintly.

"Think of it as a service above and beyond the call of duty," he said grimly.

In the past, he'd undressed her slowly and loved every moment, but now he ripped her clothes from her, shredding the beautiful gown and scattering her diamonds over the floor. Her elaborate coiffure vanished as he pulled her hair down over her shoulders, trying to make her look again like the woman he loved and less like a stranger. He tore his own clothes off in seconds and seized her in his arms, running his hands over her nakedness. "Is this a service to duty?" he demanded.

"Everything—I do—" She gasped. She didn't know what she was saying. This was what she lived for, and he was asking her to deny it even while her body ached for him. Her hot Gypsy blood began to pound in her veins, thrilled by his primitive approach. Just as Klaus was no longer making love like a gentleman, so she could abandon gentility and take him as she wanted him, fiercely and with scorching passion, asking no quarter and giving none. Now they were both naked. He lifted her again in arms that trembled, and laid her on the bed, stretching out beside her and pulling her into his arms.

"Now," he said, "let me hear you tell me to marry another woman."

She managed to say, "Your duty—" before he cut her off.

"Tonight there's no duty," he said. "Tonight there's only you and me."

He kissed her deeply, driving his tongue between her lips, and ran feverish hands over her, caressing, teasing. But now there was a new element. This time, he was dominating. Maddened by her elusiveness, he'd remembered that he was the prince, and it was for the prince to command. With every touch, he commanded her to respond to him and she obeyed helplessly. The movements of his mouth on hers commanded her to drive out all other thoughts but him, and she had no choice but to do as the prince ordered. There *was* no other man but him, nor would there be, for the rest of her life.

He made love to her hungrily, almost fiercely. For once, there was neither tenderness nor subtlety, but only a power that overwhelmed her. His arms were like a prison, the loins that drove into her were steel. The fierceness of his loving ignited a response deep in her, a response of fire. She'd been born for a man who could love like this, a man who could carry her into the heart of a furnace and keep her there while they burned up together. She fought him back, passion for passion, lust for lust. When he'd finished, she was ready for him again, reawakening his desire, inciting him on to greater vigor.

At last they both lay exhausted, like combatants who'd battled each other to a standstill, neither yielding an inch. There was a grimly triumphant look in his eyes as he looked down at her. "Tell me to marry another woman," he said, "and mean it."

She could only shake her head. She was breathless.

"Good," he said. "Then let's hear no more of such talk. For us, there's only the moment, and this moment will last a long time. My love, the night is still young...."

Laughing, she went back into his arms.

"Well, what do you think?" Reinald asked as the carriage conveyed them to the ball at the British embassy. "Will the evening be intolerably boring or merely boring?"

"Merely boring," Leonie answered with a smile. "You really dislike balls, don't you?"

He shrugged. "They're part of my duty and must be endured. But I admit I prefer to attend as few as possible."

"Is tonight part of your duty?"

He looked at her in the dim light of the carriage. "Yes— my duty to you. Klaus has to arrive and leave with Sylvana, of course, and I didn't want you to arrive alone. Your position is often very difficult."

"You make it less so by your chivalry," she said warmly. "How kind of you to think of me."

At last the carriage drew up outside the brilliantly lit entrance. Reinald brushed aside the footman to assist her himself, and together they passed in. Lord and Lady Hadden stood just inside the ballroom, receiving the guests as they were announced by the majordomo. When compliments had been exchanged, Leonie and Reinald were free to enter and mingle with the other guests.

Duffer he might be, but Lord Hadden knew how to give a party. The magnificent ballroom was at its best, hung with flowers and with every facet of the chandeliers gleaming. Most of the guests had already arrived and a buzz of conversation rose on the air. Reinald passed the time introducing her to various of his acquaintances.

Suddenly her ear picked up the sound of a familiar name. The majordomo was announcing, "The Duke and Duchess of Coniston, and their daughter, Lady Harriet Coniston."

"Harriet," Leonie said, delighted. "She wrote me that they were taking a trip to Europe, but I didn't know they were here."

"Coniston?" Reinald inquired. "Your family?"

"The family of my late husband."

Harriet had already noticed her. Forgetting decorum, she waved excitedly at Leonie, and scurried the length of the ballroom, the billowing of her white tulle gown making her look like a beautiful bird in flight, to throw her arms about her. Leonie hugged her back with equal enthusiasm.

"It's so lovely to see you," Harriet bubbled. "You look so beautiful. Are you having a wonderful time? Everyone's talking about you, even in England." She rushed on, words tumbling over one another, while Leonie laughed and vainly tried to stem the tide.

But it was Gwendolyn who subdued her daughter, simply by catching up with her and uttering her name. Harriet fell silent while her mother greeted Leonie with frosty courtesy. She was awe-inspiring in crimson velvet with the Coniston rubies about her neck. Cecil, as usual, looked as if he would have liked to shuffle out of sight. Leonie presented the family to Reinald, which slightly soothed Gwendolyn's ruffled feathers. Reinald demonstrated his loftiest courtesy and she was too pleased with herself to notice the touch of disdain in his manner.

Luckily, before she could find something else to annoy her, the majordomo announced the arrival of the prince, and everyone turned to watch Klaus enter the room with Sylvana on his arm. Behind them, at a discreet distance, came Sylvana's lady-in-waiting, and Klaus's equerry. Leonie sensed Harriet's eager start beside her, and realized that the equerry on duty tonight was Bernhard.

The first part of the evening was taken up with duty dances. Klaus opened the ball with Lady Hadden, while Lord Hadden danced with Sylvana. Leonie, whirling in Reinald's arms, saw Harriet standing in her mother's shadow like a lamb being guarded by a dragon, until at last she was claimed by an amiable courtier whom Leonie knew to have vast wealth, a great title and no brains whatever.

When at last she could dance with Klaus, he said, "I don't know what's the trouble with Bernhard tonight. He's normally excellent at his job, but suddenly I can't get his attention."

"Haven't you seen who's here?" Leonie laughed. "My granddaughter."

"Lady Harriet? But surely that was a passing fancy?"

"Well, he keeps asking me if I've heard from her. When her letters arrive, I always try to find some passage to read out to him, and he hangs on the words. If he's distracted, it's because he's hoping for a dance and he can't see any opportunity. Gwendolyn won't let Harriet dance with anyone under the rank of duke, and even a duke is a disappointment to her."

"Why, what can she be hoping for?"

Leonie raised an eyebrow satirically. "Royalty of course. Gwendolyn is related to the blood royal."

"Whose blood royal?" he asked, only half believing her.

"The house of Saxe-Coburg-Gotha, and through them the crown of England, and of Wolfenberg, too. She's sure to mention it herself. Poor Bernhard."

Klaus grinned. "Shall we see if we can get past her guard?"

"Let's."

He waltzed her over to where Gwendolyn stood talking to
the ambassador. She beamed as she saw the prince approach, and even Bernhard's immediate appearance didn't
cause her smile to fade. "How delightful to renew your acquaintance, Duchess," Klaus said, at his most affable.
"Lady Harriet." He nodded to Harriet, who blushed and
shrank back a little, overcome by awe. "I have such pleasant memories of our first meeting, in England," Klaus
added mendaciously. "I believe I introduced my good friend
Bernhard von Leibnitz."

Gwendolyn's nod in Bernhard's direction was barely ad-
equate to the situation. Before she could gather her wits,
Klaus had offered her his arm. "I know Leonie longs for a
good gossip with Lady Harriet. Perhaps you will give me the
pleasure of a dance."

Gwendolyn beamed and allowed herself to be swept onto
the dance floor. Bernhard murmured to Leonie, "Didn't I
tell you he was the best of kind friends?" But his eyes were
on Harriet.

"I feel the need of an ice," Leonie declared. "I'm sure
Harriet does, too. Would you be kind enough to bring us
two ices, Bernhard—on the terrace?"

She linked arms with Harriet and took her out to the terrace, which had been hung with colored lamps. There were
several other people out there, but few enough to give an illusion of privacy. She was of two minds about what she was
doing. She didn't want to encourage Harriet and Bernhard
in a romance that had no future, but it could surely do no
harm to let them have a few moments together under her
chaperonage.

When Bernhard returned with the ices, the two young
people said little, and their few words were conventional,
even awkward, but their eyes spoke much.

"I was sorry to hear that you'd suffered a fall from your horse," Bernhard said. "But delighted that you recovered so well."

Harriet regarded him in wonder. "Why, however did you know about that?"

"It was in one of your letters," Leonie reminded her. "I believe I mentioned it to Bernhard."

"Yes, indeed," Bernhard confirmed, blushing to his roots. "I hope you have a less dangerous horse now," he added anxiously.

"Oh, but poor Dancer isn't dangerous," Harriet said with her innocent smile. "Her hoof struck a stone, that's all. She's never thrown me before."

"I'm delighted to hear it. I—I wish I could show you some of the rides near Treuheim. I assure you they're delightful."

"Oh, I'm sure they are."

Leonie loved Harriet and was fond of Bernhard, but a very little of this kind of conversation was enough to make her eager for a diversion. Yet she forced herself to stay quiet, doing her duty "like a good grandmother," as she put it to herself. Luckily, Klaus soon appeared on the scene, Gwendolyn on his arm. Bernhard was immediately on his feet.

"It's all right, Bernhard," Klaus told him. "You may consider yourself off duty for the rest of the evening."

"Thank you, sir." Bernhard turned to Gwendolyn. "May I have the honor of leading Lady Harriet onto the floor?"

"I'm afraid Harriet is looking too tired to dance anymore," Gwendolyn said.

"How unfortunate," Klaus said, his face darkening at this rudeness. "I was about to ask her myself."

"Oh, but of course," Gwendolyn simpered. "Naturally dear Harriet is only too happy to obey the royal command. She can manage one dance."

"But the first dance rightly belongs to Bernhard, who asked before me," Klaus said. "I could only be entitled to the second. Does Lady Harriet have sufficient strength for two?"

Thoroughly outmaneuvered, Gwendolyn forced a smile and declared, "Certainly she has."

"Bernhard, I rely on you to bring Lady Harriet to me when you've finished," Klaus said smoothly.

Bernhard flung him a look of gratitude and led Harriet away. Klaus offered Gwendolyn his arm. "Will you take a glass of wine with me, Duchess?"

They found Lord Hadden in the ballroom, searching for Klaus. He ordered wine for them all and then said fulsomely, "Perhaps I might venture to touch on certain very pleasing news that I believe will be announced shortly—er—news concerning the closer ties between our two countries." He faltered a little under the black look Klaus threw him, but didn't seem to know how to stop. "I'm in constant touch with Lord Palmerston, who assures me that matters in London are going very well—yes, very well." He mopped his forehead and his voice died away. Klaus had fixed him with a stare that would have intimidated a far braver man than Lord Hadden.

At last Klaus said in a voice of steel, "I believe it's time for me to claim my dance with Lady Harriet."

Bernhard was approaching with Harriet on his arm, her face flushed, her eyes shining, but she flinched at the sight of Klaus's thunderous look. He bowed and led her back onto the floor. Their dance was a disaster. Klaus was furious at Lord Hadden's clumsiness and the reminder of what must soon happen, and although he preserved a correct demeanor, his features were still sufficiently clouded to scare the gentle Harriet. She became wooden and awkward, blushing with mortification. He was too uneasy himself to set her at ease. Somehow they endured each other until it was time for him to lead her back to Gwendolyn.

In the final dance with Leonie, Klaus demanded, "Whatever was the matter with that child?"

"You frightened her. You were at your most intimidating."

"Nonsense, I'm the mildest of men. I own I could have wrung that fool Hadden's neck. Don't heed him, my love. It's a long way off."

She sighed. "I wish I might think so, but I have a terrible feeling that something is going to burst in on us any day."

His voice became tender. "Look up at me and smile, and nothing can go wrong for us."

She raised her head. "You're right. Nothing can go wrong for us."

The words were brave but they couldn't conceal the heartache, and they both knew it. He began to whirl her faster and faster. She gave herself up to the sensation, knowing that they were dancing ever closer to the void.

On the journey home, Leonie lay back against the squabs, exhausted by the evening. Usually her energy was enough to carry her through the longest ball, but tonight was different. She'd looked into a future without Klaus, and it was bleak.

"Is Hadden the clown he seems?" Reinald asked.

"I don't think he's a man of wide vision," Leonie said carefully. "I've heard he can be effective when he's set on something."

"And you know what he's set on now, don't you?"

"He wants Klaus to marry Princess Louise."

"And he'll get his way. Klaus knows his duty. But Leonie—" his voice deepened suddenly "—have you thought what it will mean to you?"

"I have some idea," she said with a faint sigh.

"You'll be banished, thrown off, when you of all women should grace the throne."

"But I'm not a princess," she observed lightly.

"You're more than a princess. Nature has made you a queen, and if he can't see it, I can. Leonie—" He'd moved to sit beside her, taking hold of her arms. "Listen to me," he said urgently. "There's so much I must say to you—"

She tried to fend him off. "It's better if you don't."

"But I must. I've been silent too long. *Leonie*—" With a sudden cry, he jerked her toward him, crushing her in his arms and pressing his mouth against hers. She tried to turn away but he yanked her head back while he forced kisses on her mouth, her face, her neck.

"No!" she said fiercely. "Reinald, don't do this."

"I must," he rasped. "Do you think I'm made of stone, to stand by day after day and never speak of my passion? From the moment I met you, I knew you had to belong to me. I thought no woman could ever mean so much to me, but you engulf me. You possess my heart and soul utterly. I drown in you. I spend my life in torment, wondering when I'll see you again. I can't touch you without trembling. I love you to distraction, and you *will* hear me."

He crushed her mouth again before she could answer. Leonie had ceased trying to fight him. It was useless. He was beyond reason. So she let herself go limp, lying motionless and unresponsive in his arms while he covered her with burning kisses. At last he raised his head. His face was suffused and he was gasping. "Do you think you'll alienate me by lying there like a dead woman?" he asked. "You're wrong. If your body is cold now, I look forward to the day that will change."

"It will never change," she told him tonelessly.

"It has to change. It *must* change. Klaus can't marry you, can't honor you as you deserve, but I can. Leonie, listen to me. On our wedding night, I will kneel at your feet and worship you as my goddess. When we lie naked together in the darkness, I will be both your master and your slave. Then your body will come alive in my arms."

"You're mad," she told him. "You're deluding yourself."

"It's you who lives in delusion. Don't you see that Klaus is only amusing himself before he makes a marriage of duty? But I *love* you. I love you enough to set aside the world's opinion. I can wait. I know you're his as long as he wants you. I can endure the torment, knowing that you'll be mine in the end."

"I'll never be yours," she cried angrily.

The scar stood out vividly against his pale face. "Don't say that. If I thought you'd never belong to me, I'd—" A shudder shook his frame. "Don't drive me to desperation with that thought. Say nothing. Let me hope. I can wait as long as I have to."

It was useless arguing with him. Leonie drew away, and this time he released her. She sank back into a corner, away from Reinald, never taking her eyes from him. He looked different. The madness was passing and outwardly he was resuming his old self, but he would never appear the same to her again. "You mustn't wait," she said. "I can never love you."

Even to her own ears, the words sounded brutal. His pain filled the carriage, making the air itself jagged. She could never love Reinald, but she'd always liked him, and now she pitied him. She suspected that beneath a rigid front, he was a man of deep feeling, a man whose love could only be aroused by one woman. It was his tragedy that he should have set his heart on her, who had nothing to offer him because she belonged body and soul to another man. "I'm sorry," she said with heartfelt sympathy. "I don't want to hurt you, but neither will I torment you with false hopes."

The silence lasted so long that she wondered if he'd heard her. At last he spoke in a voice that might have come from a dead man. "I ask your pardon."

"Please," she said, raising a hand to silence him, "say no more. The blame may be mine. If I've ever led you to suppose—"

"Your behavior has been beyond reproach at all times," he said, still in the same lifeless voice. "No man could blame you... or think you anything but perfect." They sat in uncomfortable silence for the rest of the journey. As the carriage drew up at the palace, Reinald spoke without looking at her. "Will you tell Klaus?"

"No," she said softly.

"Thank you."

He escorted her to the foot of the steps that led to her apartments, but tonight he didn't kiss her hand. Instead, he clicked his heels and gave her a formal bow before returning to the carriage without a backward look.

She brooded about Reinald as Miss Hatchard brushed her mistress's hair that night. She'd come to like him as a dear friend and it was in tribute to that friendship that she'd promised not to reveal his secret to Klaus. It would do no good, and merely damage the trust that had always existed between the cousins. But it was sad to think that the happy days, when the three of them had often felt like comrades together, were over.

Then Klaus arrived and took her into his arms, and all other thoughts were banished.

* * *

Reinald was the first of her visitors early the next morning. He was deathly pale, with dark circles beneath his eyes, and Leonie thought she'd never seen a face so full of suffering. Miss Hatchard was there when he arrived, and after a moment's hesitation, Leonie dismissed her. "Thank you," Reinald said. "It's kind of you still to trust me."

"You're a man of honor," Leonie said quietly. "I know there'll be no repetition of what happened last night."

"Honor?" he echoed. "When I think of you, I'm no longer sure what honor means. But I'm a man of intelligence. I made a mistake last night. I spoke of my passion when I should have spoken of my love."

"Please, Reinald—" She held up an imploring hand. He moved away until there were several feet between them.

"You see, I'll keep my distance. I'll never touch you again until you give me leave. And one day, you *will* give me leave, Leonie, because love such as mine cannot go unanswered. No woman was ever loved as you are, and you're too much a woman to stay indifferent to a man who worships you."

"Perhaps if I didn't love Klaus, it might have been you," she said, torn with pity, desiring only to comfort him. "But I do love Klaus."

"It might have been me," he repeated slowly. "You admit the possibility then?"

She saw the trap he was preparing for her and flinched. "It's useless to talk this way," she told him. "I love Klaus. I cannot love you. You must try to accept that."

"How can I accept it when I think of nothing but you, night and day?" he demanded bitterly. "My home is empty because it waits for you. My bed is empty because only you will ever share it with me. Don't tell me to accept what my heart says is impossible."

"We all have to do that," she flashed. "Do you think *my* heart finds it easy to contemplate Klaus's marriage? How often have I told myself it's impossible, that he loves me? But impossible or not, I know it has to be. And when the time comes, *I will accept it.* Please, Reinald, I want you to leave. And never speak to me of this again. Go away and forget all about it."

He took a step toward her and looked into her face. "I warned you last night not to deny me hope. I warn you now not to make me your enemy. I'm a good friend, and when the time comes, I'll be a devoted and faithful husband. But don't be my enemy."

She threw up her hands in a gesture of helplessness. "I'm not your enemy, Reinald. I never will be. I hope you'll never be mine."

"I hope so, too," he said quietly. Then he bowed and left her.

Chapter Eleven

The full, glorious summer was slipping away into autumn, tipping the leaves with orange, although the weather was still warm. Now there was tension in the city because the law courts were reassembling, and Crazne would come to trial.

Leonie had made it her business to discover whatever she could about him, with Masham's help. Anton Crazne owned and ran a small newspaper in which he spoke frankly about what he perceived as shortcomings in the government. He criticized Klaus for his despotic powers, although he conceded that they were mostly used "with restraint, and often generosity." He'd written:

> But, used or not, they exist. They remain for some future tyrant to abuse. Wolfenberg can be neither free nor safe until the prince seeks advice, not merely from a few appointees, but from men who are chosen by the people as a whole.

"Treason!" Reinald had exclaimed in disgust.

Klaus grinned. "You'll never get Leonie to say so. Crazne thinks the English system is ideal. Naturally she considers him a great man."

"And, I, too, admire many things about England," Reinald said quietly, "but her system of government wouldn't do for Wolfenberg."

Once, Leonie would have answered this with a teasing jest, but the old comradeship was now gone forever. She was wary of Reinald, afraid to say anything that he could interpret as encouragement. Superficially there seemed little cause for alarm. He never spoke to her of love, and she avoided being alone with him. But sometimes, as now, he would say something with a second meaning that seemed to draw her into a secret that only the two of them shared. At such times, she came close to telling Klaus what had passed, but she always backed off, partly because she was reluctant to disturb the affectionate relationship between him and his cousin, but mostly because she pitied Reinald.

The coming trial worried her. She seldom went to The Black Dog these days, but Masham went constantly. He would talk and drink with anyone who would talk and drink with him. He could imbibe prodigious amounts while remaining more sober than he looked, and this appearance of muddled stupidity made people speak without caution. Through his reports, Leonie knew that Klaus was popular with his people, but that his popularity was tinged with resentment at his resistance to change. In the matter of Bismarck, they were with their prince. They knew well enough that unification would mean subservience to Prussia, and they admired Klaus for his determination to protect them from that fate. But they wanted him to share some of his power with them, as his ancestors had refused to do. In fact, they wanted his trust, and although, under Leonie's influence, he'd grown closer to them, trusting them was still something he found very hard.

With Masham in attendance, she went to the first day of the trial, heavily veiled to avoid recognition. There was no jury. Three magistrates sat up high, two wearing black gowns, and one in a scarlet gown and full wig, who did all the talking from the bench. When they were seated, an usher cried, "The prisoner will present himself to the court," and two guards appeared with Crazne between them. He was a young man, little more than thirty, and somehow this fact disturbed Leonie. Looking around her, she saw how many in the public gallery were also young. They were people Klaus couldn't afford to ignore.

She returned home in the late afternoon to find a message to attend Klaus in his study. She went to him at once. "Why are you swathed in veils?" he demanded. "Have you been to a funeral?"

She pulled off the hat and kissed him. "No, I've been to Crazne's trial. I thought this attire was more discreet." She looked at him impishly. "After all, you wouldn't want people to know I interested myself in such things, would you?" she teased. "Shockingly unwomanly."

He smiled at her tenderly. His ideas of what was womanly had undergone a total revision since he'd known this most glorious of women. Womanly was whatever she was, and whatever she was, was perfection. "Kiss me," he commanded.

The next few minutes were rather breathless and drove all thoughts of Crazne out of her head. When they could both speak again, Klaus said, "This was a mistake. I have a cabinet meeting in a few moments. How can I appear before my ministers in this distracted state?"

"They'll blame me."

"Quite rightly. Do you think nobody notices that I'm not the man I was?"

She laughed. "I like the new man better. He's more human."

"He's happy." Klaus said fervently. "He's never been so happy in his life, and he fears he may never be so happy again." He grew serious suddenly. "I was raised never to be afraid, or at least, never to admit that I was afraid. But with you, I don't have to pretend. I look into the coming years and have to turn my eyes away in dread. How will I endure them without you?"

"By remembering every moment that we've had," she whispered. "Just as I will."

"And will that be enough?" he asked, studying her face. "You who have the wisdom of all women, tell me—will it be enough?"

Suddenly her eyes blurred with tears and she buried her face against him. "No," she cried. "It won't be enough."

They clung together in silence. There was nothing else to do.

"Tell me about Crazne's trial," he asked after a while.

"Do you know what he's charged with?" she asked, throwing herself into a chair. "Operating an unlicensed newspaper. *An unlicensed newspaper.* Why should he need a license? And sedition—by which they mean questioning your authority. But I've been reading his paper and he says little more than I've said to you, many times. He wants a free press, free elections and an end to your power to over-rule a court's verdict."

"In all of which you agree with him, no doubt?"

"Of course I agree with him." She smiled. "Particularly when he says the vote should be open to everyone, including women."

"A true revolutionary," Klaus agreed ironically. "Do you mean that Britain lags behind in this?"

"My country needs a lot of changes, too," she said darkly.

"You should tell Crazne. He appears to believe that British democracy is the perfect model."

"He only wants a state that isn't set in aspic, and for that, he's put on trial." She threw up her hands in a gesture of frustration and anger. "It's outrageous."

"Let's wait for the verdict," Klaus said. "Things may not be as bad as you think."

Despite what he'd said, she sensed him pulling away from her a little. He'd traveled a long way, but he still wasn't ready to heed too much of her advice at one time. It was almost time for the cabinet meeting, so she discreetly withdrew.

She attended the trial over the next few days. Crazne impressed her as a patriot and a brave man. He stood upright in the dock, pale from his weeks in prison, and spoke of his beliefs with simplicity and strength. "I love my country," he told the prosecutor. "I want to see Wolfenberg free, proud and strong under the rule of its prince. But that can only be if the prince listens to his people and acknowledges the need for change."

"Treason," the prosecutor bawled. "You dare repeat your abominable doctrine before this court. You stand condemned as a traitor out of your own mouth."

Leonie was shocked. Gruber had been a traitor. To hear the same word applied to this man was disturbing. Looking around her, listening to the murmurs of her fellow spectators, she knew that they thought as she did. Crazne spoke what many of them thought, and coming now, under the shadow of Bismarck's threat, the situation was doubly dangerous.

With each day, the tension mounted. If the verdict was guilty, the court would erupt, and after that, perhaps, the country. If it was not guilty, the spotlight would be on

Klaus, who must either sign the release order, or detain Crazne by royal decree.

After five days, the three judges retired to consider their verdicts. They returned in less than an hour. The usher cried, "The prisoner will rise."

Crazne rose to await his fate. The air was alive with tension. The chief justice began to speak. "On the charge of treason, we find the prisoner not guilty—"

The rest of his words were drowned by a roar of delight from the court. The chief justice raised his hand for silence. When he had it, he continued, "On the charge of operating an unlicensed newspaper, we find the prisoner guilty. We sentence him to prison for two months. Since he has already served two months awaiting trial, he is free to go as soon as his royal highness has signed the order for release."

A murmur went around the courtroom. Everyone there recognized that these verdicts would cause the maximum difficulty for Klaus. Leonie heard the buzz and caught the seething note of expectation, of aggression waiting to break out, and knew that this presented Klaus with a threat as great as any from Bismarck. As Crazne was taken back to the cells, someone cried, "Shame!"

"Silence!" snapped the chief justice.

"Free him now!" shouted someone else.

On the journey home, Leonie brooded over what she'd seen. The incipient trouble had been quelled easily today. But tomorrow, the chorus would grow, and one day—perhaps soon—it would be impossible to silence a resentful people.

As soon as she returned to the palace, she broke all her previous rules and went straight to Klaus's study. He looked at her curiously as she hurried inside. "You look as if there's a crisis," he said.

"There is," she said urgently. "Crazne was acquitted on the treason charges. They couldn't do anything else. They found against him about the newspaper, but the sentence was only two months and he's already served that." She looked at Klaus intently. "So now it's all up to you."

"You mean, I take it, that you expect me to sign the release order?"

"It's vitally important that you sign it. If you could have seen your people as I saw them today... They're expecting the worst from you, and they won't stand for it."

Klaus stared at her, but he didn't see her. He was a boy of seventeen again, listening to the mob baying at the palace gates. One man, wilder than the rest, had hurled a stone, shattering a window. Through that jagged gap he'd heard the cry of, "We won't stand for it any longer." The words had been taken up by others, until the whole crowd was screaming, "We won't stand for it." Remembered bitterness swamped him, and he clenched his hands.

Although unable to follow his thoughts in detail, Leonie realized that she'd said the wrong thing. Klaus's jaw had set grimly at the hint that he might act under coercion from his subjects, and she cursed her clumsiness. He'd traveled far under her influence, but he was still basically the autocrat who'd ruled Wolfenberg for years in the way that he, and he alone, saw fit.

"My darling," he said at last, "I have let you advise me in much, but in this matter you must trust me to know best."

"But how can you know best when you weren't there today? You didn't see what I saw," she pleaded. "There are things happening in your country that you know nothing of."

"On the contrary, I can read about them in Crazne's illegal rag."

"But it shouldn't be illegal!" she cried. "You shouldn't be afraid of having a free press."

Another mistake. Klaus's eyes kindled. "I bear much from you that I wouldn't tolerate from anyone else," he growled. "But even from you I will not endure dictatorship. Don't ever presume to tell me what I should and shouldn't do."

Her own temper rose at being so abruptly rebuffed. "I tell you what any friend would tell you," she said crossly. "If you don't sign that release order, you're doing something very dangerous."

"In other words, you think I should obey the mob?" he snapped.

"They're not a mob yet," she told him in a firm, deliberate voice, "but they have a legitimate grievance. You haven't a shadow of excuse for keeping Crazne in prison."

"Except that I consider him a danger to the state."

"Your judges have ruled otherwise."

"Then it's as well that I've kept the ultimate power in my own hands."

"It's an oppressive power," she cried. "No man should have the power to imprison someone who's committed no crime."

"In other words, madam, you consider me a tyrant?"

"What else am I to think when you act like one? Klaus, I beg you, sign that order, and renounce your power to overrule the courts."

"Renounce my—are you mad?"

"Not mad. I merely have eyes for the future. The day when even a benign despot could justify his despotism is passing. Your people are growing up. They want a say in their own lives, they want laws that protect them—"

"I pass all the laws necessary to protect them."

"But where's the law to protect them against *you?*"

"What did you say?"

"All right, not you in particular, but your successors. Who can say what they'll be like? They might be tyrants. If—" She stopped at the sight of his thunderous expression.

"Go on," he said. "Having come so far, why stop?"

"If you grant your people a constitution defining the limits of the prince's power, it will bind your successors, too."

A constitution: the very thing the rebels had agitated for in 1848. There was even an ugly rumor that his grandfather had granted one, but had repudiated it the moment he was free on the grounds that a signature gained under duress was invalid. But it was no more than a rumor. And now she . . .

"It's the only way to convince your people that you're on their side," Leonie finished.

His face was dark with fury. *"On their side?"* he echoed harshly. "My entire life has been dedicated to my people from the moment I was born. Do you dare to suggest that I need to prove myself to them?"

"I didn't mean—"

"A lifetime of duty, and you have the unspeakable impertinence to suggest—"

Carried away by the strength of her feeling, Leonie threw protocol to the winds and interrupted the prince. "Never mind about duty," she said passionately. "You talk about duty constantly, but it's your love they want. If you loved them, you'd understand them better, and you wouldn't misjudge their mood as often as you do."

That was it, she thought, looking at the stony expression in his eyes. She'd be lucky if she didn't end up in The Fort with Crazne.

Klaus's face was frozen, shutting her out. After a long silence, he said in a hard voice, "We have a meeting in a few minutes. You have our permission to leave."

Since the start of their love, he'd never spoken to her with such stern formality, even using the royal "we" to set her at a distance. There was a pain in her heart and she longed to put her arms around him and try to soften him. But after her earlier blunders, she'd recovered some of her diplomacy, so she merely curtsied, murmuring, "As your royal highness pleases," and departed.

Klaus watched her go with anguish. For a few terrible moments, she'd been his unwitting enemy, invading him with memories of the worst time of his life, seeming to side with those who'd driven his family to flight. On that night, he'd known feelings that still tortured him, not fear, but shame and humiliation at being forced to run away. And *she*, whom he'd admitted to the innermost recess of his heart, had turned against him.

But of course, she was a British agent, sent to nanny him, to make him comply with Britain's will, and persuade him to adopt Britain's ways. He'd been a fool to forget it.

Klaus was in love, but he'd been reared as an autocrat. There were laws, both divine and natural, that ordained proper spheres for everyone, ruler and ruled, prince and subjects, men and women. A subject's rights included a generous prince who put his people's welfare above all things. A prince's rights included a trusting and obedient people. A man loved a woman but didn't allow her to interfere with serious matters. A woman didn't even try to.

But this woman acknowledged no rules but her own, and assumed that everything was her concern. With British money and British military might at her back, it had been hard to gainsay her, but today she'd gone too far. Klaus's love struggled with his rearing in the most bitter, miserable battle of his existence.

Archduke Reinald, announced a few moments later, entered to find his cousin looking pale and ill. "Good God!" he exclaimed at once. "What terrible thing has happened? Tell me!"

Klaus forced a laugh. "The most terrible thing of all," he said with an attempt at lightness. "I've quarreled with a lady."

Reinald's eyebrows rose. "With *that* lady?"

"I know of no other lady worth quarreling with," Klaus observed wryly. "I know of no other lady who can bring me so close to wringing her neck."

Reinald frowned. "What can poor Leonie possibly have done to put you in such a passion?"

"She isn't 'poor Leonie,'" Klaus said bitterly. "She's a woman with a damned sharp tongue, which she uses in matters that are not her concern."

"Politics?" Reading the answer in Klaus's face, Reinald said sympathetically, "You should never discuss such matters with a woman, even the best of them. It's fatal."

"I don't talk politics with Leonie. Unfortunately, she insists on talking them with me."

"What was the quarrel about?"

"Crazne. You've heard the verdict?"

"Yes, indeed. Most awkward. In fact, if the judges had been wanting to force your hand, they could hardly have chosen a verdict better calculated to do so. It almost makes one wonder where their sympathies lie."

"I will not let my hand be forced, by them *or* by her," Klaus said with firm deliberation.

"I suppose she wants you to sign the release order."

"How did you know that?" Klaus demanded sharply.

Reinald shrugged. "A shrewd guess. The lady's liberal sympathies are no secret."

"The release order is just a beginning," Klaus declared bitterly. "Nothing less than a constitution will do for her."

Reinald stared. "A constitution, no less? And what would this constitution say? It wouldn't make Wolfenberg a province of Britain by any chance?"

"I'm beginning to wonder."

He regretted the words the moment they were out. Some far corner of his mind knew he was overreacting and reproved him. She was his Leonie, whom he loved and fundamentally trusted, whatever he might say. But today she'd stirred up a hornet's nest, and the hornets needed time to settle before he could think of her calmly.

"Don't judge her too harshly," Reinald advised. "Remember, she's English."

"I *am* remembering it."

"I meant that the English are ruled by a queen. They're used to taking orders from women. They like it."

"Impossible."

"They do, I assure you. Leonie was reared in that atmosphere and can't come to terms with a country run by men." He waited to see if there would be any answer to this, but Klaus only scowled, so Reinald adroitly changed the subject. "Do you go to the opera tonight?"

"Yes. Leonie and I together. It should be a fascinating evening, especially as the work is the most recent composition by Richard Wagner. Gruber wanted me to ban Wagner's works from this country on the grounds that he was a '48 revolutionary. I told him that was taking matters a little far." Klaus's lips twisted bitterly. "Let's hope that touch of liberalism finds favor with my lady, although frankly I doubt she's in a mood to set anything to my credit."

Reinald frowned. "I wonder if you're wise to appear in public. If feelings are running high, there may be demonstrations."

"Nonsense!" Klaus said impatiently.

At nine o'clock that evening, Klaus and Leonie made their entrance into the Royal Theater together, with Bernhard in attendance. Each of them looked and felt ill at ease. The short journey from the palace to the theater had been eerie. Crowds had lined the street to see the royal carriage pass, but instead of cheering, they'd stood in silence. Klaus, who'd been prepared to cope with angry shouting, had found the silence unsettling. The breach with his people was like the breach with his beloved. It hurt him badly, but it didn't change his conviction that he was right.

Things appeared to change for the better as soon as he appeared in the royal box. There was a shout from below, and the next moment, the audience was on its feet, cheering and applauding him. He acknowledged the enthusiasm and glanced at Leonie to see her reaction. To his annoyance, she didn't look pleased as any rational woman would have done, but virtually ignored what was happening below. Her attention was on the upper tiers. He followed her gaze and saw what she was studying.

Below and up to the royal box, the audience was cheering him. They were the aristocracy, the ones who could afford the most expensive seats. Above them were the professional folk, bankers, lawyers, merchants. Above them, crammed against the roof, were the cheapest seats of all, taken by the shopkeepers, the servants, those who'd save their precious coins until they could afford to squeeze into the least comfortable places. From the "professional" seats upward, there was no cheering, no applause, only a repetition of the silence they'd experienced in the streets.

Klaus was shrewd enough to realize what the sharp division meant. The aristocracy were showing their relief that the prince was exercising his autocratic power, and, by extension, protecting their own. The others were showing their disapproval.

He sat down and the conductor raised his baton. In another moment, the first soft bars of *Tristan and Isolde* were stealing onto the air. He tried to give himself up to the music and forget his troubles, as he'd so often done before at the opera. But tonight it wasn't so easy. Tonight he was at odds with the woman who'd taken possession of his heart and soul, and it was torment. To quarrel with her was like tearing himself in two.

But he couldn't give in. To yield for the sake of love when he knew he was in the right would be a sign of weakness. A country couldn't be ruled on that basis. He reasoned it out endlessly, wondering how it was possible to be right and yet so unhappy.

He was roused from his reverie by the sound of applause. Somehow, an hour and a half had passed. He sighed and forced himself to applaud and look delighted.

Suddenly the air seemed to explode in a shower of white paper, coming down from the roof. Looking up, Leonie saw that people were standing in the highest gallery, tossing leaflets over the rails. She put out her hand and caught one. As she'd half expected, it said simply, FREE CRAZNE.

"Don't dignify it with your attention," Klaus growled, his face dark with fury.

"Why not? It's better to know what people are thinking," she retorted.

He ignored this. "I believe a supper table is ready for us," he said, offering his arm with a hard look that forbade her to argue.

Leonie sighed and took his arm, letting him lead her out of the box to the supper room. Georg Kanner, the theater manager, was there, full of profuse apologies. "I've sent men up to put a stop to this intolerable insult," he blustered, "but they can't get in. The doors have been locked from the other side. They'll be broken down, of course, and the malefactors arrested—"

"I desire you to do no such thing," Klaus said firmly. "No broken doors, and no arrests. These are not 'malefactors,' merely people whose opinion differs from my own."

"But, your royal highness, surely that's treason?"

"It's regrettable, but I've no intention of treating it as treason," Klaus replied. "My people are fully entitled to their opinions, as long as they understand that mine is the opinion that must prevail. My wish is that you take no action at all, and when the performance is over, no one is to stop them from leaving."

Herr Kanner bowed himself out, mopping his forehead. Reinald was at Klaus's elbow. "Is that wise? I have troops that—"

"I refuse to allow a small matter to turn into a major incident," Klaus stated. "Nor will I let them think I'm afraid of them. Let that be clear."

Reinald bowed. Klaus met Leonie's gaze. "It won't go away just because you ignore it," she murmured.

"And I will not yield to force...no matter where it comes from. Do I make myself plain, madam?"

She sighed again. "Perfectly plain."

His voice became gentler. "Don't let us quarrel. Trust me. I know my country better than you."

Leonie looked at him in despair. There was no sign of the man she'd thought she knew. His place had been taken by this stubborn stranger, deaf to reason, convinced of his own rightness.

There were no further disturbances in the opera house. Isolde sang out her passion over Tristan's lifeless form and was reunited with him in death. The curtain fell, the applause broke out. Klaus applauded for a long time, refusing to leave early by so much as a moment. No more leaflets descended, and Leonie concluded that they'd all been thrown. Perhaps those who'd tossed them over had wanted to be arrested, in which case Klaus's behavior was shrewd. But his hard stubbornness still filled her with dismay.

On the journey home, there was the silence again. She could hear nothing but the sound of hooves on the road from the cavalry that rode beside the carriage. But it couldn't last. There came the first cry. "Free Crazne!" Others took it up, and soon everyone was shouting. But not all the cries were about Crazne. *Tyrant* and *Despot* were some of the ominous words her ears picked up. She ground her nails into her palm. This was Bismarck's finest opportunity to kill Klaus. "For pity's sake, tell the coachman to go faster," she muttered.

He gripped her arm and spoke without looking at her. "Not by an inch. Not by a second," he said grimly. "I will not run away."

The next moment, everything was chaos. A small figure detached itself from the crowd and darted forward, hands upstretched to the horses' heads. One of the horsemen beside the carriage drew his sword and plunged forward. The horses reared and the carriage shuddered to a halt. The crowd was shouting, but one scream rose above all others.

"Murderers! *Murderers!*"

A woman hurled herself madly forward and dropped to her knees beside something that lay on the cobbles near the horses' hooves. The horseman dismounted, sword in hand, but before he could do more, Klaus had leaped from the carriage and seized the man's wrist. "Stand back!" he ordered furiously. "No bloodshed, do you hear? No bloodshed."

"You say that when it's too late!" the woman screamed. "She's dead. Oh God, she's dead. *Murderer.*"

Leonie had hurried out of the carriage after Klaus, one hand ready to spring the stiletto concealed in her fan. But neither Klaus nor anyone else had attention for her. They were all looking with horror at the crumpled figure of a raggedly dressed young girl on the cobbles. She looked no older than twelve, and she lay frighteningly still. For a horrible moment, Leonie thought the girl really was dead. The woman seized her in her arms, sobbing violently as she rocked the seemingly lifeless body back and forth. The air was jagged with hate and ugly tension, but Klaus ignored it. Kneeling, he gently took the child away from her mother, cradling her in his arms and stroking her face. The crowd fell silent as she opened her eyes. "Are you in pain?" Klaus asked her.

"No," she whispered.

He rose to his feet, still holding her in his arms. As if by instinct, the child steadied herself by putting her arm around his neck. "What are you doing out at this hour?" Klaus demanded. "You should be in bed."

She looked up at him. "Free Crazne," she said feebly, as though reciting a well-learned lesson.

Klaus's reaction took everyone by surprise, including Leonie. He smiled at the girl, the warm, genuine smile that he kept for his few intimates. It was full of charm and generosity, and Leonie had often wished his people could see it. The little girl gazing up into his face received its full glow. "Perhaps," he answered her. "Perhaps." He turned to Bernhard who'd been following in another carriage, and had run to join them. "Take this child to her home," he said. "Send for my own physician to attend her. Tell him to give her his best attention."

He handed her over and turned to the woman. "Go with your child. She'll be all right." The woman stared at him speechless, wide-eyed. "Go," he repeated gently. He seemed to become aware of the guard beside him, his blade still in his hand. "Sheath your sword," he ordered. "There's no need for it here."

The crowd backed away, murmuring uneasily. Klaus looked around at them and his ease dissipated, leaving him self-conscious again. "Return to your homes," he commanded. "Nothing is worth endangering your children."

They didn't answer, but their eyes were watchful as he handed Leonie back into the carriage and got in beside her. He didn't speak to her for the first few minutes, but then he said, "I told the guard to sheath his sword. You should do the same." When she looked at him, he pointed to her fan and said wryly, "Did you think I didn't know you were armed?"

"It might have been needed," she said.

"I'm coming to understand that this is how it always is with you, so soft and feminine on the surface, and underneath—the concealed weapon."

She said nothing. His words had hurt because they revealed he was still holding himself at a distance from her.

Klaus read her face accurately and leaned over, taking her hand between both his and saying in a kinder voice, "Be patient. Things look different to me now."

"Because of that little girl?" she ventured to say.

"Yes. If it matters that much to them..." His voice trailed away. Even to himself he would have found it hard to describe how his perspective had changed in those few dramatic moments. When the crowd had seemed threatening, it had merely aroused his stubbornness and a determination not to yield an inch to force. But the child's helplessness had touched his heart. It was as though filters had shifted from his eyes, throwing a new light over everything, revealing that the people were not threatening but pleading. And he'd been refusing to listen.

At the palace, he said briefly, "Stay with me," and went to his office. Reinald was already there. "I heard what happened," he said. "The guards are on alert—"

"Then you must stand them down," Klaus said firmly. "I don't take up arms against my own people. And by God, tonight I nearly did!" His face was pale. "Children! They take their children into the streets to make their demands!"

"A sign of how unstable and dangerous they are," Reinald said.

"Or a sign of how earnestly their hearts are set on this thing," Klaus mused aloud.

"A prince cannot be ruled by his subjects' hearts," Reinald replied. "I've heard you say so."

"Yes, I said so." Klaus gave a little smile. "I was blind for a long time. But perhaps now I understand more about hearts than I once did."

Reinald frowned. "Do you mean to release Crazne?"

"I mean to do more. I intend to renounce for all time my power to overrule the courts."

Leonie gave a start of joy. Klaus was looking directly at her, and she knew he was telling her that it was she who'd taught him the importance of the heart.

But Reinald still frowned. "For all time?" he echoed. "No prince of Wolfenberg has ever renounced power in such manner that his successors couldn't take it back—if circumstances made it necessary."

"That's exactly why I must do so," Klaus replied. "How can my people be free if the door is left open for my heir to put them back in chains?"

Reinald's glance at Leonie was brief, but she had the feeling he understood her part in this. "If you must do this," he said at last, "make sure you do it properly."

"What do you mean by that?"

"Don't just issue a decree. Have the matter voted on and ratified by the chamber of deputies."

Leonie was silent, but everything in her was alert. She'd studied Wolfenberg's political system, and she knew that the chamber of deputies was the closest thing it had to a parliament. It was composed of fifty men representing the country's larger towns, and it functioned largely as a rubber stamp for the prince's will. But it had one significant power. Once the chamber had ratified a decree, even the prince couldn't withdraw it.

Klaus looked surprised but pleased. "An excellent idea. Nothing could be better to convince them that I'm in earnest. But I own I hadn't expected to hear such a suggestion from you." He grinned at Leonie. "Reinald has always been even more eager to defend my absolute authority than I have myself."

"Times change," Reinald said. "It may be that good order may best be preserved by relinquishing a little power. It will certainly be a popular move."

"I've never courted popularity," Klaus brooded. "It's a fatal course for a ruler. Just the same, a little popularity might be pleasant."

"When will you release Crazne?" Leonie asked, smiling.

"Now." Klaus sat down at his desk and immediately began to write.

Reinald moved closer to Leonie and spoke in a low voice. "Do I detect your influence?"

"Very little," she answered. "His highness's own sense of justice prevailed."

"You're too modest. I recognize British liberal opinion in this."

"In other words, you think I'm interfering in politics?" She kept her tone light. "I assure you, they're beyond my comprehension."

"No, no," he said. "That affectation will do for others, Leonie, but not for me. I think very little is beyond your comprehension."

Before she had time to think of an answer, Klaus rang a small bell on his desk. A footman appeared immediately. Klaus handed him the sealed envelope. "Have this conveyed to The Fort at once," Klaus instructed him. Then, although he'd never previously felt it necessary to explain himself to subordinates, something impelled him to add, "It's the order for Crazne's release."

The look of startled delight on the man's face shocked him with its revelation that this footman had concealed a passionate interest behind an expressionless mask. And the other footmen, hundreds of them—what were their thoughts? He'd never even wondered before. But they weren't only footmen. They were men. And he was only now coming to understand what that meant.

Chapter Twelve

Crazne was released with the dawn. Masham, who was in the crowd that thronged the entrance to The Fort, later told Leonie what happened when Klaus's messenger appeared. "They knew he was carrying the release order, because he waved it at them, with a grin all over his face. I've never heard such a cheer. When Crazne appeared half an hour later, I thought they'd go mad."

But this was nothing compared to the popular clamor that ensued when it became known that Klaus was to address the chamber of deputies that afternoon. "The city is alive with rumors about what you're going to say," she told him when she returned from her drive in the park that afternoon.

"They'll just have to wait until the proclamation is posted," he said.

"What about the newspapers? Won't they report it?"

"The *Treuheim Gazette* will be sent an official report in due course."

"But won't they have anybody there to take your speech down?"

He looked so outraged that she almost laughed aloud. "Have a journalist in the chamber of deputies?" he demanded, aghast. "What will you think of next?"

"I don't know what I'll think of next," she riposted. "A free press, perhaps."

"Not in my lifetime," Klaus said with a shudder. "You've driven me as far as you're going to. Now, be off with you and put on some stunning gown for your appearance in the public gallery. And when I make my speech, try not to look too triumphant."

"I'll be a model of decorum," she promised with an impish smile, and darted away, leaving him to look after her tenderly.

Her carriage had to struggle to get to the building where the chamber of deputies met. Crowds thronged the streets and there was an air of cheerful expectancy. She traveled alone, since this was one place where the prince couldn't flaunt his favorite on his arm. Her appearance in the gallery created a sensation. She was attired with a touch of severity in a dark blue walking dress, trimmed with white. On her head was the merest wisp of a bonnet, adorned by a white feather. Tall and regal, she swept into the gallery and took the place that had been kept for her at the front.

When everyone was assembled, Klaus appeared and took his place on the podium. He spoke briefly, outlining his wish to renounce power over the judiciary, and making a formal request that the chamber ratify the decision. The next hour was taken up with speeches of appreciation from the deputies. Plainly, each man wanted his name in the record of this notable occasion. At last it was time for the vote. The speaker called for a show of hands, and every hand shot up.

"I declare the decree formally ratified," the speaker declared.

Pandemonium broke out in the chamber. The deputies rose to their feet and cheered, their faces wreathed in smiles. Klaus looked startled at this display of emotion, but after a moment, a smile touched his mouth. Only the most observant noticed that he glanced up to the public gallery. His eyes met those of a woman sitting there, and something he

saw made him relax. At last he bowed his head in acknowledgement of his people's tribute, and departed.

There was a feast in the favorite's apartments that night.
Nothing could have been merrier or more comfortable, yet
Klaus rose to leave early. "Everyone will think my star is
waning," Leonie murmured as she accompanied him to the
door.

"Then they're fools," he answered. "Get rid of them, put
on your peasant costume and wait for me."

He appeared in her room half an hour later wearing his
own peasant garb. "I have this sudden wish to visit our
friends in the woods," he said. "It came over me without
warning."

"We've often spoken of returning to them," she said demurely. Her eyes were twinkling.

"But something else always got in the way." He put his
arms around her. "When I came down here, all I wanted to
do was make love to you. But now everything is different.
Today you've done so much for me."

"No, you did it yourself."

"I did it by your light. Without you, it wouldn't have been
done." Suddenly his mood lightened and he kissed her nose.
"Come. Let's hurry."

They crept out of the palace as before, took two horses
and made their way in the direction of the woods. Once
again there was a full moon, bathing the countryside in silver light, until they reached the shadows of the trees. As they
rode beneath them, Leonie looked up and he saw her begin
to smile. "What do the signs tell you?" he asked.

"There's a wedding tonight. Everyone's invited. Let's
hurry."

They urged their horses forward and soon they could see
the glow of the campfire. "It makes a more brilliant light
than usual," Klaus noticed.

"You'll see why when we get there. This is a special night."

Soon they reached the clearing, and as they broke out from the trees, Klaus saw what Leonie had meant. Instead of one fire, there were seven, set in a circle, creating a blaze of light. "That's where the wedding will take place," Leonie told him. "In the center of the circle, to symbolize eternity."

The fiddlers were playing softly but nobody was dancing yet. Men and women were standing about in little crowds, talking in low voices. They were wearing their best clothes, the ones they used for performances, and an air of excited expectancy hung over them.

A swarm of children rushed forward to take their horses and a cheer went up as the Gypsies saw the newcomers. Uncle Silas approached, splendid in a frilled shirt and red sash about his waist, and a black velvet waistcoat, covered in luxuriant embroidery. "You're welcome," he boomed. "The fates brought you to us on this night of nights."

"Who are the bride and groom?" Leonie asked eagerly.

"Toni and Paquita," Uncle Silas said. "And their joy will be complete when they see you. When Meg told us we might go ahead, we weren't sure how to send you a message, but she said she would make you come, and she did."

"I don't understand," Klaus said. "Why did you have to wait for Meg?"

"She's the soothsayer," Leonie explained. "She reads signs and portents that nobody else can comprehend. A wedding must take place when everything is right, or the couple won't be happy. Meg will have cast their horoscopes, but that's only the start. She leaves herbs out under the moon, and much depends on how they feel to her in the morning."

Uncle Silas nodded. "She told us this morning that the day had arrived, and everyone's been in a fever since."

"What did you mean about her making us come here?" Klaus asked in a strange voice.

"She put the idea into your head," Leonie explained.

"But how?"

"Meg has her ways and her spells, but we mustn't ask about them."

"Spells? You really believe that?"

"I'm a Gypsy. I know—" she hesitated "—the things Gypsies know," she finished mysteriously.

"But surely—"

"Klaus, tell me, why did you suddenly feel you wanted to come here tonight?"

"I don't know," he said slowly. "I can't begin to explain it."

Uncle Silas led Meg into the circle of fire and clapped his hands. Silence fell. Two caravans stood at opposite sides of the circle. At a signal from Meg, two young men bearing torches went to the entrance of each caravan, and stood waiting. At the same moment, the curtains parted, revealing Toni in one caravan and Paquita in the other. They came down the steps and stood facing each other across the circle. Their eyes glowed and each seemed to see nothing but the other.

Two young women approached Paquita. One placed a chaplet of blue flowers on her head, and the other put a posy in her hand. Leonie whispered, "A Gypsy bride wears cornflowers on her head to symbolize love's abundance. In her hands she carries jasmine, for passion."

"You mean everything has a meaning?" Klaus asked softly.

"Everything. Nothing is left to chance. All the powers of the earth are invoked to turn lovers into husband and wife."

At last Uncle Silas beckoned the two young people, and they stepped into the fiery circle. Seven young girls appeared and stood by the fires. Each one had a basket under her arm, filled with herbs, and with her free hand she strewed herbs into the flames. At once, each fire crackled and threw up a heady aroma.

"The herbs are carefully chosen," Leonie explained to Klaus. "Rosemary for happiness, sage for health and beauty, mint for peace of mind, rue for self-knowledge, basil for wealth, thyme for courage and mandrake for fertility."

As she spoke, the young girls moved gracefully around the outside of the circle, tossing herbs into the flames as they passed, so that all seven herbs were burned in each fire. The air was pungent with the scent, and for a moment Klaus felt dizzy. Then the moment passed, and he was breathing in the fragrances with pleasure. Their subtle richness pervaded his whole being, raising him to another plane where magic not only existed but was natural and inevitable.

Leonie gave a wistful sigh and he reached out to take her shoulders, drawing her back so that her head rested against him. "My parents married like this," she said. "My mother told me about it. Afterward, my father insisted on having a conventional wedding in a church, so that the marriage was recognized by his people as well as hers. But she couldn't understand why he bothered. They'd been married by Gypsy rites, and she felt nothing else mattered."

"Perhaps she was right," Klaus said.

She looked up at him, smiling in surprise. "*You* say that?"

"Yes," he said, "I do. I hardly know myself, my own thoughts are so strange, as though I were another man, and that man saw and heard great mysteries . . . and understood them."

Leonie didn't speak but her eyes shone into his, and again he had the sensation of dizziness, as though the whole world had rocked on its axis, and when it settled back, there had been a subtle change. Everything looked the same, but nothing *was* the same.

The herb maidens had finished their task and withdrawn into the shadows. Meg took Paquita's hand and placed it in Toni's. Silence fell.

"Brothers and sisters," Uncle Silas cried, "Toni and Paquita have chosen each other, and we have met to witness the sealing of their choice." He pointed to the moon. "The heavens have blessed their wedding." He indicated the fires from which the herb-scented smoke rose. "The earth has blessed their wedding. And now I ask you, shall we also bless their wedding?"

A deep-throated sound came from the Gypsies crowding around. "Ohey!" they cried.

"Do we will this marriage?" Uncle Silas shouted.

"Ohey!" Klaus felt Leonie's body tremble against his as she called her assent with the others.

"Do we consent to this marriage?"

"*Ohey!*" Startled, Klaus realized that his own voice had cried out the word, not so much against his will as without his knowledge. But that didn't seem strange as once it would have. He was caught up in the spell of the occasion and the mystic belief of these people that only marriages blessed by nature were valid.

There flitted across his brain a brief memory of stately weddings he'd attended, where the bride and groom had made a "suitable" match and barely knew each other, where the guests were trying to calculate the wealth on display and guess the size of the settlement, and the bride's gown had cost enough to feed a Gypsy camp for a month. Some deep instinct in him flinched in revulsion at those vain, meaningless shows that mocked the religion in which they were celebrated. True spiritual faith was here in this "pagan" ceremony that was actually far from pagan. It showed itself in the cry to the heavens and the earth, and to the hearts and minds of fellow creatures. He, who'd lived all his life behind glass walls that cut him off from his fellowman, had been moved almost to tears by that appeal.

Toni and Paquita knelt and took each other's hands, and Toni began to speak very simply. "Let everyone here witness that you are my true wife," he declared, "in this world and the next. I shall love you and cherish you, in good times and bad, and my heart will cleave to no other."

Paquita's face was radiant as she replied in the same words.

Solemnly they kissed. As they rose to their feet, the crowd began to sing. It was an ancient melody, half sweet, half poignant, shot through with the joys and sorrows of a free people who'd traveled the open road for centuries, and it made the hairs stand up on the back of Klaus's neck. The sound rose in the scented air as the bride and groom began to walk around the circle of fire, their arms entwined, showing themselves to the witnesses as man and wife. It was not written down. No book would record the promises of Paquita and Toni, but everyone here would know, and that was all that was necessary.

The singing dissolved into applause and laughter as Toni and Paquita began to dance together. Their joy was almost a palpable thing, infusing their young bodies and making them seem to be constantly touching even when they weren't. Klaus trembled. He knew a chance had come tonight that he would never have again, and he could either seize it or regret it forever. Gathering his courage, he leaned down and whispered in Leonie's ear.

At first, she didn't move and he thought she hadn't heard him. But then she swung around to look up at him, and he knew by her eyes that she'd heard. There was shock there and disbelieving joy.

"I mean it," he said. "I want you to marry me."

"But—you can't. Your ministers would never accept it. They demand a royal bride."

"Yes, I know. I want you to marry me here, now, by Gypsy rites."

"Oh, no," she said. "Klaus, how could you ask me such a thing? I won't help you make fun of these people."

"I'm not making fun of them," he pleaded. "Your mother was right. These are the things that matter, and if you become my wife now, I swear it will be as real to me as any marriage in church. We can't tell anyone from our own world, and even if they knew, they wouldn't recognize what we do here tonight as valid. One day I'll have to make another marriage, and you—" he checked himself, and a shudder, as if of pain, went through him "—you, too, may marry again. But we'll always know that we are husband and wife. Leonie, be my wife, I beg of you."

Joy flooded her. This was right. Every fiber of her being told her so. And he'd felt it before her. The stern, taut, wary royal icon she'd first met had become a man able to listen to his own heart and hers. And this man wanted to be her husband. "I'll be your wife," she said softly, and was immediately enfolded in his arms.

They sought out Uncle Silas. When he heard what they wanted, he frowned, and Leonie saw that he shared her own feelings of a moment ago. He thought Klaus was amusing himself. "This is not good," he said at last. "You're a fine lady now—"

"I'm still a Gypsy. I'll always be a Gypsy," she insisted.

Uncle Silas was still unhappy. "I don't know," he said. "We must ask Meg."

They found the old woman sitting happily in her chair, clapping her hands in time to the music. She couldn't see the dancers but she didn't need to. She'd assisted at a thousand such occasions, and she knew that at weddings, people danced with a special passion and expectancy. Uncle Silas touched her shoulder to catch her attention. "Help us, Mother," he said. "Leonie wants to marry her man, although he's not one of us. He comes from a different world, where their marriage can't even be acknowledged. Will the earth and the heavens allow it?"

Leonie knelt beside Meg and held the old woman's hands in her own. "Is he a good man?" Meg asked.

"You know him, Mother," Leonie whispered. "He came with me before. He's a good man, and I love him."

"Let him take my hands."

Klaus, who was listening intently, stepped forward and knelt beside Meg. She took his hands and held them for a moment in a grip of surprising power. Then she asked, "If you cannot acknowledge this marriage, why do you wish to make it?"

"Because even if others do not know of it, I need it to be true," Klaus answered simply. "I need her for my wife very much."

Meg nodded slowly. Then she reached out and took Leonie's hand and sat for a moment holding them both. At last she sighed and said, "The heavens allow it. But for these two, one thing must be different. Not basil, for they have no need of wealth. Instead—monkshood."

A murmur went around the little crowd that had gathered around them. "What does it mean?" Klaus asked.

"Monkshood is to ease pain," Leonie told him quietly. "Meg has looked into the future and seen pain for us."

"Draw back," Meg advised them mournfully. "Draw back now while there's time."

"There's no time," Klaus said. "It was too late from the moment I saw her."

Meg nodded. "You're a wise man. Very well, then. Bring monkshood."

The fiddlers had fallen silent and the dancing had stopped once everyone realized what was happening. Men began throwing branches on the fires to revive them. A young man put a hand on Klaus's arm. "Come, friend," he said, indicating the groom's caravan. "You must not see her again until you meet in the circle."

Leonie was led away to the bride's caravan. The inside was almost exactly like that of the one that had been her home as a child. The thought brought memories rushing back of the day Nesta had shown her the wonders of a Gypsy wedding, telling her that one day she, too, would enter the circle of fire to give herself forever to the man she loved. And now it was happening, but in a way Nesta could never have imagined. Suddenly she could feel her mother very close to her, smiling with pleasure because her daughter hadn't forgotten her proud Gypsy heritage.

Looking out through the crack in the curtains, she saw a gleam of light, then the curtains were drawn back by two young men holding up torches to light her way. On the far side of the circle, she could see Klaus waiting at the top of the steps of his caravan. They descended at the same moment. At the foot of the steps, she paused and bent her head to receive the chaplet of cornflowers. Jasmine was placed in her hands.

Meg and Uncle Silas were in the center. He beckoned the bride and groom, and slowly they began to walk forward, between the fires. Somewhere in the background Leonie was aware that the young girls had started to circle around the outside. They were tossing herbs into the flames, herbs containing monkshood because Meg had looked into the future and seen the pain that would soon overtake them.

But tonight there was no thought of pain. Tonight she was marrying the man she loved, and her thoughts were all of him. As they neared each other, she saw his eyes fixed on her, and knew that for him, as for her, nothing else existed.

Despite her blindness, Meg reached out to exactly where Leonie was and took her hand to place it in Klaus's. A hush fell on the little crowd. Uncle Silas looked around and spoke the same words as before. "Brothers and sisters, Klaus and Leonie have chosen each other, and we have met to witness the sealing of their choice. The heavens have blessed their wedding. The earth has blessed their wedding. And now I ask you, shall we also bless their wedding?"

"Ohey!" cried the Gypsies with one voice.

"Do we will this marriage?"

"Ohey!"

"Do we consent to this marriage?"

"Ohey!"

They knelt, still holding each other's hands, and Klaus began to speak in a voice loud enough to be heard by them all. "Let everyone here witness that you are my true wife, in this world and the next. I shall love you and cherish you—" his voice trembled with emotion "—in good times and bad, and my heart will cleave to no other."

He waited, but for a moment she couldn't speak. Love for him overwhelmed her, bringing tears to her eyes. At last she calmed herself enough to say, "Let everyone here witness that you are my true husband, in this world and the next. I shall love you and cherish you in good times and bad, and my heart will cleave to no other."

He kissed her and the singing began. Under the music he murmured, "Now you belong to me, and I belong to you."

They danced together in the firelight. They'd danced so many times before, in fine clothes under glittering chandeliers, but now it was like the first time. The others watched them, smiling, and a ripple passed through the crowd. This was a true marriage, and everyone there knew it. His body was close to hers, the perfect attunement of their movements reminding her of many lovings. "My wife," he said. "Oh, my wife."

The fire was dying. The music faded. Toni and Paquita drifted away to find their own happiness in their little caravan. Klaus led Leonie to stand before Uncle Silas. He smiled at them with joy and sadness. "In a few days, we leave here," he said. "God knows when we shall meet again. But while we live in each other's hearts, we are not parted."

He embraced Leonie, then opened his arms to Klaus with the same naturalness. "One of us now," he said as they hugged. "One of us."

They made their farewells and slipped away through the trees. They rode in silence, linked by feelings too deep for words. But as they reached the edge of the woods, Leonie was suddenly seized with a strange sensation, as though she'd lived through this moment before, long ago in a half-remembered life. "What is it?" Klaus asked, seeing her face.

"I don't know—that is, I don't understand. I feel as if I've been here before."

"But you have. We rode back this way last time. And something about this place upset you then, too."

"No, I mean more than that. I was here long ago. I'm sure I was. And something happened here—something grand and wonderful."

She slipped from her horse and began to wander about among the trees, searching for some clue that would explain the bittersweet sensations in her heart. Klaus also dismounted and followed, watching her with eyes softened by love, wondering what Gypsy magic this would turn out to be. In his eyes, everything she did was marvelous.

But wherever she looked, nothing seemed to give her the answer. They'd almost left the woods now. The trees had thinned out, and gradually they reached the last one, a huge oak that stood on a little rise, its leaves rustling gently in the soft breeze. In the distance, the dawn was breaking, bathing everything around them in pearly gray. And as the first ray of sunlight touched the tree, Leonie knew when she'd first come here before, and why.

"It was just here!" she cried. "That was the tree. He was sitting under that tree—and such a smile on his face."

"Who, my darling?"

"My father. He died in this spot. I was a child—we found him here." She saw Klaus looking at her with a quizzical smile and cried passionately, "It's true. This is the place."

"But you were never in Wolfenberg before," he reminded her.

"I was only ten. I could never recall where we were when it happened. But now it all comes back to me. He wasn't the same after my mother died. He walked and talked, but he was like a ghost. I know now that he was just holding on until he'd made arrangements for me. One night, he simply walked away. We found him here next day, sitting under this oak, looking up and smiling."

"But how can you be sure?" Klaus asked gently. "You didn't remember all this last time we were here."

"Part of me did," she said. "That's why I had that terrible sensation of misery. It came from the day I discovered that he'd come here to die, and I felt he'd abandoned me. I didn't understand then—I wasn't ready to understand."

"And now?" Klaus asked softly.

She gave him a smile full of joy and profound mystery.

"Now, when you live every moment in my heart, when my life is only you, and my love for you possesses me body and soul—now I'm ready."

It had all become so clear. With her heart full of love for the man who'd chosen to be her husband, she knew that Gavin had looked up to find his beloved Nesta stealing silently across the grass toward him. And he'd smiled because the weary parting was over. She'd held out her hands and he'd put his own hands into them, letting her lead him away, leaving only the husk behind, sitting beneath the tree.

Impulsively, Leonie dropped down to lie full-length on the ground over the place where Gavin was buried. "Can you hear me, Father?" she whispered. "I know now. You could do nothing else but go with her, for your heart died with the parting, just as mine will die when I have to leave him. For so long I blamed you, but you will forgive your daughter, because at last she understands."

"Come, beloved." Klaus raised her. "Come home. Let your father sleep in peace. He has all he needs."

Leonie lay in the great bed in her apartments, relaxed and contented, as Klaus joined her. Their passion had taken many forms, sometimes leisurely, sometimes frenzied. Tonight was different again. Now they were husband and wife, bound forever by the unbreakable ties of love and commitment. Now there could be contentment mingled with the passion, and the certainty of those who'd come to the end of a fretful journey and found peace.

Klaus propped himself up on one arm, looked down at her pale, beautiful body against the silk sheets and brooded over his treasure, enjoying the way her two peoples united in her. She had the long, elegant legs of the aristocrat, combined with voluptuous hips, whose power spoke of Gypsy sturdiness. In heated nights, he'd discovered that her delicacy was an illusion. The apparent fragility hid a fiery strength. She could contend with him until morning, recover her breath and be ready to take him on again.

He laid his hand on her leg, just above the knee, and slid it slowly up the length of her thigh, taking his time, enjoying the feeling of her soft skin against his palm. Leonie put her arms behind her head and lay back, watching him with a little smile on her beautiful mouth. The smile was so enticing that he almost abandoned what he was doing and kissed her at once. But no! Everything in good time. He'd promised himself to save that treat for later.

He dropped his head to lay his lips against her throat, holding them there a moment, feeling a soft little pulse beating beneath the skin. Her perfume filled his nostrils. It was the kind that any court lady might wear, but beneath it, a thousand times more enticing, was her own personal scent, a mixture of musk and earth, flowers and air, and the special scent of arousal. He could feel now how much she wanted him and the knowledge excited him, putting new urgency into his movements.

Her eyes were drowsy, but filled with expectancy. Leonie found herself looking at Klaus with new eyes. Tonight he'd given her ultimate proof of his love and bound them together for life. She'd never felt so close to him, so truly a part of him, heart and soul and body. Tonight their love would be different, not the mating of two separate people, but the reunion of two halves of one whole. Even now, the warmth that was spreading through her at his touch was less desire than deep, intense love, love that would last a lifetime, that would make her his beyond the grave. She gave a long sigh of contentment and murmured his name for the pleasure of hearing the sound.

"Leonie," he whispered against her skin. "My Leonie . . . love me. . . ."

He was warm to her touch as she ran her hands lovingly over his body, taking a deep, sensuous delight in the shape of his broad shoulders, his torso, his hips and thighs. So much male beauty, and all for her pleasure, with the night before them. She gave a long, contented sigh.

"What is it?" he asked.

"I was enjoying my good luck," she told him. "And like a sensible woman, I'm going to make the most of it. After all, this is our wedding night."

"A night like no other," he said. "The night we finally became each other's completely, with trust and love and no holding back. As it should be."

She began to kiss his chest with subtle, purposeful movements. "How you hated me at first," she murmured.

He gave a deep chuckle. "How I hated you," he agreed. "And how little I understood. I didn't know women like you existed in the world."

She could hear the soft thunder of his heart as its beating became deeper. His breathing had slowed to long ragged breaths, and her own was in rhythm with it. She lay on her back and drew him across her, parting her legs for him in eager invitation. He came into her slowly, reverently, as if he couldn't believe how precious was the thing he held, and feared to break it. She received him with joy, feeling him find his natural place within her, uniting them in perfect harmony. He began to move in long, slow thrusts that drove pleasure deep inside. She gasped with the sweet-poignant sensation, utterly possessed by him as never before. She who'd always prized her freedom now found a new kind of freedom, melting herself into the self of her lover, creating a third self that took wing into eternity.

All good things seemed to come together in her consciousness, the glow of dawn, the burning of sunset, fresh flowing water, the running of the horses in spring, the first smile of a baby—all these things were there in the heat of their bodies' union, the giving and taking of pleasure and the bonds of love. In giving her himself, he'd given her the whole of life and made her queen of the world.

He lay close to her, his face near hers, her arms entwined around his neck. "Say that you're mine," he whispered, and she answered, "Yours—for all time."

"For all time," he echoed. "It has a beautiful sound."

Almost at once she knew his moment was coming. Her own breathing grew stronger at the same instant. The pleasure spiraled to new heights where nothing existed but the white heat of their desire. The world fell away from them. There was only this beauty, this ecstasy.

The fall back to earth was a kind of anguish, but his arms about her were strong and comforting. And his smile was there to tell her all was well. She smiled back in the last second before she fell asleep.

Leonie awoke at dawn to discover herself alone. The rumpled bed beside her showed where Klaus had lain, but there was no sign of him. Puzzled, she rose and looked around. He had never done such a thing before.

As she stood frowning, the secret door clicked and Klaus appeared. "I slipped away while you were asleep," he said, kissing her. "I needed to fetch something. Look."

He showed her a ring created from plaited strands of gold. "My father put it on my mother's hand the day they married, and removed it on the day she died," he said. "I've kept it to give to my own bride." He lifted her left hand and slipped the ring onto the third finger. "My wife for all eternity," he said.

"For all eternity," she whispered, awed by the love and humility in his voice.

He bowed his head to kiss her fingers, letting his lips linger against them. "In this world and the next," he said, echoing the words of their marriage service, "my heart will cleave to no other."

Chapter Thirteen

Klaus was to be away for four days inspecting the troops on Wolfenberg's border with Prussia. Leonie would have liked to go with him, but Reinald argued strenuously that the arrival of the favorite in a military camp would have caused scandal.

"Have no fear for me," Klaus told her tenderly. "Knowing you as I do, I'm sure my protectors are in place."

"Jack Blair's head will roll if they're not," she said darkly.

They dined in private on the last evening, and spent the night in each other's arms. There had never been such loving, brilliant, ecstatic, yet tinged with sorrow at their parting. Leonie tried to tell herself she was seeing shadows. They would be apart for a mere four days. Yet her heart was heavy with some nameless fear, and when the passion was over, she still clung to him for reassurance. They fell asleep in each other's arms.

Reinald traveled with him, intending to remain as long as Klaus did, but on the day after their departure, Reinald appeared in her apartments. It was late evening and Leonie had already undressed for bed. She was sitting in the dining room, sipping tea, wearing a peach satin robe, lavishly embroidered and adorned with lace. It was a voluminous garment that revealed less of her than if she'd been formally

clothed, but it still suggested undress, and she wouldn't
normally have chosen to appear this way with Reinald. But
when she heard his voice, she feared the worst and called out
in agitation. "Come in Reinald. Tell me quickly, has something happened to Klaus?"

"Klaus is well," he said, closing the door behind him.

"I thought you were to remain in camp with him."

"I meant to, but things are going so well there, my presence seemed unnecessary. I brought you a letter from him."
He held it out to her and she took it, smiling, and laid it
aside. "Don't you mean to read it now?" he asked with a
touch of irony. "Doesn't your impatience overcome you?"

"I can master my impatience," she said coolly. "I don't
need to prove how much I love Klaus. He knows it. Won't
you have some tea?" She would have loved to be rid of him,
but she wouldn't give Reinald even the small victory of seeing her discomposed.

As she poured his tea, Reinald said casually, "There were
a surprising number of Englishmen in the camp. Everyone
remarked on it."

"I dare say a few hotheads have come in search of adventure," she said. She already knew that English volun-
teers were attaching themselves to the Wolfenberg army.

"I think it's more," Reinald said. "England is taking a
close interest in Wolfenberg's fate. An alliance is expected
at any moment—and that means a marriage."

"I assure you I understand all the implications," Leonie
said, holding herself still.

"I wonder if you do. We spoke on this subject before, you
may remember."

"I also remember that you promised never to speak of it
again," she said sharply.

"I gave no promise. And circumstances have so changed
that now I must speak of it. What will it take to make you
see reason?"

"Reason?" she echoed. "Do you think love has anything to do with reason?"

He gave a humorless laugh. "Not for a man, perhaps. If I were governed by reason, I should never have chosen to love you. But for all their talk of love, women tend to be practical when making certain choices. Your good sense should impel you to me."

"My good sense impels me to tell you to leave," she said, rising.

He rose also and faced her. "Not until you've heard me out," he said. "And by God, you shall listen to me this time, Leonie."

"Leave at once or I call my servants." When he didn't move, she reached out to the little bell she kept on the table. But Reinald was there before her, seizing her hand in a cruel grip. "You'll call no one," he snapped.

"Are you mad? Klaus—"

"Klaus isn't here now. By the time he returns, you'll be singing a different song."

She saw real intent in his eyes and tried to call out, but he clamped a hand over her mouth before she could utter a sound. She fought madly but she was hampered by the huge folds of the gown. Reinald seized her hair and forced her to look up at him. His eyes were glittering and his breath came in harsh gasps. "You've no right to stand there so beautiful and tempting, and refuse me," he growled. "Do you understand? *No right.*"

He crushed her mouth brutally, twining his fingers deep into her hair to hold her still. She managed to struggle violently, but the only effect was to slide the gown down until her shoulders were completely exposed. With a swift movement, Reinald pulled it farther down, revealing her breasts. The sight seemed to drive him mad. He began to claw her wildly, like an animal. Frantically, Leonie drew back her left hand and delivered a blow she'd learned in the service. For a moment, it seemed to make his head spin. She seized her advantage to struggle free and make for the bedroom. He followed her, the glitter in his eyes clearly showing that he thought he'd won. But Leonie made straight for her dressing table on which lay the ivory fan with the concealed knife. A click and the slim blade sprung free just in time for her to hold it an inch from his face.

"Get out," she gasped. "I'll use this if I have to."

With most women, Reinald would have laughed off the threat, but there was something about Leonie that stopped him in his tracks. Perhaps it was the way she was holding the knife, purposefully, as if its feel were familiar to her. Or perhaps it was that she had the eyes of a woman who'd used a knife before—maybe even killed before—and wouldn't fear to do it again.

He began to back away. As he moved, he kept his eyes on her, on the glorious hair that tumbled about her shoulders, at the splendor of her naked breasts. At the bedroom door, he paused, and a cold smile touched his mouth. "Your servant, ma'am," he said, and turning, departed.

Leonie waited until she'd heard the front door close behind him. Then she pulled her clothes frantically about her, hurried back to the breakfast room and rang the bell madly. When her servants appeared, she gasped, "That man is never to be admitted to these rooms again. You understand? *Never.*"

They exclaimed in horror. With difficulty she prevented her elderly majordomo from pursuing Reinald and attacking him with his bare hands. "No scandal," she told them. "Not a word until the prince comes home."

"And I'll sleep in your room tonight," Miss Hatchard declared in an unusual show of feeling, "in case the devil comes back."

Martha sniffed. "That's for me to do."

In the end, Leonie allowed them to share the room, each taking one side of the huge double bed. She had her own bed made up on the sofa, but spent the night sitting up, covering sheets of paper with her extravagant handwriting. A lesser woman would have been sending a cry for help to her lover, but Leonie was made of sterner stuff. She was sending an urgent report to Lord William. When she'd finished, she read it through, signed it and slipped it into her reticule, ready for the next day.

Reinald returned at once to Herrenhaltz. Leonie's blow had produced an angry red mark on his face, and he had no desire to be seen at court in that state. A black look at Luther kept the little man from making any observation.

In his own room, he studied himself furiously in a mirror. Then something made him grow still. He peered closer at his reflection, and saw that his first thought had been correct. Leonie had struck him with her left hand, and her ring had left a mark. He looked at the mark for a long time. At last he left the room. "Remain here," he said curtly to Luther, who was outside.

He let himself into Sylvana's room without knocking. She was sitting up in bed, reading, and glanced at her brother with curiosity but no surprise. This wasn't the first such visit. There was no affection between brother and sister, but they'd occasionally found it convenient to be allies. When he turned up the lamp and she caught sight of his face, she burst into a coarse laugh. "Did some woman dare to say no?" she mocked. "I wonder what she looks like now? For I'm sure you gave as good as you got."

"Not yet, but I intend to," Reinald said coldly. "Be silent, and listen to me. Just how much do you hate the Dowager Duchess of Coniston?"

Sylvana was instantly alert. "What do you want me to do?"

* * *

Leonie took the air as usual the next morning. A carriage
conveyed her to the park where she alighted and sauntered
across the lawn for half an hour. Sometimes she smiled and
spoke to acquaintances. Sometimes she merely nodded in
gracious acknowledgement of a greeting. All eyes followed
her as she went regally along her way.

But not every creature treated her with respect. Today, a
young man walking a large dog was seen to lose control of
the creature, who bounded up to the duchess and pounced
on her beautiful gown with dusty paws. In fending him off,
she dropped her reticule, which was rescued for her by the
young man, full of profuse apologies. Barking gleefully, the
dog pounced again and it took their combined efforts to
make him understand that his attentions were unwelcome.
The young man apologized again. Leonie begged him not to
think of it. He returned her reticule and sped away, her letter to Lord Bracewell concealed inside his jacket, ready to
be slipped into the diplomatic bag.

Leonie returned to the palace to find her majordomo in a
flutter. "You said the Archduke Reinald was to be kept
out," he said unhappily, "but no mention was made of his
sister."

"The Princess Sylvana?" Leonie said, astonished. "Is she
here?"

"For the last hour, your grace. She insisted on coming in
and waiting for you. I hope I didn't do wrong—"

"It's all right," Leonie soothed him kindly. "As you say,
I made no mention of anyone else."

Sylvana was sitting by the window in an attitude that
might have suggested humility if Leonie hadn't known her
incapable of it. She rose when she heard Leonie enter the
room. Determined to maintain formality, Leonie dropped
into a curtsy and Sylvana immediately rushed forward to
raise her. "I beg you not to curtsy to me," she said quickly.

"Your rank prescribes it, madam," Leonie said.

"Oh, let us not talk of rank," Sylvana pleaded, her hands clasped to her breast. "Let us confide in each other like sisters."

Leonie thought grimly that if she were playing this scene—and it wasn't unlike some she'd been called on to play in the course of her career—she'd have done better than this. But Sylvana's arrogance made her incapable of successful dissimulation. In trying to appear modest, she merely became melodramatic and false. But Leonie concealed her suspicions, cast down her eyes and murmured, "Too kind...honored..."

"It's I who am honored that you deign to receive me after the terrible events of yesterday," Sylvana told her. "That's why I came when I knew you were out. I was afraid your hatred extended to our whole family and you would refuse to see me. And indeed, I wouldn't have blamed you, for my brother has confessed all to me. His behavior was unforgivable. He says so himself."

"Then I won't quarrel with his choice of words," Leonie said calmly. "I own I'm surprised that he's told you."

"Oh, but I'm his ambassador. I've come to beg forgiveness for him."

"I never want to see him in these rooms again," Leonie declared flatly.

"He doesn't ask that. I swear he doesn't. But I beg you not to tell Klaus. It would disgrace my family."

"I can make no such—" Leonie began. Before she could continue, Sylvana gave a cry and slipped to her knees on the floor. To Leonie's intense embarrassment, the princess was kissing her hand. She tried to snatch it away but Sylvana kept firm hold on it while she wept and entreated. "Have mercy on us," she sobbed hysterically. "The disgrace would kill my mother."

Leonie finally recovered her hand by sheer force. "I mean no harm to your mother," she said, fighting down her disgust at this performance. "And nor will Klaus. I have to tell him, but he's a generous man. He won't let her suffer. You have my word on that."

Sylvana stayed where she was on the floor, her head bent so that Leonie couldn't see her face. A shudder seemed to go through the princess's body, and Leonie feared a violent burst of tears, but when Sylvana raised her head, her eyes were dry. "Then I must accept your word," she said. "What am I to tell Reinald?"

"Tell him nothing," Leonie said fiercely. "I send him no message. I would prefer to forget that he exists. Please leave me now."

Sylvana rose from the floor. Her manner was calm for one who'd so recently been hysterical. "I'll bid you good day," she said, and swept out.

Left alone, Leonie went to her bedroom. The falseness of the whole scene had left her feeling shattered, as though someone had struck a cracked glass, making an ugly reverberation that had echoed through her. Through the window, she could see Sylvana get into a closed carriage and leave the palace. She kept her eyes on the carriage until it was out of sight.

"Well?" Reinald asked.

Sylvana made a face as she leaned back against the squabs of the carriage and regarded her brother. "I hope I'm well rewarded for what I've just endured," she said bitterly. "I humbled myself to her. *I* actually humbled myself to that harlot. I groveled on the floor. It makes me positively ill to think how I kissed her hand."

"Her *left* hand?" Reinald asked sharply.

"Her left hand, as you instructed." Sylvana's eyes narrowed. "And you were quite right. She wears his mother's wedding ring."

"I suspected it." Reinald touched the mark on his face reflectively. "If he's given her his mother's ring, he's in deeper than I thought."

"A secret marriage?" Sylvana demanded sharply. "It must be set aside."

"I doubt it. My guess is that they exchanged sentimental, but unofficial vows. Klaus knows his duty. And that doesn't mean his duty to you, dear sister. You should have abandoned that hope long ago."

Sylvana's eyes were hard. "If I can see that woman brought low, that's all I ask."

"That depends on how well you performed the rest of your task. Were you left alone?"

"For almost an hour. Don't worry. I've done my work very thoroughly."

"I don't doubt it," Reinald said dryly. "Then it seems as if we'll both be avenged."

Just one more day until Klaus's return. Leonie went to bed thinking of him, and found that he was there in her dreams, but a long way off, out of her reach. A terrible sense of foreboding possessed her and she struggled to awaken. As her eyes opened she discovered that Martha was shaking her frantically and calling her in a voice filled with fear.

"What's the matter?" Leonie asked sleepily.

"Wake up, please, your grace," Martha begged. "There are soldiers here. They say they've come to arrest you."

She was out of bed and throwing on her clothes in a moment. As she worked, her mind repeated the incredible words. Arrest. It was impossible. She was the prince's favorite, beloved and protected. But the prince was far away, and the sense of foreboding in the dream was still here. At a level too deep to be examined, she knew she'd been expecting trouble.

She found three soldiers waiting for her, all looking uneasy but resolute. The sergeant in charge cleared his throat and announced, "Charges of spying have been laid against you. I'm instructed to search your rooms."

"You must be quite mad to risk the prince's anger in this way," she told him coldly. The sergeant's face clearly showed that he knew it. "Who dares accuse me of spying?" she asked.

The man cleared his throat. "The order has been signed by Archduke Reinald," he said.

Suddenly Reinald was standing there in the doorway, regarding her coolly. "It's I who dare accuse you," he said. "Your devious activities have come to light, madam, and you will stand trial before the people of this country. Sergeant, I've already ordered you to search these rooms. Do your duty."

"You'll find nothing to incriminate me," Leonie told him.

"I already have one document that speaks blackly against you," Reinald said smoothly. He reached into his jacket and pulled out some sheets of paper, which he held up. Leonie started as she recognized her own letter to Lord William, handed over in the park the previous day. "A letter to Lord William Bracewell," Reinald said, "whom I happen to know is the head of British Intelligence. The contents of this letter do you no credit, madam, a series of scurrilous lies against me. For myself, I care nothing. The people of Wolfenberg know what to think of me. But what other lies have you told, and how much damage have you done?"

"I don't tell lies," Leonie said, although she already knew her protests were useless. This was a prearranged scene. "Every word is the truth, as you well know."

He shrugged. "We'll let the court decide."

"How did you come by that letter?"

"Not without some difficulty, I must admit. Your messenger was unwilling to yield it up. It was necessary to stop his obstruction permanently."

"Oh, my God! You had him murdered," she said with loathing.

"He was the unfortunate victim of an accident that wouldn't have happened if he hadn't been resisting arrest."

Leonie closed her eyes, thinking of the cheery young man who'd played out the little farce in the park.

"I've found something, your lordship."

The triumphant cry jerked Leonie back to life. She opened her eyes to see the sergeant holding up a package in triumph. Reinald snatched it from him and flicked through the contents. "Letters from Lord William," he announced, "that will doubtless reveal everything about your part in the plot to overthrow this country."

"Doubtless, since you wrote them yourself," Leonie snapped. She never kept Lord William's letters. They were read once and then burned.

Reinald gave an unpleasant, silent laugh. "Surely you can manage a better defense than that? I'd thought better of your ingenuity."

"I'd thought better of your honor."

Reinald's eyes were flints. "Leonie, Dowager Duchess of Coniston, I arrest you for spying on this country. You will be taken to The Fort and kept there until your trial and conviction."

"You've already decided that I'll be convicted."

"My dear, I haven't a doubt of it. Shall we go?"

He took her arm. She tried to shake him off but he had a grip of iron. With his fingers digging into her flesh, she was forced to walk down the stone staircase, past the place where they'd sat and talked like comrades on the night of Gruber's arrest. Leonie walked with her head up, looking neither right nor left. Even so, she couldn't help but know that every window in the palace had curious faces pressed against it.

At the bottom of the steps was a closed carriage. Luther sat on the box, smiling at her humiliation. Reinald pushed her toward it and climbed in after her. "The far door is locked," he said. "But then, where would you escape to?"

"I've no need to escape," she told him proudly. "Do you think Klaus will ever let you get away with this?"

"Klaus can do nothing about it," Reinald said simply. "He's renounced his power over the judiciary—something in which you most obligingly assisted. You'll go to trial, and there's enough evidence to convict you."

Her heart was beginning to hammer with apprehension. "False evidence, planted by Sylvana," she snapped.

"Prove it."

"All this because I rejected you?"

"Oh, no, my dear. You were coming much too close to things I didn't want you to know about. You're a very dangerous woman."

She met his eyes. "Gruber wasn't the real traitor at all, was he?" she said. "It's you."

"I object to the word *traitor*. As poor Gruber himself said, I'm a patriot. I want what's best for Wolfenberg, and that happens to be me. You'd have seen through me eventually if you hadn't happened to stumble on Gruber's activities. He was exactly what Klaus thought, a silly, deluded old man who never meant any harm. But he was lucky for me. He threw you off the scent."

"It was you all the time."

"As you say, all the time."

"You killed him, didn't you?" she breathed. "You did it that night in his cell."

"I got to him just in time. The letter he was writing would have been highly damaging to me. I couldn't allow anyone to see it. The few torn scraps they found were simply the remains of the last page. I carried the rest away with me and burned it.

"It was Gruber, by the way, who put me on your track that night. He told me you sometimes visited The Black Dog. Since then, Luther's watched you there several times. Then there was that beggar I saw you with in the park. When I heard him mention The Black Dog, I guessed he must be one of your colleagues."

"And yet you did nothing—until now."

"I expected you to see reason and turn to me. You must admit that I gave you every chance. But you were stubborn. I kept on hoping until I discovered this." He took her left hand, turning it to reveal the ring. "His mother's wedding ring."

"It means nothing," she said quickly, to protect Klaus. "The world would never recognize us as married. I'm no dynastic threat."

"My dear! As though I cared. No, it simply served to reveal how deeply committed to Klaus you were. Until then, I'd kept my hopes alive against all reason. You see what love will do to a man."

She stared at him. "You still wanted me, even when you believed me to be working against your country."

He laughed. "You're not working against Wolfenberg, Leonie. I know very well why you're here. British Intelligence sent you to keep watch over Klaus and discover who was behind the attempts on his life. What a pity that you won't get the chance to tell them."

"And do you think Klaus won't guess—after this?"

Reinald shrugged. "It might even be useful if he did. Any action he took against me, or on your behalf, would be, shall we say, highly convenient in certain quarters."

"Give Bismarck an excuse to invade," she breathed. "You monster!"

"Far from being a monster, I care only for my country's well-being. Firmness and order are what is necessary. A strong hand to keep the people in their place. Believe me, they're better for it."

"Under a Prussian jackboot?" she demanded scathingly. "It'll need Bismarck to put you on the throne."

"Of course. We made our arrangements long ago. I take the throne and lead Wolfenberg into a greater united Germany. In return, he'll leave me a free hand here."

"Then God help the people," she said bluntly.

Reinald shrugged. "The people will soon become accustomed to a new master." He drew aside one of the black leather curtains that covered the windows. "We've reached The Fort," he said.

With a swift movement, he pulled her against him and looked at her. "How bitter you look." He sighed. "I dreamed that it might be otherwise. I thought I'd hold you in my arms and see your face flushed with passion, not hard and unyielding as it is now." He paused. "Not a word? Not a hint? Very well. Let this be our farewell."

She stayed tense and stiff in his arms as he forced his kiss upon her. She was pervaded by horror, but she wouldn't give an inch. She wouldn't even give him the satisfaction of seeing her struggle. At last he drew back. "Even now, you could have begged me for mercy," he said. "One day soon, you'll regret that you didn't."

Chapter Fourteen

The cell was bare and cold. There was a narrow bed with a hard mattress, a table and one chair. Leonie was allowed pen and paper and a candle, but she ignored them, suspecting a trap. Turpitz, the jailer, was a small man with a false smile that verged on a sneer. Showing Leonie around "her new apartments," as he called them, he drew her attention to the courtyard below, which she could just see from the window. "That's where executions are carried out," he informed her. "In Wolfenberg, we do it by firing squad." It was plain he expected her to join the number of the victims.

His only redeeming feature was that he was under the thumb of his wife, a large woman with arms heavy enough to keep her husband in order. She came into the cell in time to hear his last remark and told him sharply to mind his tongue. He jumped and scuttled away.

Within a few hours, Martha appeared, having managed to get on the right side of Frau Turpitz by doing the woman's washing. In return, she was allowed to visit her mistress twice a day, and she declared her resolve to do so, ignoring Leonie's commands that she escape while she could. The others, too, had refused to leave. They'd taken advantage of the turmoil caused by her arrest to slip out of the palace, and were living in a small inn nearby. Masham

was looking for a chance to contact Jack Blair, but so far he
hadn't dared. He guessed, as Leonie did, that they were still
free because Reinald was having them watched in the hopes
that they would do something that could be used to further
incriminate her. Masham's message to Leonie was to keep
in good heart. He wouldn't fail her. She smiled at the message, but she knew it was hopeless. Reinald was an implacable enemy.

She began to understand just how implacable when Turpitz entered and threw the *Treuheim Gazette* on the table,
regarding her with a gleeful grin as he withdrew. Leonie
snatched it up. The front page was full of a lurid tale of a
British plot to invade and subdue Wolfenberg. It read:

> Under the guise of assisting us, the British secretly
> planned to seize control of the country for themselves.
> To this end, a spy was placed near the person of our
> gracious prince with secret orders to obtain informa-
> tion about Wolfenberg's defenses so that when the time
> came...

There was a lot more in the same vein, but Leonie didn't
need to read it all to know that Reinald had been fiendishly
clever. He'd simply taken the truth and stood it on its head.
The result was a witch-hunt in which cold logic had no
place.

That was confirmed when Turpitz came in an hour later,
ostensibly to bring her food, but actually to remark,
"There's a crowd gathered around the British embassy.
Someone threw a brick through the window."

She kept her face blank, refusing to let him see that she
was disturbed, but when he'd gone, she buried her face in
her hands and sent up a desperate prayer for her servants'
safety.

She was still praying when she heard the key rattle again in the lock. She looked up quickly, setting a blank expression on her face, but it vanished when she saw the man who entered and stood looking at her, his heart in his eyes. The next moment she was running across the floor to be enfolded in his arms. "My love," she breathed before his mouth covered hers.

They clung to each other for a long time, listening to the sound of their hearts beating together. Then Klaus pushed her a little way from him and studied her anxiously. "You're so pale," he said. "I've given the strictest orders that you're to be well treated, but oh my God, I should be able to get you out, and I can't." The words were a cry of agony.

"I'm being well treated," she promised him. "Martha takes care of me."

"And you'll be out of here soon," he vowed. "I'll speak at your trial and tell everyone the truth about you."

"*No,*" she said urgently. "No, Klaus, you mustn't do that. Don't ever think of it."

"My darling, it's no use trying to protect your cover now. That's all over. Your only hope is to have me tell the truth."

"The truth is that I *am* a British agent—just as I'm charged."

"But you were working *for* Wolfenberg, not against it."

"Who knows that except you? Klaus, listen to me, I beg you. I know now who's been behind the attacks on you. The real traitor is Reinald. It's been Reinald all the time. He murdered Gruber. He used Sylvana to plant incriminating evidence on me. He hates you. He wants your throne and he thinks he can get it through Bismarck."

He stared at her. "That's not possible." But he said the words mechanically. Even as he uttered them, he knew he'd already become uneasy about his cousin. Reinald's brutal arrest of Leonie had shown a side of him Klaus had never suspected, a side that had been carefully concealed. And yet...

"Reinald, hand in glove with Bismarck," he said distractedly. "I don't believe it. I can't."

"You must, for your own sake and the sake of your people. You dare not let him succeed. He's watching you now, waiting for you to do something reckless to defend me. He's convinced the people that my country is an enemy. If you admit that you've been working secretly with the British, he can make you look like an enemy, too. Prussia will invade and Reinald will reign as Bismarck's puppet. Your people will be little better than slaves. For *their* sakes, you mustn't give him the shadow of an excuse."

He was as pale as death. "What are you asking me to do? Abandon you?"

"You have no choice. My usefulness is finished."

"Usefulness?" He repeated the word as though it was strange to him. "Do you think that's what you've been to me—useful?"

She shook her head. "There are no words for what we've been to each other, but that's for ourselves alone. It's something that no one can take away from us, ever. But, my darling, our time is over. Can't you see that? From now on, you must be the prince, ready to lift an instrument or cast it away, as you need. And the moment has come to cast me away."

"No!" he said explosively. "You're telling me to betray you. How could you even think I'd do that?"

She touched his face gently. "I know that in your heart you'll never betray me," she whispered. "But I also know that you can't save me. You can only save your people, and that means saving yourself."

"I'll have Reinald arrested—"

"On what charge? You have no evidence, only the opinion of a woman arrested for spying. Arrest Reinald and Bismarck will cross your border the same day."

"Then I'll defeat him. My army is bigger and stronger now. I've used that loan to buy the best equipment—"

"And how many of your subjects would die? Not just soldiers, but civilians, men, women and children cut down in Bismarck's path. You swore to protect them. Can you let them die to save me?"

In the silence, she saw his face turn gray with horror. "I'd lay down my own life for you without a moment's thought," he whispered.

"But you have no right to lay down theirs. My dearest, there's nothing you can do. Reinald has blocked off every avenue."

"Dear God!" he exclaimed. "Once, I could have freed you by decree. Now, I can't even do that. I gave up the one chance I could have had to help you. And Reinald...he agreed so easily when I renounced that power. He even suggested that I have the decree ratified in the chamber. It puzzled me at the time, but now I see why."

"Yes, he was laying his plans against me even then. In his own frozen way, he's in love with me. When I refused him, he decided to destroy me. It's so easy to see it, now that it's too late."

"I won't admit that it's too late," Klaus said harshly. He kissed her repeatedly, her mouth, her face, her eyes, as if he were trying to store the memory of how she felt against his lips. She could sense his anguish in the trembling of his strong body, and she clung to him, trying to give comfort as well as take it. She loved him with all her heart, and now the worst anguish was the knowledge that she'd caused him such bitter grief. "I'll save you somehow," he vowed. "There *has* to be a way."

"You must keep quiet. Promise me. Don't take any risks. But do one thing for me."

"Yes," he said eagerly. "Anything."

"Martha comes here to care for me, and the others are living nearby in the Angel Tavern. They haven't charged them with anything, but they could at any moment. Make them all leave while there's still time. You can do that, can't you?"

"Yes, if they haven't been charged, I still have that power," he said grimly. "It shall be done. But who will look after you in this place?"

"I need very little. Tell me that you love me, and there's nothing left for me to want."

"How can I speak of my love now?" he demanded. "What right have I to *your* love when I'm failing you?"

A sudden light illuminated her face, making it more beautiful than he'd ever seen it. "There are no rights or obligations between us. I love you, Klaus. That's all there has to be. You don't need to do anything. Just give me your heart in return and I'll say that my life has been glorious because I was loved by you."

"Will I never stop learning from you?" he asked in wonder.

"Never, just as I will have learned from you until the last moment of my life. I've learned from your tenderness, from your strength and courage and wisdom. You've been all I needed, all I'll ever need. I've lived a whole lifetime in the few months we've had together. We've had so little, and yet so much. It can never be taken away."

He understood and his frame was racked with anguish. "*No,*" he promised. "I won't let you die. I can still refuse to sign the death warrant, and perhaps release you later."

"You could never release me. Reinald is watching your every move, ready to pounce. You could only condemn me to a living death in this place instead of a quick merciful one. Klaus, you mustn't do that. I'm a Gypsy. I must live in freedom or not at all."

"You ask me to sign away your life?" His voice was hoarse and full of agony.

"If you have to. Better that than be walled up for years, going mad. Promise me."

"No," he cried harshly. "I can't."

"You must. If you love me, promise me this."

For a moment, she thought he would refuse. His face was like death. Then he said, as if the words were drawn from him by torture, "I'll do it. I'll do whatever you want, but *oh God*, I pray it doesn't come to that."

"It will come to that," she said bleakly. "Reinald has already decided."

That evening, Martha came to her bringing fresh fruit she'd bought in the market. It was a delicious relief from the disgusting prison fare. Nonetheless, Leonie was sorry to see her. "Martha, haven't you seen the prince?" she asked worriedly.

"He keeps his distance from me and I keep my distance from him," Martha answered crossly. "The less I see of him the better. What's the use of being a prince if he can't get you out of here?"

"Don't blame him, Martha." She lowered her voice. "He came to see me and was full of wild plans to rescue me. They won't do. He must put his country first. But he promised me that he'd see to it you left."

Martha snorted. "Promises are easy. He's done precious little about that one. Nor will he."

She had hardly finished speaking when the door was flung open with a crash and Turpitz scurried into the cell, followed by three soldiers. One of them, a sergeant, stood a little in front of the other two and consulted a paper before addressing Martha. "Martha Randall, Englishwoman?"

"And who wants to know?" Martha demanded belligerently.

"By command of Prince Klaus Friederich, Martha Randall is declared an undesirable alien, and sentenced to be expelled from this country," the sergeant read.

"You can take that paper and stick it up your nose," Martha announced bluntly. "Here I am and here I stay."

The sergeant sighed in exasperation. "That's what they all said."

"All?" Leonie gasped.

"Your other servants are being expelled, too. They've been rounded up from the Angel Tavern and I've got them in a carriage outside. And every one of them gave me trouble. My orders are to get you all across the border by midnight, so come on. There's no time to waste."

But Martha set her chin and seemed to take root in the floor. The sergeant nodded to the other two soldiers, who advanced on her. "Get away from me!" she shrieked. "I'm staying with my lady." She clung to Leonie. "Don't let them take me away. What will you do without me?"

"It's best, Martha," Leonie said quickly. "I'll be easier in my mind."

"I won't go. I won't go, d'you hear?" But they lifted her from the ground and bore her from the cell, fighting and shouting to the last. Leonie could hear her indignant screams growing fainter down the corridor. When the last sound had died, she leaned against the wall, her eyes closed, almost faint with relief.

"So now you'll have to manage for yourself...if you know how," Turpitz sneered. "Thought you were going to act high-and-mighty in here, didn't you? But our prince knows how to treat a woman like you."

He departed with a final sneer. Leonie opened her eyes and looked about her at the bleak cell where she would now be completely alone. Despite everything, there was a strange sensation in her breast that was almost like joy. Klaus had taken away her last remaining comfort, her one contact with the outside world. And he'd done it because it was the only way he could show that he loved her.

Klaus knew that his best hope was Palmerston, the British prime minister who set such store by the alliance with Wolfenberg, who'd sent Leonie on her dangerous mission and who was such a notorious ladies' man that his nickname, "Lord Cupid," had pursued him into his old age. Even now, a beautiful woman could soften him as nothing else could, and his tendency to apply military pressure was notorious. He would respond to Leonie's peril in such belligerent terms that Klaus could appeal to the chamber of deputies to expel her from the country, arguing political necessity. He would never see her again, but he could live in peace knowing she was beyond Reinald's reach.

He considered writing a letter but abandoned the idea at once. If the paper should fall into the wrong hands, it would be damning. Only a verbal message would do, and only one man could be trusted to deliver it. He summoned Bernhard and told him the whole story. "Tell Palmerston that my power is limited," he said urgently, "but he can reinforce my arm. And if he doubts that you come from me, give him this." He held out the card, torn into two pieces, that had alerted him to Leonie's true reason for being in Wolfenberg. "Now come with me."

He led Bernhard to the door of the secret passage. "It's best if you depart this way," he said. "I believe there are some who may try to stop you." He embraced his friend. "God be with you!" he said fervently.

Back in his own room, he lost his temper. It was twenty-four hours since the arrest of a prominent Englishwoman, yet from the British ambassador there hadn't been a word.

He sent a sharp message to the embassy and waited for Lord Hadden's arrival.

The ambassador appeared two hours later.

"I'd expected you sooner," Klaus growled.

"A thousand apologies, your royal highness, but I had the greatest difficulty making my way here. The crowds around the embassy are extremely hostile. They called me the most unpleasant names."

"If names are the worst thing you have to worry about, you needn't be too concerned," Klaus said curtly.

"Oh, but they aren't. A brick was thrown at the window, although, fortunately, it fell short."

"Never mind, you're here now."

"I was about to call and apprise your royal highness of the sad tidings when I received your message," Hadden announced with lofty dignity. "But I gather the news has gone ahead of me. It is a tragedy for us all."

"I'm glad to see that you realize that," Klaus said. "I'd thought to hear from you sooner."

Hadden looked puzzled. "But the news only reached me an hour ago."

"You only heard that your fellow countrywoman had been arrested a day after it happened?" Klaus said angrily.

"Your royal highness's pardon, I was not referring to the fate of Lady Coniston, but to the death of Lord Palmerston."

For the first time, Klaus noticed that Hadden was wearing black. He stared at him, unable to take in the full extent of the blow. "Lord Palmerston—dead?" he echoed.

"Peacefully in his sleep," Lord Hadden intoned. "He was nearly eighty, but his health had seemed good. Now he is lost to us. It is a catastrophe that will be felt in many countries. . . ." He spoke as if he were addressing a crowd.

With a feeling of sick despair, Klaus realized that little could be hoped for from the ambassador. "Is there any news about who will succeed him?" he asked.

"There is no definite word, but I believe Lord Russell is widely expected to be the next prime minister."

Klaus's heart sank. He'd met Russell, an aloof, cold-featured man, and been ill at ease with him. He forced himself to say what was proper, then returned to what chiefly concerned him. "I'd expected to hear from you before this concerning the arrest of the Dowager Duchess of Coniston," he told Hadden.

"Ah, yes, the dowager duchess. I have of course been reading the accounts in the newspapers. Most regrettable. However, I'm happy to assure your royal highness that I don't seek to interfere with the course of justice in Wolfenberg."

"But you will make a protest?" Klaus insisted.

"I—er—oh yes. Yes, indeed, perhaps some protest is called for. I have of course read the *Treuheim Gazette* and find it most unfortunate that such things should be said about the British government."

Klaus clenched his hands, trying to control the rage growing in his breast. "The protest I have in mind concerns the fate of Lady Coniston," he said. "You naturally take the view that Lady Coniston is innocent. In fact, that is the view I take myself. I find these accusations impossible to believe."

Lord Hadden looked unhappy and Klaus's fury grew. "If you've read the papers, you must know she's been accused of spying against this country," he snapped. "You can't seriously consider her guilty."

"As a representative of the British government, there is naturally no question of my conceding that a British subject could be guilty of spying on this country," Lord Hadden declared, evidently relieved to have gotten onto a familiar track.

"Then you think her innocent," Klaus said emphatically.

"Oh, certainly—er—that is—yes."

"And you wish to protest in the strongest possible terms against this unjustified detention of a British subject," Klaus persisted.

"Er—well—"

"And you will let me have your protest in writing within the hour. Good day to you."

Lord Hadden bowed himself out. Left alone, Klaus sat at his desk, prey to sensations of horror such as he'd never known before. He recognized only too clearly that Hadden was incapable of lifting a finger to protect Leonie. His own power was severely weakened. His best hope had been Palmerston. He buried his face in his hands, picturing Bernhard hurrying to England to deliver a life-and-death message to a man who would never hear it.

At three in the morning, The Black Dog was almost empty. The last few customers were drifting away and the landlord looked up in annoyance when the stranger entered. Wasn't a man allowed to sleep? But before uttering a surly word, he paused, struck by the newcomer's clothes, which were costlier than he normally saw in here.

The man approached the counter. "I seek Jack Blair," he said in a low voice.

"Not here," the landlord grunted. "He and his friends left in a hurry two days ago."

Klaus's heart gave the lurch of near despair that was becoming so familiar to him. But something in the landlord's manner made him try again. He produced a gold coin and laid it on the counter. "Are you sure they went right away?" he persisted. "I would pay well to be taken to them."

The landlord bit the coin, seemed to find it good and grunted again. "I know nothing about this," he said cautiously.

"That's understood."

"Then come this way."

He went to the back of the tavern and pulled up a trap door from the wooden floor. Klaus followed him down a rickety flight of steps to a noisome cellar where a man sat, drinking ale by the light of a lantern. He was sitting on an upturned box, using another box to play a solitary card game, while a few sacks thrown into a corner showed where he slept. He glanced up, and in the poor light, Klaus just managed to recognize Jack Blair. Blair got to his feet when he recognized his visitor, and a knife gleamed.

"You don't need that," Klaus said quickly. "I'm here as a friend. You've heard what happened?"

"'Course I heard. I suppose by now she's blabbed everything?"

"She's told nothing," Klaus said. "Nothing at all. She doesn't care for protecting herself, but I care about protecting her. Somehow she must be gotten out of there."

Blair shrugged. "So let her out. You're the prince."

"I have no power to free her," Klaus said bitterly. "She herself persuaded me to renounce that power. I have to find another way."

"Bribe the judge."

"The judge is incorruptible. Based upon the evidence planted on her, he'll have to find her guilty. That's where you and your friends come in. You must rescue her. I know a secret way into The Fort. I can give you the key—"

"Rescue her?" Blair was staring at him. "Why the devil should I want to rescue her?"

"Because you're her colleague, her friend."

"She's no friend of mine and I'm no friend of hers."

Klaus's rage began to grow again. "But if the positions were reversed, you know as well as I do that she'd risk everything to rescue you," he said with biting emphasis.

"I know nothing of the kind. The only thing I *know* is that it was madness to send a woman on this mission, and as for putting her in charge..." He snorted.

"So that's it," Klaus breathed. "You've always resented her for being your leader. For God's sake, man, put your personal feelings aside and do your duty by her. If you and your friends—"

"My friends have gone," Blair interrupted. "Every one of them got out of here fast when the news broke. There's only me left, and I'm not mounting any solo expeditions, I can tell you."

"Then why did you stay?"

Blair didn't speak, but his malevolent eyes gleamed with sudden pleasure and Klaus felt sick. "So that's it," he said. "You stayed for the execution. Do you enjoy thinking of her being shot?"

"She won't bother me anymore after that."

Something snapped inside Klaus. Before he knew what he was doing, he'd leaped on Blair and slammed him against the wall with his hands around the man's throat. "You'd be a fool to kill me," Blair croaked.

Slowly Klaus relaxed his hold. He was breathing hard but his brain had cleared enough to know that the loathsome creature was right. There was nothing to be gained here. Feeling as though his head would explode, he stumbled up the stairs and out into the fresh air.

An hour later, soldiers arrived at The Black Dog with an order, signed by the prince, expelling Jack Blair from Wolfenberg. They saw him across the border with a warning never to return if he valued his safety.

* * *

Bernhard was gone four days. He arrived back late one evening, hollow-eyed with exhaustion, and handed Klaus a letter. "Russell is the new prime minister," he said. "I told him everything. He said Palmerston was given to 'exotic intrigue'—that was his exact expression—but that things would change now. He said the British government couldn't accept the responsibility for 'ill-considered adventures.'"

"You mean he won't do anything to save her?" Klaus demanded.

"All he's prepared to do is contained in that letter."

Klaus opened it and discovered an official protest at the detention of a British subject. It was couched in the most formal and least belligerent of tones, and had plainly been written by a man anxious to discharge his official duty and forget about the matter. Klaus read it through twice, trying vainly to extract an ounce of hope from it. Then he let his head fall into his hands.

All Treuheim wanted to see the trial, and the public seats were filled before nine o'clock. The lawyers gathered, trying to seem decorous and judicial, but talking eagerly amongst themselves, their gazes always turning back to the dock where the prisoner would soon stand. At last Judge Konrad appeared, his black robes a reproach to the crowd that had gathered to see the fun.

Finally the prisoner entered, no longer in fine satin and jewels, but forced to wear ugly gray prison garb. Her golden hair that had once taken hours to dress was now drawn severely back and confined in a snood, and her face was dreadfully pale. Yet she held her head high and gave her name in a voice that never wavered. And the spectators, pushing forward to see her, murmured that she had never looked so beautiful, then fell silent, shamed by her courage and dignity.

When she was standing before the court, there was a moment's expectancy, while all eyes turned toward a carved, gilded chair, set near the judge, but slightly apart. For a trial of such importance, the prince himself might choose to be present, and that chair was his alone. Surely, they all thought, he would appear today to see the fate of the woman who'd bewitched and deceived him? Perhaps he'd be there to wreak vengeance on her? Or perhaps he would offer her his support? But they waited in vain. There was no sign of the prince. And then they all understood. He'd abandoned her.

There wasn't one person there who didn't know that the case was hopeless, including the prisoner herself. She remained silent as witnesses came and went. The honest sergeant who'd been ordered to search her apartments spoke of what he'd found, then cast an almost beseeching glance in her direction, as if asking forgiveness for what he was forced to do. A murmur went around the court as she smiled at him, as if to say that they were both caught up by forces beyond their control.

Reinald entered the witness box. He seemed to speak more in sorrow than in anger, telling the court how the woman before them had practiced her black arts to infatuate their prince, while all the time spying against their country. He told how she'd used her wiles on himself, but he, not blinded by passion, had resisted her. Driven by love for his country and his prince, he'd tracked down the evidence that proved what she was.

When Reinald was done, Judge Konrad asked, "What does the prisoner have to say in her own defense?"

Leonie rose and stood silently looking around the court. For a moment, every man and woman there felt she was looking directly at them, but in fact, she was aware of none of them. Her thoughts were far away with the man she loved, and she was praying for the chance to do him one final service. At last she spoke, in a voice whose soft beauty vibrated in every dim corner of the room.

"My lord, I will not waste this court's time in pleading for my life, for my death has already been decided."

The judge frowned. "Do you accuse this court of corruption?"

"No, my lord. I know you to be just and impartial. But you are the victim of one man's evil, as I am myself. The Archduke Reinald has lied to this court to conceal his own design, which is nothing but the overthrow of your prince with Prussia's help. Then he'll claim the throne and rule as Bismarck's puppet. That's the danger that faces this country, and it's so great and so near that my own fate is nothing beside it."

A buzz went around the crowd at these outrageous accusations. The judge frowned, and Reinald regarded Leonie with a pitying smile. She ignored him and continued, "I never sought to use my 'wiles' against the archduke. It was he who pursued me, and turned against me when I refused him. There's only one man whom I love, and that man is your prince, whom God preserve and protect from the enemy within his own palace."

As she spoke of her love for their prince, all eyes swiveled to the empty chair that told, more plainly than words, that he'd seen through this woman's treachery and left her to her fate. She herself, they noticed, couldn't help glancing briefly at the chair, with its eloquent emptiness, and her beautiful face grew a shade paler.

But still her voice remained steady, and her bearing dignified. "You will find me guilty and condemn me to death because, on the false testimony before you, you have no choice. My life or death is of no consequence. But beware that man—" her arm shot out in Reinald's direction "—for he's Wolfenberg's enemy. He's the prince's enemy. He's *your* enemy, and he'll sell the people of this country into servitude to Prussia."

There was uproar. Judge Konrad was shaking his head as if pitying the desperate lengths to which the prisoner had been driven by her fear for her life. Reinald sat unperturbed, the smile never leaving his face. At last the judge banged with his gavel for silence.

"Prisoner, you will not wash away your own guilt by attempting to blacken a man whose name has always stood for honor in this land. Have you anything further to say?"

"Nothing," Leonie said proudly. "But in the time to come, remember my warning."

The end was a forgone conclusion. They all knew it. Death by firing squad. Sentence to be carried out early the next morning.

She stood watching as night fell on the courtyard below, until the only light came from the lamps hanging on the walls.

Finally came the sound her heart had listened for, footsteps, then a heavy key turning in the lock. He'd come. She turned to the door with her arms open wide. But she checked herself sharply, and something inside her fragmented with bitter disappointment at the sight of the man who stood there.

"You," she said, filled with loathing.

"Were you expecting Klaus?" Reinald inquired. "You'll be disappointed. He left the city this morning and nobody has seen him since. It's strongly rumored that he's gone hunting. If so, it's a wise move. It shows his indifference to you."

"Then it's no more than I advised him to do," Leonie said, trying to subdue her pain.

"Oh, to be sure," Reinald agreed. "But one may give advice and yet not be entirely pleased when it's so readily taken."

She held herself steady, refusing to let him see how his words affected her. It was true. Although she'd told Klaus to abandon her, one corner of her heart had clung to the belief that he loved her too much to do so. But it seemed he was first and foremost a prince, after all.

"Didn't you know he would desert you, Leonie?" Reinald continued. "It was always bound to happen. The only man who could offer you a future was myself. You should have taken it when it was offered."

"A future stolen from the freedom and happiness of this country," she retorted scornfully. "That has no interest to me."

"Come, no heroic airs if you please. In a few hours, you'll be dead. In Klaus's absence, I signed your death warrant myself. If ever there was a time for realism, it's now. Or are you cherishing the hope of a reprieve? There'll be no reprieve. Even now the preparations are under way. See."

He went to the window and pointed down. Reluctantly Leonie drew closer and looked where he was indicating. The courtyard below was busy. Two soldiers had appeared carrying a thick wooden post, which they drove into the ground by the wall. Then a file of ten men appeared, marching two by two, each one carrying a long rifle. They took up their positions, aiming their rifles at the wooden post. Leonie's gorge rose as she realized she was watching a rehearsal of her own execution.

"*Fire.*"

Ten shots rang out with a deafening sound. When Leonie opened her eyes, it was to see the sergeant examining bullet holes on the post and the wall.

"*Fire.*"

Again there was the explosion of sound. Reinald was watching her face carefully. "We pride ourselves on efficiency in Wolfenberg," he remarked dispassionately. "Everything must go perfectly tomorrow, so some practise is essential. You need have no fear. They're fine marksmen and they'll bring the business off in a second."

She'd chosen death over imprisonment, but faced with the reality of those marksmen, she had a moment, not of fear, but of horror. Her own terrible aloneness in the face of those bullets came rushing over her. She fought for calm, but her hands clenching on the sill betrayed her, and Reinald saw every tiny movement as though through a microscope. "Now you see what you've done," he said. "Tomorrow morning you'll stand before that post, and the guns will be pointed at you."

Her head was bent. Suddenly his hand shot out to grasp her wrist and pull her around to face him. "It need not be," he urged. "There's still a way out if you're wise enough to take it."

She was too dazed to answer him and he took her silence for attention, pulling her closer and speaking rapidly. "I vowed not to come here," he said in a shaking voice. "I thought you'd send me a message when you realized your fate was in my hands. I believed you'd beg me for mercy, and when you didn't, I swore that nothing would bring me to you. But here I am, because I can't tear you from my heart."

Leonie had recovered her power of movement and began to struggle, but Reinald tightened his grip on her. He was in a frenzy. "You *shall* hear me out. I've never loved any other woman, but you were sent to torture me. You haunt me, you obsess me. If you die tomorrow, part of me will die with you. And yet I must send you to your death unless . . ."

She stared at him. "Unless what?"

"Unless you give me your love."

"Give my love . . . to Klaus's enemy?"

"What's that to you when you're dead? In the world to which you're going, there are no enemies and no lovers. I'm offering you life. Say the word and I can arrange your escape tonight. I'll take you to a secret place and keep you safely there until we can be married, and you'll sit on the throne of Wolfenberg at my side."

Suddenly all fear and dread died within her, leaving only contempt behind. "You fool," she whispered. "You're deluding yourself with mad dreams if you think the people of Wolfenberg will tolerate you on the throne."

"Tolerate? Do you think I shall ask their opinions? I'm not Klaus to be seduced by your soft ideas. They'll be kept in order and taught who's master. But why should you care for them? I'll elevate you above all other women. Leonie, listen to me—I can give you life and love."

He finished on a hoarse cry, crushing her against him and covering her face with kisses. She struggled but he was maddened by her coldness and his own desperation. "Touch me," he commanded. "Feel that this is a living, breathing man who loves you passionately. Isn't that better than to lie in the cold earth, your heart withered, your children unborn?"

With all her strength, she managed to free herself and back against the wall, her breasts rising and falling with the effort. "Better that my children should stay unborn," she gasped, "than to carry the blood of a traitor and murderer in their veins. Leave me now, Reinald. You wasted your time coming here. There's nothing in my heart for you but scorn and loathing."

He was deadly pale as he surveyed her. "You speak bravely now, but will your courage be enough as the minutes tick past and your time runs out? Death is very final, Leonie. Perhaps I'll return when you've had time to think.

But think hard and quickly, for the longer you wait, the more difficult it will be for me to save you.''

"You need not return. I've made my decision."

"Perhaps. We shall see."

He called through the grille of the door, and a moment later Turpitz let him out. Leonie stood frozen until she was sure he was gone. Then her legs gave way and she sank onto the bench.

Chapter Fifteen

The lamps still hung on the wall in the courtyard below. One of them cast its light directly onto the bullet holes. Leonie found that her eyes stayed fixed on those holes as the minutes passed, bringing the dawn ever closer.

She guessed Reinald would return for his final answer at any moment and she dreaded seeing him. She wasn't afraid of weakening. The woman who'd known love in Klaus's arms could never belong to any other man. But she was withdrawing deep into herself, preparing her heart and mind so that when the moment came, she could walk down into that courtyard and face the guns with her head high and with no trace of fear in her manner. Reinald's coming would be an intrusion.

She heard a noise from the corridor outside and stepped away from the window to confront him. Turpitz's voice reached her next, but he sounded different—indignant and worried. His voice rose higher, as though he would shout aloud, but no shout came, only a grunt, then a clatter that might have been a chair overturning.

She peered through the grille, and in the lamplight she could make out shadowy figures moving to and fro. Turpitz lay on the floor being hastily tied up by a man whose face she couldn't discern. Beyond him, she could see the outline of the guards, also lying as if they'd been stunned, and also being secured. One of the men approached her cell, a key in his hand. Leonie gripped the bars as it dawned on her like a thunderclap that she was being rescued.

The key turned, the door was pushed open and she was facing a tall man, his face covered by a mask. But no mask could disguise the twinkle in his eyes. *"Uncle Silas,"* she whispered joyfully. "How—"

"Hush," he said quickly. "A friend of yours sought our aid, and helped us get in."

She could make out the other seven figures better now. One came close enough for her to recognize Toni, the others were minding the unconscious guards, except for one man, more heavily masked than the others, who stayed back in the shadows, watching silently. In her haste, she stumbled. One of the figures took her arm, and something in the light pressure of the fingers made her look up quickly at her helper's face. *"Paquita."*

Paquita's eyes gleamed at her. "I never let Toni out of my sight," she said mischievously.

There was no time for questions although Leonie's mind was seething with a million of them. "Reinald was here," she said in a low voice. "He could return at any moment."

"Then we'll be going," Uncle Silas said, taking her arm.

"Too late. How lucky I chanced to be here."

Leonie's heart lurched at the sound of Reinald's voice. She could see him now in the doorway of the antechamber. The flickering torches on the walls gave his face a demonic aspect, and an unpleasant smile touched his face. With an unhurried movement, he drew his sword and pointed it directly at Leonie. "Get away from her," he ordered. "I said get away."

Then the man who'd been standing back in the shadows moved forward and put himself in front of Leonie, sword in hand. "Stand aside," he commanded. "She comes with us."

A black mask covered the lower part of his face leaving only his eyes visible, but a thrill went through Leonie. She knew that voice. It was the voice she loved, that would live in her heart all her days. Her lips framed his name silently, but she made no sound. She was caught, as they all were, in the tension of the moment.

Reinald moved so suddenly that everyone was taken by surprise except Klaus. He parried the deadly thrust, moving back a step to balance himself, then drove forward with a force that sent Reinald staggering against the wall. Klaus took advantage of the moment to throw off his long black cloak. Now he was lighter, more agile, ready to deal with Reinald as he came storming back. Klaus had learned from his duel with Gorstein. Since then, he'd practiced constantly with the foils, and now there wasn't a finer swordsman in Wolfenberg—unless it was Reinald himself. The Gypsies were silent as the two perfectly matched duelists advanced and retreated, slashing at each other with deadly intent.

Klaus had no illusions. This bout must end in death for one of them. Reinald's cold, merciless eyes left no doubt that it was kill or be killed, and now Klaus was defending Leonie's life as well as his own. When all else had failed, he'd slipped out last night to seek the Gypsies. It had been a hard search for they'd moved on from the woods, but at last he'd tracked them down and there, for the first time, he'd found help. Their readiness to risk everything for her sake had made him love them, but he knew now that if he didn't defeat Reinald, he'd have led them into a trap.

The thought lent strength to his arm and he advanced, thrusting and parrying with all the skill and power at his command. To his satisfaction, he could see that his enemy was becoming unnerved. Uncertainty was written on Reinald's face and his movements grew wild. He tried a desperate move, failed, and saw his sword go spinning from his hand. The next moment, he was flat against the wall with Klaus's blade at his throat.

"Kill me," he croaked. "You know you have to. You can't risk letting me live to tell the world how you helped a convicted traitor escape. Kill me if you dare!"

Klaus's eyes grew frantic. He'd been prepared to slay Reinald in the heat of battle, but not like this, not plunging his sword in cold blood into the breast of a disarmed man. Yet it was true, Reinald knew too much to live. To save Leonie, he must kill his cousin in a way that made him little better than a murderer.

"You can't do it," Reinald jeered. "You see the need but you can't soil your hands with blood. That's the difference between us. I can sweep away what stands in my path. Doubts and scruples are for weaklings." His voice rose to a scream as he saw the horror in Klaus's eyes. "Kill me, I say, if you da—"

A deafening explosion cut off the last word. Reinald slid to the floor, blood pouring from a hole in his chest. He came to rest in a sitting position, his eyes staring into the distance while life drained out of his face.

Klaus whirled in time to see the gun raised again, this time aimed at Leonie. He moved faster than he'd ever done in his life. He hurled himself against her and carried her to the floor just in time. A split second later, the bullet hit the wall where she'd been standing. Everyone stared at the doorway where Luther stood holding the smoking gun, his hate-filled eyes glittering in the dim light. Then he vanished.

Klaus raised Leonie. "Tell me that you're unhurt," he pleaded, enfolding her in his arms.

"I'm unhurt. Oh, Klaus, you came for me."

"Did you think I wouldn't? Could I see you die and not raise a finger? Come, hurry. We haven't much time. Those shots will have raised the whole fort." He drew her quickly to her feet. The others dragged the guards and Turpitz into her cell and locked the door behind them. Already in the distance, Leonie could hear shouts and the sound of running feet. "This way," Klaus said urgently, leading them toward the passage by which Reinald had entered.

After a few yards, the passage forked. They had just taken the left branch when the sounds grew louder, coming from the other branch. "Get back," Klaus whispered, pressing her against the wall. The others all flattened themselves and turned their heads to see the guards go by. "They'll raise the alarm," Klaus said. "Hurry."

The ground was becoming uneven. She stumbled and Klaus held her. She clung to him, the one fixed point in a shifting world. He lit a small torch and she found they were approaching a heavy door. "It's never used," Klaus explained. "It was locked years ago. Luckily I kept a key."

The door groaned horribly on its hinges as he opened it a crack, and she was forced to squeeze through the narrow space to avoid having to open it farther. She found herself in a narrow street. It was deserted except for a small carriage, completely closed, with the blinds pulled down, and a coachman on the box, swathed in scarves. Klaus hurried her toward it. Behind it stood a group of horses held by a boy. "Wait," she whispered urgently. Turning to Uncle Silas, she held out her arms to him. He hugged her fiercely.

"No words," he said. "It's all been said. Now be off with you."

"But what about you?" she asked worriedly.

"The caravans are already safe across the border." He indicated the horses. "The best horses we ever had. Straight from the royal stables. We'll catch up with them in a couple of hours."

Klaus reached inside the coach and brought out a heavy bag that chinked as he held it out to Uncle Silas. "And this will help you," he said. "It's gold, good anywhere."

Uncle Silas shook his head. "This was for Leonie," he said.

"Then for Leonie's sake, take it," Klaus insisted. "It'll ease her mind to know you'll have enough funds."

"Ah, well . . ." He took the bag.

Above their heads lamps were being lit in the fort. Uncle Silas blew her a kiss and turned away to where his companions were already climbing onto their mounts. Leonie embraced Toni and Paquita, then Klaus pushed her into the coach and got in with her, slamming the door. The vehicle took off so fast that she was almost thrown to the floor, but Klaus was there, holding her steady, drawing her against him, kissing her with a need that blotted out all memory of grief and danger, leaving only him and their love.

The outside world fell away. She was in his arms, the only world that mattered. His lips were just as she remembered them, only infused now with new passion and tenderness. They'd nearly lost each other forever. Now they'd regained each other, and in that searing joy, it was possible to forget that their reunion was only the precursor to a final parting.

"My love...my wife," he whispered, "dearer to me than all the world. Did you think I'd forgotten you?"

"Never in your heart," she managed to say. "Never that—" Then words failed her and she clung to him, desperately trying to imprint the feel of his body on her own so that the memory might last through all the lonely years to come.

The blinds shut out almost all light, except now and then the gleam from a streetlamp through a crack. In those brief moments, they caught glimpses of each other's faces. "Never to see you again," he said hoarsely, "never again to hear you say you love me—"

"I shall always love you," Leonie whispered. "Always. All my life and beyond. And every moment of every day, I shall tell you in my heart that I love you. And if your heart listens, you'll hear me."

"But I want more," he said. "You're my true wife and I can have no other—"

"You must. We've always known that."

"Yes, I must," he said in agony. "And you'll hear about my marriage. Promise me, swear to me that whatever you hear, you'll never stop knowing that I love you, that you're my only wife, now and forever."

"I promise, always in my heart—"

"Always, always," he said against her lips.

The carriage rocked and swayed over the cobbles. In the distance, they could hear voices calling. "We've nearly reached the river," Klaus said. "Bernhard is waiting. He'll take you the rest of the way. He'll stay with you until you're safely in England. Hold me, my darling. We have only a few moments left...just a few moments...for all our lives...remember...all our lives...." His grief drowned the rest of his words.

"Yes," Leonie said. "All our lives, always together, even when we seem farthest apart. Whenever you think of me, I'll be with you."

"Then you'll be with me always. There won't be a word that isn't you, not an action, not a thought, not a breath, not a dream that isn't you."

The carriage came to a sudden stop. Leonie felt herself lost in his arms, his mouth on hers. They'd had so little time together to last them a lifetime apart.

The door was pulled open. Bernhard was there. "Come quickly," he urged. "The barge must leave at once."

Klaus would have come with her to the edge of the water, but she prevented him. "No," she said urgently. "Go back. Don't let them find you missing. Your part in this must never be known."

"I won't go until I see you on board," he said.

"Goodbye then . . . goodbye."

There was time for only one fleeting kiss before Bernhard was hurrying her away. As she climbed aboard the barge, she looked back at the carriage, where she could dimly see Klaus, and a terrible anguish came over her. "My love!" she called. "Goodbye. *Goodbye.*"

Leonie's memory of the journey back to England was vague. She recalled the river and Bernhard hustling her onto a barge, making her lie down and covering her with sacking. Then there was a gap in her recollection, as if she'd fallen asleep or passed out, because the next thing she knew they were floating down the Rhine, and she could see daylight creeping between the weave of the sack. Bernhard was there beside her, whispering that she should keep still until he told her to move.

They stopped for a long time while voices came and went overhead. She heard enough to understand that they'd come to the border and customs officers were checking the barge, which was carrying coal. But were they also looking for an escaped prisoner? Her heart hammered against her ribs as the delay went on and on. But suddenly they were moving again, and she realized that she'd left Wolfenberg behind, left Klaus behind, and was drifting into a void.

After another hour, Bernhard pulled the sacks away and told her they were safe enough for a while. There was no sign of pursuit. She ate something without tasting it, and sat watching the banks go past until darkness fell. The next three days passed like this, later blurring into one in her mind, until they had reached the mouth of the river, where a ship was waiting to ferry her across the channel.

For the last leg of the journey, Leonie tried to distract herself from her grief by picturing her daughter-in-law's face when she turned up like a bad penny, but she was denied that satisfaction. Gwendolyn was far away in the northern county of Yorkshire, bringing comfort and consolation to Rose, her eldest daughter, whose wayward husband had, not for the first time, "finally gone too far." So there was only Cedric and Harriet at home when the door was opened by an astonished housemaid to reveal Bernhard standing with his arm about Leonie, who was leaning on him, wild-eyed and exhausted.

It soon became clear that Leonie had taken a chill from the journey. She'd kept her courage up as long as it was needed, but now that the danger was over, she felt herself sinking into blackness. Occasional flashes of brilliance revealed faces and scenes that vanished again at once. Reinald was there, his eyes staring horribly, his face livid in death. Uncle Silas danced with her in the flickering light of the campfire. Luther fired the pistol at her heart. But above them all was the face she loved and would probably never see again. He regarded her sadly and opened his arms to her. She ran to him, longing to be held against his heart, but however fast she went, the distance between them stayed the same. In anguish, she called his name, and he vanished.

At last Leonie's fever abated and she awoke. She was weak, but when she heard that Bernhard was still in the house, she asked to see him. He entered eagerly, full of news, Harriet just behind him. "I have so much to tell you," he said. "The Wolfenberg ambassador has been showing me the coded wires he receives. Luther's body has been fished out of the river. He'd committed suicide by weighing himself down with a heavy strongbox chained around his waist. Inside the box were letters to Reinald from Bismarck."

"You mean—"

"They prove that Bismarck and Reinald were hand in glove, just as you said. Reinald was to get rid of Klaus and assume the throne with Bismarck's help."

"Thank God!" she said fervently. "Now they know."

"Yes, it's all out in the open at last. The only thing I don't understand is why Luther tried to take the letters with him. I mean, if he hated Reinald enough to kill him, you'd think he'd want his treachery known, wouldn't you?"

It would be useless to try to explain to this pleasant but uncomplicated young man the tangle of possessive love and murderous jealousy that had made up Luther's feelings for his master. Leonie supposed that when Reinald declared his love for her, it was more than Luther could bear. She merely said, "Luther worshipped Reinald. He killed him, but it broke his heart, and even then, part of him wanted to protect his master's reputation. Poor wretched little man."

"How can you be sorry for him?" Harriet demanded. "I think he sounds perfectly horrid."

Leonie smiled at her granddaughter's naive indignation. Bernhard smiled at Harriet, too, and Leonie held her breath at the look in his eyes. It was fervent and adoring, and and she was suddenly filled with fear for them. Harriet was standing in the window, bathed in the golden glow of a late-autumn day, and in her radiance she seemed to embody everything that was young, beautiful and innocent. "How long is it since we arrived?" Leonie asked.

"A week," Bernhard told her.

A week, she thought, for these two heedless creatures to forget everything but each other. If only their love might be allowed to prosper! She slid back into sleep.

After a few more days recovering her strength, she finally awoke feeling normal. Bernhard hurried in with a Wolfenberg newspaper. "You're a national heroine," he said. "Look."

Klaus had lost no time in publishing the truth. On the front page, the paper described the damning contents of the strongbox and reminded everyone how Leonie had tried to warn the country about Reinald from the dock. The editor thundered:

It must be a matter of infinite regret that the Duchess of Coniston was forced to suffer at the hands of the traitor. This brave and noble English lady was falsely accused by a man who feared she suspected his evil secret. In her hour of greatest peril, her thoughts were not for herself, but for Wolfenberg. We all owe a debt to her, and to those unknown heroes who rescued her at the last moment.

"Those unknown heroes," Leonie echoed.

"One of whose identity must *never* be known," Bernhard added significantly. "I have a further piece of news for you. The Gypsies all made it safely across the border."

"Thank God!" Leonie said.

An attack of awkwardness seemed to swamp Bernhard. "Duchess, if I might speak to you on another matter...."

"Harriet?" she asked with a sympathetic smile.

He took a deep breath and blurted, "I think Lady Harriet is the most glorious, perfect—I mean, if I dared to think of—but of course it's impossible."

"Does Harriet say it's impossible?"

"Naturally, I haven't presumed to speak without her father's approval."

"Since when were words necessary when people love each other?" she murmured, half to herself.

In an instant, his face was illuminated with joy. "Then you think she loves me? You think I have a chance?"

"With Harriet. *Not* with her mother."

"But surely it's her father's decision?"

"Not in this house."

"The duke seems a very decided man to me," Bernhard declared in the tone of a young man trying to reassure himself.

"That's because Gwendolyn isn't here. We can all be brave when the enemy's out of sight. Unfortunately, the enemy has a way of coming back into sight, especially if rumors should reach her in Yorkshire."

His self-confidence seemed to collapse. "Then what am I to do?"

Leonie made a lightning decision. The pain of parting from Klaus had shed a new light on the world. She knew now that only love mattered, and any action, no matter how reckless, was justified to help it triumph. "Listen," she said urgently, "get Cedric's consent now and have your betrothal announced in *The Times*. The more settled it is before Gwendolyn can interfere, the better. Ask Klaus to write to her giving his blessing."

He beamed. "Of course. Then everything will be splendid. I'll do it now." He hurried away.

Barely an hour later, Harriet herself came flying into the room. "Well?" Leonie asked in a teasing voice.

"Leonie—*oh, Leonie*. I'm so happy, so blissfully, utterly happy. He loves me. He wishes me to be his wife. He's talking to Papa now, and I know Papa will give his consent."

"Let's hope your mother doesn't overrule him."

"Oh, but Bernhard's got a plan. He's going to announce our engagement in *The Times* immediately. Then it will be too late for Mama to object."

"Bernhard worked all that out?" Leonie asked, with an admirably straight face.

"Yes, isn't he clever? He thinks of everything."

That evening, Leonie left her bed to dine with the others. It was a happy meal. Harriet and Bernhard's joy glowed, illuminating everyone around them. When dinner was over, Leonie took Cedric to the library to draft the announcement to *The Times*. The young people took refuge in the conservatory where they held each other close. "Can't you remain for one more day?" Harriet pleaded.

"I dare not." He sighed. "I've stayed too long, but I know the prince will forgive me when he knows the reason. I only wish that he could be as happy as we are. But I don't see how he can ever be, now."

"Are he and Leonie very much in love?"

"Very much, almost as much as we. He was different with her, as though he'd discovered joy for the first time. And he was allowed to know it so briefly. Since I've found happiness with you, I feel for him more than ever."

His love rushed over him with sudden force and he kissed her with passion. Harriet responded eagerly, letting her head fall against his shoulder. After a very long time, she opened her eyes slightly, and what she saw through her lashes made her cry out with horror.

Gwendolyn was standing there, watching them.

Bernhard rose to confront the woman whose cold, harsh face made even his brave heart quail, but Gwendolyn brushed past him to slap her daughter viciously. Harriet screamed and Gwendolyn slapped her again so hard that Harriet collapsed, sobbing.

"You, sir," Gwendolyn said in a voice of steel. "You *dare* to make your filthy overtures to my daughter—"

"My intentions are entirely hon—"

"When a dear friend wrote to inform me what was going on under my roof, I found it beyond belief." She turned on Harriet. "But you behaved like a trollop!"

"Lady Harriet has consented to be my wife," Bernhard declared, very pale. "And her father has given us his blessing."

Gwendolyn flung her most scornful look at her husband who trembled in the doorway. "Her father never did have any sense of what was due to this family," she snapped. "But *I* say that royal blood does not ally itself with commoners."

Leonie hurried in and sped across to take Harriet in her arms. "For heaven's sake, Gwendolyn," she said, "do forget that royal nonsense."

"I am descended from the house of Saxe-Coburg-Gotha," Gwendolyn informed her arrogantly, "the same royal house that produced the late prince consort. Through that blood I'm related not merely to the royal house of England, but to many others all over Europe, including Wolfenberg, a place whose prisons I understand you know well."

It was terrible, monstrous, but there was no stopping her. Even Leonie was briefly silenced by the stream of bile and vindictiveness that flowed from Gwendolyn, but she recovered before either of the men. "Bernhard von Leibnitz is a man of noble birth," she said emphatically, stressing the "von" as the sign of Bernhard's aristocratic lineage, "and the intimate friend of Prince Klaus—"

"As indeed you were yourself," Gwendolyn sneered. "A *very* intimate friend. But the most intimate friendship comes to nothing when royalty loses interest—as you've discovered. It's blood that counts. Royal blood. And if Bernhard *von* Leibnitz has royal blood, I have yet to hear of it." She turned to Harriet. "Go to your room, miss. I'll deal with you later."

Harriet raised a streaming face. "Oh, Mama, please don't be angry," she pleaded wildly. "I'm not shameless, I'm not a bad girl, I swear I'm not, but I love him so much—"

"*Go to your room.*"

Leonie helped the sobbing girl to her feet and supported her as she made her way from the conservatory. At the door, Harriet turned and looked back at Bernhard who was regarding her with a face full of love and agony. For a moment, she touched her fingers to her lips in farewell. Then her head fell on Leonie's shoulder and she let herself be led away.

Bernhard appealed frantically to Cedric. "Sir, you gave your consent."

Cedric shifted his feet uncomfortably. "Well... perhaps I was a little hasty. We'll talk later, hey?"

"Herr *von* Leibnitz," Gwendolyn said, "is leaving immediately."

"Is that your decision, sir?" Bernhard asked, emphasizing "your" in a way that made Cedric mop his forehead.

"Well, the fact is, I hadn't realized how time had passed," he managed to say. "Very grateful to you for bringing Leonie home safely... er, aren't we, my love?"

"Ecstatically," Gwendolyn snapped.

"But all things come to an end, eh?"

"But my engagement to Lady Harriet—"

Gwendolyn gave a loud crack of laughter and swept from the conservatory. Bernhard thought his chance had come, but Cedric was too demoralized to do more than offer the services of his valet to assist with Bernhard's packing, and mention a number of hotels.

"Thank you, but I shall go to the embassy," Bernhard said with dignity.

Leonie had taken Harriet to her own room, where she tried to calm the girl's frantic weeping. But with her resilience depleted by illness, she, too, was feeling shattered by Gwendolyn's descent on them. Within a few minutes, the door was flung open and Gwendolyn stood on the threshold. "I ordered you to your room," she said to Harriet.

"Mama, please—" Harriet broke off with a scream as her mother seized her wrist, yanked her to her feet and dragged the hysterical girl away. Leonie followed them into the corridor, and saw Gwendolyn thrust Harriet into her room and lock her inside. From the sounds that came through the door, she guessed Harriet had fallen to the floor and lay there sobbing. "You must be the most inhuman woman on earth," Leonie raged.

"I want you out of this house, madam," Gwendolyn said through gritted teeth. "You won't see or speak to Harriet again because she'll stay locked in that room until you've gone."

Leaving Gwendolyn standing there triumphantly, Leonie ran downstairs to where Bernhard was waiting to leave. "I'd meant to write a letter for you to take to Klaus," she said breathlessly, "but there's no time. Oh, Bernhard, tell him I love him. Tell him I'll love him all my life."

They hugged each other. Then he was gone.

That same night, Leonie departed for a hotel, but she didn't remain there. By the following evening, London was abuzz with the tale of how the Princess of Wales had personally arrived at the hotel to carry off "her dearest Leonie," to stay at Marlborough House. And there, to Gwendolyn's boundless fury, she remained.

Chapter Sixteen

The palace was suddenly very silent and still, as though its heart had ceased beating. During his last moments with Leonie, there'd been no time for Klaus to think. In the days after her escape, he'd lived in dread of her recapture. When that didn't happen, he gave prayers of thanks, but it was as though she'd vanished into the void.

At last there came a telegraph from Bernhard in London, announcing in their prearranged code that his grandmother had endured her long journey well but was suffering a severe chill. Klaus sent a return wire ordering Bernhard to remain until his grandmother was well.

But when the first euphoria of relief had passed, he realized afresh that Leonie was gone. Forever. And it was only now that he fully understood what she'd become to him. He'd called her his wife because she'd entered the deepest recesses of his heart in a way that no other woman had done or ever could do. But she'd been more than a wife, more than a lover. She'd been a friend and comrade, something he hadn't believed possible with a woman. She'd built a bridge to his people and shown him the way across. She'd laughed at him and with him. She'd melted in his arms, giving to him from a boundless generosity. She'd seen past the defensive shell that covered his heart, and discovered the lonely man inside. She'd taken that man's hand and led him out into the sun. But now she was gone.

He tried to concentrate on his work, and at first it helped him, because he could do something for her. The discovery of Luther's body and the strongbox with the papers that proved Reinald's treachery beyond doubt, enabled him to clear her name. He showed the papers first to his cabinet, then to the chamber of deputies, who passed a resolution condemning Reinald and praising Leonie. Then he did something that would once have been unthinkable. He sent for two men—Jan Heinrich, the editor of the *Treuheim Gazette,* and Anton Crazne, now producing his small, independent paper unhindered—and laid all the evidence before them with permission to print whatever they liked. "I want no secrecy," he declared. "My people are entitled to know the truth."

The story spread across Europe like wildfire. In Treuheim they danced in the streets. Klaus, watching them from his window held up his glass in salute, and they cheered him. None of them knew that he was really toasting the woman who'd made this moment possible, the woman who would live in his heart until the day he died.

He began going out at night, mingling with his people as she'd shown him how to do. It seemed strange to go alone, without her there to "protect" him. He managed to smile at that thought, but then he realized that she had indeed protected him, not physically, but by throwing a warm cloak of love and humanity around him.

One night, he returned to The Golden Bear. The summer had passed into autumn, and already chill breezes brought the first sign of winter. Now the customers were wrapped up warmly, and Klaus, with his collar turned up against the cold, could sit quietly in a corner, his identity concealed from all except Hal Kenzl.

Hal filled the prince's stein. "First-grade," he whispered, venturing a wink. Klaus smiled back and raised his stein to toast the landlord. Suddenly a young man stood up under the bare tree and began to sing.

Sad is my heart beneath the summer moon,
Sad for soon I must leave you.
Soon there will be only the moonlight,
And my memories.

He sang in a high, sweet tenor, full of youth and poignancy. Gradually the others joined in until they were all singing softly. The aching melancholy of the tune was more than Klaus could bear. Suddenly the moonlight was hard and cold and the memories brought only torment. He slipped quietly away.

In his own room he poured himself a brandy and sat sipping it slowly. Then he looked up at the sound of a voice outside his door, and the next moment he was on his feet, striding across the floor. *"Bernhard!"* he exclaimed joyfully. "Come in, man. Tell me that she's safe and well."

"She's safe and well," Bernhard said. "I'm to tell you that she loves you and always will."

The surge of joy that possessed him was powerful enough to sweep away the ache of her loss. She was well. She loved him. Nothing could be wrong.

He saw that Bernhard was looking haggard and wretched, and pulled him toward a chair, removing his friend's cloak with his own hands, and pouring him a brandy. As he drank, Bernhard told the story of the flight to England and the events at Coniston House. Harriet's name began to appear more often. Klaus smiled, but his smile faded as the story reached the end.

"I have no hope," Bernhard said simply. "None at all."
Suddenly he roused himself. "Forgive me, your highness. I had no right to speak of my own affairs."

"A man should speak what's in his heart," Klaus said quietly. "It's the same for both of us."

"I know she loves me still," Bernhard said, "and she always will. But to go through life without her—"

"I know," Klaus said somberly. "I know."

They sat in silence as the candles flickered down.

Two days later, Klaus summoned a meeting of the chamber of deputies. When everyone was assembled, he appeared and took his place on the podium. He looked pale and tired. "I thank you for attending, gentlemen," he said. "I'm going to ask your agreement to things that have never been done before in Wolfenberg.

"The world is changing, and this country must change with it. From this day, debates in this chamber will be attended by representatives of the newspapers. They will be free to report whatever they hear, without censorship. Furthermore, in future, no newspaper will need a license, and the complete freedom of the press is guaranteed."

There were gasps in the chamber as the full import of this was taken in. But Klaus's next words were even more staggering. "I intend to grant a constitution, limiting the power of the Crown, and defining its rights and duties in relation to the citizens of Wolfenberg, and their rights and duties in relation to the state."

This time there was no gasp. His listeners were stunned.

"The power of decree will exist no more," Klaus continued. "But today I have one final use for it. Henceforth, the people of Wolfenberg will be known not as subjects, but as free citizens. A small change, but, I believe, a significant one. I thank you for your attention." The finish was so abrupt that it took everyone by surprise. For a moment there was silence. Then the chamber erupted in roars and cheering that went on and on, dwarfing even those that had greeted Crazne's freedom. For a moment, Klaus stood rigid, but at last a faint smile touched his mouth. He inclined his head toward his deputies and left without another word.

The news spread rapidly and all Wolfenberg was astounded and joyful. The free press he'd granted expended gallons of ink speculating on the prince's motives for this unexpected move. In England, *The Times* did the same, and concluded that it was a brick in the wall of defense against Prussia, "in which matter this country is happy to offer his royal highness our warmest support." From Bismarck there was a brief letter saying, "You have done a dangerous thing."

But none of them, not the newspapers, the well-wishers or the enemies, ever guessed the truth. There was one woman whose name never passed his lips, but her letter of joy and pride was worn over his heart night and day.

Lord Bracewell called on Leonie at Marlborough House and praised her achievements. "The revelations about Archduke Reinald came as a severe embarrassment to Bismarck," he told her. "The Prussian kaiser feels it reflects badly on him. He's about to make a public statement, declaring friendship for Wolfenberg. Diplomatic humbug, of course, but it ties Bismarck's hands. He can't risk an assassination scandal."

But now that her identity had been revealed, Lord Bracewell had no further work for her. He also killed the hope that had been flickering in her heart since she learned that her name had been cleared in Wolfenberg. "I left so quickly," she said as casually as she could manage, "with no time to say goodbye to my friends. Perhaps I could make a return visit?"

"Duchess, I beg you to do no such thing," Lord Bracewell said in alarm. "Between ourselves, her majesty has at last been persuaded to agree to allow Princess Louise to marry Prince Klaus. The betrothal will be announced at any moment. For the prince's—er—favorite to reappear in Wolfenberg at this delicate time could undo months of negotiation."

And Klaus needed this marriage, Leonie thought. For his sake, she must deny herself even one last meeting.

Within days, reports of the new freedoms in Wolfenberg appeared in *The Times*. Everything Klaus had done carried her stamp, and every word she read was like a love letter. She knew now that she had been of real benefit to him, and that, at least, was a comfort.

She wrote to tell him of her pride in him, and her undying love. He wrote back speaking of his own love, and also paying full tribute to her part in his actions. "It makes me feel that you are still with me," he wrote. "God bless and keep you." It was all she had to give her courage to face the empty years ahead.

Daily she looked for the announcement of his marriage, but none came. In the spring, her hosts left on a tour of Scotland, and Leonie rented a house in Park Lane. Every day she appeared in her carriage in Hyde Park at the fashionable hour, and there was always a crowd of men eager to ride alongside her.

She'd stopped to flirt with two or three of them one morning when suddenly Harriet, with a pale face and a distracted air, appeared, running and out of breath. She clutched the carriage door, crying, "Oh, Leonie, please, I must talk to you." Leonie immediately assisted her into the carriage and ordered the coachman to get them home.

"Whatever's the matter?" she begged. This was the first time she'd seen Harriet since she'd left Coniston House, and she was shocked by the wretchedness of the girl's appearance. Something terrible must have happened to make the delicately reared Harriet so breach decorum as to actually *run* in the park, and without a maid.

Once inside the house, she hurried her upstairs to her bedroom. As soon as the door was closed, Harriet dropped to her knees beside Leonie's chair, buried her face in her lap and burst into violent, hysterical sobbing. "Harriet, please, try to tell me what's wrong," Leonie pleaded.

"Oh, Leonie, save me, please," Harriet implored. "I can't bear it. I'll die if Mama forces me."

"What is your mother trying to force you to do?"

"She wants me to marry—to marry—Prince Klaus."

The whole world seemed to shift violently on its axis, tossing everything into chaos, so that it was a surprise a moment later to find the objects about her in their right places. "It can't be true," she whispered at last. "He's going to marry Princess Louise."

"No." Harriet wept frantically. "At the last minute, the queen changed her mind. They were going to announce it this week but she refused and they need another bride quickly, to avoid the insult to Wolfenberg. Mama went to see Lord Russell. He says it's my duty to accept, and Mama has told him that I will, although, she knows I love Bernhard. Oh, Leonie, I know it's a terrible thing to say, but I think I hate my mother."

"It's not terrible," Leonie said grimly. "Anyone of any sensitivity must hate her."

Harriet seized Leonie's hands. "You'll help me, won't you? You can hide me somewhere where nobody can find me?"

"Gwendolyn will think of this house first," Leonie said, frantically trying to think.

As if to prove her worst fears, they suddenly heard the doorbell being mercilessly attacked. Gwendolyn's voice reached them from the hall below. Then the door to Leonie's room was flung open and Gwendolyn stood on the threshold, wearing the smile of a cat who'd swallowed the cream. "My *dear* Leonie," she purred. "I meant to come to see you today to tell you of Harriet's impending marriage, but the darling child was so eager that she ran on ahead of me. *What* a triumph for her!"

"You must be quite insane if you think you can force this through," Leonie said furiously.

"Now, now, you don't want everyone to know you're jealous, do you?" Gwendolyn turned to her daughter who was watching her as if despair had turned her to stone. "Come, my dear."

"If you imagine I'll let you drag Harriet from my house—" Leonie began, but Harriet stopped her with a thin hand on her arm.

"It's all right, Leonie," she whispered. "In my heart I knew there was never really any chance."

"There *is*," Leonie urged. But Harriet was already moving toward the door with slow, dispirited steps. Leonie recognized that Harriet's gentle, yielding nature made her unfit for prolonged battles. She'd managed a brief rebellion against her mother, but she couldn't hold out in a long siege.

The next day, the newspapers carried the official announcement of the betrothal of Prince Klaus Friederich to Lady Harriet Coniston. The wedding was set four weeks ahead. Leonie's heart ached more for Harriet than for herself. A juggernaut had started and now it would go on its way, unstoppable, crushing everyone beneath its wheels.

But another shock awaited her. One morning, she returned from Hyde Park to find the Wolfenberg ambassador patiently waiting in her library. "You're a heroine in my country, Duchess," he said, beaming, "and its people desire to honor you. Prince Klaus Friederich has decided to invest you with the title of Archduchess of Wolfenberg.

Your presence at his wedding will provide the ideal opportunity—"

"Wait, please wait," Leonie interrupted him distractedly. "Surely you realize that I won't be attending the wedding?"

The ambassador stared. "But—the ceremony in your honor—everything is planned. Any refusal would be interpreted as an insult to the people and Prince of Wolfenberg."

She tried to protest again, but the ache of longing in her breast was too strong. To behold him once more, just once more, even if it meant the pain of seeing him married to Harriet—to look again into his eyes and see there warmth and tenderness for her—she could carry this in her heart for the rest of her life. Hardly conscious of what she said, she promised to attend the wedding.

The ambassador took an envelope from an inner pocket. "I am instructed by his royal highness to present you with this. Good day to you, Duchess."

At first she couldn't open the envelope, her hands were shaking so much, but at last she calmed down sufficiently to get the letter out. Then, as she read, her heart began to beat wildly. What Klaus had written was impossible. And yet...

The Prince and Princess of Wales were visiting Alexandra's parents in Denmark and would travel to Wolfenberg for the wedding immediately afterward. So they weren't with the party that left England. That was comprised of the bride, her parents and Leonie.

The royal train of Wolfenberg was waiting at Calais to meet them as soon as they disembarked from the steamer to begin the journey across Europe. At every stop, guards stood to attention, and they had to descend while the local mayor made a speech. Gwendolyn was in seventh heaven and her manner became increasingly haughty and smug. Her daughter's misery merely caused her to scold. "Harriet, if you go around with such a long face, people will take offense. We've been shown most proper attention, and I'm sure I don't know what more you want."

"I don't want more, Mama," Harriet said faintly. "Indeed, I never wanted so much."

"Such remarks are not what is expected of a princess. Let there be an end to these die-away airs."

"Yes, Mama."

At the Wolfenberg border they were to be met by the prince's representative, Count Voder. But behind the title was a face they all recognized with varying degrees of shock.

"Bernhard von Leibnitz," Gwendolyn snapped, stiff with outrage.

Pale but composed, Bernhard addressed her. "The prince gave me the position of his chief aide, and bestowed on me an old title that had fallen into disuse." He proceeded with a formal speech of welcome. His eyes didn't linger on Harriet, but it was clear to everyone there that he was intensely conscious of her.

Carriages conveyed them to the royal barge that was tied up on the Rhine. A dais had been set up on the deck where Harriet was to stand so that the people of Wolfenberg could see their future princess. As the barge began its journey, Leonie could see the crowds on the bank, and hear their cries of welcome. The cheers from the riverbanks weren't all for Harriet. Many had recognized Leonie standing a little behind her, and her name began to drift over the water. Klaus had done his work well. They knew this was the heroine who'd almost lost her life defending their country. As the shouts of "Coniston" grew louder, Gwendolyn began to scowl.

Not so Harriet. There was no jealousy in her gentle nature, and she was delighted that her dear Leonie was being

acclaimed. Smiling, she drew her forward to stand beside
her and acknowledge the crowd.

At last Leonie caught sight of the landing stage at Treuheim. Klaus would be there. She would see him again after
the long months of loneliness, but who would she see? What
had the terrible time apart done to him? She could hear the
band playing, people cheering. Then she saw a tall man in
the uniform of the Wolfenberg army. He was still too far
away for her to discern his face, but his bearing was familiar, and the sudden mad pounding of her heart told her the
rest.

Slowly the barge drew in to the landing stage. A red carpet led up to the dais where the court was gathered. Leonie
strained for a better look. Klaus was in front, with several
of his senior ministers standing behind him. She watched
him for any sign that he was searching for her, but he stared
straight ahead.

He advanced slowly along the red carpet and stood waiting as the wedding party descended from the boat, Harriet
in front. When she reached Klaus, she began to curtsy, but
he lifted her at once and bent his head to kiss her on each
cheek. There was something like a smile on his face, but it
wasn't the smile he gave when someone touched his heart,
the smile he'd given Leonie many times, that she would
surely see from him now when he met her eyes.

Klaus looked up and gave a nod that included the entire
wedding party. Then he offered his arm to Harriet and
turned to lead her away. The crowd of curious onlookers,
agog to see how he greeted his one-time favorite, buzzed
with the news that he'd virtually ignored her.

On the night before the wedding, a thousand people
crammed into the Glass Room to see the investiture of Lady
Coniston as an archduchess of Wolfenberg. When everyone was present, the master of ceremonies rapped his staff

on the ground. The huge glass-paneled doors at the far end of the room swung open and Prince Klaus Friederich, his future bride on his arm, began the long walk down the room to the throne.

Behind Klaus walked the Prince and Princess of Wales, and after them came Cedric and Gwendolyn. Everyone was aware of the gaps: Reinald, dead for his treachery; Sylvana, pleading illness, but rumored to have been banished to a distant estate for crimes unknown; Eugenia, tending her "sick" daughter. Slowly the little procession made its way to the dais where gilt chairs awaited them.

The master of ceremonies rapped again and all heads turned to the doors where Lady Coniston had appeared on the arm of the prime minister. She was a vision in cream satin and lace, glittering with diamonds. Her eyes were fixed on the prince's face as she neared him, but not a trace of emotion showed on her face, nor on his.

She dropped a deep curtsy, causing her gorgeous gown to swirl out around her. Klaus leaned toward her and took her hands in his, raising her to her feet. She fought not to tremble at his touch. Bernhard was beside him, holding a velvet cushion on which lay the heavy blue sash adorned with a glittering star. Klaus spoke the words that made Leonie an archduchess of Wolfenberg. As he lifted the sash, she bowed her head for him to fit it around her, then turned to face the crowd and listen to the applause.

Then came the dancing. How often had she whirled in his arms in this very ballroom, seeing herself reflected a hundred times in the glass panels? Now she was forced to watch as Klaus led Harriet into the dance.

She smiled as she took the floor with the prime minister, accepting his awkward compliments gracefully. Count Lemberg was a recent appointment, and she hadn't met him before. He was reputed to be of formidable intelligence, but his appearance was weedy and he was shy in company. His awe of her brought out her protective instincts and they were soon on cordial terms.

She was to have the second dance with Klaus, and already her heart was beating with hope mingled with apprehension. But as Count Lemberg led her to the dais, she became aware of trouble. Klaus appeared to be urging Harriet to dance with Bernhard and she was hanging back. It was a measure of her desperation that she was opposing Klaus, but at last she obeyed him.

The strains of a Strauss waltz floated through the ballroom as Klaus led Leonie onto the floor. She was in his arms again as she'd dreamed of so many times, but his face was unyielding. At last she ventured to say, "Was that wise? This is so difficult for Harriet . . ."

"It's difficult for each of us," he replied somberly. "Harriet must play her part, as we all must."

"It's so hard to talk like this," she murmured. "If we could only meet privately—"

"Impossible," he said quickly. "Nothing remains a secret in this place. You surely realize that the whole court is watching us to see if I'm still in thrall to you. They must see that I am not. You are here to be honored as an archduchess of Wolfenberg. I'm on the verge of marriage to another woman. The world must see what it expects to see."

"But—not a word—a smile—"

"We must not," he said quietly.

She sighed. "I look down the road of the future and my heart is full of fear."

"You were never afraid. I remember you in prison, defying the world, defying death itself."

"Death was easy to defy. But the thought of the future—"

"Be brave, as I must." He turned his eyes to Bernhard and Harriet, dancing in each other's arms as if in a dream. "As we all must," he murmured. "When I look ahead, I don't see a straight road. I see a winding one that may take me where I don't want to go but can't avoid. Or it may give me my heart's desire. Do you remember what I wrote to you in my letter?''

''Every word,'' she said softly.

''Then if ever you prayed in your life, pray for me in the next few hours. Pray for all of us. There, the music is ending. Our duty is done.''

Late at night when the ball was over, Klaus settled down to work in his study, and it was there that Bernhard found him. ''I hope the matter is important, Bernhard,'' Klaus said, looking up impatiently. ''I have much to do.''

''I've come to tell your highness that I can't continue in your service. I must ask you to release me at once.''

''Out of the question. I need you more than ever these days. Consider your request refused. Is that all?''

Bernhard took a deep breath. ''I regret having to displease you, but I *must* leave. Surely you understand why.''

''I'm not concerned why,'' Klaus declared. ''You will remain.''

Bernhard took his courage into his hands. ''You can't have forgotten what I once confided in you—that I was in love with Harriet and—and that she loved me.''

''Very few people are allowed to marry for love.''

''But can't you see that it would be easier for her if I was gone?'' Bernhard demanded passionately.

''Not at all. You and Harriet are little more than children, and the love of children—such as it is—passes quickly. It was a charming romance, but it faded long ago.''

''That isn't true,'' Bernhard cried. ''I love her more than ever.''

''Nonsense! A man who loved her would never have allowed things to get to this pass. The secret passage through the favorite's apartments is still open. If your love was worth anything, you'd have used it to snatch Harriet from under my nose. But you've made no effort to claim her."

"But—she's betrothed to you," Bernhard stammered.

Klaus shrugged. "If such considerations trouble you, your love is very feeble."

"*You* say that? What about duty?"

"The duty you speak of binds me, not you. I can't defy convention, but you can. At least, you could have, if it wasn't—almost—too late. Now kindly leave. I have much work to do still."

Leonie sat at her bedroom window, listening to the hours tick away. Next morning, Harriet would leave for the cathedral, dressed as a bride. By midday, she would be Klaus's wife and Leonie's life would be over. The hope that Klaus's letter had seemed to hold out, and that had sustained her until this moment, had proved false. Now, somehow, she must find the courage to endure tomorrow.

Twelve hours to go. Eleven hours to go. Ten . . . nine . . .

Something was shaking her. She awoke to find that she'd dozed on the window seat and Martha was trying urgently to awaken her. "Your grace," she said, "there's a message from the prince. He wants you in your old apartments quickly."

"Now? What time is it?"

"Four in the morning. The message said to hurry."

As soon as Leonie approached the apartments, she heard agitated voices coming from inside. Puzzled, she hurried in. The room was crowded. There were Harriet and Bernhard, clinging together. There, too, were Gwendolyn and Cedric and the Prince and Princess of Wales, all in dressing gowns as if they'd been torn from their beds. Everyone else was fully dressed, including Count Lemberg who looked deeply worried. Harriet and Bernhard wore cloaks and at their feet were two traveling bags. But Leonie's eyes sought Klaus who was giving her an intent, searching gaze, as if reminding her to be careful....

"What's happened?" Leonie asked cautiously.

"The wedding is canceled," Klaus announced. "I caught my bride attempting to elope with another man." He indicated Bernhard.

"But nobody knows about it," Gwendolyn almost wailed.

"*I* know about it," Klaus declared sternly. "I repeat, there can be no marriage."

"I don't understand," Leonie said.

"They tried to escape by the secret passage in this room," Klaus told her. "Luckily I discovered them."

"You were waiting for us," Bernhard protested. "When it was you who—"

"*Be silent!*" Klaus roared.

Leonie touched Klaus's arm. Before she could speak, he bent his head to her. "For God's sake, keep quiet and trust me," he said in a fast whisper.

Count Lemberg gave an unhappy little cough. "Your royal highness, I beg you to reconsider this hasty decision. We *must* have the alliance. If you cancel the wedding, England will be insulted. Think of the consequences."

"I have thought of them," Klaus declared somberly. "As you say, we can't afford to offend England, nor to postpone the wedding. So we must act quickly to avert disaster."

"But—how?" Count Lemberg stammered.

"It's very simple. We must find another royal English bride in the next few hours."

"Impossible," the Prince of Wales said. "Mama won't shift on Louise and my other sisters are too young."

"Then some other family with royal connections," Klaus said. Inspiration seemed to come to him. "Like the Conistons."

"Unfortunately, both my other daughters are married," Gwendolyn said through gritted teeth. She couldn't resist adding, "Although, of course, Rose's husband enjoys very poor health."

"I'm afraid we can't wait for Rose's husband to make her available," Klaus said. "I need a bride by tomorrow. Are there no better suggestions?"

The Prince of Wales, succumbing to a huge yawn, was startled by a dig in the ribs from Alexandra. "Perhaps," he said quickly, "the answer lies with the Dowager Duchess Leonie, who, by a happy coincidence, is also an archduchess of Wolfenberg, and very popular with your people."

Klaus turned to regard Leonie with surprise, as though nothing could have been further from his thoughts. "Archduchess Leonie would be an excellent choice," he agreed. "She's a Coniston and therefore related to half the royalty in Europe."

There was an audible gasp from Gwendolyn, for whom this was the final outrage. Klaus was wise enough to continue before she could collect her wits. "She's also English and can bring the alliance with her." His face fell as he seemed to discover a snag. "But perhaps she herself would be unwilling to come to the rescue of a country that has ill treated her in the past."

Leonie's heart was hammering but she tried to speak calmly. "Since Wolfenberg has been so kind as to honor me, there is nothing I wouldn't do to protect her interests."

"No!" This howl of rage and anguish came from Gwendolyn. "I won't allow this," she said frantically. "Do you think I'll stand by while she takes my daughter's place?"

"A place that your daughter doesn't want," Klaus reminded her.

"Just give me five minutes alone with that girl and I'll tell you what she wants," Gwendolyn shouted. She was almost gibbering as she took a step toward Harriet. But she halted in alarm as she found herself confronting Bernhard, his face so dark that even Gwendolyn faltered.

"Good," Klaus said approvingly. "A man should protect his wife."

"Wife?" Gwendolyn raged. "She's not his wife, nor will she ever be."

"On the contrary," Klaus said. "They're going to be married within the next hour in my private chapel. I can't ally myself with a family touched by scandal, so the scandal must first be wiped out by their marriage."

But that wasn't the real reason, Leonie knew. He was protecting the two young people by marrying them quickly. She looked at Klaus with new eyes, seeing not only a man she loved with her whole heart but also an adroit fixer. He'd planned the whole thing, and was using all his skill to bring it to a successful conclusion.

Klaus turned to Count Lemberg. "Of course, I also require my prime minister's approval," he said. "I'm sure you realize, Count, that this is the only way to avert an international incident."

Lemberg pulled himself together. He knew now what was expected of him. "Archduchess Leonie has done much for our country," he said with a little bow. "I know I speak for the people of Wolfenberg when I say that if she is willing to do this one thing more, we shall all be eternally grateful."

"Very fine," Gwendolyn sneered. "But you'll sing a different tune when you know the truth about her mother. What do you say to having a Gyp—"

She never got the rest of the words out. For the first time in his marriage, Cedric asserted himself, placing his hand firmly over his wife's mouth. "One more word from you," he growled, "just one more word... I have thirty years of your tyranny to make up for. Do you hear me, woman?"

"Remove your wife, Coniston," Klaus ordered. "And don't let her open her mouth for the rest of the time she's here."

"Out," Cedric commanded, pointing to the door. Gwendolyn stared at him wildly before scuttling away.

The Prince of Wales came forward and kissed Leonie on both cheeks. "Now I must try to catch a little shut-eye," he said, yawning. "Heavy day tomorrow. Big responsibility, giving the bride away. That was what you wanted me to do, wasn't it, Klaus?"

"You're the best of good fellows," Klaus said warmly.

"And I shall be matron of honor," Alexandra said, beaming.

Wales winked at the assembled company. "Make it all look good, eh? Come along, m'dear." He ushered Alexandra out.

"I'm afraid you're going to have a busy night, Count Lemberg," Klaus said. "My other ministers must be roused, and you must explain to them how your brilliant change of plan averted disaster."

Even Lemberg's adroitness briefly deserted him at this revelation. "Er—*my* brilliant plan?" he stammered.

"You thought of the whole thing," Klaus said blandly. "And naturally, like a good constitutional sovereign, I accepted my prime minister's advice." And then, incredibly, Klaus winked.

Lemberg drew himself up straight. "I'm delighted to hear that your royal highness intends to be a good constitutional sovereign," he muttered.

He departed, leaving just the four of them. Klaus immediately went to Harriet and seized both her hands in his. "My dear Harriet," he said warmly, "tell me that you forgive me for exposing you to all this. I'm sure you realize that I was fighting for your happiness as well as my own."

Harriet's answer was to stand on tiptoe and kiss Klaus on the cheek. "I used to think you were very grim and stern," she confessed. "But you're not, after all. And—and Leonie is very lucky." Then she blushed at her own forwardness.

"I hope she is," Klaus answered her. "I know that I am."

"To think that I hated you," Bernhard said, grinning. "You practically ordered me to run away with Harriet, and then stopped us and acted the outraged bridegroom."

"I thought you'd have done it without waiting to be ordered," Klaus grumbled. "I threw her into your arms at every conceivable opportunity, simply to remind you how much you loved each other. But I underestimated your loyalty to me. When nothing happened, I grew desperate. In a few hours, it would have been too late." He clasped his hands with his equerry. "Bernhard, I want you to take Harriet directly to the chapel and wait there. By the time her mother sees her next, it will be too late."

When they were alone, he turned to Leonie. Now there was no further need of words. He simply drew her toward him. Leonie's arms were about his neck, her mouth on his, her body melting into his warmth. "My dearest wife," he murmured.

"You did it," she said exultantly. "When you wrote saying you had a plan that would enable us to marry despite everything, I couldn't really believe it. So much was against us."

But now you see that I can scheme and connive with the best of them. I determined long ago that nothing would make me give you up. You're my wife for all time, and tomorrow the world will know it." He kissed her again fiercely, and when they could both speak, he said, "But by God, it was a close-run thing. It so nearly didn't work."

"Will it work?" she asked anxiously. "Will we get away with it?"

"We'll get away with it because I haven't given anyone time to think."

"I have no royal blood," she reminded him. "It's a shocking misalliance."

"Nonsense!" he declared with a grin. "I'm marrying the heroine of Wolfenberg, the woman who saved the country. Lemberg will whip my other ministers into shape, and by the time they start worrying about your ancestry, it will be too late. You'll be my princess and no one will dare open their mouths to protest it." He held her tight. "My darling, there's going to be much to fear in the years ahead. Bismarck isn't going to give up."

"But we can fight him together."

"With the help of three regiments of English soldiers who slipped into Wolfenberg as wedding guests and went straight to the border. I used to get angry when you said I needed England's strength, but now I'm not too proud to be glad of it if it keeps my people free."

But Leonie shook her head. "It will be you who keeps your people free," she said. "You've won their hearts and minds, and that's a far stronger weapon than any regiment of soldiers. Oh, my darling, when I heard what you'd done, I was so happy. I knew then that I'd given you something."

"You gave me everything," he said fervently. "Whatever I have of value comes from you. And so it will be throughout all our lives. Wolfenberg will be lucky in its princess—as lucky as I am in my wife."

The room was growing lighter. With a swift movement, Klaus went to the window and threw back the shutters. "Look," he said, "the dawn is breaking already. A new day for Wolfenberg. A new day for us—a day full of light and gladness."

He took her into his arms and laid his lips on hers in a kiss that had all the passion and tenderness she'd yearned for and never thought to know again.

"Come, beloved," he whispered. "This is our wedding day."

* * * * *